HUNG OUT

MARGARET WEIS
& DON PERRIN

A ROC BOOK

ROC
Published by the Penguin Group
Penguin Putnam Inc., 375 Hudson Street,
New York, New York 10014, U.S.A.
Penguin Books Ltd, 27 Wrights Lane,
London W8 5TZ, England
Penguin Books Australia Ltd, Ringwood,
Victoria, Australia
Penguin Books Canada Ltd, 10 Alcorn Avenue,
Toronto, Ontario, Canada M4V 3B2
Penguin Books (N.Z.) Ltd, 182–190 Wairau Road,
Auckland 10, New Zealand

Penguin Books Ltd, Registered Offices:
Harmondsworth, Middlesex, England

First published by Roc, an imprint of Dutton NAL,
a member of Penguin Putnam Inc.

First Printing, August, 1998
10 9 8 7 6 5 4 3 2 1

 REGISTERED TRADEMARK—MARCA REGISTRADA

Printed in the United States of America

XRIS IN CRISIS

"Everyone in place?" Xris was asking in low tones. Soft responses from Jamil and Quong.

"Just putting on my lipstick now." That was Raoul.

"Here goes." The squeak of the front door hinges.

Xris sounded grim. "Who are you and what do you want?"

"Xris Tampambulos?" This was a man's voice.

"Who wants to know?"

"Agent Jonathan Fist, FISA. This is Agent Rizzoli. I have a warrant for your arrest."

"What's the charge?"

"The murder of Dalin Rowan, senior agent with the Federal Intelligence Services Agency."

"Oh, dear God!" Darlene whispered.

No bird soars too high,
if he soars with his own wings.

—William Blake,
    "Proverbs of Hell"

CHAPTER 1

The use of a trick or stratagem permits the intended victim to make his own mistakes.
Carl von Clausewitz, *On War*

The buzzing was annoying, seriously annoying.

Annoying because the buzz was letting Jafar el Amadi know there was something he should do and he didn't want to do it. He wished the buzz would stop, and it did for a moment; then, just as he was starting to drift back to sleep, the buzz began again.

His wife, stretched out in the bed beside him, gave him a punch in the back. "It's the phone," she said drowsily. "Answer the phone."

Amadi woke up, peered bleary-eyed at the phone on the nightstand beside his bed.

"What time's it?" his wife mumbled.

Amadi rubbed his eyes, brought the clock into focus. "Two in the morning."

The buzzing continued, insistent.

"It's probably a wrong number," he said.

"Uh-huh." His wife pulled the blanket over her head, rolled away from him. "Tell them you're retired."

Amadi lifted the phone. "Yeah?"

"I'm calling about that order you placed, sir," said a female voice at the other end.

"Do you know what time it is?" Amadi snapped. "It's two o'clock in the morning!"

"Sorry, sir. I just thought you'd want to know, sir, that the item you requested has been located."

"What item? What the hell are we talking about? Is this some goddam vidalog company? Because if it is—"

"I have the order here, sir. Your authorization: Delta 750-6711-9."

Good God! It was the Bureau.

"Oh." Amadi was now very awake. That was his authorization code, but what the hell were they talking about? "What's it in regard to?"

"Body parts for a cyborg, sir. Would you like to go ahead and place your order, sir?"

"I need more details—color and size and all that."

"Very good, sir. I'll give you a number to call for customer service. Ask for order number 7/66/807/9. Sorry I woke you, sir, but this was marked 'urgent.'"

The other end clicked. The connection was broken.

Amadi sat and frowned at the warm green glow of the clock for another moment, then he slid his feet into his bedroom slippers and eased himself out of bed. His wife was used to late-night phone calls, used to him roaming about the house at all hours, used to him leaving in the middle of the night. Of course, that had been before he had retired, when he had still been with the Bureau.

It had been years since he'd received a late-night phone call, probably one reason it had taken him such a long time to respond. In the old days, he would have been wide awake at the first buzz. But at age seventy, he'd come to relish his warm bed and a good night's sleep.

Giving his wife a customary reassuring pat on the shoulder—a pat she probably didn't feel because she'd gone back to sleep already—Amadi grabbed his robe, threw it on. Yawning, he left the bedroom, visited the john, then went downstairs. The dog, lying with his back pressed up against the front door, opened one eye, thumped his tail against the floor, and raised his head to see if he was needed.

"Go back to sleep, Charlie," Amadi said, moving through the hallway, heading to the kitchen.

The dog obeyed gladly. He was an old dog and he, too, appreciated his rest.

In the kitchen, Amadi brewed coffee, freshly ground, made the old-fashioned way in a drip pot; none of that muddy water the replicator turned out. He mulled over the cyborg matter as the coffee brewed. The risk was immense, but he had already considered and discounted all his other options. He cut himself a piece of pound cake—gone were the days when he could drink six cups of coffee on an empty stomach—then carried cake, a cup, and the coffeepot down another flight of stairs to the rec room. Behind the vid, mounted on the wall, was a sensor device.

Amadi considered briefly attempting to juggle cake, cup, and pot in one hand while he activated the sensor, but rejected the idea. His wife may have been patient with late-night phone calls and her husband vanishing for weeks at a time on some secret assignment, but she took a dim view of coffee stains on the rug. Amadi placed his breakfast on an end table, passed his hand twice over the sensor device, which was no more than a tiny hole in the wall.

A door disguised to look like part of the oak paneling slid aside. Amadi retrieved his breakfast, making a mental note to himself to bring the cup and coffeepot out of the room when he was finished. His wife would be extremely irritated if one of her best china cups went missing, as it had upon one occasion, only to turn up two weeks later with a fine growth of mold on what was left of the coffee.

The door slid shut behind Amadi.

The room was small, soundproofed, fireproofed. It contained a desk, a chair, a computer. Seating himself in front of the computer, Amadi gave it his password. Once he and the Bureau were linked and each had admitted that they knew the other, he went through more security procedures. At last, the Bureau conceded that he had the right to be where he was and to acquire the information he needed. He gave the "order" number, which he had—from habit—committed to memory as the agent rattled it off. He munched cake while he waited, drank his coffee, and yawned.

A woman's face appeared on the screen. He didn't know her, but that wasn't unusual. He'd been retired for ten years. He knew few people in the Bureau anymore.

She was human, mid-twenties, lean and mean, with skin the golden color of olive oil, short-cut black hair, high cheekbones, an upturned nose, full lips. Adjectives came to Amadi's mind: new, pert, hungry.

The voice belonging to the face was the same voice that

had spoken to him on the phone. She was seated at a desk in an office cubicle, probably her own cubicle, for there were pictures stuck to the fabric wall behind her. Family pictures. Mother and father. Three young men standing together grinning at the cam with wide smiles. Probably brothers. A white fluffy cat.

"Agent Rizzoli, sir. Petronella Rizzoli."

"Rizzoli." Amadi nodded, swallowed pound cake. "What do you have for me?"

"We've located former agent Tambam . . . Tampambulos, sir," she replied, stumbling over the name.

"Good work, Rizzoli. He's not an easy person to track down. You have the warrant? Is all in order?"

"A few local problems, sir."

Amadi frowned, displeased. "The reason I lured him to that planet was because the locals promised there would be no trouble. Where's he staying?"

"Where you said he would stay. He's at the home of his ex-wife, Marjorie Tambamp . . . Tamp—damn that's a hell of a name to pronounce. And any rate, that's where he is, sir. At her home."

"Excellent. That's where I was hoping he'd go."

"We could never have removed him from Olefsky's world," Rizzoli agreed. "Not without a fight."

"And they don't have the death penalty on Solgart," Amadi added. "So what's he doing with his time in his ex-wife's house?"

"We intercepted several calls made to various parts of the galaxy. They were all encrypted, unbreakable, but we believe that he's assembling the Mag Force 7 team. He's also been in contact with the Royal Navy, one of the lord admiral's adjutants, a Commander Tusca."

"Probably doing a job for them."

"Will that present a problem, sir? When we arrest him?"

"The Navy won't like it, that's for damn sure, but they'll drop him like a hot rock if we threaten to go public with the facts. Especially when they hear the charge. How does the warrant read?"

"Murder, sir. First degree. The murder of his former partner, Dalin Rowan."

Amadi closed his eyes. He wished he hadn't eaten the pound cake.

"He *is* a murderer, after all," Rizzoli continued. "And while the Navy may hire murderers with impunity, they don't want it broadcast on the six o'clock news."

"Is the Navy keeping an eye on him?"

"No, sir."

"Are you sure about that?"

"Yes, sir. It's a quiet neighborhood, sir. Our agents have him under surveillance, of course. We could spot one of their agents easily."

"And I'll bet that Tampambulos has spotted you," Amadi observed. "He was a good agent, you know. One of the best."

"I doubt it, sir." Rizzoli was confident. "We've never even been near the house. All visual surveillance has been carried out by our system of satellites. We're monitoring everything going in and out of that house from a base twenty-five kilometers away. We pick up every signal, every phone call. And if a mouse crawls underneath the garage door, we see it on the satellite report.

"The new orbital spectral analysis system allows us to 'see' to a resolution of one centimeter, even through solid objects, such as the roof. We could tell you if former Agent Tampambulous has a problem with irregularity, sir. Which he doesn't. Every morning at around 0830, after he has his coffee, he takes the morning paper into the john and—"

"Spare me the details," said Amadi. "I get the picture and, frankly, I wish I hadn't." He had seen Xris when they'd first brought him to the hospital, seen what was left of him.

"If you want my advice, Rizzoli, you'll arrest him now, this minute. Don't wait until his friends show up. They're a dangerous bunch."

"We'd like to, sir, but there's a problem with the warrant."

Amadi had forgotten. He was going to have to start doubling up on his old-age hormone injection shots. "Local police force giving you grief?"

"No, sir. They're eager to cooperate. The chief wants to see her name on GNN. It's the legal system. We can't arrest him on a Crown warrant alone; we have to have a local warrant as well."

Amadi dumped the remaining pound cake in the trash. "They want to review the case, I suppose."

"Yes, sir. We've provided them with all the files, but they're taking their own sweet time over it. The chief is putting pressure on the prosecutor, though. She told us to expect the warrant by Monday."

"And when the hell is that? I'm half a universe away, you know."

"Sorry, sir. Twenty-four hours, sir."

"Twenty-four hours. Time enough for his whole blasted personal army to show up. Well, it can't be helped."

"We plan to go in at about 0400, sir, when everyone's asleep. We'll use the standard flash-bang—"

"No, absolutely not!" Amadi said firmly. "These people are trained mercenaries. They're armed and they're experts. What do you think they're going to do if they wake up to find they're under attack? Especially if you surprise them!"

"Well, sir, what do you suggest?"

"It's a suburban neighborhood," said Amadi. "Upper middle class. Kids playing in the front yard next door. Tampambulous won't want to endanger innocent civilians. He's not the type of person to start gunning down toddlers. Go to the front door, ring the bell, hand him the warrant. He'll come along peacefully. I guarantee it. I want him alive, Rizzoli. Alive. He's no good to me dead."

What was her first name? Amadi wondered. Petro-something. He'd forgotten that, too. Damn odd first name.

"Yes, sir." Rizzoli was all business, cool and professional. "Don't worry, sir. We're taking extra care on this one. He killed one of our own. We want to see him in the disrupter."

"Keep me posted." Amadi ended the meeting.

He finished off the entire pot of coffee, then sent a memo to a man he knew well—Andrew Robison. Formerly Amadi's boss in charge of the Hung investigation, Robison was now head of Internal Affairs for the Bureau.

Robison was investigating Amadi, an interesting development and one that Amadi wasn't supposed to know about.

The memo to Robison was headed, *Tampambulos. Warrant issued. Arrest imminent.*

"There," Amadi muttered to himself. "That should make the son of a bitch happy."

CHAPTER 2

. . . there is something about him, which even
treachery cannot trust.
                    Public Advertiser, 22 June 1771, "Junius"

"So the message he sent me is accurate? Are you certain?"

"Yes, sir. I'm certain." Petronella smiled. "He assigned the grunt work to me: issuing the warrant, arguing with the locals, all of that."

Head of Internal Affairs Andrew Robison frowned at the electronic notepad he held in his hand, a pad that held all the details of a murder case. After almost ten years, there'd finally been an arrest.

"I recorded our conversation, sir," Petronella told him.

"Secure?"

"Yes, sir. Of course, sir," Petronella replied coolly. She was not accustomed to having her work questioned.

Robison gave a grunt that was tantamount to an apology.

Petronella, knowing her boss, accepted the grunt and went on. "Here are the codes to the encryption."

Robison pulled up the encrypted file, observed the conversation with Amadi from Petronella's viewpoint. Robison frowned most of the time during the conversation.

Petronella nodded. "Amadi thinks I'm a bumbling fool," she told Robison. "As do most of my co-workers." She gave a sigh that, fortunately, Robison didn't hear. He was replaying the vid.

Petronella liked her co-workers and respected them. They were, for the most part, hardworking, dedicated, and loyal. They liked Petronella, but they considered her young, inexperienced, and, on top of all that, a Talisian who could not control the weird energy surges common to those born on her home world. What they didn't know was that she could control them, but chose not to do so. The fact that wherever Petronella Rizzoli went chaos followed added immeasurably to her cover and it was one reason she'd been recruited to work for FISA Internal Affairs. With all the assignments she'd handled over the past five years, no one had ever suspected she was a plant.

Petronella regarded Robison, her boss, with affection and a certain amount of sympathy, though she was careful to reveal neither to him. Robison was strictly professional and he expected his people to be the same. But she was aware that this particular assignment must be tough on him. He had once been Jafar el Amadi's chief superintendant. Robison and Amadi had been close friends as well as co-workers. And now Robison was placed in the position of exposing as a traitor a man whom he had once admired.

There could not be two more different men, Petronella thought idly, as she watched Robison watching Amadi. Jafar el Amadi could trace his ancestors back to the Bedouins who had roamed the deserts of Old Earth. Amadi was intensely proud of his heritage. His home was filled with Arabic artifacts, decorated with paintings of men in flowing robes riding magnificent and long-extinct Arabian stallions.

Looking at Amadi's face, with its hawk nose and fierce black hawk eyes, Petronella could easily picture him riding among the dunes and she thought it a pity that he should have betrayed such a noble lineage.

Robison, by contrast, was far more suited to an English tea room than the wind-blown desert. Blond, with blue eyes and a thin face marked by a very handsome acquiline nose, Robison was younger than Amadi by ten years—a fact that some men might have resented, considering that Robison had been Amadi's boss. If Amadi did, he didn't show it, although perhaps that could have been the reason why he'd gone over to the enemy camp.

Watching Amadi on the vid, listening to his voice, Petronella wondered again what had driven him to commit such heinous crimes: marked his own agents for death, aided and abetted in the deaths of thousands of innocents, worked for one of the most ferocious, cruel, murderous criminal organizations in the history of the galaxy.

For what? Money? Jealousy? Ambition?

No one knew. No one had been able to prove Amadi's complicity, although, according to Robison, the Bureau had long suspected him.

"Amadi was clever enough to lay low when his bosses were going to prison," Robison had told her at the beginning of this investigation. "He took retirement soon after that. We could never prove anything. The only person who might have been able to tie Amadi into the Hung was a man named Dalin Rowan. The victim of the murder."

"What I don't understand," Petronella said, after Robison had played through the vid a second time and was sitting, frowning, at the frozen image of Amadi on the screen, "is why Amadi is risking exposure by bringing this to light again after all these years."

Robison's thin lips, outlined by a pencil-thin mustache, tightened. He regarded her speculatively, as if making up his mind whether to tell her or not. Petronella might have been offended at this seeming lack of trust, but she had become accustomed to going into cases without knowing all the details. Andrew Robison never fully trusted anyone. The joke among his staff was he entered data into his computer with his eyes shut, so that he wouldn't reveal anything to anybody, himself included.

"I'll tell you why," Robison said finally.

Petronella regarded him in astonishment. She hadn't really expected an answer.

"Dalin Rowan isn't dead."

"He's not, sir?" Petronella was amazed.

"No, at least that's what we suspect. Why? Because the Hung are looking for him. We know that much from our informant. And Amadi's looking for Rowan, too."

"But . . ." Petronella was momentarily speechless, gathering her thoughts. "But Amadi has a witness, a nurse . . ."

"Fake. Phony."

"Then why is he having Tampambulos arrested for something he knows he didn't do?"

"Because Rowan's in hiding. Naturally enough," Robison said dryly. "The number of people who would like to kill

Dalin Rowan would fill a football stadium. Amadi hasn't been able to find him and neither have the Hung. He figures this way he'll force Rowan to come out in the open."

"From what I've read about Xris Tampambulos, he's not that easily intimidated."

"He won't be. I can guarantee it. I knew him in the old days. He was one of my agents. And Amadi knows Xris as well or better than I do."

"So finding Rowan isn't the only thing Amadi's after?"

"That's what Amadi's going to make it look like. But I don't believe flushing out Rowan's the reason he's after Xris. Here's the file on Dalin Rowan."

He passed over a disposable electronic file pad. Petronella activated it, scanned swiftly through the contents until she reached the end.

"Good grief," she said, gasping.

"Yes." Robison had no need to ask what she'd come across.

"But he's . . . she's . . ."

"Yes," Robison said again. "You see why it was so difficult to locate him. Her."

"Good grief," Petronella repeated, dazed.

"She's now going by the name of Darlene Mohini. Here are your instructions. . . ."

CHAPTER 3

The family—that dear octopus from whose tentacles
we never quite escape.

Dodie Smith, *Dear Octopus*

Xris hadn't meant to sit down.

He hadn't meant to sit down and he hadn't intended
to remain sitting after that. He hadn't meant to sit here
doing nothing. Doing nothing when he had a hell of lot
to do.

"It can wait," he said aloud, startling a seagull that had
hopped up onto the patio in hopes of stale bread.

The bird gave a squawk of irritation, then settled down
on the edge of the deck, hope springing eternal.

Xris eyed the seagull, which was eyeing him, not the least
bit afraid, confident in the possession of strong wings and
an offshore breeze. Xris knew this gull. It had only one
foot, probably a congenital defect. The lack of a foot didn't
bother the gull, although the deformity made its landings
real nose-bumpers, as Harry Luck would say.

Beak-bumpers would be a better term, Xris decided. He
had taken to feeding the one-footed gull, though feeding
one meant that twenty more always showed up and now
the deck was covered with gull shit. Marjorie wouldn't like
that, not in the slightest. Xris would clean it up before
he left.

"At least," he told the gull, "they didn't stick you with
a metal foot." He looked down at his own metal foot,
propped out in front of him.

The bird didn't seem to appreciate its good fortune. It
ruffled its feathers and turned its head rapidly from side to

side, as if as to say, *Cut the chatter, buddy, and bring on the bread. I got things to do, even if you don't.*

Xris had things to do. The house was a mess, for one, but he hadn't had time to clean. The Mag Force 7 team had been hired for a job, mercenary work. High pay, with only a moderate amount of risk. He had decided on the basic plan, but he had to work out details. The rest of the team would be arriving soon, traveling in from the various parts of the galaxy they called home, to hear his presentation. It had better be complete. If Dr. Bill Quong asked a question Xris couldn't answer or if Jamil caught Xris in a miscalculation, he'd never hear the end of it. And if Raoul discovered a wet towel on the bathroom floor . . . well, Xris didn't even like to contemplate that eventuality. But it could wait. The plan. The housekeeping. The grocery order.

It could all wait.

He couldn't remember the last time he'd done nothing. He was always doing something and he liked it that way. He liked keeping his mind occupied. When it was thinking about useful things, interesting things, it didn't have time to brood on things over which he had no control. Things such as the fact that he couldn't sit and listen to his heart beat, like most people. He had to listen to his heart hum, like the fine-tuned machine it was, which then reminded him that most of the rest of his body needed a lube job and an oil change every fifteen thousand kilometers.

Xris lounged in a chair on the back deck and watched the sunlight ripple over the surface of the water. He wouldn't think about his heart or anything. The ocean was calm today, almost flat, the offshore breeze smoothing the waves. The teenage surfers stood around in gloomy knots on the beach, but the younger children were happy, paddling in the gentle waves that washed up on the shore— waves that would usually knock them over when the wind blew in from the sea.

Three pelicans flew in perfect formation, like a squadron of spaceplanes on maneuvers. The seagull, a supremely independent bird with a mind of its own, cast the pelicans a scornful glance. Growing impatient, it hopped over on its one foot to remind Xris of its presence.

He hadn't brought the bread with him, not having intended to stay out here in the hot afternoon sunshine. He'd come out on the deck to rearrange the furniture in preparation for tonight's barbecue. Instead of lifting a chair, he'd sat down in it.

If he had to put a name to what he was feeling, he'd have to name it peace. He was at peace, with himself and with the universe. The feeling of peace was a rare one and he intended to prolong it, luxuriate in it as much as possible. It wouldn't last.

He was surprised to find himself feeling peaceful here, for by rights he shouldn't. This place should be painful for him, which was why he'd first turned down Marjorie's invitation to use her beach house while she was away. His turn-down had been an automatic, knee-jerk response. He and Marjorie had once dreamed of owning a house like this on this very stretch of beach. They used to vacation here, and for fun on rainy days they'd walk up and down the beach, pick out lots, plan their dream vacation home.

The dream had ended in a nightmare of flame. The explosion in the illegal Hung munitions factory had left Xris half metal, half man—and he was the lucky one. His partner had ended up half bone fragments and half charred flesh. Marjorie had made the decision to keep Xris alive, to turn him into a walking soup can. And then the first time he touched her with his fake hand, she'd flinched. Xris had walked out on her. But he hadn't divorced her. And she hadn't divorced him. He told himself she was after his money, for Xris was now a very wealthy man. But he knew deep inside, somewhere around his plastic heart, that this wasn't the reason.

She still loved him. This beach house—which was built exactly along the lines they'd planned—was the proof. He'd turned down the invitation because he knew it would hurt her. He'd turned it down because he was afraid it would hurt him. And that was the reason he'd called her back to accept. It was pretty darn stupid to be scared of a beach house.

This was the ideal place for the Mag Force 7 team to meet to discuss the new job. The security wasn't as tight as he usually liked it; not as tight as the Exile Café, or his own home on Bear Olefksy's planet Solgart. But this job didn't require tight security. The team wasn't doing anything illegal; they weren't planning to assassinate a Navy officer, for example, or plotting to steal an antique robot. They were merely going to help overthrow a government.

Xris had accepted Marjorie's invitation and he had expected to be uncomfortable, hadn't planned on staying long. He now realized he was going to be sorry to leave. He was already looking forward to coming back.

Maybe even when Marjorie was home.

Except that, in many ways, she *was* home. Her presence was everywhere, in the books in the bookcase, in the sea paintings on the walls, in the feather pillows that she liked but which always made him sneeze, in the perfume on her dressing table, in the heavy old ratty bathrobe—the same bathrobe, he'd swear to it—hanging in the closet. The scent of her bath oil that clung to it. Ten years and she still used the same fragrance; something to do with the sea. Xris couldn't ever remember the name. But he remembered the scent. It brought her back to him in full color, brought back her smile, her laugh, her voice . . .

There had been a day when that picture of her would have hurt him, angered him, infuriated him. But time heals, time and therapy and the grudging acknowledgment that maybe Marjorie hadn't reacted to the ugly metal on the outside as much as she had reacted to the ugliness deep inside him.

He enjoyed having part of her around. It was rather like entertaining a friendly ghost.

Maybe, once he got used to this part of her . . .

The doorbell rang.

The melodious sound drove away the seagull, which flapped off with a croak expressive of its extreme disappointment.

Xris rose from the chair, his own feelings similar to that of the gull. He had enjoyed the brief interlude of doing nothing and was sorry to see it end. Returning to the house, he entered the living room, which faced the beach. French doors opening onto the patio provided a spectacular view of the ocean. He left the living room, walked into the front hallway—picking up a half-read newsvid on his way and depositing it in the recycler. Reaching the door, he glanced at the vidscreen on the wall to see who it was before he opened the door.

Xris wasn't particularly worried that a person or persons unknown might be waiting on the porch to accost him. This was a secure community; the guards at the front gate would stop anyone who didn't have a pass. But he was afraid Raoul might have arrived early and Xris had just realized that he was tracking sand all over the living room rug.

Prepared to swear that he had been interrupted in the act of turning on the cleaning 'bot, Xris was relieved to see that it wasn't Raoul. A woman in a rumpled skirt, a plain blouse, and a well-tailored suit jacket stood smiling into the cam. Her shoulder-length hair had been brushed at least once today, but no more. She had apparently started to apply her makeup and had then been interrupted in the process, for she had penciled in one eyebrow but not the other and she was only wearing one earring. Glancing at her feet, he saw that both shoes matched, which meant that she'd actually taken a certain amount of care with her appearance.

He opened the door. "You were supposed to call me from the spaceport. I would have picked you up. It's too dangerous—"

"I was fine, Xris." Darlene waved away his concerns. "Not an assassin in sight. I rented a hover. It's great driving in civilized lands again."

He shook his head, frowned to show he was angry. She grinned to show she knew he wasn't, and the two shook hands.

"Were you followed on Adonia?" he asked as he ushered her inside the house, taking her overnight bag from her. He knew better than to offer to carry her computer case.

"No, but that's not surprising," Darlene said, smiling at him. She shook her hair out of her eyes to see better and glanced around the house with approval. "You should try following someone in Adonia. It cannot be done. The Adonians have no concept of air lanes. They float their hovers all over the sky, going every which way, mainly because they're not paying the slightest attention to what they're doing. Either they're putting on makeup, fixing their hair, changing their clothes, drinking champagne, admiring the view, entertaining guests, making love, or a combination of all those. If someone *was* tailing me, my guess is that he either died in a midair collision—I've seen some beauts— or that he just went quietly insane. Not that anyone would notice *that* on Adonia."

All of which, thought Xris, is her polite way of telling me that she has the situation under control, that she would know if she were being followed, and that she'd know how to handle it. I should butt out. Fair enough. He was about to ask if she'd been followed from the spaceport, changed that to:

"Do you like the house?"

Darlene gazed around with approval, nodded. The beach house was small. From the front entryway, she could look left into the kitchen, straight ahead into the living room and down a hallway to the three bedrooms on her right. The view of the ocean from the living room was worth the hefty price Marjorie had paid.

"This place is great, Xris. Really wonderful." Darlene shifted her gaze back to him, studying him closely. "The sea air appears to be good for you. You should visit here more often."

"I'm thinking about it," he admitted.

"Really, Xris?"

Reaching out, Darlene gave his good hand a squeeze. "I'm glad to hear it. I'm very, very glad."

Of the Mag Force 7 team, Darlene was the only person who'd known Xris back in the days when they had both worked for FISA. Darlene had been his partner and his best friend. She hadn't been Darlene back then; she hadn't even been a she. She had been Dalin Rowan. She—or rather he—had known both Xris and Marjorie, liked them both. Rowan had been truly sorry to hear that they had split up.

"I'm so glad," she said again.

"I've put you in the back bedroom. I'll show you." Xris started down the hallway.

"I can stay in the hotel with the others—" Darlene began to protest.

"Nothing doing." Xris was firm. "I only agreed to let

you come here on the condition that you live in the house where I know it's safe. Unless, of course, you'd rather have Harry sleeping across your hotel room door with his beam rifle in his lap?"

"No, thank you. The back bedroom will be fine. Dear Harry. How is he? It's been two months since I saw him—or any of the team, for that matter. Not counting Raoul and the Little One, of course. Though they've been out of town for the last two weeks. There was some sort of vid festival and Raoul's favorite actor—Rusty Nails—"

"Rusty Love," Xris corrected.

"Yes, that's it. Anyway, this Rusty Love was going to be attending in person and Raoul went in hopes of meeting him or stealing his underwear or something along those lines. I'm not clear on the details. I didn't like to ask too many questions."

"Good idea," Xris agreed. "Raoul might have supplied you with the answers."

The doorbell rang.

"I'll take care of this. Thanks." Darlene retrieved her overnight bag and flung it on the bed. "You mind if I take a shower? I must smell of at least twenty different brands of Adonian perfume. The transport was crowded as hell."

"Is that what that smell is? I thought you'd been mugged by a gardenia bush. Sure, go ahead. Down the hall, last door at the end. If you need a robe, there's a couple in the closet in my room."

Darlene gave a vague nod. She was busy setting up her computer. In many ways, she was more machine that he was. Darlene never truly came to life until her computer screen did the same. The computer had been packed with tender care, while her clothes—which were leaking out of the partially un-Velcroed bag—had been tossed in haphazardly. Xris took one look at the untidy, wrinkled, and confused mass of jeans, shirts, and sweaters poking out of the sides of the bag and hoped again that he wouldn't soon find Raoul on the doorstep.

The doorbell rang again and this time whoever it was kept his finger on the bell. Xris had no need to look at the vidscreen. Only one of the team members would not have patience enough to wait even a few seconds for a response to the announcement of his arrival.

"Hello, Doc. Good to see you."

Xris and Dr. William Quong shook hands. Quong brought in two traveling cases—one for his clothes and one for the instruments of his trade. He gave a perfunctory glance at his surroundings, a glance that took in the hall, the living room, the kitchen, and the bedrooms. If Bill Quong turned around and walked out now, he would be able, twenty years later, to provide a detailed diagram not only of the house but of the placement of the furniture, down to the kitchen trash-masher.

He made no comment on the beach house, which didn't really interest him, but focused on Xris, who did.

"How are you feeling?"

"Fine, Doc. No complaints."

Quong grunted and frowned, clearly not believing his patient's diagnosis. "We will see. You look flushed."

"I've been out in the sun—"

Quong ignored him. "My guess is that your thyroid levels are off. I will need to take a blood sample. Where may I set up my equipment?"

"Doc, I don't—"

"In the kitchen? The table is small, but I suppose that will have to do. Where is your disinfectant? And don't tell me that you don't have any."

"Fine, Doc, I won't tell you," Xris muttered, and left Quong opening and shutting cabinets and poking around beneath the sink, all the time making comments about proper hygiene and the strong likelihood that they were all going to come down with salmonella poisoning.

Quong's personality was irritating, his bedside manner a bit too abrupt and calculating for most of his patients to tolerate. He was easily and often offended. But he had kept Xris alive and well and firing on all cylinders for a number of years now. For all his irascibility, Quong was an excellent medical doctor. He was also a genius with mechanics, mainly because he preferred machines to people. A fanatic about diet and exercise, he was also deeply and occasionally annoyingly religious—and he was a damn good shot with a beam rifle.

Xris went to answer the doorbell, which was ringing again. He noted, in passing, that Darlene was hunched over her computer, a familiar, intense, interested expression on her face—an expression rarely seen except when she was working. She had forgotten about taking the shower.

Xris opened the door to find Jamil and a delivery man—a delivery man that second glance revealed to be Harry.

"What the hell?" Xris stared.

"Harry's been thinking again," Jamil said in grim tones.

"Harry." Xris was disappointed. "I thought you knew better."

"The guards at the gatehouse wouldn't let him in," Jamil continued. "He'd been standing there arguing with them for fifteen minutes."

"I thought I should come in disguise," Harry mumbled.

Xris shook his head. "I gave the guards your name and description, Harry. Well, what I thought was your description. All you had to do was present your passport. I didn't realize you'd found a new line of work."

Harry looked sullen and aggrieved. He was the team member who'd been with Xris the longest. One of the best pilots in the galaxy, the moment Harry Luck set foot inside a spaceplane, he became a different person. In essence, he became a spaceplane himself. But on land, as Xris was wont to say, he'd been hit in the head with a stun gun once too many times.

The delivery man's uniform was a size too small. He'd already burst a button on his broad chest and a seam was splitting out on his thick thigh. He had actually put enough thought into his disguise to bring along a beaten-up-looking package, which was tucked under one arm. Unfortunately, the FASTER-THAN-LIGHT INTERPLANETARY DELIVERY SERVICE label on the package didn't match the GALAXY AT YOUR DOOR insignia on his uniform.

"You gave them my real name?" Harry asked accusingly.

"Well, yes. What name was I supposed to give them?"

"An alias! Suppose someone's after us?"

"No one's after us, Harry. We're clean for a change. Well, most of us are. Darlene still has to take a shower."

He paused, then added, "That's a joke."

Harry wasn't laughing.

"Come inside," Xris said. "I let it be known among the neighbors that I was having a barbecue for some old friends."

"Maybe they'll think Harry's with the caterer," Jamil said, and entered the house. He glanced around appreciatively. "Nice. Very nice. Mind if I give myself a tour?"

"What about Darlene?" Harry continued stubbornly, as Jamil walked out the back door to view the deck. "Is she okay?"

"She's here," Xris said, gesturing into the bedroom. "Safe and sound. See for yourself."

"You didn't give them *her* real name?" Harry asked anxiously.

"No, of course, not, Harry! For God's sake—"

Xris pulled out his golden cigarette case—a gift from His Majesty the King—and removed a particularly strong and obnoxious form of tobacco known as a twist. Putting the twist into his mouth, he bit off the end, also biting off the words that would have hurt Harry and done little good anyway.

"Look, Harry, for the tenth time, if the job requires you to put on a disguise, I'll let you know! And I'll supply the disguise. What's in the package?"

Harry handed it over. "Cookies. My mom sent them. Did you check for bugs?" He peered worriedly up at the light fixture.

Xris opened his mouth, shut it again, clamped his teeth down hard on the twist. "No, Harry. I didn't think of it. Go ahead and take a look. Doc's got the equipment."

Harry brightened. "Sure thing. I'll get right on it." He wandered into the kitchen, bent down on his haunches to converse with Quong, who was still searching for disinfectant.

"Is Xris okay?" Xris heard Harry ask in what he probably considered to be an undertone.

"His thyroid levels are off. I am certain of it," Quong replied.

"Oh, gee." Harry cast Xris a glance of alarmed concern before he began wandering around the house with a frequency analyzer looking for any sort of miniature transmitter.

"Charming," said Jamil, coming back from the bed-rooms. "I'm thinking of building one of these vacation houses myself. Larger, of course, and not so close to the water, with a better view, a bigger garage, and located in a more upscale neighborhood. But other than that, this is very close to what I was considering."

"Glad you like it," Xris said, chewing on the twist.

A former officer in the Army, Jamil had been relegated to the job of teaching recruits how to prepare for zero-G combat. Xris had spotted Jamil's true talents and had suggested early retirement from the military, a suggestion Jamil was glad to take. Handsome, charming, with ebony black skin and melting brown eyes, he was now second-in-command on the Mag Force 7 team. He was attractive to women and extremely good with explosives.

Darlene emerged from the bedroom. "What the hell's Harry doing?" she demanded. "He told me I had to shut down!"

"He's checking for bugs," Xris said dryly.

"But didn't you—"

"Sure I did. But it keeps him occupied. Unless, of course, you have any packages that need to be delivered."

"I'm going to take a shower," Darlene muttered. Retreating to her room, she grabbed her robe and marched down the hallway. The next moment they heard her say firmly, "I don't care if there are bugs in the bathroom, Harry! They can wait until I've had my shower!"

"Gee, Darlene's in a bad mood," Harry commented on his return. "I didn't find any bugs in the house, Xris. But then I haven't checked the bathroom yet. You want me to look in the garage?"

"Sure, Harry. Jamil, I— Ouch! What the devil?"

"Blood sample," said Quong, walking off with an extractor and a tube filled with Xris's blood.

Xris swore softly, rubbed his arm.

The doorbell rang. And rang. And rang.

A vision in a purple vest, a frilly blouse, and purple satin pants slit up the sides to reveal his shapely legs, Raoul stood on the porch, his finger pressing the bell, an expression of ecstasy on his face. His eyes, beneath purple eye shadow, were dreamy and unfocused. A strong smell of citrus and rose wafted from the Adonian; his was a race noted for their beauty, their love of pleasure, and their lack of morals.

Standing beside Raoul, a drab planet to Raoul's gorgeous sun, was his partner, known only as the Little One. A large fedora covered the Little One's head, the brim shading his face. He wore a long raincoat that dragged the ground, and he kept the coat collar turned up. All that could be seen of the diminutive figure were two bright eyes.

The Little One never spoke. An empath and a telepath, the Little One was Raoul's friend and constant companion. The two made a good team. The Little One sheltered beneath the umbrella of Raoul's habitual, drug-induced euphoria, while the Little One's intelligence gave direction to Raoul's butterfly mind.

The Little One offered his hand to Xris, who shook it gravely, and then entered the house. Raoul remained on the porch, enjoying the synthesized music of the doorbell.

"Raoul," Xris said loudly between rings, and at last the name penetrated.

"Xris Cyborg!" Raoul cried, recognizing him with surprise and delight. "Whatever are you doing here?"

"I live here," Xris said patiently. "I was the one who invited you here. Remember?"

"No, but then why should I?" Raoul asked lightly. "Don't kiss me. You'll smudge my makeup."

"I wasn't going to—" Xris began, but gave up. Raoul had wafted past him into the hallway.

"Greetings, all! Jamil. I love your suit. Sardoni, isn't it? You can always tell. William Quong. I hope and trust that you are not conducting your ghastly experiments on the kitchen table.

"Darlene, my dear." Raoul kissed the air near her chin. "Don't ever wear that style bathrobe. It makes you look pudgy. Or maybe it's those chocolate eclairs you've been having for breakfast. Sorry, I'd love to stop and chat, but I really must visit the little boy's room. Where is it? Down the hall?" He headed that direction, paused a moment to gaze with horror at one of the paintings on the wall, shook his head—gently, so as not to disturb his long black hair—shuddered, and disappeared into the bathroom.

Quong emerged from the kitchen. "Your thyroid levels are fine, Xris. The white blood cell count is slightly elevated, however. I'd like to take another—"

"Xris," Harry shouted from the back door. "Is there any way to get under the house?"

"I am *not* pudgy!" Darlene stated indignantly. She looked at herself worriedly in the hall mirror. "Am I?"

"The patio's all wrong," Jamil was saying, "and the kitchen's much too small. I'd add a second story—"

A shriek came from the bathroom. "There's a hair in the sink! You people are barbarians!"

Xris grinned. It was great to have the family back together again.

They watched the sun melt into pink and gold and slide into the ocean. Couples walked along the beach, picking up shells. Children poured salt on a jellyfish. Xris's seagull returned, was introduced to the group, and accepted potato chips from Darlene's hand.

Raoul emerged from the bathroom, still upset over the state of the sink, but determined to bear his hardships bravely. He had changed his clothes—purple satin not being considered appropriate for barbeques—and his new outfit had done a great deal to console him.

Dr. Quong did eventually discover some sort of chemical imbalance—not with Xris, but with Harry. Quong held forth about half an hour on the value of proper nutrition, bombarding Harry with a barrage of references to folic acid, antioxidants, glycomates, zinc, and beta-carotene.

Harry sat listening dumbly, looking shell-shocked, and only said, at the end of the lecture, "Thanks, Doc. But I *like* french fries!"

Xris fired up the barbeque. Jamil brought out a platter of steaks.

"I told the doc they were a soy product," he said.

"Did he buy it?"

"Hard to tell. He's still furious over the french fries." Jamil was silent a moment, fidgeting, his hands in his pants pocket. "Look, Xris, maybe I'm getting as paranoid as Harry, but you see those two men walking along the beach?"

Xris glanced out. "Yeah. What about them?"

"Have you ever seen them around here before?"

"No, but then I haven't really been looking. Why?"

"Because they've passed this house four times now."

"Probably just out walking off dinner," Xris said. "But just in case, ask Darlene to stay indoors, will you? Don't let on why. Say the mosquitoes are bad. She hates mosquitoes. I'll keep an eye on those men."

The afterglow filled the sky, but shadows were gathering on the beach and it was difficult to see. Adjusting his cybernetic eye for night vision, Xris studied the two men. They were dressed in sweatpants and sneakers, wearing sweatshirts, big and bulky. They were in their late thirties, maybe, and engaged in conversation. One bent down, picked up a shell, and chucked it into the sea. Both paused to look with interest at the shriveled-up jellyfish. One patted a child on the head. They continued on down the beach.

Xris couldn't say positively that they weren't Hung assassins; those oversized sweatshirts could have concealed anything from a beam rifle to a small missile launcher. But he put the odds against it, at about seven to one. Hung assassins didn't stroll about in the open before making a hit. And why would they wait to attack when Darlene was surrounded by friends, instead of catching her alone, as she had been on the way from the spaceport?

"Ten to one against," he said to himself, and stuck a fork in the steaks.

CHAPTER 4

Fear and Hope are—Vision
William Blake, "The Gates of Paradise"

Harry Luck didn't like it. Not one damn bit.

He squirmed in his chair on the deck, looked over his shoulder, peered back into the house. Standing up, he tried to see over the pink-flowered hedge that circled the house on three sides, but he couldn't manage it. Imagining assassins lining the block, laser weapons taking aim, he slumped back down disconsolately in the chair, only to start up again when a bell dinged.

"Egg rolls are done," said Jamil, giving Harry a soothing pat on the shoulder as he walked past him into the kitchen.

"Drink this," Raoul said, skimming by in a flutter of pink silk. He handed Harry a drink the same color, with clusters of frosted grapes. "It will settle your nerves."

Harry took hold of the glass automatically, but he didn't drink it. He made it a practice never to eat or drink anything the Loti handed to him if he could help it. Not that Raoul would poison him deliberately, but there was always the possibility that something lethal could have slipped in by accident. Raoul was always fully stocked wherever he went. He had lipstick that could kill a full-grown man in under three minutes, while the contents of his pillbox could have served to instruct a graduate-level class on toxicology, and there was no telling what was hidden underneath his long, fashionably painted fingernails.

Harry didn't know what to do with the drink. He didn't dare pour it out; Raoul was frightfully sensitive. Harry sat with the icy, fruity drink freezing his hand until the Little

One shuffled up and switched the pink drink with the grapes for a cold beer.

Harry was grateful for the beer, but he still didn't like the situation and he didn't know what to do about it. He wandered into the kitchen, where Darlene sat, avoiding the mosquitoes, a pink fruity drink in her hand, a drink she was obviously enjoying.

Harry, with a nervous glance at the pink concoction, offered to bring her a beer.

"Thank you, Harry," Darlene answered with a smile, "but I've never tasted a pink flamingo before. It's really good. Would you like a sip?"

Harry shook his head. He spent a few anxious moments expecting to see Darlene double over, clutching her throat, her last words, "There's something wrong with this drink!" Instead, she sucked on an ice cube.

Harry thought Darlene one of the most attractive women he'd ever met. The fact that she had once been a he didn't bother Harry, who had only the vaguest concept of how that had all worked anyway. So Darlene was a miracle of modern science? Big deal. Harry's own mother, often mistaken for his sister in dim light, was the product of a prominent Dorasian plastic surgeon. In Harry's mind, the two were much the same. He was fond of Darlene and he worried about her.

Hung assassins had tried twice before to kill her. The Little One's telepathic abilities, Raoul's pharmaceuticals, and her own wit had saved her.

"What's wrong, Harry?" Darlene asked.

Harry would have liked to have answered her, but he couldn't put his feelings into words. It was all wrong, that's what it was. From the waves crashing on the beach, which was practically in their backyard; to the flowered hedge, the patio, the sliding glass doors; to Jamil serving hot egg rolls, Raoul mixing drinks from the wet bar in the living room, Xris flipping steaks on the barbecue outside.

Harry cast another anxious glance at Darlene and said in a low voice, fearful of being overhead, "What kind of a place is this for us to meet?"

Darlene smiled. "I think it's a very nice kind of place,

Harry. The weather is beautiful. Our swim this afternoon was outstanding. And those steaks smell wonderful."

"It is amazing what they can do with soy products these days," Dr. Quong observed.

Harry was not to be lured off course. As Jamil had once remarked rather caustically, once a thought finally wandered into Harry's head, he clung to it as if it might be the last one ever.

"There's no protection," he restated. "We're out here in broad daylight—"

"It's evening now," Jamil corrected.

Harry ignored him. "The neighbors have seen you, Darlene. They've seen all of us."

"Sometimes the best hiding place is out in the open," Quong stated, helping himself to an egg roll, having first ascertained that it was baked, not fried. "Relax, Harry, my friend. I'm going to have a fruit juice. Would you like anything?"

Harry shook his head.

"I think I'll go with Doc," Darlene said. Pausing, she stared out the front window.

"Looking for snipers?" Jamil asked.

Darlene laughed a little self-consciously. "Yes, I guess I was, to tell the truth. You know how it is—if someone says it's Monday and they keep saying it's Monday, even if you know for a fact that it's Tuesday, you check your calendar. Harry's making me jumpy, that's all. I'll go help Raoul with the drinks."

Jamil walked over to Harry, bent down, tray in hand. "Egg roll?"

"Are there snipers out there?" Harry asked.

"Unless the Hung are employing toddlers, no," Jamil answered.

"Tycho should be on the roof with his rifle," Harry said, and scooped up a handful of egg rolls.

"Tycho's dead, Harry." Jamil frowned down at the now empty tray. "Did you get enough?"

"Are there more?" Harry asked.

"No." Jamil sounded cold. "There aren't."

"That's okay, then. Thanks. And I know Tycho's dead. I was there when he died. It's just that we're stuck here out in the open with no protection. No security cams, no shields. Anything could hit us."

"We're in a house, Harry, not a Stiletto bomber. Very few of these homes in this neighborhood are equipped with blast shields. We have a smoke detector, a carbon monoxide detector, a radon monitor, and an excellent burglar alarm system. You should know. You checked it out yourself. We're perfectly safe."

"Tycho should be on the roof with a rifle," Harry maintained glumly. "Someone should be on the roof."

"I'm sure the neighbors would love it. We're supposed to be blending in with suburbia, not scaring the hell out of them."

"He could wear a disguise," Harry suggested.

"As what? A vid receiver? Santa Claus? Eight tiny reindeer?"

"There *are* eight of us," Harry said, intrigued. "No," he amended after a moment's thought. "I guess there's only seven, now that Tycho's dead. Even so, I don't think the roof is big enough for all of us. Thanks, Jamil, but I don't believe that will work."

Jamil muttered something it was just as well Harry didn't hear and tossed the empty tray into the sink.

Harry roamed outdoors, onto the deck, where Xris was cooking and Dr. Quong was looking on with displeasure.

"It has been determined that charring food over an open flame has caused cancer in laboratory mice."

"That's why I didn't invite them over for dinner," Xris said.

Quong appeared puzzled.

"The mice, I mean," Xris explained. "It's a joke, Doc."

"Uh, Xris, don't you think it would be a good idea if you wore your weapons hand?" Harry asked, gazing down at the steaks sizzling on the grill.

Xris was a cyborg. His right side was mostly human, his left side mostly metal. It was hard to tell his age for that very reason. He was one of those men who looked old at twenty, young at sixty. He was bald, his head scarred, one of his eyes was his from birth and the other came from a factory. A twist dangled almost perpetually from his mouth.

If he wasn't smoking one—which he usually didn't, out of deference to his friends—he was chewing it.

His left hand was detachable; he had specially made weapons and tools that fit onto his arm. But today he wore only the plastiskin, fleshfoam hand that looked and felt real; would even bleed fake blood. He held nothing more deadly than a long-handled fork in one hand and a can of beer in the other.

Xris took a swig of his beer. "It's kind of hard to flip steaks with an anti-tank rocket launcher, Harry. Don't worry. This is my ex-wife's house. It's a lot safer than my own, mainly because no one's looking for me here."

"Safer, Xris?" Harry repeated, dumbfounded. "In your house you've got more security than the king has in the whole fucking Royal Palace. How can this be safer?"

"Language!" Raoul admonished in shocked tones, pointing to the children playing in the waves and feeding the seagulls.

Harry stared down gloomily at his empty beer mug, wondered what had happened to the beer. He couldn't remember drinking it.

"Jamil says to tell you, Xris Cyborg," Raoul continued, holding a hand over his face, shading his complexion from the ravages of the moonlight, "that the hors d'oeuvres went faster than he expected." Raoul cast an accusing glance at Harry. "You can serve dinner anytime."

Xris stuck his fork in one of the steaks, lifted it, peered at it. The meat was blackened; blood ran from the prongs of the fork.

Raoul glanced at it, made a retching sound, covered his mouth with his hand.

"Cut the dramatics. Go tell everyone the steaks are done, will you?" Xris said, sniffing appreciatively.

"For those who want to add unsightly bulges to their hips and tummies, the burned animal flesh is ready," Raoul called, traipsing back to the patio, his high heels making small indentations in the lush green lawn. "I have, of course, made one of my special olive, goat cheese, bean sprout, artichoke, and anchovy salads for those of us who are concerned with our appearance. I hope you'll have some," Raoul said to Darlene. "I made it 'specially for you."

"I am not pudgy," Darlene insisted irritably.

"Flesh?" Dr. Quong repeated incredulously, coming to stand beside the barbecue. He regarded the steaks with deep suspicion. "What does he mean, 'animal flesh'? Jamil told me this was a soy product." He shook his finger at Xris. "You know your cholesterol count!"

"Yeah, Doc, I keep it written on the back of my hand," Xris said, winking at Harry. "I guess I was mistaken. These are real beef. Must have picked up the wrong package. Sorry about that, everyone."

"We forgive you," said Jamil, grinning. "Trust me on that."

"Grab a plate and line up," Xris ordered.

Harry juggled his plate nervously.

"Xris, I really think—"

"Harry, stop it," Xris said. His tone was stern, his expression grim. "For the last time, there's nothing wrong. There's no one watching us or bugging us or tailing us. You're making Darlene nervous. Hell, you're making me nervous! Now sit down and eat your dinner."

"Yeah, Xris. Sure. Sorry." Harry carried his plate inside.

"Your problem is clogged pores," said Raoul, accosting Harry as he walked past. "Try my salad. There's nothing like goat cheese to open the pores."

Raoul heaped salad onto Harry's plate. Blood running from the rare meat mingled with the anchovy salad dressing. Harry sat down at the table, stared at the pink swan napkin in front of him, wondered what he was supposed to do with it.

The Little One, seated to his Harry's left, flicked the napkin open with a deft hand and flung it onto Harry's broad lap, then dumped most of his salad onto Harry's plate when Raoul, his attention captured by the wind chimes, wasn't looking.

"So, what's all this about?" Jamil asked between mouthfuls. "What's the job, Xris?"

"No business discussed during meals," Dr. Quong said sternly, tapping his finger on the table. "Bad for the digestion."

Xris glanced around at the others, winked, and started on his steak. The talk became general—a discussion of Rusty Love and his latest vid, the current problems facing the Prime Minister, an argument over the changes made in the wing configuration of the new model Rapier spacefighter.

Harry gave a deep sigh. He stared down at his plate. He had eaten not only the steak but the salad as well. He had a vague impression that the anchovies had been disgusting, but he didn't remember any of it. At least he'd won Raoul's heart.

"I'm so glad you liked my salad!" Raoul gushed. "I've got *lots* made up! I'll send some home with you."

"Sure," said Harry, not paying attention. "Thanks."

He knew now what was really, truly bothering him. He didn't know how he knew, he just knew.

Xris was wrong about them being safe. Someone was out there watching them, stalking them, waiting to nail them. For the first and only time in all the years they'd been together, Harry knew that Xris was wrong.

Harry could only hope Xris wasn't dead wrong.

CHAPTER 5

If the lion was advised by the fox, he would be
cunning.

William Blake, "Proverbs of Hell"

"We'll have our coffee and dessert inside," said Xris.
"And then we'll talk business."

Jamil and Darlene served coffee and cheesecake as the
rest of the group gathered around a vidscreen. Xris slid in
a memory cube. A space map appeared on the screen, complete with locator numbers and names of prominent stars.
An arrow pointed at one tiny planet orbiting one of the
stars. Xris zoomed in on this planet.

A city appeared, a dot of white floating on green, surrounded by blue.

Xris began his briefing. "For those of you who don't
recognize it, and I don't expect any of you do, this is the
planet Del Sol, located in the Osiris system. The planet is
small, but it has a large population, mostly gathered in one
major city. This is the capital."

They flew closer, viewed, from space, a large grid configuration. "Three-fifths of Del Sol's population lives in this
city, known as Rianus. The other two cities are on a different continent and are mostly agrarian in nature. Basically
they exist to feed Rianus. They're ruled by governors ap-
pointed by the dictator of Rianus, a man called Kirkov.
Harry, what the devil are you doing?"

Harry jumped, dropped the phone, which he had been
dismantling. "Uh, nothing, Xris. I forgot to check the phone
for bugs—"

Xris looked grim. Quong put the phone back together.
Harry slumped unhappily on the sofa.

"Now, here's the plan," Xris said, when order had been restored. "Del Sol is ruled by this guy Kirkov. He's a dictator, a psychotic who thinks he's a god. Because he thinks he's a god, he has decided that he outranks King Dion. Kirkov's formed a small hegemony in the Foravis Arc, which is here, next to the Hormel Cluster. They call themselves the League of Nine Sisters. The league, led by this nutcase, has pulled out from under Imperial control. They refuse to let the Royal Navy in their sector, which, as you can see"—Xris brought up the map of the galaxy again—"is a sector that has a certain strategic value."

"The Royal Navy should go in and kick some ass," Jamil stated. "Send a few big cruisers in there like the *King James* and this Kirkov would come out yelping with his tail between his legs."

"The Royal Navy would like nothing better," Xris said. "There is a problem, however. Darlene, would you care to explain?"

Darlene Mohini had been a high-ranking officer in the Navy, a part of RFComSec, involved in handling all the secret codes, making them and cracking them. Her departure had been abrupt and unexpected, causing the Navy considerable alarm and inconvenience. All that was behind her now. The Navy, if not thrilled that she was now a civilian, was at least no longer threatening to have her shot on sight.

"This sector doesn't just have a *certain* strategic value," Darlene told them. "It has *major* strategic value."

"What's that?" Jamil argued. "It's far from the Void, which means it's far from the Corasians. Of course, if the information's classified—"

"It is. How can I put this?" Darlene's brow furrowed in thought.

Raoul shook his head sadly and whispered recommendations for cream of cucumber.

"Let's imagine that there's a sector in the galaxy where some very delicate scientific experiments are being conducted—"

"The Bulgarvian wormhole!" Quong said, snapping his fingers. "I recall reading about that. Nothing was ever discovered, however, and it was all discounted as so much theoretical nonsense. I had no idea anyone was still pursuing that. So the reports of its nonexistence must have been—"

"Delicate scientific experiments," Xris said loudly, overriding Quong. "Of a most important nature. Believe me, the Royal Navy does not want to draw the galaxy's attention to this particular area of space."

"If they have to send in the big guns, they will," Darlene agreed. "But they'd rather try other means first."

"The 'other means' are where we come in, I take it," Quong said.

"The people of Del Sol are not keen on being ruled by a psychotic god. But Kirkov has a very effective, highly efficient force of secret police. It is said that you can't take a crap on Del Sol without the secret police barging into the stall to hand you the toilet paper."

"I could make the god go away," Raoul offered, and licked his lips suggestively. "Like the wretched Madame President on . . . where was it?" He held one of his silent conversations with the Little One. "Yes, Modena. Thank you, my friend."

"I know you could," said Xris. "That was my first idea. Unfortunately, the politics aren't as simple as they were on Modena. Kirkov has his people in every level of government. Not only that, but they also run the banks, which means that he controls the economy. And he has a successor chosen, ready to step in when he attains godhood. These people of his have things very good right now and they won't be easy to dislodge."

"It would take me some effort, but it could be managed," Raoul said.

"Don't you think a bunch of bureaucrats all dropping dead at the same time would tend to make people suspicious?"

"It's been done before," Raoul observed with a flutter of his eyelashes.

"Yes, but not by us and not by the Royal Navy. We want to avoid bloodshed, if possible," said Xris firmly. "Now, there's another factor at work on Del Sol. The planet's original inhabitants, a race known as the dremecks—"

"Dremecks. I have never heard of them," said Quong,

whipping out his electronic notepad. "Let me have all the details."

"Sorry, Doc, but I wasn't able to acquire much advance information. What I do know is that they're gentle and peace-loving and they are now enslaved. And while the scientists and military experts are concerned over the wormhole that they won't admit exists, His Majesty is concerned about the dremecks. Not just the fact that they're slaves, although that's bad enough. They're about to become dead slaves."

"Genocide? In this enlightened age?" Quong was skeptical.

"It's been done before in enlightened ages, Doc," said Xris. "His Majesty's intelligence has uncovered a plot by Kirkov to load all the dremecks into transports, haul them off into the next quadrant, and space them."

"What a waste," Raoul lamented. "He could sell them to the Corasians for meat and make several million quite easily."

The other team members stared at him.

Raoul blinked. "Sorry," he murmured. "Did I say that out loud?"

"Is Intelligence certain of its information?" Darlene asked. "I'm afraid I agree with the Doc. It seems impossible to imagine."

"You were in Intelligence," Xris said. "You tell me."

Darlene bit her lip, shook her head, and sighed.

"The humans on Del Sol may live in a police state, but won't they be just the least little bit upset when they wake up one morning to find an entire population missing?" Jamil demanded.

"Kirkov's got that figured out. He's already starting to talk about 'relocating' the dremecks to 'an environment more suited to their needs.' He'll probably put out fake reports showing the dremecks frolicking on a beach somewhere."

"Not to disparage Intelligence"—Dr. Quong bowed to Darlene—"but I tend to agree with Raoul, the Master forgive me. It seems a terrible waste of resources. This Kirkov has a cheap labor force. Why get rid of them?"

"Because dremecks are running Del Sol," Xris answered.

"That is not logical, my friend. If they are running the planet, then they are in no danger."

"I don't mean running as in controlling. I mean that they are literally running it. The dremecks are very clever people. The humans have been turning over all the 'menial' labor tasks to them, along with a lot of low-level tech jobs. The dremecks have become essential to the workings of the nuclear power plants, the electrical substations, the commlinks—you name it. Kirkov is afraid that one day the dremecks will shut Del Sol down, hold the planet hostage. If he gets rid of them himself, sure, things'll be chaotic for a while, until the humans can figure out what the dremecks have been doing, but at least Kirkov will be in control."

"Poison," said Raoul, tapping his perfectly manicured nails against a small golden case he had removed from his purse.

"No," said Xris. "Revolution. Mag Force 7 has been hired to aid a rebellion. The humans are afraid to rebel against Kirkov, but we have word that the dremecks are not. The dremecks need weapons, training. That's where we come in."

"Time frame?" asked Quong.

"We're— What's the matter with him?"

Xris spoke to Raoul, but he was referring to the Little One, who appeared distraught.

"He is picking up on disturbing emotions," Raoul said, and looked accusingly at Harry.

"Harry," said Xris severely, "you're thinking again."

"Sorry." Harry ducked his head.

"Time frame. The dictator plans to space the dremecks on the night of his birthday, a little present to himself. Twenty-one space-time days from today."

Jamil raised his hand to indicate he had a question, and without waiting for Xris to acknowledge him, fired it in. "What's our take on this?"

"A small amount up front, with a promise, in writing, for more when the job's done."

"Who's hiring us?"

"I can't say," Xris hedged. "As you can imagine, this has to be handled with extreme delicacy. Certain people can't be known to be involved."

"You can't tell us who's hired us and they're paying us with promises. No offense, but I think Doc's right. You've got a chemical imbalance somewhere."

"If we pull off this revolution, this person will make the payment," Xris said confidently.

"What if we don't pull it off? What happens then?"

Xris shrugged. "When have we failed?"

Raoul raised his hand.

"That time doesn't count," Xris snapped.

Raoul lowered his hand.

Xris continued. "First we train the dremecks into a disciplined, crack fighting force—"

"Did you say we're fighting for King Dion?" Harry interrupted. He had been thinking of something else, but thought he should say something to make Xris think that he—Harry Luck—hadn't really been thinking at all.

"No, Harry, I didn't say that," Xris said patiently. "I didn't say anything about His Majesty, or if I did I didn't mean to and so you just forget it. All right?"

Harry nodded.

"Good. Jamil, you and Harry will be in charge of training the dremecks.

"Raoul, you and the Little One will infiltrate the Ministry of Internal Security and keep them from finding out about our rebellion. If they do catch on to us, your secondary mission is to pass along the warning."

"Internal Security," Raoul said, tasting the words on his tongue. He evidently didn't like the flavor, for he came as close to frowning as he possibly could without actually harming his complexion. "They sound frightfully . . . secure. Are you certain I am going to enjoy this?"

Xris took this opportunity to put a twist into his mouth, which also allowed him to count to whatever number he currently required to restore his patience.

"You're not being paid to like it," Xris said finally, chewing on the twist.

"I'm not?" Raoul was agog. "Then why ever am I doing it?"

The Little One gave his friend a thump on the thigh with his fist.

Raoul massaged his leg. "That may do wonders for cellulite, my friend, though thus far—thank the gods of thigh cream—I do not suffer from that malady. But I take your point."

Raoul gave a magnanimous nod and subsided. Xris waited a moment to make certain he wasn't going to suffer from further interruption, then proceeded.

"Darlene, you will be in charge of subverting the local media. The population has to believe that there's the rebel equivalent of four Imperial Marine Divisions ready to take the city, and you're the one who's going to make them believe it. In addition, you'll plant a few bugs in the communication system of Kirkov's Army, make it tough for them to put together a military response to our actions."

Darlene nodded, smiling.

Xris shifted the twist from one side of his mouth to the other. He looked grim. "Doc, I saved the messy, dangerous part of the job for you."

"Of course," Quong said calmly. "You know that I am the most capable of handling such assignments."

Jamil snorted. Quong cast him a disparaging glance, sat up even straighter.

"I want you to gain entrance into Del Sol high society, Doc."

"Yes, and then whom do I assassinate?"

Xris took the twist from his mouth. A corner of his lip twitched. "You don't assassinate anyone, Doc. You get chummy with the rich and the powerful, find out who's discontented with the current regime, who would be willing to provide influence and backing when our brave rebel forces march down the streets of Del Sol." Xris waved the twist. "Promise them a share of the next government, if you want."

"Dangerous assignment, Doc," said Jamil, chuckling. "Watch out that your black tie doesn't strangle you. And think of all the champagne you'll have to drink to keep your cover! I'm sure Raoul can teach you the latest dance steps—"

Raoul was patting the air with his fingertips, a sure sign that he was distraught. "Champagne! Black tie! The rich and the powerful! And you are sending in a man who wears cranberry-colored socks with a red cummerbund! I protest most strongly—"

"I told you, I dressed in the dark! And no one could see my socks anyway!" Quong returned, offended.

"*I* knew they were there," Raoul replied in sepulchral tones. "And they ruined my evening."

"Well, as long as we're being honest"—Quong bristled— "the feather boa *you* were wearing made you look like a—"

The doorbell rang.

Jamil looked at Xris, silently asked if he was expecting someone.

Xris shook his head.

The living room was located in the rear of the house, provided no glimpse of what was happening in front. There was no way they could see who was out there.

The doorbell rang again.

"Aren't the gate guards supposed to notify you if anyone is coming?" Jamil asked softly.

Xris nodded. "Unless someone told them not to. Doc, check out the back."

Quong padded soft-footed through the darkened living room to the sliding glass doors overlooking the deck and the beach.

Xris turned to the Little One. "Who is it?"

The Little One grabbed hold of his fedora, pulled it down over his ears almost to his small shoulders, and shook his head violently.

"He says that whoever is out there is surrounded by what I can only describe as a . . . a mental dust storm," Raoul said. "The dust storm prevents my friend from obtaining any sort of reading."

"Dandy. Just dandy," Xris muttered.

"I told you we should have set out the security cams," Harry pointed out.

"Thank you, Mr. Luck. You can be team leader next week, okay?"

The ringing was repeated, more forcefully.

"Xris," reported Dr. Quong, returning from his recon-naissance mission, "there are two men walking slowly along the beach."

"Sweatshirts? Sweatpants?"

"Yes, those are the ones."

Xris swore softly, rose to his feet. Raoul reached languidly and casually for his purse, which contained his special lethal lipstick. Jamil drew a .44-decawatt gun from a holster he wore on his belt in the small of his back and padded soft-footed into the hall, positioning himself for a clear line of fire out the front door. The Little One placed his hand inside his raincoat, brought out a blowgun—his favored weapon—and crept behind the couch. Quong drew his .44 and placed his back against the wall, keeping a watch out the patio doors.

"Harry, you're with Darlene!" Xris whispered.

He looked at the vidscreen, which provided a view of the porch, but all he could see were wavy lines: some sort of interference.

"Sorry, I can't come to the door right now," he said through the speaker. "I just got out of the shower and I'm dripping wet with no clothes on. Who is it?"

"I'm a friend of your wife's," was the response in a cool, feminine voice.

"Sorry. Marjorie's out of town. Leave your name and I'll tell her you called."

"I know she's out of town," the voice returned. "I know where she is, in fact. Do you?"

Jamil sucked in his breath, let it out in a low whistle.

Quong frowned and pursed his lips.

"What is it? What's wrong?" Raoul whispered. He turned to his friend. "Do you know what's wrong?"

The Little One made a low, feral growling sound in his throat.

Xris said nothing for a moment. He removed the twist from his mouth, stared at it, then tossed it into an ashtray.

He was on the intercom again. "Look, give me a moment. Let me put some clothes on." He turned, issued orders. "Harry, take Darlene to the garage. The hover's parked inside. Switch on the computer, but don't fire the engines. Just be ready to if I give you the word. You and Darlene might need to make a fast departure." Xris tapped his head. "Listen for my orders over the commlink. Got that, Harry?"

"Commlink?" Harry was puzzled.

"The one behind your ear! The one Doc implanted! Tap it twice to activate it!"

"Oh, yeah. Sorry, I forgot. Sure, Xris. You can count on me." Harry drew his handgun from its shoulder holster.

"The two men have changed direction." Quong was keeping an eye out the back. "They are now approaching the house."

"Weapons?"

"None in sight."

Xris looked back at Darlene, who was standing stubbornly in the middle of the room, not wanting to leave.

"Harry, carry her if you have to," Xris said grimly.

Darlene glanced at Harry, who was quite prepared to carry out Xris's least order, and she stalked off to the garage.

The hover, a newer model, stood on its pads. Harry went to take a discreet look out the garage's front windows. Expecting to see the street lined with helo-tanks, he was astonished to see only one vehicle parked outside, a hover painted an unassuming gray. Unfortunately, the hover was parked directly behind Harry.

"Don't worry, Darlene." Harry eased himself into the front seat, studied the instrument panel as Darlene climbed into the passenger seat. Harry was pleased with what he saw. This was a good machine. He located the control that would open the garage door, considered whether or not it would be best to use it or just blast his way through. "We'll get you out of here."

"Sure, Harry. Thanks," Darlene said quietly. She was nervous, but not for herself. She was worried for Xris.

"We're all set here," Harry reported in.

No answer.

"Tap it," Darlene reminded him.

Harry tapped the communicator device—a small metal commlink inserted beneath his skin behind his left ear. He could now hear what was happening back in the house.

"Everyone in place?" Xris was asking in low tones.

Soft responses from Jamil and Quong.

"Just putting on my lipstick now." That was Raoul.

"Here goes." The squeak of the front door hinges.

Xris sounded grim. "Who are you and what do you want?"

"Xris Tampambulos?" This was a man's voice.

"Who wants to know?"

"Agent Jonathan Fisk, FISA. This is Agent Rizzoli. I have a warrant for your arrest."

"What's the charge?"

"The murder of Dalin Rowan, senior agent with the Federal Intelligence Services Agency."

"Oh, dear God!" Darlene whispered.

CHAPTER 6

The fox condemns the trap, not himself.
William Blake, "Proverbs of Hell"

Xris had experienced a lot of unpleasant surprises in his life. The time when a munitions factory had blown up in his face. The time when he had discovered there were two assassins out to kill the king, when he'd only expected one. The time a deadly antique robot that wasn't supposed to work, worked. This unpleasant surprise ranked right up there with the worst of them.

"What was that remark you made about my wife?" Xris demanded.

Two agents stood on the porch. The two men approaching the house from the beach were undoubtedly connected with the Bureau as well. Standard procedure, in case the suspect tried to escape through the back. The Bureau didn't expect trouble from Xris, however. Fisk didn't have his gun drawn. Neither did the agent behind him, an attractive, energetic-looking, and excited young woman, who was trying hard to look cool and professional. This was probably her first field assignment.

Fisk was obviously an old hand at this. Middle-aged, with a roll of fat around his middle, he didn't look cool and professional. He just looked bored.

By now it had occurred to Xris what was going on. Amadi—that son of a bitch! So this is how he's going to get to Rowan. He knows darn good and well I didn't kill Rowan because he knows dark good and well Rowan's not dead! I hand her over to prove I'm innocent. Nice try, ex-boss, but it won't work.

So what to do? The team was ready. Xris knew without

looking that Jamil had moved to a better location, was now taking aim through the kitchen window. Quong was guarding the rear with a beam rifle from the cedar chest in the bedroom. Xris had only to say the word and Fisk and the pretty, perky agent would be smoking corpses on his front lawn, with two smoldering agents on his back deck.

And what then?

Fisk cheerfully filled in the details.

"This is a nice house," he stated. "Nice neighborhood. I'm sure you wouldn't want to do anything that would upset your neighbors or damage your wife's reputation. She teaches school near here, doesn't she? They're very particular about the people they hire to teach our kids. And I hear she's been accepted by some high-powered university for graduate work. Universities like publicity, but not that kind. Not GNN interviewing a student who's also the wife of a murderer—a cop-killer." Fisk's voice grated. "So tell your people to put down their guns."

"Xris!" Darlene spoke urgently through the comm. "I'll turn myself in. I'll explain everything."

"Nobody fires!" Jamil ordered. "Nobody moves. Everyone stays put until Xris gives the word."

Give the word. And what happens? Xris knew well what would happen. Four bodies. Four dead federal agents. Sir John Dixter would renounce him. The king himself would be forced to sign the order for Xris's execution.

And not just *his* execution. Jamil, Quong, Harry . . .

"You're a clever bastard, Amadi," Xris muttered to himself. "Choosing the one place where you knew I wouldn't be able to put up a fight. How did you know Marjorie would invite me here? Unless . . ."

No, Marjorie never would have agreed to trap him. He knew that. But what if she didn't know? What if she hadn't been the one to send the invitation? What if, after all, she didn't really give a damn . . .

Stop it! he ordered himself. He couldn't be distracted.

"I'll come to the Bureau with you," he offered. "Just promise me that my wife won't be involved. You can make that promise, can't you?"

He stared hard at Fisk, who didn't blink an eye.

"Yeah, I can promise that."

"I don't want her name on the vids or splashed all over the mags."

"We don't want publicity over this case any more than you do, Mr. Tampambulos," the woman stated.

"Rizzoli's right," Fisk reiterated. "We don't want anything about you on the nightly news. We don't want the public to know about a rogue agent, a traitor to the force. A man who murders not only another agent but one who was his best friend." His voice hardened. "Not the type of publicity the Bureau wants. And just so you know, Mr. Tampambulos, I can call in all the firepower I need, have it here the moment I touch this button. I repeat, tell your mercenary pals to put away their guns."

"Give the word, Xris." That was Quong. "I have a clear shot."

"My people are not involved in this," Xris said. "They had nothing to do with any of it."

"We're aware of that, Mr. Tampambulos. They'll be asked to come down to the office for routine questioning, but after that they'll be free to leave the planet. They'll be encouraged to leave, in fact," Fisk added dryly.

Harry's plaintive voice came over the communicator. "What's the deal here? Xris didn't kill Rowan. Rowan's sitting right next to me."

"Cut the chatter," Jamil returned tersely.

"Jamil, Quong, put down your weapons," Xris ordered.

Harry was baffled. Darlene Mohini, who used to be Dalin Rowan, was pale and shocked and distraught, but she was most definitely not dead.

He started to say something to her, but she pinched him on the arm—hard, it hurt—and gestured to the commlink. Harry went back to listening.

"You have the right to remain silent," Rizzoli was saying. "You have a right to retain counsel. Anything you say may be used in evidence against you. Do you understand these rights?"

"Yes." Xris sounded tired. "I understand. Look, I'll make a deal with you."

"You're not in much of a position—"

"Yeah, Fisk, I know all that. I used to be on the other side of that badge. But I also figure you'd like to wrap this up without any trouble. If you've read my files, you know the reputation of the people in this house. You know that if I decide to refuse to cooperate, my people will back me up. You might capture me—*might,* I say—but I guarantee you'll lose some good people in the process, not to mention the fact that this lovely neighborhood will look like a war zone when we're finished."

"Are you threatening us, Mr. Tampambulos?" Fisk demanded. "I have to warn you that this will be taken into account at your trial—"

"What the hell did *you* do to me? That business about my wife! Oh, yeah, it was a good ploy. It got my attention. But wait until *my* attorney hears about that one! Can you spell *coercion*?"

Fisk was silent a moment, then said, "What's the deal?"

"Let me walk out of here without restrainers—"

"You're a goddam murder suspect—"

"A murder that happened ten years ago!" Xris returned. "Look, Fisk, *if* you've read my file, you know that there aren't any restrainers made that can hold me if I want to bust loose."

Harry could hear the whine of machinery and guessed that Xris was flexing his fake hand.

"I don't want the neighbors to see me being hauled off like a common criminal. My wife has to live here."

"Anything else we can do for you, Mr. Tampambulos?" Fisk had gone from cold to sarcastic. "Maybe we should send for a limo."

"Let me have one minute to talk with my people."

"Absolutely not—"

"We'll hold our conversation right here on the front porch. You can see everything, hear everything."

The sound of a crash exploded in Harry's communicator.

"Xris!" he shouted, then drew his gun and jumped out of the hover.

"Harry, stop!" Darlene made a grab for him, but missed.

Harry could move with surprising speed for a man built along the lines of an armored bunker-buster.

"Harry!"

He ignored her.

Noise and confusion were the only sounds coming over

the commlink now. Harry dashed through the door into the kitchen, gun raised. Quong had his beam rifle aimed at the patio doors. The two beachcombers were nowhere in sight. They had disappeared, probably run around the sides of the house. Jamil, his back against the wall, held his .44-decawatt lasgun in both hands. At the word, he'd turn and fire down the hallway. The Little One had his preferred weapon, a blowgun that fired poisonous darts, in his hand. He was deadly accurate. Raoul was applying a second coat of lipstick, either to enhance its deadly effectiveness or because he thought the color was a shade too pale. It was hard to know.

And then Xris's voice, strong and urgent, came over the comm.

"Stand down! Everyone! It's only a broken flower urn. Stand down! That's an order."

Jamil glanced at the others, shook his head peremptorily. He and Quong maintained their positions. Catching sight of Harry, Jamil motioned him to keep back out of sight. Harry did as he was told, flattened himself—and there was a lot of himself to flatten—against the refrigerator.

"What the hell did you do that for?" Xris demanded angrily. "You nearly got us all shot!"

"Sorry about that," said Fisk, chagrined. "It's Rizzoli. She's a Talisian. Why don't you go wait in the car, Rizzoli? She's great with computers," he said, by way of apology. "The Bureau will reimburse your wife for the damages, of course."

"Since when did the Bureau start hiring Talisians?" Xris demanded. In an undertone, he spoke two words into the commlink, "Rizzoli. Computers."

"His Majesty's new nondiscrimination act," Fisk was saying. "Talisians can supposedly control their weird kinetic energy field with medication, but that doesn't seem to work with Rizzoli." He sounded resigned. "I'll give you your minute's meeting, Tampambulos. Right here. Where I can keep an eye on you. And I'll invite my friends to join us, if you don't mind." He lifted his wrist, spoke into a commlink. "Move in."

Harry looked to Jamil. This was their chance.

Jamil jerked his head toward the patio door. Harry

sneaked a peek around the fridge and through the pass-through window that opened into the living room. Two men could be seen coming from around the side of the house. Dressed in sweatsuits, they looked like ordinary tourists, except for the guns in their hands.

Harry lifted his shoulders slightly. There were only two of them.

"Xris?" Jamil asked over the commlink.

"No!" was Xris's urgent response. "Come out here on the porch. I've got instructions for you. Put your weapons down and come out. All of you."

"He's got a plan!" Jamil whispered. "Follow orders."

Replacing his gun in the holster he wore at his waist, gun at his back, he smoothed his shirt and walked down the hall. Quong tossed the beam rifle he'd been holding on the sofa and followed Jamil. Raoul came after, being quite careful not to lick his lips. The Little One shuffled along in Raoul's perfumed wake. Darlene entered through the garage door. She had regained some color in her cheeks, looked almost relieved.

Harry couldn't figure it out for a moment, then the light dawned.

"Ah," he said to himself. "We're going to take them out bare-handed." He shoved his gun back into its holster and moved from the kitchen into the hallway.

The team gathered on the porch, grimly eyeing the agents, who stared just as grimly back. The team formed a ring around Xris, with the Little One crowding close to his legs. They were silent and dour, except for Raoul, who took a mincing, fluttering step forward.

"What a very charming friend you have. Please introduce us, Xris Cyborg." He pursed his lips. His eyes, usually dreamy and drifting, were sharply gleaming, alert, focused.

"No, Raoul!" Xris said.

Jamil strong-armed Raoul, dragged him back.

"You don't need to be introduced," Xris said. "Not now."

"I don't! Are you sure?" Raoul asked with dangerous sweetness.

"I'm sure."

"If you say so." Raoul shrugged his shoulders delicately. "By the way, Jamil, you're hurting me."

"Sorry." Jamil loosened his grip on the Adonian's wrist.

"Don't be," Raoul said softly.

"You have one minute," Fisk barked.

Xris faced the team. "First, Jamil, contact the team's attorney. I want Parker himself, not one of his flunkies."

Jamil nodded.

"Second"—Xris's gaze encompassed all of them—"carry on with the job. Looks like we might need the cash to fund my legal expenses."

"It's not funny, Xris," Harry said.

"I know," Xris said, adding lamely, "I'm sorry."

Jamil glowered. Quong looked stern and severe. Raoul's lashes were lowered, but he kept his gaze on Fisk. The Little One, holding tightly on to Xris's pants leg like a child about to be parted from its mother, peeped at the agents from beneath the fedora.

Harry waited for Xris's signal. He would take out Fisk with a shoulder to the gut. Jamil and Quong could deal with the other two agents. Then—

"Good-bye. Good luck." Xris gave them a final glance.

"Xris!" Darlene took a step forward. "I'm going to—"

Xris caught her in his arms, gave her a kiss, and hugged her to his chest.

"Good-bye, sweetheart," he said loudly. In a harsh whisper that could only be heard over the comm, he said quickly, "Listen to me, all of you. Someone's set me up and he's done it for a reason. My guess is Amadi. He knows Darlene's not dead. He told me so."

Fisk, on the sidewalk, rolled his eyes. "C'mon, Tampambulos. Your minute's over. You can send your girlfriend a postcard from the lockup."

Xris held on to Darlene a moment longer, speaking through the cover of her hair. "Darlene once discovered someone high up in the Bureau was tied into the Hung. This may be our chance to find out who! Not a word until you hear from me. Promise? Rowan?"

"I promise, Xris," Darlene said reluctantly.

Xris released her with a kiss on the cheek. "All right, Fisk. I'm ready."

His jaw set, his face colder than his metal body parts, Xris walked down the stairs. His feet crunched on pieces of the broken stone urn. Watchful and wary, Fisk accompanied him.

Harry tensed, ready to jump. He expected Xris's "Now!" to explode among them like a grenade, wrecking havoc.

A gray hover vehic, unmarked, was parked on the landing site. Rizzoli, looking embarrassed, stood near the door on the passenger side. She held the door open. Xris entered the hover without a backward look. As he was climbing into the vehic, sliding across the seat, he spoke very low, but with such vehemence and force that every syllable was clear.

"None of you knows any connection between Dalin Rowan and Darlene Mohini. Remember that! I'll be in touch."

Rizzoli climbed into the hover, seated herself next to Xris. Fisk climbed in the front, next to the driver. The two agents in sweatshirts, who had been guarding the back of the house, came around to the front.

"Sorry for the disturbance," said one politely. "We'll arrange a time for you to come downtown tomorrow"—he glanced at his watch—"make that today—for questioning."

"Just routine," said the other. "And if any of you were thinking of taking a trip, I should tell you that your passports have all been revoked. Don't worry. They'll be reinstated as soon as we have all the information we need. Then you'll be free to go. Good morning."

With a cool nod, the two sauntered, at a slow pace, down the sidewalk.

Harry cast a pleading, stricken glance at Jamil.

Jamil shrugged. "We have our orders," he said bitterly.

Turning, he walked inside the house. The others followed, with the exception of Harry, who waited on the lawn.

Harry watched the hover lift up, make a graceful turn in midair, and glide at slow speed along the marked hover routes that ran between the houses. He had a fleeting memory of his old neighborhood—all the would-be teenage space pilots buzzing the housetops, flying under bridges, playing chicken with occasionally disastrous results. The hover sedan flew sedately around the corner and that was the last Harry saw of it.

Head down, his feet kicking at bits of broken urn, Harry returned to the house, slamming the door loudly on his way inside.

The sun was starting to rise, shining in the sky like a hot pink penny. Hard to believe it was dawn already.

They stood staring at each other. No one moved or spoke.

"I don't know about the rest of you," Jamil said at last, "but I could use a walk on the beach."

Harry blew up. "A walk on the—"

Jamil flashed a warning glance at him.

"Oh." Harry subsided. He understood. A little late, but he understood.

"I'll go remove my lipstick," Raoul said. "And change into my beachcomber outfit. I won't be a moment."

"Wait a minute, Loti. Did the Little One get anything out of Fisk?"

The Little One growled and pounded himself on the head, making a dent in the fedora.

"Fisk was using a mind block," said Raoul.

"Damn," muttered Jamil.

CHAPTER 7

A dead body revenges not injuries.
William Blake, "Proverbs of Hell"

The team reassembled out on the beach, about a mile from the house. The early morning breeze blowing off the ocean was pleasantly cool. Jamil built a driftwood fire, over Raoul's indignant protests that now his clothes would reek of smoke.

"Sit upwind," Jamil snapped. He was not in a good mood.

"It won't help," Raoul protested. "Smoke follows beauty, you know." He drew a fan from his purse and plied it frantically.

"Xris and Harry both checked the house for bugs," Jamil said, "but we've got to assume they missed one."

"Satellite surveillance," Quong said.

"Yeah, you're probably right. I didn't think of that."

The fire danced among the driftwood, the salt in the wood causing the flames to burn with vibrant colors of blue and green.

"We have to tell them the truth," Harry said. "We have to tell them that Darlene Mohini is Dalin Rowan!"

"We can't, Harry," Jamil returned. "You know what will happen to Darlene if her cover is blown."

"Her cover's already blown," Harry argued stubbornly. "The Hung know who she is. They've tried twice to kill her. Her cover doesn't matter now. We can't let Xris go to the disrupter for Dalin Rowan's murder when he—'scuse me, Darlene, I mean *she*—is sitting right here!"

Darlene said nothing. She stared into the flames, seemed not to have heard.

"We have thrown the Hung off Darlene's trail," Quong observed. "They don't know where she is at the moment."

"But they sure as hell will know where she is if she shows up on the vids!" Jamil said. "Besides, you heard Xris's order, Harry. Or at least I assume you heard it. You *did* have your communicator on this time, didn't you?"

"I had it turned on," Harry said defensively. "I keep telling you guys, the one time that happened I had popcorn caught in my tooth and it interfered with reception. This time there was nothing caught in my teeth. I heard his order fine."

Jamil frowned dangerously. "Then are you saying we disobey it?"

Harry couldn't imagine disobeying Xris. He'd been with Xris a lot of years, more than anyone else on the team. Harry admired Xris. Harry thought Xris was the smartest man he'd ever known, the smartest and the bravest and the best. Harry had once even thrown himself on a grenade to save Xris's life. The grenade had been filled with sleep gas and Xris had not been in any danger—except of taking an unforeseen snooze—but, as Xris himself had said, it was the thought that counted.

"Xris wasn't himself. He wasn't thinking straight." Harry looked up hopefully. "Maybe he could plead temporary insanity."

Jamil rolled his eyes, turned to Darlene. "What Xris said at the end—about you discovering that someone high up in the Bureau was working for the Hung—what was that all about?"

Darlene continued to stare into the fire. She had her knees drawn up to her chin, her arms resting on them. And though she was wearing a sweater and sitting close to the blaze, she shivered.

"After the explosion at the factory, the explosion that killed our partner Ito and maimed Xris, I went undercover and infiltrated the Hung's operations. I knew that one of our agents, a man named Armstrong, had been working for the Hung. He was the one who set up Xris and Ito to die in the explosion, and he tried to kill me. He thought he'd succeeded.

"I managed to get enough evidence to prove that Armstrong was on the take. He was about to be arrested, but someone beat us to him. Armstrong was murdered. The official word was that the Hung had been afraid he was going to turn on them, and killed him before he could talk. But I knew better. I was working for the Hung at the time and I knew that no orders had been issued by them.

"Armstrong had been taken out because he was going to reveal someone higher up in the Bureau who was being paid by the Hung. Someone who had a lot more to lose than that wretch Armstrong.

"I couldn't find out who it was, though. Not with Armstrong dead. I guessed that whoever it was knew I was on his trail. He would take care of me the same way he had taken care of Armstrong. That's when Dalin Rowan died and Darlene Mohini came into existence.

"Xris thinks—and I guess I have to agree with him—that this is why he's being arrested. The person I suspected then and the person I suspect now is a man named Jafar el Amadi. I still don't have any proof, though." Darlene sounded discouraged.

"Who's this Amadi?"

"Our former boss. He was in charge of the Hung investigation. Amadi worked against the Hung for years. He knew more about them than anyone. He retired, but his boss, a man named Robison, brought Amadi back on the case. Despite the fact that their leaders are in prison, the Hung are still in business. And they're afraid of me, as evidenced by the fact that twice they tried to kill me. The Hung know that Dalin Rowan is still alive and they now know that he's not Dalin anymore, but Darlene." She glanced around at all of them. "Amadi knows that, too. He knows that Dalin Rowan isn't dead."

"The hell he does!" Jamil exclaimed, startled. "Then why arrest Xris for a crime he knows he didn't commit?"

"Because Amadi knows Xris can't tell the truth!" Darlene said helplessly. "If he did, as you said, he'd blow my cover. He wants something from Xris and he figures he'll use this to pressure it out of him."

"If Amadi was working for the Hung," Dr. Quong said, "why did he permit you to go undercover and expose them? Why did he let the Hung leaders go to trial and then prison?"

"There wasn't anything he could do to stop it. Not without revealing his hand." Darlene shrugged. "And let's face it, the Hung were only put out of commission temporarily. Someone saw to it that the Hung leaders were transferred to a high-class, luxury prison known as Jango. Their operation is ongoing, even expanding. And because they're in prison, no one hassles them. It's a pretty sweet setup."

"What do you think this Amadi is trying to gain by arresting Xris?" Quong asked.

"My first guess was that Amadi was going to use this phony arrest to pressure Xris into giving me up," Darlene said slowly, thinking out loud. She rested her chin on her knees, stared into the fire as if, like the ancients, she could read the answers to her questions in the flames.

"Just what is it you know about the Hung, anyway?" Jamil asked.

"It's not what I *know,* exactly." Darlene hedged. "It's what they *think* I now. They think I know the location of the Hung's secret bank account. The one they're using to fund their operations."

"Do you?" Harry blurted out. "Where is it?"

Darlene avoided his eyes. Biting her lip, she picked up a stick and started poking at the fire. Sparks flew up in a shower that caused Raoul to squeal in protest.

"She can't tell us, Harry," Jamil said shortly. "In fact, she *shouldn't* tell us. I certainly don't want to know."

"Nor do I," Quong agreed. "They will be asking us questions today, and the less we know, the better." He frowned. "In fact, we probably know too much already. They will be giving us truth tests."

"Not to worry," Raoul called out, having removed himself as far from the conflagration as possible yet still hear what was being said. "I have a little concoction of my own that you can take with your orange juice this morning. You will be so relaxed during their questioning that you can lie without the least possibility of their detecting it. If they ask you if Xris Cyborg is your mother, you can answer yes with a clear conscience and no perceptible agitation in the brain waves."

"Check it out, Doc. If you think it's okay and it won't turn us into mindless zombies, we'll take it," Jamil instructed.

Raoul took offense. "Mindless zombies!" He sniffed. "I assure you it will do nothing of the sort. I take the drug myself on occasion, such as when Darlene and I go shopping for clothes."

Jamil grunted. "All right. We never heard of Dalin Rowan. We never heard of this Amadi guy and we never heard of the Hung. Got it, everyone? You got it, Harry?"

Harry frowned. "Yeah, but I don't want it."

Darlene looked up. The fire had been of some inspiration, after all.

"There might be a way to work this," she said. "When that Talisian broke the urn, Xris spoke two words into the commlink."

"*Rizzoli* and *computers*. Yeah, I heard him," Jamil said.

"That's right. If this Rizzoli is the office computer hound, then there might be a way to use her." Darlene hesitated. "I'll have to think about this. I'm not sure. . . ."

"What's wrong? Sounds like a good idea to me," said Jamil.

"There's one aspect to this that doesn't make any sense," Darlene explained. "The Hung know that Dalin Rowan is Darlene Mohini. If Amadi's working for the Hung, he must know that, too!" She spread her hands helplessly. "Why not just arrest me along with Xris? Amadi wants Xris and he wants him for a reason. I thought it was me, but now I'm not so sure."

"There's the death penalty on this planet," said Harry Luck.

Startled and alarmed, they all stared at him.

"Where the hell did you come up with that?" Jamil demanded.

"I read about it in one of the vidmags on the transport," Harry said loftily. "I'm not stupid. I do read. I read lots, as a matter of fact."

Darlene had gone extremely pale.

"Could that be the reason?" Jamil asked uneasily.

"Xris wouldn't let matters go that far," Quong predicted.

"*I* won't let it go that far," said Darlene.

"Yeah, well, it's a little late now, isn't it?" said Harry angrily. "We should have done something when those buzzards showed up on the doorstep! We never should have let them take Xris. We've been in tougher spots than that! We escaped from a Corasian mothership, for the love of God! We should have done something."

"What *could* we have done?" Jamil retorted. "The agents had the drop on us. So we start a firefight. What about those kids outside playing on the beach? What happens to them when the lasguns and beam rifles start blasting? Not to mention Xris. He would have been the first casualty. Remember what Fisk said about pushing a button? They had backup somewhere. You can bet on that. Snipers, most likely."

"Satellite prowlers," said Quong. "They could have incinerated the house—"

"All right, all right. I get it," Harry mumbled disconsolately. He poked a stick in the fire.

"What's the plan now?" Quong asked.

Jamil scratched his jaw. "I'll contact our lawyer, arrange for him to see Xris—"

"A lawyer!" Harry cried furiously. He jumped to his feet, kicking sand on Raoul, who bleated in irritation. The Little One shriveled up in the heat of Harry's rage, curled into a ball on the sand, and pulled his hat over his head.

"A lawyer? A fucking lawyer? We should be planning to break Xris out of the Feds' lockup right now! A lawyer? What the hell is the matter with you people?"

"Harry," Jamil began, exasperated, "this isn't the time to go in with guns blazing! There's a time for subtlety—"

"Jamil is right, my friend. Look, Harry," Quong added, "let us suppose for the sake of argument that we succeed in breaking Xris out. Let us suppose that we get him away safely. This Amadi will simply say to the world, 'See there. We were right! He is guilty!' As it is, with a good attorney, Xris may win the court case. Then he will be cleared of these charges for life. And Darlene will be safe."

"And if he's not?" Harry demanded. "If they send him to the disrupter? Or maybe they won't even wait for that! Maybe he'll be 'shot while trying to escape.' Then what?"

No one had an answer to that.

Harry glared at them, sitting around the fire, so damn complacent and smug. They didn't care about Xris, none of them.

"You and your subtleties and your fucking attorneys and your friggin' satellites." Harry coughed, had to pause a moment to clear his throat. "Goddam smoke," he muttered. He rubbed his eyes, wiped his nose. "All I know is that Xris wouldn't let one of you sit for five goddam minutes in a prison cell without trying to do something! And it wouldn't be hiring a goddam lawyer! You people disgust me."

Harry turned on his heel, heading for the house.

"Harry, where are you going?" Quong demanded.

"Back to the hotel."

"Harry, remember!" Jamil said sternly. "You can't say anything about Darlene!"

"I won't," Harry retorted. "Her secret's safe with me. As for the rest of you, call me when you grow some balls."

"Certainly not a very tactful thing to say under the circumstances," Raoul admonished, with an arch of a finely plucked eyebrow and a glance at Darlene.

Harry stomped off, trudging through the soft sand, slipping and sliding. He could still hear the rest talking, and wondered why for a moment. Then he realized he had his commlink on.

"You know," Jamil was saying in quiet, thoughtful tones, "Harry's not as dumb as we think."

"He has a certain native perspicacity," Quong agreed.

Harry paused on his way into the house, waited to see if they might change their minds and decide to do something besides insult him.

All he could hear were the waves, rushing into the shore, then rushing back out.

Goddam cowards.

Harry stomped through the house, slammed the front door on his way out.

And as for him having perspicacity, he knew better.

He showered every morning.

CHAPTER 8

This ain't the shop for justice.
　　　　　　　　Charles Dickens, *Oliver Twist*

"You've got to give me more to work with, Xris. You had the motive—God! Did you have a motive! You had means. You had the opportunity. You've got to respond with something more than just 'I didn't do it'!"

Nathaniel Parker, attorney at law, paced about the small prison room where prisoners were permitted to meet with their attorneys. Parker was in his fifties, short, thin, gray, and balding. He and Xris were old friends, having met years ago on a case, when Xris was with the Bureau. Parker had been doing legal work for a local private detective, a big fat guy with an ego to match. The detective had earned his ego; he'd steered Xris right on the case. It was during dinner at the detective's house—a gourmet dinner so marvelous Xris had never forgotten it—that Xris had met Parker.

When Xris formed Mag Force 7, he'd hired Parker as his attorney.

Nathaniel Parker had a gentle demeanor and a soft voice, which he used to his advantage. Juries liked him immediately, tended to trust him. His mild, unassuming appearance said to them, *Look, would I be defending this person if I didn't believe him?*

In reality, Parker was as tough as a frozen piece of beef jerky.

"Look, Xris, I'm used to my clients protesting their innocence, whether I believe them or not, but I'm not used to a client protesting his innocence and then going silent as hyperspace on me."

Xris, dressed in a lime-green prison uniform, sat awkwardly propped up in a chair. Since he was a cyborg, the authorities had taken extraordinary precautions with him. They had made him remove his cybernetic leg—a leg that could easily kick through a wall, a leg that held an assortment of weapons in its many compartments. They had taken off his cybernetic left hand for the same reason. They had considered forcing Xris to shut down his entire cybernetic system, but the prison doctor, who'd been brought in on consultation, maintained that this would imperil the prisoner's life.

The authorities contented themselves with taking his leg and his arm and forcing him to turn off his enhanced-vision eye. Now crippled and partially blind, Xris felt like a bug that had its wings pulled off or a turtle tipped upside down.

On top of this, he was dead tired. He'd spent a day in prison unable to talk to anyone, unable to find out what was going on. This was followed by a restless night. The cells were noisy, with men all around him snorting and snoring. A security light in the corridor shone right in his eyes. Since he hadn't been able to sleep, he spent the night wondering who was doing this to him and why.

Xris's thoughts paralleled Darlene's, if he had only known it. He reached very nearly the same conclusion she had.

Amadi. It had to be Amadi.

But what did he want?

Surely not Darlene. If the Hung knew Darlene was Dalin, Amadi most certainly knew. He could have picked her up as a material witness (to her own murder!) at the same time he arrested Xris. But then, of course, if Amadi had Rowan, he couldn't have Xris, because that would mean Xris hadn't murdered anybody. . . .

Xris finally fell asleep when it was almost morning, only to be roused out of his slumbers by the call to breakfast or what the prison termed breakfast. He dragged himself down to the cafeteria on crutches and sat where he was told to sit. He stared at the coagulating oatmeal for thirty minutes, ignored all attempts by his fellow inmates to make conversation, then dragged himself back to his cell, where he sat stoically, silent and bitter, waiting to talk to his lawyer.

"I didn't do it," Xris said again. "I didn't kill Rowan."

Parker snorted in frustration. "You said that. Twenty times. And, of course, you don't have to say even that much once we go to trial. You have the presumption of innocence. It's up to the Crown to prove you are guilty. But I've told you what evidence they have. You have to admit it's damning."

Xris shifted the stump of the leg to which the cybernetic unit was normally attached. The empty pants leg dragged across the floor. The guard had pinned his empty shirtsleeve across his chest.

"You haven't got a twist on you, have you?" Xris asked quietly. "They took mine."

Parker glared at him in exasperation. Standing up, he began to repack the notepads and his portable computer into his briefcase. "When you decide to take this seriously, let me know. I'm beginning to think you *want* to walk into the disrupter!"

Xris waved his hand—his good hand, his only hand at the moment. "Sit down, Nate. I'm sorry. I didn't get much sleep last night. As for the evidence, it's all circumstantial. Dalin Rowan died in a hospital undergoing routine surgery. He wasn't murdered. I've seen the file. He died on the operating table."

"He died in the same hospital where you were a patient. And he *was* murdered. The files you saw were phony. Doctored, if you'll forgive the pun."

Xris sat in silence, digesting this.

Amadi. It all keeps coming back to Amadi.

"Files were inserted into the hospital's computer to make it appear as if Rowan had died on the table," Parker explained. "In reality, his body was discovered in his room. There was an autopsy—"

"Body? Autopsy?" Xris gave an incredulous laugh.

"Yes, what about it?" Parker eyed him, but Xris said nothing more.

Shaking his head, Parker continued. "According to the autopsy report, Rowan died of an overdose of his pain medication. He had enough in him to kill three people. An empty injector was discovered under the bed."

"They're lying," said Xris. "It didn't happen like that. Not according to what the detective told me, anyway. It was Rowan who screwed with the files. He inserted his own death notice."

"Did he?" Parker was intrigued. He took out a notepad. "What proof do you have?"

"I can't tell you."

Parker closed his eyes, massaged his temples. "Very well. Give me the name of this detective agency and give me permission to look at their files."

"No, sir. I can't." Xris was adamant.

Parker tried a different angle. "Rowan was working on a top-secret case for them just before he died, wasn't he? He was working on the Hung case."

"Yes."

"Perhaps he found out something that would have been very embarrassing to the Bureau. . . ." Parker watched Xris intently.

Xris shifted his position again. It was damn uncomfortable, sitting in that chair. His torso was part metal, part flesh and blood. He was off balance. The crutch they'd given him wasn't much help. The pad on which he rested his weight dug painfully into his armpit. He'd tossed it, in a fit of temper, into a corner when he entered the room. Now he couldn't reach it and he wasn't about to ask for help.

"There could not have been an autopsy, because there wasn't a body," Xris said at last.

Parker looked startled. "But there *was* a body, Xris. We have the certificate from the funeral home. The body was cremated."

"That's not possible." Xris shook his head. "They're framing me."

"Good. Now we're getting somewhere." Parker sat down in the chair. He switched on the computer's recording device. "Tell me. What really did happen to Dalin Rowan? Why do you think they're framing you?"

Xris shrugged. "I don't know why they're framing me. And I can't tell you what happened to Rowan."

"Oh, for the love of—"

Parker switched off the recorder. Standing up, he walked once around the room, came back and sat down. "All right, Xris. Have it your way. I'll go over their evidence with you again. Maybe we'll find a crack."

He pulled up the files. "You were a patient in the same hospital where Dalin Rowan was a patient—the Kurt Lens Hospital. You'd been a patient in that hospital for many months. You knew your way around, knew the routine. You knew most of the staff. You could have easily gained access to a uniform."

"Yes, I was in the hospital, but I was in rehab! I was still weak from the accident."

"Were you? Then explain this." Parker turned the computer for Xris to read the file.

Xris glanced at it. "Yeah? So what?"

"You will see that you checked out of the rehab ward at 1500 hours on the afternoon in question and didn't check back in until last rounds at 2330 hours. According to the Bureau, Dalin Rowan died at 1800 hours. You had plenty of time to get the job done.

"And"—Parker brought up another file—"your doctor's report from the previous day indicates that your cybernetic implants were functioning very well for such a short time in your body, and that you showed a very good range of motion. But here's what's really damning. A psychiatrist says that while your body was recovering, your mental state was not. All you could talk about was revenge for the death of your partner. All you could talk about was how much you wanted to kill Dalin Rowan."

Reaching out, Xris tapped a key on the computer, shut down the files. "Who the hell are you working for, Nate? The prosecution?"

The attorney slammed his hand on the desk. "No, damn it! I'm *your* attorney. But the prosecution is going to bring up these facts and I'm going to have to refute them. You've got to tell me the truth."

"Sorry, Nate, but that's the one thing I can't do."

Parker sighed. "Let's start at the beginning. Where did you go that day?"

"How should I know, Nate? That was over ten years

ago! I was in the hospital for damn near a year. The days were all alike with the exception of sometimes my body worked and sometimes it didn't. And sometimes I hurt like hell and sometimes I only hurt like a little piece of hell."

"Xris," Parker said gently. "I'm trying to help."

"Yeah, sorry. I could have been anywhere. It was routine for me to check out for an afternoon or an evening. I went to bars, I went to the vids. I went to the Bureau to see if they'd turned up anything on Rowan."

"If you had gone to the Bureau, you would have logged in, right? That was standard procedure. They'd have a record, wouldn't they?"

"If they did, I'll bet they don't anymore," Xris predicted.

"Well, I'll check it out." Parker made a note. "Did you know then that Rowan had gone undercover to take out the Hung?"

"No, I did not," Xris said emphatically. "I only found that out when I hired the private eye to track down Rowan. The Bureau knew where Rowan was, but Amadi—"

"Who's that?"

"Jafar el Amadi. He was my boss, the big boss. There was only one guy above him and that was Robison. Andrew Robison."

"The current director of Internal Affairs?"

"Yeah, that's him. Amadi's retired now, but he used to be in charge of the Hung investigation. He lied to me about Rowan. When I went looking for my former partner, Amadi said they had no idea where Rowan was. According to him, they suspected that the Hung were putting Rowan up in a tropical paradise as a thank-you for all his help. In reality, Amadi knew Rowan was sitting in a courtroom behind laserproof glass ripping the heart out of the Hung operation."

"So they lied to you about Rowan's whereabouts. I'm afraid that doesn't help us much. The Bureau had good reason for keeping him undercover. What happened after that?"

"When I was discharged, I quit FISA. I searched for Rowan for a year, then I ran out of money and I had to find work. Because of my special 'talents' I was offered a job in the old Democracy. A corrupt senator had been kidnapped and it was my job to either rescue him or, if I couldn't do that, I was to see to it that he didn't spill what he knew to his captors.

"I put a team together, some people I'd come across during my years in the Bureau. We handled that job to the satisfaction of all parties, with the exception of the senator, and our reputation spread. In the meantime, I invented some missiles that were effective against the energy-sucking Corasians. Then I joined up with Lady Maigrey Morianna and Lord Derek Sagan. I helped bring King Dion to power and made a fortune in the process.

"Now I had the cash necessary to hire the best agents in the galaxy. They tracked down Rowan, told me that he had died in a hospital *during routine surgery.*" Xris emphasized the words. "They gave me the death certificate. I have it at home. I framed it."

Parker was grim. "Say things like that and the jury won't even have to leave the jury box to deliberate. They'll just pronounce you guilty on the spot. So you quit searching for Dalin Rowan?"

"Yes," Xris lied calmly. "There was no reason to search anymore. I knew where he was."

Parker gave a wry smile. "I think that's the first completely true statement you've made to me."

Xris smiled, a smile that warmed the shadowed eyes, if it didn't quite make it all the way to his mouth. "What more do you want me to tell you?"

"I want you to tell me the truth," Parker answered, frustrated. "The whole truth! Not a bunch of half-truths and evasions. Even if it looks damning. You claim you're being framed. All right. Perhaps I can find a witness or—"

"I *am* telling you the truth!" Xris said. His shoulders slumped in fatigue. His body sagged, a spasm of pain contorting his face. He clenched his jaw, braced himself on the table with his good arm, forced himself to sit up straight.

"Look, Nate, I was *searching* for Dalin Rowan! Don't you think if I'd have known he was in the same hospital I would have met with him, talked to him—"

"Killed him."

Xris was silent, then said, "Yeah, maybe."

Parker rubbed his hand over his face. "The Bureau has

a witness who says that you *were* in the hospital that night, Xris."

"Of course they do," Xris said bitterly.

"Not only that, but this nurse swears that she saw you going into Rowan's room. Fifteen minutes later, Rowan was dead."

"Planned it out real well, didn't they? Have you read the witness's statement?"

"Yes. I've got it, if you want to see it. The prosecution provided it."

"What sweethearts! Doesn't that strike you as odd, Nate? Since when does the prosecution hand over all the incriminating evidence to the defense?"

"Sure it's odd! This whole blasted case is odd!" Parker stood up again, walked around the small room again, his hand rubbing the back of his neck. He turned to face Xris. "Damn it! Tell me what you know."

Xris met the attorney's gaze straight on. "I can't."

"You'll go to prison. You could end up on death row."

"So I'll go to prison."

"What about execution?"

Xris was silent.

Parker sighed, shook his head. "Whatever you're hiding, whoever you're shielding—it had better be worth it."

"It is."

The attorney sat back down. Bringing up another file on the computer, he activated the file for Xris to see and hear.

"This is her statement."

A middle-aged woman appeared on the screen. She was stout, with iron-gray hair cut short. She looked very competent, very professional, very believable. She sat stiffly upright and glared into the vidcam as if she dared it to contradict her.

Some unseen person began asking questions. The voice sounded like that of Agent Fisk.

"Are you Ms. Ella Rothschild, age fifty-seven, currently head ward nurse at the Lester Smith Mercy Enlightened Hospital?"

"I am," she replied.

"Now, then, Ms. Rothschild, I want you to understand—"

"The next few minutes is all legal stuff." Parker fast-forwarded the file. "This is it."

The nurse was nodding her head. "Yes, sir. I was a shift nurse then, working at the Kurt Lens Hospital for Corrective Surgery. I was doing my rounds when a man—well, I call him a man, but he was really more machine than man—entered the ward."

"Go on, Ms. Rothschild," Fisk said.

"He was dressed in a janitor's uniform and he was repairing one of the cleaning 'bots. I remember thinking to myself that he was new—I didn't know we had any cyborgs on staff. Also that he was there ahead of the time the janitorial staff normally came on duty. I didn't pay much attention to that, because I just assumed that since he was new he wanted to make a good impression."

"Look at this vid shot, Ms. Rothschild. Is this the man?"

"Yes, that's him."

"Note for the record that the witness has identified Xris Tampambulos. Please, go on. What did the cyborg do, Nurse Rothschild?"

"He worked on the cleaning 'bot, made a few adjustments to it. Then he said he wanted to watch the 'bot operate for a while, to make certain it was okay."

"Just a moment, Ms. Rothschild. Had you noticed the cleaning 'bot malfunctioning before this?"

"No, I had not." She stared coldly at him. "But then I wasn't being paid to notice the cleaning 'bot at all, was I?"

"No, I suppose not, Ms. Rothschild. Please continue."

"He escorted the 'bot down the hall and I heard it start up. I finished my rounds and was entering the patient's files into the computer when I noticed that the janitor—I mean the man I thought was the janitor, the cyborg—"

"We know who you mean, Ms. Rothschild. Please continue."

"Anyway, I noticed that he wasn't around. And the cleaning 'bot had gone completely out of control! It was spewing water and disinfectant all over the floor. I went to find out what was going on and that's when I saw him come out of the patient's room."

"Who did you see come out of the room, Ms. Rothschild?"

"The janitor! The cyborg! That man, there!" She pointed.

"Please note that the witness has again identified a vid of the suspect Xris Tampambulos. Now, Ms. Rothschild, what happened then?"

"I told the cyborg to take the 'bot down to maintenance, then come back and clean up the mess it had made."

"How did the cyborg react when you saw him coming out of the patient's room?"

"He seemed agitated, upset. His face was flushed as if he had a fever and he was breathing heavily. I thought perhaps he was upset because the 'bot was misbehaving. Perhaps he thought he was going to be fired."

"What did he do?"

"He grabbed hold of the 'bot and lifted it up off the floor with one hand. Those 'bots are heavy! I don't mind telling you I was frightened. He looked so wild and fierce and he acted so strangely. He mumbled something I couldn't understand and then he left, hauling the 'bot into the elevator with him."

"What did you do then?"

"I was shaken. I sat down at my desk to recover. I'd only been sitting there a few moments when the alarm went off in the patient's room, the alarm which indicates cardiac arrest. We reacted stat, but there was nothing we could do. The patient was dead."

"Do you recall the patient's name?"

"No, I do not. That was a long time ago. I suppose there are records."

"Does the name Dalin Rowan sound familiar?"

"It might. I don't know. I don't remember."

"I see. What makes the cyborg stand out in your mind, Ms. Rothschild?"

"First, he murdered my patient. I knew that the moment I entered the room. The patient had been recovering nicely, no problems. The next moment, he was dead. The cyborg murdered him."

"But there was no murder investigation. The police have nothing on their files about this case, Ms. Rothschild."

"That was the other reason I remembered it. I wanted to go to the police, but I was told by the hospital administrator that if I did, my job would be in peril. I needed that job. I was a single mother with two children to support."

"Yes, Ms. Rothschild. What did you think had happened?"

The nurse stiffened. "It was my guess that the hospital administration was afraid that they'd be sued. After all, it was one of their own employees who'd gone berserk and murdered a patient. So I kept quiet. It wasn't any of my business anyway. I wasn't about to lose my job over it."

"Let the record note—" Fisk began.

Parker shut him off.

"Well?"

"She's a damn good actress," Xris said. "It's obvious. The Bureau hired her, told her what to say. Do you think I'd do something that stupid? Be that clumsy? I was a trained government agent, for God's sake! I was trained to—" He saw where that was going and stopped.

Parker finished for him. "You were trained to kill people. Now, there's a wonderful defense! And if that nurse is a liar, she's a good one. The jury will believe her, no doubt about it. That was a nice touch, her not wanting to lose her job. The jury will be able to identify with that in a heartbeat."

"What do you mean, *if* she's a liar?" Xris asked, his tone hard.

"Let's say I believe you. Let's say that after ten years or so the Bureau decides to track you down and prosecute you for a murder that never happened, only now they say it did happen and they've cooked up files and hired actresses to prove it. Why are they going to all this trouble, Xris? Just to put you under the disrupter? A guy standing on a street corner with a blaster is cheaper and easier."

Xris smiled, a smile that touched both his eyes and the thinly drawn lips. "Yeah, I can see your point. Sorry, Nate. I guess if I can't present a case solid enough for my own attorney to believe me, then it'll be pretty tough for me to convince a jury."

"We can try. The Lord knows I'll give it my best. But I have to be honest, Xris, it doesn't look good. And this is a capital offense and this is a planet that uses capital punishment. You still refuse to tell me what you know?" Parker regarded him hopefully.

Xris sat in silence.

Parker sighed. "Very well. Here's the way I see it. If we take this before a jury, the odds are good they'll come back with a guilty verdict and they'll recommend death."

"I understand," Xris said.

"I hope so," Parker said coldly. "They don't fool around with the death penalty on this planet. They allow one appeal and it goes through the judicial system at light speed. Most people sent to death row are put to death within three months of sentencing. Tell me what you know, Xris! Whatever you say to me is confidential. Who are you shielding?"

Xris smiled again. "You'd be surprised to hear me say I was shielding the corpse, wouldn't you?"

"All right, if that's the game you want to play—"

"What about a plea bargain?" Xris asked abruptly.

"On a murder charge?" Parker frowned.

"I've been doing some thinking," Xris said. "It's just a hunch, but my guess is that the Bureau doesn't want me to go to trial. They don't want me dead. Hell, like you said, they could've taken care of that themselves years ago. They want information. I'll agree to provide it, but it has to be on my terms."

"I don't know. . . ."

"First, I talk, but only to Amadi. Not to Fisk or that kinetic whirlwind Rizzoli."

"You said Amadi had retired."

"Yeah, well, I know for a fact that he isn't spending all his time on the golf course. I talk to Amadi or I talk in open court and to the press. See which they like better."

"It can't hurt to ask. How do you spell *Amadi*?"

"Like it sounds. Next," Xris continued, "tell the Bureau to reduce the charges. Manslaughter, maybe. Or murder second degree. If they do, I'll plead guilty."

"So you did kill Dalin Rowan?" Parker asked.

"In a manner of speaking," Xris said quietly, "yes, I did."

CHAPTER 9

Lastly, even the ultimate outcome of a war is not always to be regarded as final. The defeated state often considers the outcome merely as a transitory evil, for which remedy may still be found.

Carol von Clausewitz, *On War*

"Hullo, Jamil. This is Harry."

"Where have you been?"

"Never mind. This line secure?"

"Probably not."

"Oh." A moment's silence. "Oh, well. This is important."

"Harry—"

"Listen, Jamil. Xris is being sentenced tomorrow. You know what that means?"

"I'm no lawyer, Harry, but yes, I know what that means."

"It means he's going into the toilet!"

"Harry—"

"We got to bust him out of there, Jamil."

"No, Harry! Absolutely not! That's an order! Do you understand me, mister?"

"Jamil—"

"Listen to me, Harry, and try to get this through the cornmeal mush you term a brain. First, the security in the courthouse is tighter than Raoul's girdle."

From the background, in indignant tones, "I have never worn a girdle!"

"Second, if we went in there, as the Doc said, with guns blazing, we'd lose half the team and probably get Xris killed in the process. Third, you heard Xris's orders. Do I have to repeat them?"

"Naw, Jamil." A moment's pause. "So what are you guys gonna do? You going to show up for the sentencing?"

"No, Harry. The fact is, we're getting off this planet as soon as our passports come through. I advise you to do the same."

"Is *that* an order?" Harry demanded, belligerent.

"No, Harry. It's not an order." Jamil said. "It's advice. Good advice."

"I want to go the sentencing, Jamil. I want to be there for Xris."

Jamil sighed. "Fine, Harry. You do that. We're going to Adonia. To Raoul's place. A little R&R."

R&R! With Xris in the slammer.

From the background Harry could hear Raoul's voice. "Is Harry thinking of traveling to Adonia by himself? Without my guidance and supervision? The gods of *haute courtier* help us! He'll never get through customs! Oh, dear. This is awful! Give me a moment. I'm trying to think what he has in his wardrobe. . . . I know! Let me speak to him! Harry! Harry! Wear your—"

Harry ended the transmission. He liked Raoul, he truly did. But he just didn't feel like having a discussion on menswear. Not right now. Xris was being sent to prison or the disrupter for a crime he hadn't committed and there was nothing Harry could do to help his friend.

Nothing at all.

The courtroom was ugly, cold, and sterile, designed that way purposefully as if to assert that justice was blind to everything, including a sense of style. The judge's desk, on its raised platform, was encased in plastisteel—there had been several attacks on the judiciary in the courthouse— and looked like an artillery bunker. His Honor sat behind his fortifications, lobbing judgments onto the accused below. The jury—when a jury was empaneled—appeared to be engaged in trench warfare, for little more than their heads could be seen peering above the high walls of the shielded jury box.

Those people admitted to the public viewing area were searched and questioned and generally treated as if they were prisoners of war, caught in the act of spying on the enemy, rather than citizens exercising their rights. Harry answered as a prisoner of war would, giving them nothing more than his name and the license number of his rental hover, which he'd left in the public lot across the street at the exorbitant rate of twelve credits per hour.

The audience in the gallery was at least safer than the attorneys and the accused, who sat in the middle of no-man's-land on open, level ground with no cover, other than their desks. Occasionally, if the verbal shelling from the front bench was heavy, the attorneys had been known to drop an electronic stylus behind the desk, duck down in order to retrieve it, and gain a brief respite from the barrage. The public gallery was shielded from the action by a laserproof shield of plastisteel.

Harry was the only person in the gallery that day. The seats reserved for the press were empty. Had this trial gone to the jury, it might have garnered some interest, but it hadn't. The murder had happened ten years ago. The prisoner had confessed and was said to have made a bargain with the Crown. He had escaped the death penalty, though what good his life would be to him, spending the next twenty years on Sandusky's Rock, was subject to debate. He was to appear in court today for sentencing and wasn't expected to put on a show. A murder in the courtroom down the hall—a murder involving aliens, prostitutes, a food processor, and the possible bribery of a high public official—was of much more interest to viewers of the nightly news.

Harry glanced around the courtroom, hoping that perhaps some of the other team members would change their minds and show up. The last time he'd seen them had been at the questioning. Although they'd come in together, they were all questioned separately. Harry had been extremely nervous. He was a terrible liar. Fortunately, Quong had solved his problem. Catching him in the hallway, the doctor had drawn him to one side, given him some advice along with a bottle of orange juice.

"What's this?" Harry had asked, referring to the orange juice.

"You need your vitamin C," Quong had replied. "To prevent scurvy."

"Oh, uh, sure. Thanks, Doc. I read about scurvy once. Your teeth fall out and—"

"Look, Harry," Quong had impatiently interrupted, "I want you to think about something for me."

"Sure, Doc." Harry had been pleased. People were always telling him *not* to think. "What do you want to know?"

"When you first met Xris, he was already a cyborg, wasn't he?"

"Yeah, Doc," Harry had replied, disappointed. "Is that all?"

"You didn't know him when he was with the Bureau, did you?"

"No, Doc. What's all this about?"

"Be patient with me, Harry. You never knew Dalin Rowan. You never met Dalin Rowan, did you?"

"I know Darlene—"

"Listen to me, Harry." Quong had frowned at him most severely, had repeated sternly, "You never did know Dalin Rowan, did you?"

Harry had considered the matter and the more he considered it, the more he liked it. He had never known Dalin Rowan. He could be completely honest about that when they asked him.

"Just concentrate on that, Harry," Doctor Quong had whispered, his frown easing, "and you'll do fine."

"Sure, Doc, but how's that going to help Xris?" Harry had asked anxiously.

"Follow his orders, Harry," Quong had replied. "That's all we can do. Just follow his orders. And drink your orange juice."

Whenever Doc was stern like that, it usually meant he was covering up because he was nervous, so the conversation hadn't been of much comfort. Harry had followed Quong's orders, however, although he didn't drink the orange juice. Scurvy or no scurvy, orange juice gave him gas. Harry had come through the questioning fine, however, perhaps because the investigating agent—the Talisian, Rizzoli—hadn't been all that interested in what he had to say. Once she had established the fact that Harry had met Xris two years after the alleged murder, that he hadn't known

Xris while he was with the agency, and that he'd never known Dalin Rowan at all, Harry had been free to go.

Harry had made an unsuccessful attempt to visit Xris in prison. Xris wasn't being allowed visitors, except his attorney. Having found out the name of the attorney from Jamil, Harry camped out in Parker's office, which he used when trying a case on this planet. Arriving wearing a new suit that he'd bought just for the occasion, Harry looked so unhappy and bereft that the receptionist took pity on him, and though she wouldn't let him see Mr. Parker, she had brought Harry replicated chicken soup and had given him what information she could.

Which was how he had found out about the date of the sentencing.

Harry had again dressed in his new suit, which, after four days of constant wear, was wrinkled and stained with mustard and looked even worse than when he'd first put it on, if that was possible. He had made the trip to the courthouse. He had found a seat in the front row, close to where he thought Xris might sit. Harry was half an hour early.

The room was empty, for this was the first case on the docket. The chairs were uncomfortable, had evidently been constructed for some alien race not blessed with a tailbone. Harry's tailbone was well cushioned, for he was a big man, but even he could not sit in the same position for long without his legs going numb. Despite the discomfort, he doggedly held his ground, stayed at his post.

Eventually the courtroom came to life. Technicians wandered in and switched on the vids that would make a recording of the proceedings. The prosecution entered; Harry glared balefully at the enemy and made a loud snorting sound expressive of his disgust. Prosecuting counsel gave him a bored glance and turned away.

Mr. Parker entered, accompanied by an assistant. Harry sat up quite straight and nodded his head violently several times, to let the attorney know that he, Harry Luck, was present and could be relied upon in an emergency. Mr. Parker glanced at him in some astonishment.

The guards brought in Xris.

He was wearing prison lime-green coveralls and they had permitted him to use his cybernetic leg, although they had not let him have his arm. He wore restrainers around his ankles. Controlled by a guard, the restrainers would shut down the nerves in Xris's good foot if he tried to run and at the same time short out his cybernetic leg. He wore another restrainer on his good arm. He looked grim and dangerous and the guards were taking no chances. They held the restrainer controls in plain sight.

At Xris's entrance, Harry stood up and began yelling and beating on the plastisteel shield. "Xris, I'm here—"

A guard 'bot that had been hovering nearby zipped through the air and came eye level with Harry. The 'bot was dish-shaped, about twenty centimeters in diameter, and was referred to affectionately among the courtroom staff as Frisbee. It was armed with small lasers known as nerve poppers.

"You are not permitted to speak to the prisoner," said the 'bot, fixing Harry with a glassy eye. "Please sit down or you will be forcibly escorted out."

Harry was fond of robots. He could get along with any 'bot in the galaxy, generally because he didn't patronize them or treat them as nonentities, as did some humanoids.

"Oh, hullo there, little fellow." Harry was polite. "I just want to say a few words to my friend—"

"You are not permitted to speak to the prisoner," the 'bot repeated, and a grinding sound in its workings gave the words a menacing tone.

"But I just—"

"Sit down," said the 'bot, "or you will be forcibly escorted out."

"Now, look—"

The 'bot was finished arguing. It emitted a brief but brilliant burst of laser light and Harry sat down in his chair, sucking the back of his wrist where a red welt was forming, and trying to force his fingers to stop twitching. The 'bot hovered near him a moment, making certain he had seen the light, so to speak.

"All right," Harry muttered. "I'll be quiet."

Assured that the malefactor would cause no further trouble, the 'bot returned to its post. But it was definitely keeping its optics on Harry.

Xris must have heard the altercation; Harry was certain

of it. The attorney, Parker, turned back around to stare, then leaned over and spoke a few words to his client. Xris shook his head, did not turn around. Parker went back to his notes.

Harry hunched down in his seat, his rumpled and ill-fitting suit collapsing around him. He was desperately unhappy. Harry knew Xris had seen him. Xris had looked straight at him when he'd entered the courtroom. Looked at him. Then looked away without apparent recognition.

"All rise!" A bailiff 'bot brought everyone to their feet. The near empty courtroom echoed with shuffling sounds and the scraping of chairs.

The 'bot alerted the combatants to the arrival of the judge at his bunker. Everyone sat back down. The judge began to talk, shooting them with big legal words. The lawyers for both sides took turns standing up in the line of fire and, as nearly as Harry could make out, were almost always gunned down. There was some talk about "waving"; Xris was doing a lot of waving, apparently, which Harry found difficult to credit since Xris was missing a hand and the other was clamped down tight in a restrainer.

Harry sought refuge in a small nap, indulging in a pleasant dream. Jamil was driving a Devastator into the courtroom. The tank was crunching up the chairs; Quong was firing his beam rifle at the guard 'bot, who was hunkered down behind the judge; and he, Harry, had just picked up Xris in one strong arm (Xris being conveniently comatose at this juncture), while firing a lasgun. Harry was carrying his friend out the door—

"Sentence you to twenty years' penal servitude on Sandusky's Rock. Case dismissed."

A gavel slammed down with a bang like an exploding mine and jolted Harry awake. He jerked upright in his chair to see Xris rising painfully and awkwardly to his feet. His attorney was saying something, whispering in his ear. Xris wasn't paying attention.

The guard 'bot, anticipating trouble, hovered near Harry. He didn't care. It could pop every nerve in his body.

Standing up, Harry bellowed out, "Xris!" in a battlefield shout, meant to be heard over the whine of lasguns, the crunch of cannons, the cries of the dying.

Everyone turned to look, including the judge, who stuck his head up out of the bunker.

Xris looked, shrugged, and smiled wanly. Then he looked away.

The guards led Xris out of the courtroom, guiding his shuffling, hobbled footsteps. His attorney followed.

Harry remained in the room, alone and unhappy, until the guard 'bot, who had a vengeful nature, zapped him in the rear end, burning a hole in the new suit.

Wounded, outnumbered, and outgunned, Harry was forced to retire from the field.

CHAPTER 10

It is quite a three-pipe problem.
  Sir Arthur Conan Doyle, *The Adventures of Sherlock Holmes,* "The Red-headed League"

Petronella Rizzoli leaned against the pliant backrest of her office chair and regarded her computer screen in perplexity. Automatically, without thinking about it, she hooked her foot under the leg of her rolling chair to keep the chair in place. She'd done this ever since the time one of her kinetic shifts had sent her chair rocketing backward out into the hallway, where it had run down a passing secretary. Petronella had just risen from the chair prior to its unexpected performance, and so had escaped injury herself. The secretary had not been quite so fortunate. She was off work for three days with bruised shins.

Petronella came from the planet Talisia, which had been colonized by humans in the midyears of their explorations into space. Talisia was rich in minerals, ores, particularly iron and uranium, as well as gold and silver and diamonds. The planet's value was such that its inhabitants overlooked the strange fluxes and shifts that occurred in the kinetic energy, completely defying Newton's Three Laws of Motion and sending physicists scurrying to the planet to investigate.

Objects at rest did not necessarily stay at rest on Talisia, but whizzed through the air, rolled along the ground, or tumbled from the skies. Scientists eventually discovered that the problem was not with Talisia itself but had been brought to the planet by its human colonists. Their own small energy fields clashed with the Talisian fields, resulting in eddies and whirlwinds that swirled around the humans, doing little harm to them—in the eye of the storm, as it were—but wreaking havoc on the world around them.

Scientists developed the means by which those early humans living and working on Talisia could do so without bringing down a hailstorm of pots and pans on their heads or sending complex mining equipment into a mechanical arm-waving frenzy. The treatment proved effective on the Talisian home world. Unfortunately, when the treated humans left Talisia to venture out into the rest of the galaxy, their altered kinetic energy fields were likely to send luggage skimming over the heads of hapless hotel clerks.

Later, scientists discovered that, given the human propensity to adapt to their surroundings, the third generation of humans born on the planet had the peculiar kinetic energy field encoded into their systems. They were able to live and work on Talisia without having to take the treatment. But they hit the rest of the galaxy like small tornadoes.

There are not many opportunities on Talisia for employment, if one does not want to work in the mining industry. Young Talisians looking for other career opportunities have to seek them in the galaxy beyond. Medication helps some to function normally, but it does not work well with all and Talisians were often the victims of discrimination. Antidiscrimination acts had made it illegal to refuse employment to aliens in the human workplace, humans in alien workplaces and Talisians anywhere.

Thus Petronella, who had wanted to go into law enforcement since the days of her childhood—when she had been punished for locking up the neighbor boy in the closet until his parents could produce bail—had applied to FISA and had been accepted.

She had worked for Internal Affairs for five years now, ferreting out bad apples, although, according to her cover story for this particular job, she was a new recruit, eager to prove herself. She let it be known that the medication she took controlled her kinetic fields fairly well, but sometimes a tendril of energy would escape, whip out, and fling a wastebasket at someone's head.

Such an infirmity tended to limit her social life.

Petronella didn't care. She was interested in her career,

not in relationships. The reason she often worked late was to obtain advancement in her chosen field, not to go home to an empty apartment—literally empty; Talisians don't indulge in knickknacks, for obvious reasons. What furniture they own is solid, heavy, and bolted to the floor.

Following the explosion of the flower urn at the suspect Tampambulos's house, Petronella had voluntarily removed herself from field assignments, offered to return to the job of systems operator. Since her strange energy fluxes had no effect on computer operations, and maintenance had seen to it that the machine itself was firmly fixed in place, her superiors had been only too happy to accede to her request.

The hour was late, so late that most of her co-workers had already gone for the day. Petronella hadn't noticed the time, nor the fact that she hadn't eaten anything except a bagel snatched at lunch. She had come across an oddity that aroused her curiosity, and with her characteristic tenacity, she was determined to find a solution before she left for home.

On her terminal were displayed the contents of her most recent search on the transmission logs of the FISA satellite uplink. She had backed them up, as customary. The problem was, the backup had taken less time than usual. A lot less time.

The backups always took the same amount of time, give or take a second, because there was always a similar amount of data to back up. Why was the time shorter—significantly shorter—today? Petronella soon discovered the answer. The transmission log for the satellite uplink was only a twentieth of the size that it should have been. The report should have contained a complete list of Bureau activities for the day. Instead, in essence, all it said was: *Today, nothing happened.*

Unless the whole damn Bureau had suddenly taken an unscheduled holiday, that wasn't likely.

Petronella saved the file, removed it from the disk, and then tried to recover the file as if it had been accidentally erased. She succeeded in bringing up a second log file that had probably been the original file—it was about the same length as normal. But why had it been overwritten?

She studied the file. Buried deep amid transmission requests and routine permissions was a request from a Naval shipyard for high-level permissions access. The request had been denied immediately, but while the error routine for the denial had been running, a second attempt by the same shipyard had come in. The system should have kicked this second attempt out as well, but apparently it hadn't.

Petronella investigated further and discovered a bug in the system that allowed only one subprocess to access the error routine at a time. Since the subprocess was already busy denying the first request, the other request slipped by unnoticed. The second request spawned another subprocess, and then left before the first subprocess was completed with the error system. When the error system finally came back on-line, it found nothing there. The second request from the shipyard was gone. Everything went on as normal.

Petronella had been about to sign off when she discovered that the system had sent out a series of data files to a particular net access, requesting a certain number of named files. These files had been sent. Since the system itself had requested the new files, the permission system allowed them to come in. Petronella tracked them down, found to her amazement that the names of the newly transferred files had been erased.

Feeling a stabbing pain in the back of her shoulders, Petronella realized that she'd been sitting hunched and tense over her computer for so long that her shoulder muscles were in knots. She did a few stretches, rolled her head from side to side, tried to ease the stiffness. All the while she wondered: Why bother to erase data from a log that had been erased and hidden anyway?

There could only be one reason. She was peeling off layers of an onion, had gone through two and found a third. Yet another log had been overwritten. There could only be one explanation.

Someone outside the Bureau had hacked into the system, inserted new files, then was trying to cover his or her tracks.

This was the first time Petronella had ever run across a real computer break-in. Excited, she forgot the pain in her shoulders and told her growling stomach to go get a life. She tried the same trick of recovering the original log, found that the area of the halo-array used to store the file had been partially reused. She could only reconstruct a small amount of the original log.

She compared the two logs. There was only one area in which the two logs differed. One of the logs contained a name for a file and the other didn't. The new file was labeled: HUNG ACTIVITIES FOR THE PERIOD 1412232D TO 1412266D. Petronella did a search for the file and found it easily. The file was a deep archive, used only for retrieval of out-of-date information on closed cases.

Petronella brought up the file. It had been declassified, but no one had requested the file for perusal since declassification. She read it over. The file detailed the movements of weapons from a factory in the TISor system to Hung operatives on other worlds. The information contained in the file was nothing but tracking data and appeared to be of no significance.

Unless, of course, you had just happened to have arrested a former agent who had been caught in the explosion of that very factory.

"Curioser and curioser," Petronella muttered.

Just to make certain, she asked for the names of the agents working on the TISor weapons factory case and cross-referenced them with any recent activity for the Bureau. Two names came up.

Dalin Rowan and Xris Tampambulos. Petronella already had Xris's file on hand. She called up Dalin Rowan's file. It was labeled DECEASED.

Dalin Rowan had been a brilliant computer expert, Petronella read. He had worked for the agency to crack the crime syndicate known as the Hung. Xris Tampambulos had been the lead field agent on the case.

Just to refresh her memory, Petronella brought up Xris's file and read through it. She reached the end—or what should have been the end. But it wasn't the end. Not anymore. Something had been added.

Startled, she reread the last paragraph, realized it sounded familiar, and went back to Rowan's file.

Yes, that was it. The last two paragraphs were new and they were identical.

Typed in neatly, concisely, at the end of both files was

the fact that Xris Tampambulos had pleaded guilty to the murder of Dalin Rowan in return for a plea bargain of twenty years' hard labor on Sandusky's Rock.

Petronella considered the possibility that she herself had typed in that information and, due to lack of sleep or PMS, didn't remember having done so. That was possible, she supposed, though not very probable. Besides, she knew darn good and well that she hadn't added that paragraph to Dalin Rowan's file. That wasn't her job. Whoever handled records in the main Bureau would take care of that.

Further investigation convinced Petronella that she wasn't crazy, wasn't suffering from a nutritional imbalance or hormonal changes. According to the time stamps, the files had been appended within a second of each other, yet the files had been housed in two separate computers in different areas of the building in which she herself was working.

Petronella rubbed her eyes. She'd been staring at the screen so long the letters were starting to blur. She left the computer, went to the break room to pour herself a cup of coffee, absently pausing on the way out to right an overturned potted palm.

The break room was dark, the coffeepot empty. Petronella brewed another pot; the agents liked their coffee real, not replicated, though Petronella thought personally that this was mere affectation. She couldn't tell the difference and she didn't see how anyone else could, either. Still, waiting for the coffee to brew gave her time to think.

This was all very strange. Damn strange. Someone had gone to an awful lot of trouble just to insert two innocuous paragraphs at the end of two files. Why? What was the reason? To prove that they could crack FISA's security? Well, they'd done that, all right. Petronella would see to it that the bug in the system was eliminated. . . .

"Wait a minute!" Petronella said aloud.

She set down the coffeepot and hurried back to her office, ignoring the crash that sounded in the break room after her departure and the peeved voice of security demanding to know what the hell was going on up there, ending with, "Is that you, Rizzoli?"

Petronella was back on her computer, pulling up textbook files from a high-level course she'd taken on computer security.

And there it was. Fifteen years ago, an agent had discovered a bug in the main terminal access system of the Model 233. He had found a way to confuse the error-handling system and, in so doing, gain access to the main file, which would otherwise have kicked him out. He had discovered that the error-handling system could only deal with a single error at a time. While its attention was fixed on the first error, a second illegal command could be given and the system would honor it. The error system that should have caught it was busy with its first job and would never notice.

This was exactly what had happened to her transmission log.

The agent who had originally discovered the bug had come across it in a mainframe computer system. Apparently the agent had not checked to see if the security risk would be the same for a transmission system.

Either that or he'd known all along that it was the same, that he'd left this door open in case he ever needed to use it.

And there was the name of the agent who had discovered this bug. Not only discovered it but had received a meritorious citation for research excellence from the Gibbons Foundation for Computer Security.

Dalin Rowan.

By God, Petronella thought, exultant. Robison was right! Rowan's taken the bait.

CHAPTER 11

Suspicion all our lives shall be stuck full of eyes;
For treason is but trusted like the fox.
    William Shakespeare, *Henry IV, Part 1*

All she had to do was reel in her fish. Her hands were on the keyboard preparing to do another search when hot coffee sloshed over her fingers, deluged the keyboard.

"Shit! Ow!" Petronella snatched her hands back, sucked on a burned knuckle, and swore. She righted the overturned cup, regarded the soaked keyboard in dismay. The system had shut down—safety precaution. She would have to dry out the keyboard, find another, replace it, retrieve all the files. . . .

The hell with it. Obviously, the gods were trying to tell her something. Go home, Rizzoli. Go to bed, Rizzoli. You're too tired. The medication's not working anymore. She had learned long ago that exhaustion seemed to have a pronounced effect on her kinetic energy fluxes.

She wondered what time it was, guessed it was probably close to midnight. She looked at her watch, but couldn't read it. The numbers were a green blur. She rubbed her eyes.

She had just enough energy left to clean off the keyboard and leave it upside down to dry. Keeping a tight grip on her kinetic energy field, she moved carefully down the hallway, trying not to leave disaster in her wake. Her boss's office was next door. Sometimes he worked late. She supposed she should report this break-in. He'd be certain to find out about it and it would look strange if she hadn't told him first.

No one in the department, not even her boss, knew she was working for Internal Affairs.

Petronella knocked on the cubicle door, but no one answered. Glancing outside, she saw that it was pitch-dark. No hovers zipping past. Not even a cop. She squinted at a clock on the wall.

0330.

She tapped her watch, spoke into it. "Connect me with voice mail for Senior Agent Tom McCarthy, Computer Operations." She waited a moment, then heard a faint beep. "Agent McCarthy, this is Agent Rizzoli. I found some strange inconsistencies in the log tonight during backup. I think someone tampered with our transmission logs. It looks like the work of one Dalin Rowan, a former agent. I'd lay odds of a thousand to one that it was him, but then I'd guess I'd lose. He's dead, you see."

Petronella laughed at her own joke, realized it wasn't particularly funny and that Agent McCarthy would think she'd been out drinking.

"Look, sir, I've been awake for twenty-four hours now, and I have to get some sleep. Look over the files I've saved in my home directory. See what you think. I'll be in again when I wake up, which may be next month."

As an afterthought, she added, "If you need me, call me. Only please not before noon!"

She tapped on the watch, ended the transmission. Ten minutes later, she exited the building through the last security checkpoint. The guard at the main gate stopped her.

"You look like hell, Rizzoli. No offense."

"Thanks. I love you, too, Henry."

"You know that we got other agents on the payroll, Rizzoli. You don't have to crack every case yourself. You ain't gonna drive home, are you?" he added in concern, seeing her fumble for the remote that would send her hover skimming up from the parking garage.

Petronella rubbed her red eyes, trying to clear her blurred vision. "Yeah," she said carelessly. "I have to. I gave the chauffeur the night off."

"And we'll end up picking pieces of you off the transmission tower." He took the remote from her hand. "Let me get the duty driver to take you home."

"No, please. Don't bother—"

"No bother. He's got nothing to do this time of night. Just sittin' around watchin' the sports mags."

A minute later, a hover pulled up. Petronella climbed in, gave the driver her address, made certain he knew where it was. Then she sank back thankfully into the leather cushions. This was real luxury, usually reserved for the higher-ups.

"I could get used to this," Petronella said, and prepared to enjoy the ride.

A microsecond later, the driver was jostling her shoulder. "Wake up, ma'am. You're home."

There was an irritating buzzing sound in her ear. A childhood experience involving a bee and a doctor with long pincers disturbed her dreams. She could still feel the bee flying around inside her skull.

Except it wasn't a bee. It was her watch. She'd fallen asleep with her wrist beneath her head.

Rolling over, she tapped the watch. " 'Lo?"

"Good morning, Rizzoli," came a damnably cheery voice. "McCarthy here. We're sending a hover to pick you up."

"Huh? Wait! I—"

The connection ended.

Petronella climbed out of bed, noticed that she was still dressed. She had no memory of entering her apartment, much less going to bed. The buzzing started again. This time, it was the front door. She peered through the security hole.

"Yes?"

"Driver from the Bureau, ma'am." He flipped his identification.

Interesting. They weren't wasting any time. Petronella opened the door, invited him inside.

"I just woke up," she said apologetically.

He glanced at her rumpled clothes and tousled hair and the red marks on her cheeks, marks left by her blanket.

"Yes, ma'am. McCarthy sent me. He figured you'd need a ride, since according to the log you left your hover in the parking lot."

"What time is it?"

"It's 1430, ma'am."

Petronella sighed. Well, at least he'd let her sleep past noon.

"I can't go into the office looking like this. I'm going to take a shower and change my clothes. Help yourself to coffee or whatever you want." She waved a vague hand in the direction of the kitchen. A standing floor lamp, perhaps taking her gesture as an invitation, wobbled about two meters that direction.

The driver looked at the meandering lamp and said he thought he'd wait in the car.

"Suit yourself." Petronella headed for the shower.

Twenty minutes later, the driver dropped her at the front entrance to the FISA building. She thanked him and went inside, feeling much better than she had when she'd left.

She passed through the two security points, rode the lift to her level, reported to Senior Agent Tom McCarthy's cubicle.

He was sitting behind his desk, reading a report. Petronella stood quietly, not wanting to interrupt him. A chair slithered across the floor, making an odd scraping sound.

McCarthy didn't even look up.

"That you, Rizzoli? Have a seat."

She retrieved the errant chair. "I take it you got my message."

He looked up from the report. He was in his forties, had curly red hair, freckles, and wore thick-lensed glasses, either for effect or because there was something wrong with his eyes that lasers couldn't cure.

"You sure as hell stirred up a hornet's nest, Rizzoli. The head hornet himself buzzed in this morning. Chief Superintendent Amadi wants to see us both as soon as you're here, and, well, you're here."

"Amadi? He traveled all that way?" Inwardly, Petronella grinned. Outwardly, Petronella sighed and said wistfully, "Am I really in that much trouble, sir?"

McCarthy shook his head. He patted her hand sympathetically. "No, nothing like that. Amadi used to be the case supervisor for the Hung Syndicate job years ago."

"I know, sir. I've been making my reports on the arrest of Tampambulos to him. But I never thought he'd come here in person. Especially since the case is wrapped up. Why now?"

"Who knows? He's a chief supe. He doesn't have to have a reason." Rising to his feet, McCarthy shrugged. "Maybe there's a golf course on this planet he likes and he's using us as an excuse. They've stashed him in Entworth's old office." He glanced at her. "You *did* take your medication today, didn't you?"

"I'm tired, sir," Petronella returned irritably. "It doesn't work well when I'm tired."

McCarthy shook his head. "Just try not to drop a potted plant on the head of our boss's boss's boss's boss, will you, Rizzoli?"

The lift took them up four more levels to the executive offices. Real offices up here, with carpet and wood and a flesh-and-blood receptionist, who asked them to be seated while she informed the chief superintendent they were here.

Amadi didn't keep them waiting. He walked out of his office personally to meet them. He was every bit as attractive in person as he was on the vidphone. Attractive for an older gentleman, Petronella corrected. His black brows were an interesting contrast to his iron-gray hair, which was thick and wavy. The brown eyes were cool and penetrating, his handshake firm, his greeting cordial.

Attractive . . . for a traitor.

Amadi ushered them into the office, indicated two cushy chairs, then walked around to seat himself behind his desk.

As Petronella sat down in the chair, a potted plant on a brass and glass stand beneath a window tipped to the side, fell over, dumping dirt onto the carpet.

Amadi stared at it. "That's damn odd. What made it do that? You're not subject to tremors on this planet, are you?"

McCarthy shot Petronella a glance. "No, sir."

At least the pot didn't fall on his head, her look said back to him. Aloud she said, her voice strained, "It's my fault, I'm afraid, sir. I'm a Talisian—"

"Ah!" Amadi appeared highly gratified. "That explains

a great deal! No, don't worry about cleaning it up, Agent. I'll send for the maintenance 'bot when we're finished."

He glanced around his desk. Picking up a heavy brass paperweight, he slid it in a drawer. "Possible lethal projectile. Now . . . Agent McCarthy, is it?"

"Yes, sir."

"You found this security breach—"

"Uh, no, sir. Actually it was Rizzoli here who first ran onto it. She passed it up to me—"

"I see. Thank you for coming, Agent McCarthy. You can return to your duties. I don't need to tell you, of course, that this is all highly confidential. We don't want word getting to the press that we've had a security breach."

McCarthy looked startled. He sat in his chair a moment, thinking Amadi might change his mind.

Amadi regarded him in polite silence. McCarthy stood up.

"Yes, sir. I understand, sir." He looked uncertainly at Petronella. "If you need me, sir . . ."

"Thank you, Agent. I know where to find you."

McCarthy left the office, closing the door quietly behind him.

Amadi accessed a computer, brought up a file, presumably the file on the security breach. He studied it intently.

Petronella sat in her chair, stared out the window at the vast panorama of the city of Guarma. She worked hard to appear nonchalant, confident, at ease. The minutes slid by and Amadi continued to read in silence. The room was cold. Petronella's hands and feet grew chilled. A hovertaxi flew in too close. Red flashing lights on the building warned the taxi driver he'd ventured into restricted airspace. The taxi veered, made a steep, diving turn that must have piled his passengers one on top of the other. No tip for him.

Amadi finished reading. He looked up, leaned back in his chair.

Petronella tried a smile, didn't like the way it felt—too frivolous. She twitched her mouth to serious, attentive.

"Good job, Rizzoli. I'm impressed with your skill and even more with your tenacity. Not many people would have been conscientious enough to track this down."

Petronella would have taken that for a compliment, except for the deepening of the frown line between Amadi's black brows. She'd struck a nerve. The saliva in her mouth dried up. Her heart rate increased. The empty chair beside her made a skittering motion. Quickly, Petronella put out a hand to halt it.

"It wasn't right, sir. It was my job to track it down."

"Certainly it was, Rizzoli." Amadi smiled at her. "I'm very pleased. I'd like to hear your account in person. Go ahead, Agent. When did you first notice the anomaly? And how did you find it?"

Amadi was affable now, but Petronella wasn't fooled.

"Yes, sir. It began when I was downloading the transmission log last night. I noticed that it was shorter than usual. And so I . . ."

Fifteen minutes later, she wrapped it up. Amadi was a good listener. He didn't interrupt, watched her attentively and, from what she could see, approvingly.

At the name "Dalin Rowan," however, he frowned again.

"Are you certain, Agent?"

"Yes, sir," Petronella said, carefully respectful. "I know it doesn't make sense, but Dalin Rowan is known for discovering this particular method of breaking into a supposedly secure file and altering data. We learned his technique at the academy."

"And so did several hundred other agents," Amadi pointed out.

"That's true, sir, but what reason would another agent have for breaking into our files?" Petronella argued.

"Hard as it is to imagine, Agent Rizzoli, we do have our share of discontented employees."

"Sir, a copycat would have followed Rowan's original plan and broken into a LoadMaster 2800, because of the error-handling routine. This person moved a step further, took advantage of the same weakness in the transmission log handler. Someone had to really work at that, sir. Someone who knew all about the first minuscule crack in the armor, knew that it had been fixed, and knew enough to look for and to find a second, even smaller crack. And what did that person do when he found it?"

She answered her own question. "He went after the files

directly pertaining to Xris Tampambulos *and* Dalin Rowan."

"Tampambulos, then. He could have broken in before we arrested him."

"No, sir. The break-in occurred yesterday. Tampambulos is sitting in lockup, awaiting transport. He couldn't have had access to a computer. Besides, according to his files, he doesn't have the know-how to pull this off. Of the two of them, Rowan was the only one who could have done this."

Amadi smiled again, indulgently. "Nice detective work, Rizzoli. Fine deductive reasoning. The only problem we have here is that Dalin Rowan couldn't possibly have been the one to break into our files. He has the galaxy's best alibi. He's dead."

"Yes, sir, I know." Petronella shook her head, unconvinced. "But if it's not Rowan, than who could it be? And why go to all the trouble? Whoever it was didn't erase the files or damage them or alter the data. He made a little addition. That's all."

Amadi considered the matter. "Here's a suggestion, Agent. Let's say that some stressed-out entry-level clerk is told to add this attachment to the files. He forgets about it. That night, he wakes up at 0200 and remembers. He figures he better take care of it before the boss finds out. He uses this way of correcting his oversight, imagining that no one will be the wiser. How do you like that as a solution to your little mystery?"

Petronella thought she should make an effort to try to like it. He was supposedly her superior, after all. But she figured she shouldn't give up too easily.

"It's not very plausible, is it, sir?" she said with a show of reluctance. "He could have just added the data in the morning when he came to work. There was nothing of an urgent nature about it."

"Well, well. I think our poor stressed-out entry-level clerk is more conscientious than you give him credit for, Agent. Maybe he has a terror like me for a boss."

Amadi chuckled to show he didn't mean it and stood up. The interview was at an end.

Petronella rose quickly, her chilled feet prickling. She wondered what she was supposed to say in answer to that, finally decided that the best she could do was keep her mouth shut.

"Thank you for coming, Agent," Amadi said, escorting her to the door. "We'll take over from here. Delete those files and don't worry about it. As I said, I don't think we've got anything more serious than a little lapse in efficiency, but I will ask that you keep this confidential, especially since this information affects a recently completed Crown trial. The press is always looking for a chance to make us look bad. You understand?"

Petronella nodded sympathetically. "Yes, sir."

He shook hands with her again. The brown eyes were shadowed by the heavy brows, but even so there was an odd light in them as he gazed at her. She was reminded uncomfortably of the light the ophthalmologist uses to see through the eye into the brain.

"Good work, Agent," he said, and shut the door.

Thoughtful, she headed for her cubicle, hoping to be alone. McCarthy was lying in wait for her, however.

"Hey, Rizzoli. How'd it go? Who's the crazed lunatic messing with our obituaries? This gonna bring down the government?"

She entered his cubicle. Muzzy from lack of sleep, strung out with the tension of the interview, she was in no mood for jokes. "Amadi thinks it was some overworked and underpaid clerk who screwed up, got nervous, and diddled with the file in the middle of the night. You buy that?"

McCarthy wrinkled his nose, which caused his glasses to wobble up and down. He shoved them back. He was always fooling with his glasses. "I suppose it's possible. . . ."

"Anything's possible," Petronella said tiredly. "Including the fact that I might fall sound asleep in this chair."

"Take the rest of the day off," McCarthy said magnanimously. He glanced at the clock. "You've only got another couple of hours until you're off duty anyway."

"No, thanks. If I sleep now I'll wake up at midnight. I'll be in my cube, if you need me." Petronella made a wry face. "I have some files to delete."

Jafar el Amadi stood for long moments staring out the window. He was not contemplating a carefree afternoon of golf. He was wondering what to do about Rizzoli.

She was lean and she was hungry and, as Caesar had so astutely noted, the lean and hungry types were trouble. His plans were balanced on a knife's edge; a breath could topple them. And Rizzoli wasn't a breath, she was a typhoon.

As yet, she hadn't done anything to impede him. She'd been a help to him, in fact, and he couldn't really justify dismissing her or having her transferred. Such a move would call unwanted attention to himself. It would also make Rizzoli suspicious, give her cause to dig deep.

Digging reminded him of the overturned plant. He strolled over to gaze down at the plant stretched out on the carpeting, its roots exposed, surrounded by moist dirt. What a mess.

Amadi made up his mind. In some cases, inaction was preferable to action. Pick up the ball and throw it and you could break out a window. Let the ball go and, if you're lucky, it'll roll down the street and fall into the sewer.

A knock on the door interrupted him.

"Yes," Amadi called.

A janitorial 'bot rolled in, looked to him for instructions. Amadi pointed to the potted plant.

The 'bot trundled over, began sucking up the mess with its vacuum system. This finished, the 'bot dumped the pot's remaining dirt onto the floor, sucked it up as well, then thoughtfully and tenderly replaced the already wilting plant back in the empty pot.

The 'bot set the pot carefully on its stand and, task completed, trundled out.

'Bots. Amadi had no idea why people put up with them. Probably the entertainment value.

He buzzed the receptionist.

"Arrange for me to meet with convicted criminal Xris Tampambulos. He is being held on the Umbra Detention Transit Point, in preparation for delivery to the maximum-security facility on Sandusky's Rock."

After a considerable delay the receptionist was back on the line. His tone was apologetic.

"Sir, your meeting with the prisoner is arranged for 0800 hours two days from now."

"Why so long?" Amadi demanded irritably. "I can be there today. I'll take one of the Bureau shuttles."

"I'm sorry, sir, but no Bureau shuttles are available at this time. I've booked reservations for you on the midnight shuttle to Zeta Orbital. From there you will make the daily prison run to Umbra."

"Is that the best you can do?"

"Yes, sir. I'm sorry, sir. One of our shuttles is in maintenance and the other—"

"Never mind. Extend my reservations at my hotel."

Amadi started to leave his office. Remembering the doomed plant, he picked it up and carried it out, made a mental note to purchase a bag of potting soil.

Petronella drove herself home this time, landing the hover without incident in the garage attached to her apartment building. Yawning, she entered her apartment, went straight to the replicator, and pushed a button.

A cup of black coffee appeared. Petronella drank a sip and looked at the clock. She planned to force herself to stay up until 2000 hours, then she would go to bed. If she went to bed now, as she longed to do, she'd be up at 0300.

She sat down at the computer, intending to check her E-mail—she was expecting a note from her mother—when the phone buzzed.

"Oh, God! Please don't let it be work," she said as she answered. "Yes?" She invested the word with grumpiness, hoping that if it was McCarthy, he'd take the hint.

A voice said, "It will be to your advantage to complete the daily quiz."

"What?" Petronella demanded.

No answer. A click ended the call.

A phone scam, Petronella figured. They were illegal, but a good con artist could always find a way around the law. She should report this, except what did she really have to report? What daily quiz? The caller hadn't said. Which was odd, for a con. She would have expected the usual: Pay two thousand credits and win a free trip to the center of the galaxy.

She filed the incident in the back of her mind, under the heading "Strange occurrences, save for future reference," and sat down at her computer.

She brought up her E-mail, read the note from her

mother: Her brother had been accepted to the university on Talisia. Petronella wrote back, adding congratulations. She scanned the rest of the mail: a note from her college roommate, some junk mail which she deleted, and the daily quiz.

Petronella stared, startled, excited, and gratified.

First the phone call. Now this.

Hurriedly she brought up the message.

Complete the daily quiz and win a free, all-expense-paid trip to Adonia, vacation paradise!

"How very interesting," said Petronella. A lamp tipped over, then righted itself due to the strong spring attached to its base. She ignored it, scrolled down to the first question.

Name the twenty-fourth letter of the English alphabet in use during the twentieth century.

Petronella had flunked ancient history. She brought up her encyclopedia, entered the requisite information, and there was the answer.

X. The same as in their current alphabet. She supplied the letter, and a yellow circle with eyes and an insipid smile appeared on the screen.

Congratulations! You have answered the first question correctly. Move on to Question 2.

Well, at least she'd learned something today. She went to the next question.

Definition: Of persons: Doing no evil; free from moral wrong, sin, or guilt (in general); pure, unpolluted. What is the word?

Petronella pondered a moment, then typed in *Innocent.*

Again, the grinning yellow circle.

You have correctly answered two questions: X, Innocent. Proceed to question three.

The first letter of the Roman alphabet.

Even Petronella knew that one. She typed in *A.* Her screen lit with starbursts and, appropriately, Roman candles.

Question Four: *A word that describes Benedict Arnold. Soldier in North America, Earth, late eighteenth century.*

Petronella typed in *GNN news reporter,* but no fireworks erupted. The yellow circle appeared again, but this time the mouth was frowning. It looked gravely disappointed in her.

Wrong. Try again.

Petronella again had to retreat to the encyclopedia, where she located Arnold. She typed in *American,* but the unhappy yellow circle informed her she had once more chosen incorrectly. Studying the information, she at last tried *Traitor.*

She made the yellow circle very happy.

The next two questions were back to the alphabet.

Fourth letter in the alphabet, it originated in an Egyptian hieroglyph that represented a hand.

That turned out to be *D.*

The next question was rather puzzling.

What is the first initial of your name?

Petronella entered *R,* and apparently that was correct. At least the yellow circle thought so.

And finally, the last question.

If you are not dead, you are?

Alive, typed Petronella.

Fireworks burst on her screen in dazzling colors. Rockets whizzed past. Bombshells exploded.

You're a winner! appeared, followed by a summary of the winning answers:

X, Innocent

A, Traitor

D, R, Alive

Petronella sucked in a breath.

"Well, well, well," she murmured. "Imagine that."

And there on the screen was an E-ticket for a first-class seat on the next space transport leaving for Adonia.

Petronella typed a single word to a special code known only to her and Andrew Robison: *Success.*

Then she put in a call.

"McCarthy? Petronella here. I'm not feeling very good. I'm going to take a few days' leave. . . ."

CHAPTER 12

. . . I have heard the key
Turn in the door once and turn once only
We think of the key, each in his prison
Thinking of the key, each confirms a prison.
Thomas Stearns Eliot, *The Waste Land*

"I said I didn't want any visitors."

The guard grunted. "In case you hadn't noticed, X447/990, this is a prison cell, this is a force field, this device"—he exhibited a stun-stick—"is my little persuader. Not one of us gives a damn what you want. You got a visitor. On your feet." The guard grinned maliciously. "Or should I say, *foot*? Hurry it up."

Xris leveraged himself up from the metal cot form on which he'd been lying. He moved slowly, not out of defiance—defiance doesn't quite come off when you have only half a body—but because it was impossible for him to move fast.

"I said hurry." The guard waved the stun-stick close to Xris's shoulder.

"You want me to hurry, give me back my leg and turn my juice on." Xris reached out his good hand, fumbled for the metal crutch leaning against the wall.

The crutch slipped out of Xris's grasp and fell to the steel floor with a clang, landing just out of Xris's reach. The guard wasn't a total bastard, apparently. He shoved the crutch with his foot, sent it scooting toward Xris.

"Thanks," Xris said as he leaned over to pick up the crutch.

A jolt of electricity tingled painfully from his shoulder

down his good arm, causing the hand reaching for the crutch to jerk spasmodically.

"What the hell was that for?" Xris demanded, rubbing his shoulder.

"Just in case you had any ideas about using that crutch for a club," the guard responded.

"I didn't until now," Xris muttered. "Much obliged."

The guard didn't respond. He waved the stun-stick. "Move it, X447."

Xris slid his cybernetic arm through the rings of the crutch, grasped the handle, and, after a few misses and with no help at all from the guard, managed to struggle to an upright position. He lurched forward awkwardly, lost his balance, and came crashing up against the wall. He hadn't yet become accustomed to the crutch.

He'd be damned if he was ever going to become accustomed to it.

At last Xris managed to hobble out of his cell. The guard followed him. When he didn't think Xris was moving fast enough, he sent another jolt sizzling into Xris's right butt cheek. His good leg went frighteningly numb for a split second. He teetered, fought to retain his balance, determined not to give the guard the satisfaction of seeing him fall, not if it took every ounce of strength left in his body. He held on.

"Cut the sympathy act," said the guard, growing bored with his game. "And get moving."

Xris limped along the tubelike corridor of the holding center, blinking in the bright blue-white fluorescent light that beat down from the ceiling and shone up through the floor grates. The same blue-white sterile light lit the prison cells that lined the corridor. Darkness was a privilege, one that the prisoners were denied. They learned to sleep with the light on or they didn't sleep.

The other prisoners awaiting transportation looked out their cells as Xris stumped past. Most of the other prisoners were too preoccupied with their own miseries to pay any attention to his, but as he was walking slowly and painfully past one of the last cells in the block, the prisoner stood up, moved over to stand close to the force field that kept them inside.

"Hey, cyborg," said the prisoner in a loud voice that carried clearly up and down the corridor. "I hear you were a cop."

This news had every man in the cellblock on his feet, peering out his cell, trying to see.

Xris ignored them, shuffled ahead.

"Hey! Maybe you still are a cop, huh?" the prisoner called out. "Maybe you're a fuckin' spy!"

"You know what happens to fuckin' spies, cyborg?" another prisoner shouted. "They get their fuckin' necks broke!"

"Yeah, you better be real careful, cyborg. You might trip and have a nasty fall someday. A real nasty fall."

Xris reached the end of the cellblock. He was now out of sight of the other prisoners, and their threats died off to mutterings and harsh laughter.

"Good thing you're shipping out of here tomorrow," observed the guard.

"It won't matter," Xris said. "The news will get to Sandusky's Rock."

"Yeah, you're right." The guard was laconic. "I wouldn't want to be in your shoes. Make that *shoe*." He grinned, gestured with the stun-stick. "In here."

Xris entered another tube, this one vertical, and so small that he could barely squeeze his broad shoulders into it. The door slid shut. A light came on. He was being scanned—inside and out—for weapons.

The scan complete, the door slid open on the opposite side of the tube. Two guards were waiting for him. They took hold of him, helped him step out. These guards were armed with beam rifles, not stun-sticks. They entered another tubelike corridor. Xris expected to be taken into the visitors' tanks, so called because they were designed like fish tanks, with the prisoner and his visitor peering at one another through steelglass, talking via commlinks.

The guards marched Xris right past the tanks, however.

"What gives?" Xris asked. "Where are we going? I thought someone said I had a visitor."

The guards didn't answer. No snappy foot jokes from these guys. They were all business. They exited the cellblocks, moved down a quiet, more soothingly lit corridor, and entered the administrative wing of the facility. Judging by the curious glances and a few startled looks from the employees, it was not customary for prisoners to be in this part of the complex.

Xris passed a window, glanced out to see a grassy lawn, sun shining, trees. A picnic table was set up on the lawn. Several employees were basking in the sun, taking their coffee break. He tried to steer close to the window, which was open a crack, hoping for . . . what? Not escape. The very idea was ludicrous. The window was likely made of steelglass. It would take a missile to smash through it. What was he after?

Nothing much. Just a whiff of fresh air. A need to smell something besides sweaty bodies, urine, and disinfectant.

The alert guard spotted the move, was having none of it. He stepped between Xris and the window, shoved Xris back brutally and impersonally, using the butt end of the beam rifle.

"Wrong way," he said.

The guards marched Xris to a room that was probably not normally used for meeting visitors, but had obviously been chosen with great care. There were no windows, no vents, and only one door. All the furniture had been removed, except for two metal chairs.

Escorting Xris into the room, the guards pushed him down into one of the chairs. They took his crutch from him, placed a restrainer on his good leg, another on his good hand, then left. The restrainers short-circuited all nerve impulses in his foot and his hand. Xris tried wiggling his fingers, but they refused to obey. Helpless, he sat alone in the room and waited.

The wait wasn't long. The door opened. A man entered, accompanied by a guard. The man looked at Xris. Xris looked at the man. Neither said anything. The man glanced around the room, nodded once in satisfaction.

"This will do."

The guard nodded, left the room. The door shut behind him. There was a slight thump as he and the other guard took up positions outside the door.

The man walked over to the other chair, moved it around so that it faced Xris. But instead of seating himself, the man reached into the pocket of his expensive suit and took out a small device, which he placed on the floor at his feet. Xris recognized the device—a sonic scrambler. Within a two-meter circle around the device, sound traveled normally. Outside of that, the device would distort sound waves. Someone might hear their conversation, but no one would understand it.

The two regarded each other in silence, then Xris said, "Hello, Amadi."

"Hello, Xris," Amadi returned with a tired smile. He blinked his eyes against the light. "It was a long flight."

"My heart bleeds," Xris said. "The blood's fake, but it's the thought that counts."

"Always the smart-ass. How are you? Anything you need?"

"A twist. You haven't got one on you, by any chance?"

"Sorry, smoking's not allowed. Smoking's not allowed on Sandusky's Rock, either, I hear. But then, smoking's a bad habit. It could shorten your life."

"So could a lot of things. Disrupters, for one. My fellow inmates, for another. Have you come all this way to talk about my bad habits, boss?"

"I've come to talk about murder," Amadi replied. "The murder of Dalin Rowan. Mind if I sit down?"

"You can fly around the room backward for all I care," Xris said, adding, "You know I didn't murder Rowan. You know that nobody murdered Rowan—although the Hung have tried. Twice. So why have me arrested? If you think you'll make me turn over Rowan, forget it. I'll do twenty years on Sandusky's Rock before I tell you where to find him."

"Don't you mean her?" Amadi asked, with a quirk of his eyebrow.

Xris didn't answer.

"Twenty years," Amadi mused. Leaning back, he asked conversationally, "Do you know anything about our penal colony there?"

Xris shrugged, noncommittal.

"Let me tell you. It's an asteroid. They don't mine ore on Sandusky's Rock. They mine ice. Which means it's cold on that asteroid, Xris. I hear that you never get used to the cold. You always feel it.

"You want to know how they treat cyborgs there, Xris? The guards hand you your leg and your arm when you go out to the mines. The guards remove your leg and your arm when they put you back in your cell. There you lie— alone, defenseless. How long do you figure you'll last on Sandusky's Rock, Xris?" Amadi regarded him reflectively. "Now that they know you were once a cop."

"So that's how the word got out." Xris snorted. "Thanks a lot, Amadi, you bastard. Well, before you transport me, maybe you should know something.

"There's a file on a certain computer we've left with Bear Olefsky. You know him? Friend of the king? This file has information in it pertaining to the Hung and one Agent William Armstrong. You remember him? Agent Armstrong made everyone think he was working for us, when all along he was really working for the Hung, handing them all kinds of key information, which they used to build their criminal organization into one of the richest, most powerful syndicates in the galaxy."

"Armstrong's dead," Amadi said coolly. "The Hung murdered him."

"So everyone would like to believe," Xris said. "We happen to know differently—Rowan and I. Rowan and I *and* Bear Olefsky. Armstrong was murdered, but not by the Hung. Oh, I don't doubt that he was on their list. His cover was blown. His usefulness to them had run out. But someone else got to him first. Someone inside the Bureau. Rowan was there. He saw the body. He's got proof. If this proof is handed over to the press—and I've left instructions for Bear Olefsky to hand it over if anything happens to me—how are you going to look, Amadi?

"You were Armstrong's boss. Either you didn't know he was a traitor, in which case you look like one of the guys who goes prancing around in pointy-toed shoes, wearing a cap with bells on it, or you did know he was selling secrets to the Hung, in which case you and I might get to be cell mates."

Xris attempted to scratch his shoulder by rubbing it on the back of his chair. "You don't snore, do you, boss?"

Amadi regarded Xris with unblinking eyes for long moments. Then he said quietly, "I killed him."

Xris stared, startled. Whatever he'd been expecting, it wasn't this. "I'll be damned," he said.

Amadi stood up. Turning his back, he walked across the room until he reached the wall. He stood there, staring at the paint, then he pivoted.

"I had no choice. He'd hung us out to dry!" Amadi said bitterly. "No pun intended."

"You had a choice," Xris countered. "You could have arrested him, brought him to trial—"

"Break the news that one of our own agents had been handing our plans to the Hung? Tell the press that this one agent had thrown a laser spanner into I don't know how many operations, that a number of agents had been killed because of him? And that this had been going on right under my nose for about five years? You're right. I could have done that. Maybe it's what I should have done, but I didn't.

"My career—thirty years—shot. My pension shot. And where the hell was I supposed to get another job? At my age?"

Xris didn't respond. There didn't seem to be any answer for that one. He stared down at the restrainer on his good leg and thought about Amadi losing a comfortable retirement; about Ito, losing his life.

"And then there'd be the trial." Amadi shoved his hands into his pants pockets. His fists were clenched into tight balls. "Much of our evidence against the Hung had passed through Armstrong's hands. We brand him a traitor and where would that leave us? We'd have to toss out everything and start over! Flush an investigation that had been ongoing for years down the toilet.

"I looked at those two roads, Xris. I saw one road filled with crap and muck, leading exactly nowhere, and I saw the other road as clear, as bright as . . . as . . ."

"A single shot through the head?"

"Yes." Amadi was grim. "A single shot to the head. That's all it took. One shot and you were avenged. Mashashiro Ito was avenged. All those others who gave their lives were avenged. The trial went on. It was successful. The Hung were put away."

"And your afternoons on the golf course were assured," Xris said.

Amadi regarded him coldly. "And what would you have done if you'd gotten to him first, Xris? Tell me that."

Xris looked up, smiled. "The same, boss. I'd have done the same. Except I wouldn't have made it so clean and quick. I would have pulled his legs and arms off first, so he would have known what it feels like."

He was quiet a moment, thinking. "So that takes care of Armstrong. That's one of my questions answered. The other is: Why am I here? If it was to hear your confession, you ought to know that I've been defrocked."

Amadi returned to his chair. The room was growing uncomfortably warm and the smell of disinfectant wafted from Xris's prison uniform, mingled with his body odor. He was only allowed to shower once every other day.

Amadi leaned closer, a truly heroic gesture.

"The Hung leaders are in prison, but their organization's doing business as usual. Even better than usual. You know that for yourself."

"Yeah," Xris said. "I know. So does Rowan."

"We thought we had taken them down, but we were wrong. They had financial resources tucked away somewhere. The Hung leaders laid low a couple of years—long enough for us to look the other direction—then they started up operations again. They began small, but they're not small any longer. They had good people after Rowan, didn't they? Experts? Spared no expense?"

Xris nodded.

"I told you last time we talked that I thought Rowan knew the location of the Hung's stash and—"

"I asked her," Xris said, interrupting. "She doesn't."

"Maybe I believe you. Maybe I don't. The fact is, the Hung do. They think that Rowan either knows or could find out. She's a threat to them and their operation and she'll be a threat as long as she's alive. And there's not much you can do to stop them, is there, Xris? You and I both know that if someone wants to kill a person and he works at it actively, with a modicum of intelligence and luck, he'll succeed."

Xris kept silent.

"My guess is that you must be feeling pretty helpless about now," Amadi continued. "You can't protect Rowan while you're in here. Oh, they may have lost her trail for now, but sooner or later they'll find her. And she's not helping matters by playing 'tag, you're it' with one of my agents."

"Oh, yeah?" Xris thought he should look surprised.

Amadi scratched at his left eyebrow. "You remember that Talisian agent, Rizzoli?"

"The human hurricane?"

"That's her. She discovered someone had hacked into the Bureau computers, tampered with a few files—you can guess whose. The hacker left his, or should I say her, footprints all over the place. You never want to take Rizzoli shopping for good crystal, but she's got brains. She latched onto Rowan right off."

"What did she do with the information?" Xris asked, though of course he knew. If his heart hadn't been surgically glued in place, it would have sunk down to his shoes.

Make that shoe.

Amadi smiled. "She gave the info to her boss—me."

"And you did—"

"I handled it. I had a talk with Rizzoli. I told her to drop it. I said she was getting all worked up over nothing more ominous than a forgetful file clerk. I was nice to her. She's young, eager. Wants to make Bureau chief. I didn't tromp all over her illusions."

"You'll be canonized someday, Amadi," Xris assured him. "I only hope I live to see it. Did she drop the case?"

"Of course." Amadi appeared amazed that Xris would even consider otherwise. "I'm her superior. What else would she do? She deleted the files."

Well, so much for that idea. Still, it wouldn't be like Rowan to give up. He just hoped she didn't stretch her neck out too far.

Xris tried to sound sympathetic. "I'm sorry Rowan's bothering your employees during business hours. If you'll drop the charges and get me the hell out of here, I'll have a talk with her."

Amadi was shaking his head. "I can't do that, Xris. I wish I could, but I can't. There's a reason you're in here, a reason which you've probably already guessed."

"You want to help me stop smoking? Thanks, Amadi, but—"

"Would you quit being the comedian and listen for one goddam minute?" Amadi shouted.

Xris had never before heard Amadi raise his voice, had never before seen him lose his cool, calm demeanor. Amadi was stressed, stretched good and tight.

Here it comes, Xris thought. He shut his mouth, thinking he'd never wanted anything as much in his life as he wanted a twist right about now.

Amadi rose abruptly, paced the length of the room, one hand rubbing the back of his head. He looked like someone trying to steel himself to jump into a pool filled with sharks.

Xris would have been only too happy to give his former boss a shove. What the hell did Amadi want? Not Rowan; that much was clear.

Amadi spent perhaps five minutes pacing the room. Suddenly he stopped, turned, faced Xris.

"I want you to do a job for me."

Xris cast a glance at his restrainers, the stinking prison uniform, the crutch. Shaking his head, he grinned.

"You could have just hired me, Amadi. I admit that I don't come cheap, but I would've given you a cut rate. For old time's sake."

"No, I couldn't hire you, Xris. Not for this job."

"Why not? Hell, I'll do just about anything for money. Provided it's legal, of course."

"Of course." Amadi smiled sourly. "Like stealing robots. Never mind. You wouldn't have done this, not for all the money in His Majesty's treasury. That's why I had to set you up. I need you, Xris. You're the best. You're the only one I can trust."

"What's the job?" Xris was wary.

"Breaking the leaders of the Hung out of prison."

CHAPTER 13

Don't fight forces; use them.
Richard Buckminster Fuller, *Shelter*

So. We were right, Rowan and I. It is you. You're the one at the top. You're the one holding hands with the Hung. And now you're going to spring your buddies from prison. What's the excuse? So they'd be killed in the escape? So they'd lead you to the money? This should be entertaining.

Careful, Xris, careful, my friend. This is your chance. Your chance to expose Amadi and take care of the Hung all at the same time. But he's got to believe you. . . .

"How much?" Xris asked.

Amadi looked surprised, then disappointed.

"What's the matter, Amadi?" Xris's mouth twisted in a bitter smile. "Did you think I'd do this for love of king and country? You're asking me to spring the slugs who killed Ito and made me into the Tin Man. I'll squat on Sandusky's Rock until my innards rust before I'll do that unless . . . *unless* you make it worth my time. *Well* worth my time."

"You've got it all wrong, Xris! I swear it. At least listen to what I have to say."

Xris thought he should allow himself to be persuaded. He glanced pointedly at his restrainers. "You have a captive audience."

Amadi sat down across from Xris. Amadi tried his hardest to look at Xris, but his eyes didn't find the view to be particularly pleasant, for they kept shifting. Sometimes to a point over Xris's left shoulder, sometimes to the blank wall, sometimes to Amadi's own hands, resting white-knuckled on his knees.

"The Hung leaders were sentenced to a labor prison—

not Sandusky's Rock, but one like it. That was back in the days of President Robes, when anyone and everything in the government was for sale. The Hung were able to purchase an upgrade. They managed to get themselves transferred to Jango—a white-collar, executive prison designed for the 'right' sort of criminal who doesn't hurt anyone. Like accountants who've embezzled money from their firms and left a couple thousand of their fellow employees to stand in unemployment lines. Or crooked stockbrokers who swindle the elderly out of their pensions. Those who aren't a real danger to society."

Xris snorted. "You can save the righteous indignation for your interview with GNN. Don't waste it on me."

Amadi smiled, shrugged. "All right, Xris. Plain and simple. The three Hung leaders are living in a comfortable penthouse cell, complete with vids, mags, and monthly conjugal visits from their wives and/or girlfriends. They have access to a library. They attend classes taught by university professors. One of the gentlemen even went for his Ph.D. at taxpayer expense. They have their secret stash of funds. They're conducting business as usual. Better than usual, because they have the perfect alibi. They're in prison. Who can touch them?"

"And now they want out?" Xris was skeptical. "Why? Doesn't the Ph.D. want to wait until he completes his thesis?"

"I don't know," Amadi said, looking worried. "I'm not sure. A combination of circumstances, maybe."

He knows damn well why these men want out. Xris had no choice, however, but to appear helpful.

"Rowan," he said.

"Undoubtedly," Amadi agreed. "The Hung know their agents failed to take her down. They believe that Rowan knows the location of their funds. That means Rowan could ruin them, put them out of business, this time for good. Their lieutenants have botched the job. Maybe they figure that it's time they got personally involved. Maybe they want to do that *and* move their stash to a new and safer location."

"Why not have their contacts on the outside do that?"

"Would you give a subordinate—a subordinate you know

to be crooked because he's working for you—access to forty billion golden eagles?"

"That's what they're worth?"

"A conservative estimate," Amadi said dryly.

And how much of that is lining the pocket of that expensive suit you're wearing? Xris wondered.

"Then they won't miss a couple of million," he said aloud. "Which is what I charge for breaking bastards out of prison. One question: Why don't they use their own people to bust them loose?"

"This job requires specialized training and equipment. The Hung employs smugglers, drug traffickers, murderers, thieves, and corrupt politicians. Not the sort who can disable the surveillance satellites surrounding Jango or fly the spaceplane that has to outrun Navy gunships or provide the muscle and brains, skill and resources that's going to put this plan together. They have to look for outside talent. Your name happened to come up in conversation."

Xris was polite. "Thanks, Amadi, but you shouldn't have gone to all that trouble. Here's what I want. Six million gold eagles. Cash. Nontraceable. Half up front. Half when the job's done."

Amadi appeared uneasy. "That's alot of money, Xris."

"Damn right it is! This job will cost a lot of money. And I get a certain satisfaction out of thinking that the Hung will pay for it. That's the deal. Take it or leave it. By the way, my lawyer thinks I've got a real good chance of getting out on appeal."

"All right," Amadi said reluctantly. "Give me an account number. The money will be there. I'll be honest with you, Xris—"

"Yeah, you do that, Amadi. And hurry it up, will you? My butt's going to sleep."

"The Hung are a thorn in our side. Thorn?" Amadi sighed. "Make that a plasma burst torpedo! These three have murdered enough people to populate a small planet. The drugs they sell have left others wishing they were dead. The Hung have screwed up the economies of any number of nations with their counterfeiting operations. We *have* to shut them down."

"You don't need to sell me, Amadi. I'm highly in favor

of the idea. So how about this? I go into Jango with a small quantity of a very deadly substance that a friend of mine makes—"

Amadi laid his hand on Xris's good arm. "Don't even think about it, Xris. Three important prisoners turn up dead in their cells and you think no one's going to ask questions? Once they discover your connection, you *will* be walking into the disrupter."

"Accidents happen," Xris argued. "More people are killed slipping in their bathtubs every year—"

"Oh, stuff it!" Amadi was growing impatient—also exceedingly nervous. He kept glancing at the door. "The Hung leaders have heirs, people all set to step in and take over. They're like a damn troll in my grandkid's vid game. Cut off the head, the body still keeps going, and eventually it even grows a new head! We have to kill the entire body. And the way to do that is to shut off the blood supply to the brain.

"You help them escape, Xris. They lead me to the money. I arrest them."

"You? You're going to be there?"

"I'll be on the same spaceplane with you. *And* them."

So that's the plan, Xris said to himself in satisfaction. The money. Nice to know I haven't lost my touch.

"And you put them right back in their cushy cells."

Amadi smiled, but the eyes were shadowed. "Not necessarily. I don't think they'll let themselves be taken alive."

Gee, I was right on both counts! I'm a fucking genius. Xris had to restrain himself from laughing in Amadi's face.

"So that's why you didn't pick up Rowan," Xris said, pretending to have just figured this out. "She's of no use to you now. You don't need her anymore."

Amadi shrugged, noncommittal. "I have a date for the breakout arranged. Nineteen days space-time from today. Can you be ready by then?"

Nineteen days. Xris did some calculations. "Kirkov's birthday, huh?"

"Who?" Amadi appeared puzzled.

"Come on, boss. Listen to your surveillance tapes again. You know damn good and well the team's got a job to do and—surprise, surprise—they go into action on that day.

What a coincidence. Are you afraid my friends will interfere?"

Amadi didn't reply.

"Oh, I trust you're keeping what you overheard confidential. You don't want to piss off the Lord of the Admiralty."

"Dixter and I have spoken," Amadi said. And that was all he said. Obviously whatever lie he'd told Dixter, the Lord of the Admiralty had believed, otherwise a troop of Marines would have arrived to haul Xris's ass out of jail.

"I'll give you a minute to think it over." Amadi stood up, walked to the opposite end of the room, and stared at a fly crawling up the wall.

So Dixter's written me off, too. I can see the headlines now, Xris thought. CYBORG'S HEAD BLOWN OFF HELPING CONS ESCAPE. You can't think I'm that stupid, Amadi. But maybe you think I'm that greedy. . . .

Amadi turned back to face him. "Did you say something?"

"Yeah. I'll take the job."

"Good! Glad to hear it." Amadi was pleased.

"On my conditions."

Amadi wasn't so pleased. "I'm paying you six million in gold already—"

"This has nothing to do with money. Condition one: Move me from that death trap of a cellblock. I'm in with two other guys—one who's made a crossbow out of bed springs. He's a psychopath who happens to have a grudge against cops. He was real interested to hear that I'd been one."

"A crossbow." Amadi shook his head. Pulling out his electronic pad, he entered a notation. "Just think what these people could do if they would only put their energy into honest pursuits."

"Be grateful, Amadi. He'd probably have your job."

Amadi glanced up, startled.

Xris grinned, then went back to business. "I want my own cell, nice and private, maximum security, until the transport to Jango arrives. Condition two: I want to be reassembled. Leg, arm, hand, hearing, eye, full power."

"You can't have your own cybernetic limbs," Amadi

stated. "Even I couldn't get you inside Jango with that armaments warehouse you call a leg. The guards will turn you inside out when you arrive, looking for weapons. And if you get past them, you go through a body scanner every time you leave or enter your cell."

"I thought this was a luxury joint, filled with refined gentlemanly types. I thought we attended literature courses in the morning and made pottery in the afternoon. Jeez, Amadi." Xris was aggrieved. "I was counting on getting my high school diploma!"

Amadi was not amused. "Jango may not be the ice mines, but it's still a prison."

"All right. Furnish me with a leg off the rack, but I want my own personal physician to fit it. I need a proper fit," Xris explained. "Otherwise it rubs. You wouldn't want me to chafe, would you?"

Amadi noted—with a fine show of serious attentiveness—the name and the intergalactic vid number of one William Quong, M.D., a show Xris watched with cynical amusement. Amadi knew Quong as well as or better than Xris by now. FISA probably had an agent tailing the Doc this very moment. Xris could have made a smart remark, but he owed Amadi, who was handing out presents like it was Xris's birthday. The least Xris could do was to play the party games.

"Anything else you want?" Amadi didn't bother to hide the sarcasm.

"That's all for the moment. If I think of anything, how can I contact you?"

"*I'll* contact you." Amadi rose to his feet. "I'm glad we could work together on this case again, Xris."

He held out his hand.

Xris hesitated; the Hung's money wasn't the only thing that had blood on it.

Forgive me, Ito, Xris said silently. I have to play along. But soon, buddy. Soon. . . .

He tried to reach out, but the restrainer wouldn't permit it. Amadi clasped Xris's limp hand, shook it solemnly.

"I'll send in the guard," Amadi offered.

"By the way, what's my story? What have you told the guards about me?"

Amadi's smile broadened. "That you're a cop. Take care of yourself, Xris. Oh, by the way." He half turned, glanced at Xris over his shoulder. "You or the members of your team might get a visit from someone in Internal Affairs."

"Oh, yeah?" Xris was careful not to appear too interested. "Who's head of that now?"

"Robison. Andrew Robison. You remember him?"

"Our boss. Former boss. Used to head up our division."

"That's him. He's been promoted. He's now head of Internal Affairs, and between you and me, he's become one hell of a nuisance. Just now, he's sticking his nose into this matter of the Hung. Pass the word for your friends to be careful what they talk about, Xris. People do slip in their bathtubs every day, and as you said yourself, we don't need Dalin Rowan anymore."

He switched off the scrambler, thrust it into a pocket, and knocked twice on the door.

"Guard!" Amadi shouted. "I'm finished."

That's right, you treacherous son of a bitch, Xris told Amadi's backside. You are.

"One more thing, Amadi," Xris said.

He hadn't been going to ask this; he'd made up his mind he wasn't and he was startled and disappointed in himself to hear the words come out.

"Did Marjorie . . . did she know about the setup? Was she in on it?"

Amadi turned to look at him and Xris saw the pity in the man's eyes, saw it before Amadi could hide it.

He didn't reply, but then he didn't have to. Xris knew the answer. Marjorie hadn't invited him to her house. Probably she'd be furious to hear he'd invaded her privacy.

"Yeah, well. I just wondered." Xris shrugged it off.

Amadi had the grace to look away.

CHAPTER 14

Beware of robbing a wretch,
Of attacking a cripple.
Amenemope, *The Instruction of Amenemope*

"Lights out," came the announcement over the loud-speaker. "Settle down, you men."

The voices that had been talking loudly dropped to mutters, mumbles, and whispers, punctuated by the occasional harsh laugh.

Xris wondered what anyone could find to laugh about in here, wished they'd shut up. Trying to sleep was hard enough. Xris didn't sleep all that well under ideal conditions. It's difficult to curl up in a nice, comforting fetal position when half your body is metal. And there was no cuddling close to another warm soft body in the darkness. Cuddling with Xris would be tantamount to cuddling with some ancient refrigerator; about as cold and about as noisy.

He thought of Tess, a woman he'd met during the ill-fated mission to steal that dratted robot. He'd spent an enjoyable two weeks in the sun and surf of a very romantic hideaway with her. She'd been jolted out of a sound sleep every time the machine that maintained the correct balance of chemicals in his body hummed into action.

Tess had been honest and open about it, they'd laughed about it together, and for once in his life Xris hadn't felt bitter, hadn't let the laughter hurt him. But he could have, if he wanted to. He could do so now, thinking back on it. Hurting would be easy.

Of course, now he didn't have the problem of sleeping with his cybernetic body parts. He didn't have to worry about rolling over the wrong way onto his metal arm and bruising the hell out of his ribs or accidentally shoving his metal foot through the bedboard during a bad dream. Although he was in a private cell, as he had requested, and they had permitted him to activate his eye and his hearing, they still hadn't given him back the use of his cybernetic limbs.

"But we won't charge you for the crutch," the guard had assured him.

"Damn generous," Xris had sneered.

He couldn't sleep. Not in this cell, lying on a metal bed that still had metal springs. Lying in the darkness that wasn't really dark because of the security lights. Lying here with the smell of disinfectant in his nostrils, the smell of disinfectant trying to mask the smell of urine. Lying here listening to the grunts and coughs, snores and whispers of the men in the cells around him, the measured footsteps of the guards and the whirring sound of the 'bot that passed by every thirty minutes, taking a body count.

Xris could do something about the noise, at least. He could shut down his augmented hearing. Imagining the sweet silence washing over him, soothing him into much-needed rest, his right hand was reaching for the minuscule controls located behind his left ear when his instincts rebelled, ordered him not to be a damn fool.

He closed his eyes and tried to drown out the sounds by remembering Tess's laughter, reliving the fun of those two weeks. Nothing would come of the relationship. They'd both known that going into it. Neither of them was looking for anything to come of it. Tess was an undercover operative, working out of the Lord Admiralty's office, with a brilliant career ahead of her. She had put serious relationships on hold.

"Some people plan to spend their old age on the golf course," she had told Xris. "Others plan to travel. Me—I'm going to fall in love!"

"I'll wait for you," he had said.

"No, you won't!" She had laughed. "You'll be with your wife, chasing after grandkids."

That picture was one he'd torn up, ripped into shreds, ten years ago. But Tess had given him confidence; she had let him know that he could love and be loved. He had thought about trying to paste the picture back together again.

And that was why, when the E-mail had come from Marjorie, he'd decided to spend some time in the beach house the two of them had dreamed about together.

Except that Marjorie hadn't sent the invitation.

So much for . . .

So much . . .

He was sitting on the deck. The waves rolled in. Broke against the shore. Rolled out.

It was actually comfortable, lying in bed without the cybernetic limbs, he thought drowsily. He'd never tried it before, mostly because it made him feel like the helpless cripple he was. But now he could roll over, curl up. Nothing dragged on him, nothing weighed him down, nothing poked him or prodded him.

The waves rolled in and out, but their roar was receding. All he could hear were footfalls in the sand. . . .

Xris was awake, suddenly, completely.

Footfalls in the sand, my ass! Footfalls in the corridor. Footfalls trying to be as quiet as feet walking on sand. They would have been, to the normal ear. But Xris could hear the slight whisper made by tiptoes creeping along the tile floor, the faint whiff whiff sound caused by the stiff fabric of the prison uniform rubbing against itself, the sound of breaths indrawn, exhaled.

Pad, pad. Whiff whiff. Breath.

Of course, Stealthy Feet could be looking for anybody in this cellblock. Perhaps he had a boyfriend.

Pad, pad. Whiff whiff. Breath. Snick.

Xris knew that sound. Only one thing made a sound like *snick*. Arming a bolt gun.

Unless this was a lover's quarrel, the boyfriend theory was out.

The security light bathed the bed, a large patch of floor, the wall opposite, and Xris in bright white light. One hell of a beautiful target. And if he wasn't in bed, if he was, say, flopping about, a helpless cripple, on the floor, the assassin would simply readjust his aim.

A man moved into Xris's view, halted outside his cell. Xris could see the man in detail. He was tall, stocky, dressed in a prison uniform, and he carried an all-plastic eighteen-micron bolt gun in his right hand. Reaching out with his left hand, the man hit the controls that operated the force field. The red light, which let the guards know at a glance that the force field was operational, winked out.

Xris grit his teeth, forced himself to lie still when his instincts were urging him to crawl through the metal wall of his cell.

The man stepped inside, raised the gun . . .

Xris lurched off the bed, fell heavily onto the floor as the assassin fired the bolt gun into the bed. He knew the moment he pulled the trigger that he'd just killed a mattress.

"Son of a—"

Xris rolled across the floor, barreling his body into the man's legs. The assassin toppled forward. He was an agile bastard, unfortunately. His head missed the metal bed frame by a centimeter; he landed on his hands and knees and managed to maintain his hold on the gun.

"Guard!" roared Xris, lying on his back on the floor.

His metal crutch was in the corner next to the bed—an arm's length away. He could reach it, but the assassin was in front of him, already back on his feet—both feet—twisting his body as he moved, the gun coming to bear.

Xris swung his leg. His foot connected with the man's hand, sent the gun flying across the cell. It landed on the floor somewhere behind Xris.

"Guard!" Xris shouted again.

The assassin dove for the gun.

Xris had a split-second decision to make. He could either go after the gun or his crutch. He could see his crutch, which was right in front of him, and he had no idea where the gun had landed. From the scrabbling sounds and muttered curses, the assassin wasn't certain himself.

Still on his back, Xris lunged across the floor, propelling his body with his good leg. He grabbed the crutch by the toe, hefted it like a club.

The assassin had found his gun. He turned, aimed it at Xris.

Xris swung the crutch, hit the assassin in the jaw.

The man fired; his shot went wild. A bolt slammed into the floor next to Xris's head.

The man staggered backward, blood running from his mouth. But he wasn't stunned, as Xris had hoped. The assassin raised the gun again.

Xris lashed out. The crutch smacked the gun from the man's hand and this time the gun was gone for good, skittering underneath the bed.

The attacker reached for something under his arm—a backup weapon, probably a knife.

Rolling onto his side, Xris leveraged himself up on his right arm. He used the crutch like a battering ram, thrust forward. The toe of the crutch smashed into the man's groin. Xris jabbed and twisted, making sure.

The assassin had only one thought and that was to try desperately to ease the white-hot pain spreading up from his groin and flaming out the top of his head. Clutching at himself, he dropped the knife and toppled to the floor, rolling in agony.

Xris struggled to his feet. Make that foot. Thinking it was only right to put the poor bastard out of his misery, Xris punched him.

The man's head struck the hard concrete wall. He slumped to the floor and didn't move.

Silence, throughout the cellblock. No more grunts and coughs. He couldn't even hear anyone breathing. They might have all died in their beds.

"Any more of you?" Xris shouted between gasps for air.

His shout echoed through the hushed corridors, came back to him.

Xris drew in a breath. "Guards!"

Again, no answer. He didn't step out of his cell, even though the force field was shut down. He knew better than to try to escape. They'd be waiting for him.

"Guards!" he yelled, and when again no one came, no one responded, Xris picked up the bolt gun, aimed, and fired at the security cam in the corridor.

Shattered glass rained down on the concrete floor.

Xris tossed the bolt gun onto the pile. Someone in another cell laughed.

The guards came then. On the run. Red lights glared in

the cellblock. Alarms sounded. Now the prisoners were up and talking, yelling and shouting and tossing objects against their force fields to make them sizzle.

Guards filled the corridor.

The head guard arrived and everything quieted.

He came to stare at the shattered cam. Reaching down, he picked up and pocketed the bolt gun. At his orders, another guard held a beam rifle on Xris, who was sitting on the bed, waiting for his heartbeat and his breathing to return to normal. His cheek stung. Putting his hand up to it, he felt blood and realized just how close the bolt had come to smashing through his head.

Two more guards bent over the assassin, decided to call in the medics.

The head guard entered the cell, glanced around coolly. "So . . . what happened here? A lover's quarrel?"

"You know what happened," Xris returned, wiping blood on his uniform. "You saw the whole damn thing. And what took you so long to get here? Firing that bolt gun must have set off every security device in this building!"

"Malfunction," said the head guard impassively, shrugging. "System's always malfunctioning."

"Yeah, right. I want to talk to the warden."

"Sure. In the morning."

"Now," Xris grated.

"In the morning," the guard repeated. "Believe me, you don't want to wake up the warden. Puts him in a real bad mood. And why'd you shoot the cam out?" He sounded personally hurt by the incident. "Now I got to activate a guard 'bot, all 'cause you shot out the fucking cam."

"I don't see that it'll make all that much difference," Xris returned. "You weren't paying any attention to the cam anyway."

He glanced up at the man. "Or maybe you were. Maybe you were watching and enjoying the show. Except it didn't end like you'd planned. So who gave you the popcorn, huh? Who paid you to sit there on your fat ass and do nothing while this creep puts bolts into me?"

"You were a cop. Everyone knows it." The head guard shrugged.

The medics entered, examined the assassin, and after a

brief consultation they rolled him onto a stretcher 'bot, ordered the 'bot to haul him to the infirmary.

"Some of the boys don't like cops," said the head guard.

Xris opened his mouth, shut it again. Might as well save his breath. One of the medics came to examine Xris's cheek.

"It's pretty deep. You better come to the infirmary. I'll seal it for you."

Xris shook his head.

"It'll leave a scar."

Xris looked up at the man.

The medic glanced at what was left of Xris's body, muttered something unintelligible, and left Xris's cell. The head guard stepped outside, reactivated the force field.

"Excitement's over, fellas," he called harshly. "Go back to bed. You know 0500 comes pretty damn early."

The guards departed. A robot trundled over to stand in the ruins of the security cam. The light of its optic sensors glowed yellow, while a red beam moved from left to right and then back right to left. Xris was familiar with the model. Its armor could supposedly withstand a direct hit from a Devastator cannon. It was armed with electronic stunners that could fell a man in nanoseconds, leave him writhing on the floor in nerve-jangling agony. The 'bot could also release sleep gas, enough to flood the entire corridor in less than five seconds.

"Where were you when I needed you?" Xris asked the 'bot.

It looked disdainful, didn't reply.

Xris laid back down on his bed. At least, with the 'bot standing right outside his cell, a 'bot who couldn't be bribed or threatened, he felt relatively safe. But sleep would be a long time coming.

Someone had tried to murder him. And *not* because he'd been a cop.

That attack had not been made by a prisoner with a grudge. A prisoner with a grudge uses crossbows made from the bed springs. He doesn't have access to the codes that operate the force fields. He doesn't have the cash needed to bribe the guards. He doesn't use a new model eighteen-micron all-plastic bolt gun, a weapon that had to have cost several thousand credits. Specifically designed to be smuggled inside secure areas, the gun would make no blip on a routine metal scan. It was obviously a piece of a well-planned-out puzzle.

Whoever ordered this had money and clout and access.

"Amadi," Xris said to the darkness.

But that didn't quite feel right. Why would Amadi go to all the trouble of coming to meet Xris, setting up this job with the Hung, if he just wanted him dead? Why wait until now?

Whoever wanted him dead had decided to see to it *after* his talk with Amadi and *before* he left for Jango.

The Hung?

No, he was going there to help their beloved leaders. Sure, Amadi had claimed that this was a trap, but Xris didn't believe it and he was certain that the Hung wouldn't believe it, either. Amadi was in their pocket and had been for so long he'd never be able to climb out.

If not Amadi and if not the Hung, who?

"Oh, hell, it had to be Amadi!" Xris muttered, and, rolling over, he made a determined effort to get some sleep.

But before he dozed off, he'd ruled Amadi out.

CHAPTER 15

Expect poison from the standing water.
> William Blake, "Proverbs of Hell"

Petronella set the autopilot of her rental hover to take her to the address she had been provided, along with the round-trip ticket to Adonia. She had traveled to Adonia before, once to a convention and once on assignment. The first time she'd visited the paradise planet, she'd been moved to tears by the beauty. After she'd been there twenty-four hours, she'd been moved again—this time in another part of her anatomy—by the ugliness she'd seen lying, rotting, beneath the surface.

Petronella was not at all surprised, therefore, that her mysterious correspondent had chosen Adonia for a clandestine meeting. No one on Adonia gave a damn about what anyone did on the planet, as long as they did it with style.

The graceful palm trees, the azure sky, the pink-tinged clouds, the rainbows over the green mountains, the glistening black cliffs, the white sand beaches—none of these could tempt Petronella from her serious musings. Neither could the incredibly gorgeous women and the equally beautiful men of Adonia, who were seated beneath colorful umbrellas in quaint cafés, drinking chocolate coffee and shading their faces from the sun.

Adonian laws against ugliness are strictly enforced. Adonians do not permit ugly people to live on their planet. Ugly people are allowed to visit—tourist money is life's blood to the Adonians, who deem all other kinds of work as being bad for the complexion. Ugly people were therefore welcome, provided they wore masks over their faces, so as not to offend the sensibilities of the populace. The

unfashionably dressed were often held in quarantine until
their wardrobes could be adjusted.

Petronella had passed through customs quite easily, with
only a hint from the customs agent that cucumber cream
would help deal with the unsightly bags under her eyes.

The bags came from not sleeping well. Petronella hadn't
slept well since she'd taken this assignment. I should be
used to it, she admonished herself. I should be used to the
idea that some people, who look so fine on the outside, are
filled with maggots on the inside. A person loses her innocence fast in this job, her innocence, and her illusions. I've
become cynical, even paranoid. I can never trust anyone.

Petronella had once discovered herself thinking about
McCarthy, dear honest-to-a-fault McCarthy. How much
would it take to buy you? she had wondered, and she knew
for certain that he would have his price.

Everyone had a price. Sometimes she felt nervous
about herself.

The hover broke in on her gloomy musings with the announcement that she had arrived at her destination. The
hover lowered itself to the landing pad, tucked in its legs,
and settled down carefully onto the ornamental rock set in
a mosaic pattern.

Petronella climbed out of the hover.

"Are you sure this is the right place?" she asked the
hover.

The hover rattled off the address. Petronella checked.
Yes, this was it.

She stared at the magnificent chateau on the picturesque
cliff overlooking the stunningly beautiful ocean. The view
was gorgeous, but then every view in Adonia was gorgeous.
Expecting a back-alley rendezvous, she wasn't sure how she
felt about this.

Petronella took her time walking to the front of the mansion. She admired the hanging gardens, the swimming pool,
the white columns of the porch against the pink marble of
the chateau, the red-tiled roof, black shutters, clinging ivy,
splashing fountains. Admired them and looked the locale
over carefully, marking exits in case she needed to make a
quick getaway.

Ascending the stairs, she entered the shade of the ornate portico. Delicate scents of hibiscus drifted over her.

The doorbell played a few bars of a Mozart concerto. The carved wood double doors, decorated with a sun's beaming face, were opened by a man so handsome, elegant, and refined that Petronella assumed he must be the owner of the mansion. She was nonplussed to discover he was the butler, Hoskins.

Hoskins ushered her inside. Cool shadows washed over her, soothing after the brilliance of the sun. She had an impression of green marble, huge, wonderfully colored vases, whispering silken curtains.

"Petronella Rizzoli," she said. "I'm here to see . . ."

She paused, looked suitably helpless. Presumably, she had no idea who she was here to see. During the pause, a vase teetered on its stand. Hoskins, acting quickly, steadied it with a hand.

"I'm terribly sorry," Petronella began.

"No need to apologize," Hoskins said smoothly. "It is not Madam's fault. This area is subject to tremors. If Madam will accompany me, they are waiting to receive you on the patio."

The house was charming, the decorations perfect. She stopped to examine a particularly fine statue of a nude woman and a swan, until she saw what it was the two were doing. She had considered herself past the age of blushing, but apparently not. She moved on, carefully avoiding looking too closely at the rest of the statuary.

French doors opened onto an exquisite patio. Several people were seated at a table beneath a large umbrella.

"Ms. Petronella Rizzoli," the butler announced.

The people rose to their feet. Petronella blinked in the bright sunlight, tried to focus. And here they all were, just as she'd expected. She located an exit, put her hand over the lasgun hidden in the pocket of her suit jacket, and waited.

One of them, the woman, came to meet her. The woman kept her hands in plain sight. She wasn't carrying a weapon, that Petronella could see. The woman extended her hand.

"How do you do, Ms. Rizzoli?" said the woman. "My name is Darlene Mohini."

"Yes," said Petronella coolly. "I recognize you from the files. I recognize the rest of your gang, too. What is it you people want with me?"

"Only a little talk," said Darlene, squinting up at Petronella in the bright sunshine. "Won't you sit down? Raoul, I think our guest might be thirsty."

"I have never been referred to as a 'gang,' " said Raoul. Smoothing his black hair, so black that it glistened in the sun with rainbow hues, he remained seated. "The term has such a very common quality about it."

He glanced at her, glanced away. "I don't believe I like her."

"I'm sure Ms. Rizzoli didn't mean *gang* in a negative sense," Darlene said in soothing tones. "She's just a bit nervous. New surroundings. She doesn't know us, after all. Perhaps one of your pink flamingos. They are so refreshing. . . ."

"They are, aren't they?" Raoul said.

He was dressed in white diaphanous garments that flowed around him, and was so incredibly beautiful, and looked so very hurt, and so little like the professional assassin and expert poisoner that he was according to his file, that Petronella found herself apologizing before she quite knew what she was doing.

"The trip was very tiring. And going through customs can be so stressful—"

"Very well, my dear," Raoul said, coming closer to her and enveloping her in a breathless wave of gardenia perfume, "I forgive you." He kissed the air near her cheek and drifted off. "Anyone else want a flamingo?"

Everyone assured him that they did, which appeared to gratify Raoul immensely and put him in an excellent humor. Darlene introduced the other members of the *team,* laying emphasis on the word.

Petronella knew them from their files. Jamil Khizr, the ex-Army officer and far more good-looking than even his file photo.

"Petronella," he said, with a charming smile. "Do they call you Pet?"

"Only once," she assured him.

Dr. William Quong, who bowed politely, then asked if it was true she was a Talisian.

"I've done a cursory study on your people and I have a few questions—"

"Not now, Doc," Darlene said.

The last person was a small figure enveloped in a raincoat and fedora, who peered up at Petronella from beneath the brim of his hat with a pair of exceedingly bright and intelligent eyes. This was the telepath. Petronella didn't have to worry about him, her, or it—the file didn't offer much information on the personage known only as the Little One—because whatever it was about Talisians that caused the strange energy fluxes also scrambled their brain waves, making it impossible for telepaths to read them.

"We're expecting one more team member," Darlene said. "Harry Luck. In fact"—the Mozart concerto was playing again—"that may be him now."

"I'll answer the door, Hoskins!" Raoul could be heard calling. "You refill the ice bucket."

"Very good, sir," was the butler's response.

The next moment, a piercing shriek cut through the air. The shriek rose to a high-pitched wail, ending in a strangled gurgle.

Jamil's lasgun appeared in his hand with a rapidity that impressed Petronella, who was still reaching for hers.

"Keep her here, Darlene," Jamil ordered. "Maybe she brought friends. Doc, you're with me."

The two ran for the house, stopped short at the sight of Raoul staggering through the French doors. His hands covered his eyes, as though he'd been blinded by a disabler. Giving a moan, he collapsed at their feet. Petronella took a step forward, only to feel a lasgun pressed against her side.

Darlene smiled at her apologetically. "I think you should stay here with me, Agent Rizzoli. Hand me your gun, will you?"

Petronella handed it over.

"What's the matter with him, Doc?" Jamil asked, bending over the prostrate bundle of white. "Has he been shot?"

"No. He has merely fainted. He has received a severe shock of some sort."

Hoskins, the butler, appeared in the doorway. He was as pale as was considered fashionable and trembling in every limb.

"What is it, Hoskins?" Jamil demanded. "What's happened."

"Oh, sir!" Hoskins said faintly. "It . . . it's coming this way. . . ."

A large blond man dressed in a polyester suit that was much too small for his portly figure crashed through the French doors. He had his lasgun drawn and was looking around wildly. "What's the matter? Are we under attack?"

Harry Luck, according to his file.

Jamil looked at Harry, especially at Harry's suit. Sighing, Jamil holstered his weapon.

Dr. Quong also looked at Harry. "Ah, now I understand." Quong lifted Raoul gently in his arms. "Where can I put him?"

"In his bedroom. Where he can see his wardrobe on awakening. The master always finds that soothing. I will show you, sir," said Hoskins, delicately raising a hand to shield Harry from his view.

"It's all right, Hoskins," Quong said. "I know the way. You don't look too well yourself. Perhaps you should go lie down."

"I think, sir, under the circumstances," said the shaken butler faintly, "if you are quite certain that the master will be all right, I will retire to my quarters for a brief restorative."

"Put the gun away, Harry," Jamil said in exasperation. "We're not being attacked. It's your suit. Come out here on the patio where you can't hurt any innocent bystanders. Where did you buy that thing, anyway? Murphy's House of a Thousand Suits?"

"Yeah, I did!" Harry was impressed. "How'd you know that? There was an outlet right next to my motel. Murphy's offers a real bargain. You get two pairs of pants with the jacket. Your choice. I picked these out myself. The salesmen said the plaids didn't match and the colors clashed, but I think they look fine." Harry gazed down at himself admiringly. "I could take you there, Jamil, if you're interested. This suit attracts a lot of attention."

"I'll bet that's true," Jamil said. "Let me hazard a wild guess—you didn't wear that through customs, did you?"

"No. I didn't want it to get wrinkled on the ship. I changed in the men's room."

"You walked through the spaceport wearing it?"

"Sure, Jamil. You have to walk through the spaceport if you're going to get to the rental agencies. What's the problem? Oh, I get it. You think I was followed. I wasn't. I kept a lookout."

Jamil sighed. "Hoskins! There you are."

The butler was tottering by with a large snifter of brandy in his hand. "Yes, sir?"

"Just check with the police, will you? See if they've put out an arrest warrant for Harry yet? If they have, tell them we have the suspect in custody and we'll deal with the matter."

"Yes, sir. May I say, sir—the sooner, the better." Hoskins continued on his way, adding pointedly, "Garbage pickup is every Tuesday."

"Sorry about that, Agent Rizzoli," said Darlene, returning her lasgun to the holster she wore at the small of her back. "This is Harry Luck, one of the best pilots in the galaxy."

"Aw, I'm not that good," Harry said modestly, his face flushing. He was a big man and might have been handsome, but for the tiny frown line in the center of his forehead, as if he were continually perplexed by life in general, and his cheerful grin which said that he'd given the matter a lot of thought and declined to accept responsibility.

Blinking in the sunlight, he peered at Petronella. "Who's your friend, Darlene? You know, it's funny, but I think I've seen her before." Suddenly his expression hardened, darkened. "Hey, do you know who that is?"

"Yes, Harry—" Jamil began.

"That's the bitch who arrested Xris! What the hell is she doing here?"

"Harry—" Darlene tried to explain.

"Oh, I get it!" Harry relaxed; the grin was back. "We're holding her hostage." He rubbed his hands. "That's great! When do they release Xris?"

"Hostage!" Petronella exclaimed. "Listen to me! If you think that for one moment—"

"He didn't mean it!" Jamil assured her. "The fumes from the polyester must have affected his brain. We're *not* taking you hostage. You can leave now, if you want to."

"And I must admit I wouldn't blame you," Darlene added with a wry smile. "You haven't exactly seen us at our best. We don't intend to harm you in any way. In fact, we have some information that will be of interest to you. Please, won't you sit down? Oh, and here's your gun back."

Petronella accepted the gun. According to the files, the team was a strange bunch, but they'd pulled off some pretty impressive feats, such as rescuing a group of humans being held hostage by the Corasians, and saving His Majesty the King from an assassin. There was the rumor that they had even managed to break into a top-secret, heavily guarded Navy base, but that was unconfirmed.

"What information?" Petronella said, thinking it wise to maintain the appearance of suspicion.

"My name is Darlene Mohini now. But, in a former life, I was Dalin Rowan."

Petronella did her best to look astonished. She wasn't supposed to know this, after all. "But . . . Dalin Rowan . . . is . . . was a man. And anyhow, he is dead. Was dead."

"It's a long story. I think you better sit down, Agent Rizzoli. I'll try to explain everything."

"Just in case anyone cares," Harry Luck interrupted, glowering, "Xris got twenty years on Sandusky's Rock."

"Yes, Harry, we know. Parker called us," Jamil said.

"And you're all sitting here drinking lemonade! With her!" Harry glared at Petronella.

"Take a seat, Harry." Darlene's voice was crisp, whip-like, and Harry, though red in the face, meekly obeyed, looking like a recalcitrant lion being put through his paces by his trainer. "I'm trying to explain."

But before she could start, Mozart was playing once again.

"What now?" Darlene demanded, exasperated.

"Maybe it's the cops coming to arrest Harry," Jamil said. "I'll take care of it." He pointed a dictatorial finger. "Mr Luck, you stay here, out of sight!"

Harry sat down, plainly unhappy. Darlene fidgeted, drumming her fingers on the table and glancing often in the direction Jamil had taken.

Petronella caught herself staring at Darlene, trying to see if she could detect any male features—Adam's apple, rough-cut chin. Realizing that this was simply voyeuristic curiosity and had nothing whatsoever to do with her job, she shifted her gaze to two swans circling an ornamental pond.

"How is Xris, Harry?" Darlene asked, either trying to fill the awkward silence or perhaps elicit Petronella's sympathy. "Did you see him before you left? Did you have a chance to talk to him?"

"I tried." Harry sulked in the shade of the umbrella. "But they wouldn't let me. You should have seen him at the trial, Darlene," he added abruptly, glaring again at Petronella, who suddenly felt unaccountably guilty. They were using the cyborg, after all. Tampambulos was nothing but bait to lure Amadi into Robison's trap.

"Xris looked real bad. He had to use a crutch to walk. They wouldn't even let him put on his hand."

"He *is* a murderer," Petronella said loftily.

"Not if I'm the one he murdered," Darlene said dryly.

"That's true," Petronella conceded, looking confused. "*If* what you say is true. And if it is true, then why didn't he tell someone? Why would he let himself get locked up for a crime he didn't commit?"

"That's part of what I have to tell you. You see—"

Jamil emerged from the house carrying a tray of drinks.

"Well, was it the cops?" Darlene asked. "Perhaps Harry can plead temporary insanity."

"Very funny," Harry growled.

"Naw, it was the pool cleaner. I couldn't find Hoskins, so I told the guy to go ahead. Here, I fixed iced tea."

"Iced tea," Harry said gloomily, staring into his glass. "Xris is probably chopping away at ice now himself. And none of you give a damn."

The pool cleaner walked by, carrying his equipment with him in a bag. He wished them good afternoon and sauntered across the patio toward the pool. He was wearing swimming trunks and a white T-shirt that accentuated his golden tan and showed off his well-developed muscles. Like everyone else on Adonia, he was gorgeous. Petronella allowed herself a moment to admire the view before returning to work.

Darlene clasped her hands on the table, was looking at Petronella earnestly. "I know this is going to be hard for you to believe, Agent Rizzoli, but Xris and I are convinced that our former boss, your current boss, Jafar el Amadi, is a traitor. We believe that he is working for the Hung and has been working for them for years."

Good God! Whatever Petronella had been expecting Rowan to say, it wasn't this! She was caught off guard, didn't know how she should react. Fortunately, her stunned expression could be taken for shock at the information.

"You're right," she said at last. "I don't believe it."

"Then why did you come here?" Darlene smiled. "One of the answers to the daily quiz was, 'A—traitor.' Don't tell me that Amadi didn't cross your mind."

Petronella was noncommittal. "I'll listen to what you have to say."

"Fair enough." Darlene leaned back, made herself comfortable. "Here's the story."

Half an hour later, Darlene was describing to Petronella how Dalin Rowan had found Xris and what was left of Mashahiro Ito in the burning ruins of the Hung ammunitions factory. She went on to explain how Armstrong had tried to kill her in the shuttle and told how Amadi had ordered her to keep quiet about the entire affair, how all the records had disappeared.

Petronella listened in silence. Everything tallied exactly with what she already knew. Darlene told her story calmly, but with pain in the eyes that were watching her past rewind. Petronella could hear the anguish in Darlene's voice and she could see, through those pain-shadowed eyes, the blood-covered, mangled body of Xris in the wreckage of the factory, could see the bits of charred flesh that were all they ever found of Ito. Anger stirred in Petronella again, just as it had when she'd first read the file.

But she couldn't let them see that she believed them. Not yet.

Darlene interrupted her story for a long swallow of iced

tea. Petronella discovered that she was stiff from sitting so long in once place without moving. She sat back in the shade and sipped at her tea, which had gone tepid.

Dr. Quong emerged from the house, in company with the Little One.

Jamil looked around. "How's Raoul, Doc?"

"He has suffered a severe shock. I trust there will be no damage to the central nervous system, but at this point it's too early to tell."

"You're kidding, right?"

"He is an Adonian. What more can I say? I've given him a sedative. Now, my friend." The doctor reached for Harry's wrist to take his pulse. "You look terrible. What's the matter with you, beyond a deplorable lack of fashion sense?"

"I've just come from Xris's sentencing," Harry said, his voice high-pitched and strained. "They've given Xris twenty years. On Sandusky's Rock. He—"

The Little One suddenly lifted his head and twisted around to gaze in the direction of the swimming pool. Turning back, he reached out and grabbed hold of Darlene's arm. He made a stabbing gesture with his stubby finger.

"That? It's the pool cleaner," said Darlene.

The Little One shook his head with such violence that the fedora fell down over one eye.

Darlene looked at Jamil, who looked at Quong.

"He says it's *not* the pool cleaner."

Jamil was on his feet. "This has been a busy day. Doc, you're with me. Harry, you stay with Darlene. Careful, Doc. Don't tip him off that we're on to him."

"I understand perfectly the finesse required for this particular situation," Quong returned, nettled. The two strolled casually across the patio in the direction of the pool. "I don't need a retired Army officer to explain it to me."

"Fine, Doc, fine. Keep your voice down and if you have to shoot, shoot low. We need to talk to him."

"Harry!" said Darlene, exasperated, "I appreciate your concern, but there's no need to use your body as a shield. Could you please move out of the way? I can't see!"

Harry shook his head. He had planted his large body in

front of Darlene and seemed prepared to take root and flower.

According to the file, Hung assassins had tried twice to kill Darlene Mohini. Petronella drew her own lasgun, hid it swiftly beneath her purse.

Harry Luck regarded her with narrowed eyes, but Darlene said softly, "It's all right, Harry. She's on our side."

"If you say so," he muttered, and turned to keep a close watch on the alleged pool cleaner, who was down on his hands and knees, taking water samples.

Petronella didn't argue. She wasn't exactly on their side, but she'd be damned if she'd let some Hung assassin kill her star witness.

Jamil and Quong were sauntering over to the pool. The pool cleaner, intent upon his samples, was bent over his work.

At that moment, Raoul wandered out the French doors—doors that opened almost directly onto the swimming pool and brought him into close proximity with the bent-over pool cleaner. Cheek by jowl, as it were.

Delightfully relaxed from the sedative, which would have put most humans into a sound sleep for a week, but which merely gave the Loti a feeling of pleasant euphoria, Raoul gazed directly at a most interesting and attractive portion of the pool cleaner's anatomy, perfectly showcased in spandex swimming trunks.

"Ah!" cried Raoul, staring at this vision which, after the paralyzing shock of Harry's suit, seemed a gift from the gods. "You're not the *usual* pool cleaner!"

The man leaped to his feet.

"Damn!" Jamil cried, and broke into a run.

The pool cleaner took one glance behind him, saw Quong and Jamil coming for him. Reaching into the water, he grabbed hold of something, then sprinted for safety. He shoved Raoul roughly out of his way, scaled the wall that encircled the pool, was up and over the side and had dropped down to the ground below before Jamil could fire his lasgun or Raoul could get his name and phone number.

They heard the roar of a hover engine firing and by the time Jamil had pulled himself up onto the wall for a look, all he could see was the back end of a truck soaring over the tops of the palm trees.

Jamil dropped to the ground, brushed the dirt from his hands, and gazed ruefully at the stains on his good trousers.

"Did you get the name?" Quong asked.

"Yes," Jamil began. "Except—"

"Oh, good!" Raoul cried, clasping his hands.

"But," Jamil continued, glaring at Raoul, "you can be damn sure that the truck was stolen. Ah, Hoskins."

The butler appeared, looking much more relaxed, though he swayed slightly on his feet and the air was tinged with the strong smell of brandy.

"Yes, sir. I heard the commotion—"

"That was the pool cleaner, making a quick exit."

"Yes, sir. I was just going to say, sir, that he was not the usual pool cleaner and that today is not the day when the pool is customarily cleaned. The pool cleaners are not scheduled to come until tomorrow, and while I have known them to be late on countless occasions, I have never once known them to be early."

Quong went to examine the pool equipment, which the man, in his mad dash, had left behind. Jamil, in no very good humor, returned to the table.

"We lost him," he lamented. "He left in a van that was probably stolen. He's likely ditched it by now. Should we report it?"

"On Adonia, they'd only arrest him if he left the van parked in a flower bed," Darlene said dryly.

"Maybe we could tell them he was the one who sold Harry that suit," Jamil growled. "Except that then they'd shoot to kill."

Raoul joined them, keeping his hand carefully over his eyes, avoiding looking at Harry.

"Why did you frighten him away?" Raoul complained.

"Because he was a Hung assassin, that's why," Jamil snapped.

"Nobody's perfect. Just part of him." Raoul smiled sadly at the memory.

"He was *not* an assassin, my friends," said Dr. Quong.

In his hand, he held a boom microphone electronic listening device disguised inside a vacuum hose.

"He was a spy. There was probably a microwave recording unit attached to it. See where one would fit in here? He recorded our conversation and when he was exposed . . ."

Raoul gave a wistful sigh.

". . . he fled, taking the recording with him."

"But that's not very plausible," Darlene argued. "Why would the Hung send someone to spy on me when he could just as easily have killed me?"

The Little One shook his head, sending the fedora toppling into his eyes, and pointed a jabbing finger.

Everyone turned to Petronella.

"The pool cleaner was not spying on Darlene," Raoul said, after he and the Little One had held one of their silent and eerie communications. "He was spying on Agent Rizzoli."

CHAPTER 16

The easiest person to deceive is one's own self.
Baron Lytton, *The Disowned*

"Are you sure?" Petronella demanded. She didn't need to act startled. She *was* startled. "Why? How? No one knew I was coming here. . . . It doesn't make sense. . . ."

A patio chair skittered across the flagstone, landed with a splash in the swimming pool.

"Did I really see that?" Raoul asked.

The Little One nodded the fedora.

"I had to make sure. These days, it's so hard to tell," Raoul said.

Dr. Quong brought out his notepad. "I assume that you are taking the standard medication prescribed for Talisians off-world? Obviously the medicine's not working all that well for you. My guess would be that, in your case, unlike other Talisians I have treated, the kinetic fluxes do not roll off you in waves, but rather they whip out like tendrils. Perhaps that's why. Now, if I could check your blood pressure—"

"Not now, Doc," Jamil said impatiently.

Petronella tried to figure out how to play this. Of course, they'd staged it, but why? For what reason?

"But who could be having *me* followed?" Petronella asked, glancing at them all uncertainly. "You don't think—"

"Amadi," Darlene said coolly. "It has to be."

The Little One caught hold of the sleeve of Raoul's blouse and tugged on it urgently, drawing his friend back reluctantly from whatever world he was currently visiting.

"What is it? Oh, yes." Raoul gazed at Petronella with

dreamy, unfocused eyes. "The Little One says that the pool cleaner was, in reality, an Adonian private detective hired by someone—he's not clear who it was—to keep watch on you and to record what you said and to whom you said it."

"Which explains why he ran at the first sign of trouble," Jamil said. "An Adonian detective. His biggest case before this was probably trying to track down smudgy mascara."

"If it was Amadi, wouldn't he have sent his own people?" Quong wondered.

Both Darlene and Petronella shook their heads.

"The Bureau doesn't station agents on Adonia," Darlene explained. "The local authorities are afraid that the Bureau's presence might interfere with bribery, kickbacks, roll-overs, and the Adonian good life in general.

"If there's a reason for the Bureau to be on Adonia, they can either send in agents good-looking enough to pass through customs, or they hire Adonians. That's a last option, because they're not terribly efficient. As it was," Darlene admitted, "this one was pretty damn good. He was here for almost an hour, caught us telling Agent Rizzoli everything there is to tell."

"And you couldn't get any reading on who hired him?"

The Little One opened his hands, smacked himself on the forehead.

"The agent was not thinking about who hired him. Why should he?" Raoul asked. "He was thinking about the loveliness of the clouds in the sky, the beauty of the swans reflected in the pool, the spicy fragrance of the hibiscus, so conducive to love, how attractive he found his reflection in the water, his blond hair tousled just so. . . ." Raoul sighed. "We could have been soul mates!"

A Beethoven violin sonata began to play.

"The phone," said Raoul, looking up hopefully.

Hoskins emerged.

"For me?" Raoul cried.

"No, sir. I fear not. It is for Dr. Quong. His answering service."

"Excuse me." Quong left them.

Why were they going to such lengths? Petronella wasn't certain. They were probably hoping to trap her into revealing something.

Quong emerged from the house. Walking straight up to Harry, he rested his hand on the big man's shoulder. "You do not have to worry about Xris anymore, my friend."

"I don't?" Harry sprang to his feet. "He's been released!"

"No, they have not released him," Quong said. "But he has been transferred. He is not going to the ice mines on Sandusky's Rock. He is being sent to the correctional facility for antisocial behavior on Jango. He has asked to see me and the authorities have given me permission to attend to him. I must go pack my things."

"Jango," said Darlene, startled. "That's . . ." She let the sentence hang.

"That's what?" Jamil asked.

"Interesting," said Darlene lamely.

"Not to me!" Harry protested. "Why's the Doc going? Why can't I go? What about me?"

"Shush, Harry," Darlene said softly, with slight tilt of the head in the direction of Petronella, a glance and tilt that Harry missed, but which Petronella caught and which further increased her suspicions.

"I think I should go," Harry said stubbornly.

"Shut up, Harry, and sit down," Jamil ordered. "You need any help, Doc?"

"Thank you, but no. Agent Rizzoli," Quong said, turning to her, "it has been a pleasure meeting you."

Petronella gave a cool, curt nod and stood up. She had a call to make.

"I have to be going as well. Good-bye," she said. "It's been . . . interesting. Of course, I think you're completely mistaken about Jafar al Amadi. He has an exemplary record. But I'll keep what you told me in mind. If you receive any more information, you know how to contact me," she added wryly.

She walked off, conscious that she had made an abrupt exit and that she had left them all staring at her.

"Very rude," came Raoul's voice. "She never even said thank you for the vacation, and after we purchased tickets for her and everything. I *told* you I didn't like her."

Entering the living room, Petronella nearly knocked over

Hoskins, who must have sprung up from the marble-tiled floor.

As Hoskins gravely and silently escorted her to the front door, the vase that had teetered earlier now lurched off its black marble stand and crashed to the floor.

Gulping and looking stricken, Petronella gasped. "I'm so sorry. I'll pay for the damages—"

Hoskins was gracious, though haggard. It had been a difficult day. "Never mind, madam. The master was not particularly fond of that Ming vase anyway."

"If you're certain—"

"Quite certain," Hoskins said firmly.

Taking hold of her elbow, he steered her rapidly to the front door. "Next time Madam visits, perhaps Madam would be kind enough to warn us in advance. I could then pack away all the breakables."

He shut the door on her.

Petronella ran down the stairs. As she climbed into the hover, she heard a piercing scream come from the mansion.

Well, she wouldn't be invited back here again.

Departing in haste, Petronella returned to her hotel by a circuitous route, keeping watch.

No pool cleaner trucks were in pursuit. No one was following her.

Not that this proves anything, she said to herself. If that man *was* following me, then he must have picked me up at the hotel. Why didn't I check like I usually do? That was careless. Damn careless.

They *must* have staged it, she repeated. And the very fact that she repeated it meant that she wasn't believing it.

Motive. The Bureau was very big on motive. And for the life of her she couldn't figure out any motive for why the Mag Force 7 team would try to convince her that she'd been tailed by a pool cleaner in disguise.

Amadi, then. He was on to her.

Once she reached her room, she did a quick calculation of the time difference. It was late, but Tom might still be in the office.

"McCarthy here," he answered, sounding harassed.

Petronella wasn't fooled. He always sounded that way, a method he used to get rid of annoying callers.

"Hello, Tom, it's Rizzoli."

"Oh, hi, Rizzoli. How are you feeling? Any better?"

"Yes. Well, no, not really. Say, Tom, could you do me a favor? I heard on a news broadcast that the prisoner Tampambulos is being sent to Jango. Could you check that out for me? It sounds fishy."

"I'll say. Since when do convicted murderers go to a resort spa like Jango? Unless they can afford it, of course. Just a sec. . . . I'll be damned, Rizzoli. You're right. Here's his transfer authorization. He's being sent to Jango. Well, isn't that a kick in the face."

"Who authorized the transfer, Tom?" Petronella asked.

"The chief supe. Amadi."

"Thanks." Petronella ended the link.

She kicked off her shoes and lay down on the bed, having first taken the precaution of moving the table lamp to the floor and making certain the vid set was bolted to the dresser.

Jango. It sounded familiar. Why? She couldn't recall where she'd heard that name before.

Petronella called room service, ordered dinner. No cheap in-room replicators for this fancy hotel.

Lying on the bed, she activated the long-range and extremely sensitive listening device she'd placed under the table when the team had been distracted by the chair tumbling into the swimming pool.

The first voice she heard was Darlene's, and here was one of Petronella's answers.

"The Hung leaders are in prison on Jango."

CHAPTER 17

O lost, and by the wind grieved, ghost, come back again.

Thomas Wolfe, *Look Homeward, Angel*

"The Hung leaders are in prison on Jango," said Darlene. "This is starting to make sense."

"Not to me," Harry grumbled, hurt. "Why does Doc get to go see Xris and I don't?"

"Because Doc's going to fit Xris with a new cybernetic leg and arm, made to spec, if you take my meaning."

"Oh, yeah. I get it." Harry brightened. "A new leg with files and stuff inside so he can cut through the bars of his cells."

"Something like that," Darlene said gravely.

"You knew that, too, Jamil?"

"Yes, Harry. I knew."

"But how did you guys figure that out?" Harry's brow furrowed in deep concentration.

"Logical deduction, Harry. Inferences," said Darlene. "Do you understand?"

"No," Harry said bluntly. "I thought inferences were what you used to see in the dark."

Jamil and Darlene exchanged glances. Darlene hid her smile, but Jamil was forced to leave hurriedly, mumbling something about checking to see if all the snooping devices had been removed from the pool.

"I don't see what's so funny." Over the splash of the fountain, Harry could hear Jamil laughing.

"I'll explain, Harry," Darlene said kindly. "You said yourself that they'd taken Xris's cybernetic limbs. Doc gets a call to his service. Xris leaves a message saying he needs a new leg and a new arm and can Doc come and fit them. Any cybertechnologist could have fit Xris with a new leg. The fact that he asked specifically for Dr. Quong indicates that he would like a little something extra."

"But we don't know what," Harry protested.

"True. My guess is that Quong is on my computer right now, researching the security devices at Jango and trying to figure out how to get around them."

"You're really smart, Darlene," Harry said.

"Thank you, Harry." She smiled at him and rested her hand over his.

Night was coming to Adonia, bringing with it cool air, the perfume of night-blossoming tropical flowers, and the sounds of merriment from the chateau belonging to one of the neighbors. Raoul wandered onto the patio, looking distraught, disheveled, and tragic.

"What a ghastly day," he said faintly, and sinking down into a chair, he rested his forehead on his hand, gave a heart-melting sigh. "Raj Vu is giving another party, and did he invite me? He did not. The Little One is in bed with a severe headache. He says he feels as if he has been pelted with bricks. And we must make do with leftovers for dinner. I had to give Hoskins the night off and he has threatened to give notice if that tornadic female returns."

Raoul gazed with pleading eyes at Darlene. "You don't consider it likely, do you?"

"I doubt if Agent Rizzoli will be back to see us," Darlene replied somberly. "I don't think we did a very good job of convincing her."

"What about the guy tailing her?" Jamil asked, returning to the table. "That would have convinced me."

"She probably figures we staged it. We could have, you know," Darlene replied, shrugging. "Hopefully we've given her something to think about, at least. She's the type who likes to ferret things out, that much is obvious, since she tracked down the files I altered. And she's energetic and she doesn't mind taking risks."

"She's a menace to society," Raoul said in a low, tremulous voice. "And should be locked up."

"What happens if she doesn't come through for us?" Jamil asked.

"Then it's up to Xris," Darlene replied. "He has something in mind or else he wouldn't be where he is right now. You ready to go, Doc?"

"I have booked a flight for 2200 this evening. I am to meet with Xris at 1200 day after tomorrow."

"Do you know what he wants?"

"I do not care what he wants," Quong replied stiffly. "I intend to provide him with what he needs. I—"

Mozart sounded with damnable cheeriness through the night.

"The gods save us!" Raoul proclaimed, his face ashen. "Maybe it's *her* again! Don't answer."

"It might be her," said Jamil, with a wink at the rest of them. "Or it could be Raj Vu with a party invitation."

"I'm coming!" Raoul cried.

"Harry, go with him," Jamil ordered.

"Absolutely not!" Raoul said, turning on them. Fire flickered in the depths of his usually drug-drowned eyes. "You would scare poor Raj Vu into fits. In that suit, you would frighten Death himself. I will call you if I need you," he added, and left to answer the door.

Jamil removed his lasgun from its holster, laid it out on the table, Quong, who should have been leaving for the spaceport, had drifted over to where he could see Raoul through one of the windows. Darlene drummed her fingers nervously on the glass tabletop. Harry scratched his head. He had more important matters on his mind than unexpected visitors in the night.

"What does Raoul mean by leftovers?" he asked worriedly. "Those icky toadstools we had to eat for lunch?"

"Truffles," Darlene corrected.

Mozart played again.

"What the devil is Raoul doing?" Jamil demanded impatiently. "Why doesn't he answer the door?"

"He's fixing his makeup," Quong reported, peering through the glass, "and brushing his hair."

Jamil muttered something beneath his breath.

Quong continued to watch. "He is opening the door—"

A piercing scream shattered the night, split their eardrums, and probably would have finished off the Ming vase if Petronella hadn't gotten to it first.

"In the name of the Maker!" Dr. Quong gasped, staring, wide-eyed. He dropped his briefcase.

"I knew it!" Jamil was on his feet, lasgun in hand.

Harry was right behind him and Darlene was behind Harry, although Jamil ordered her repeatedly to keep back.

They found Raoul prostrate on the marble floor of the entryway, picturesquely composed, his hair flowing around him, apparently unconscious. The Little One, his hat tossed on his head backward, was bent over his friend, but his gaze was riveted in astonishment on the being standing in the doorway.

The being was a tall—well over two meters—humanoid, with skin that had been as dark as the night through which he'd traveled, but which now was gradually lightening, taking on the taupe color of the walls in the entry hall.

"Tycho!" Jamil gasped.

The chameleon, for that's what his people were called, due to the fact that their skin changed color to match their surroundings, looked at them all and grinned with pleasure.

"You know me!" he said, speaking through a translator. "I wasn't certain you would remember!"

CHAPTER 18

BERNARDO: It would be spoke to.
MARCELLUS: Speak to it, Horatio.
William Shakespeare, *Hamlet,* Act I

"Tycho—you're . . . you're dead!" Jamil was the only member of team able to find his tongue. The rest were still searching through the general astonishment for theirs. "You were blown to bits by a grenade! I saw the body."

"Yes, of course," said the chameleon. "An immeasurable sorrow. Why are you pointing that lasgun at me, Jamil?"

Jamil was suspicious, grim. "All right, you know *my* name. Who the hell are you?"

The chameleon appeared confused. "I am Tycho. You must know *me.* I know all of you. Quong, Darlene, Harry Luck, Raoul, the Little One. But"—he glanced around— "where is Xris Cyborg?"

Keeping the lasgun trained on the alien, Jamil grabbed hold of a handful of the Little One's raincoat and shook him. "Who is this bastard really?"

The Little One slapped himself back and forth on the side of his head several times and performed a shuffling dance step.

Jamil watched in frustration. Raoul, the only one who could understand his friend, was only semiconscious, making low moaning sounds and fitfully requesting that someone bring him a dry sherry.

"Doc," Jamil asked, "can you translate? What's the Little One saying?"

Quong joined the rest of them in staring in amazement at the stranger who claimed he wasn't. Then he looked at the Little One.

"I have no idea."

"Wake up sleeping beauty, then," Jamil said harshly. "You, Tycho, or whoever you are, don't move. Do what you can for him, Doc. We need Raoul to translate."

Quong kept his gaze on the chameleon, who was now starting to appear uneasy, his skin color fading from taupe to a sort of sickly gray. The doctor knelt beside Raoul and gave him a not very gentle slap on each cheek.

"The rubber hose," Raoul murmured, smiling beatifically. "Don't forget to bring the rubber hose to suck the . . ." His eyelids fluttered. He looked up and his smile froze. "You're not the pool cleaner."

Quong grunted, shoved Raoul to a seated position.

Raoul took one look at the chameleon and promptly screamed.

"Don't faint! And that's an order!" Jamil motioned to the chameleon. "Who is this?"

Raoul and the Little One looked at each other. Both looked at the chameleon. Both looked at Jamil.

"Tycho," said Raoul, and the Little One nodded.

"But that's not possible!" argued Jamil.

"Why, sure it is, Jamil," said Harry. "We learned about that in church. 'On the third day he rose again from the dead.' Maybe it took Tycho here a little longer, but hell, he's an alien! Cut him some slack!"

"I am not questioning Harry's theological beliefs," Quong said, confronting the chameleon, "but I saw Tycho die. I pronounced him dead and I do not make mistakes. Yet you claim to be Tycho, our former team member, an expert sniper—"

"I am not a sniper," said the chameleon, anxious to make certain there was no misunderstanding. "That was Tycho's specialty. I, Tycho, am trained in field engineering, with expertise, if I may say this without appearing prideful, in improvised detonators. I am also adept at acquiring access to secure environments."

"Field engineering. In other words, an explosives expert," said Dr. Quong. "And he can break into buildings. I think I'm beginning to understand."

"Then explain it to the rest of us," Jamil demanded.

"I cannot do so yet," said Quong with maddening imperturbability. "I require more facts."

"I'm not sure which of you to shoot first," Jamil muttered.

"I have the contract, if you wish to verify my nonentity," offered the chameleon.

"Identity," murmured Quong to Darlene. "Apparently he has the same translator problems that afflicted our other Tycho."

Blissfully unaware of his mistake, Tycho brought forth an electronic contract pad—the type Xris always used—and handed it to Jamil.

Darlene peered over his shoulder as Jamil activated the device.

"That's Xris's DNA signature, all right," Jamil said. He looked up, frowning. "But this contract is made out to Tycho."

"And that is why Tycho is here," said the chameleon with a tentative smile. "To fulfill the contract. According to my elder brother—"

"Ah-hah!" cried Dr. Quong. He turned, gazed at the others triumphantly. "Jamil, put the gun away. Tycho is a *family* name. Like Luck, as in Harry Luck." Quong elaborated: "For example, Harry, your older brother—"

"I don't have an older brother," Harry corrected him. "I got a sister, though, if that helps."

"Your older brother," Quong repeated loudly, frowning, "would be known as Luck—"

"I beg your pardon, Doctor, sir." The chameleon broke in apologetically. "You are nearly correct, but not quite. I had assumed that my elder brother would have explained this to you, but apparently he did not. Tycho is the name given to the senior male member of the family. My elder brother, Tycho, is dead, and I am now the senior male. I am now Tycho. The contract was made with Tycho, the senior male member of the Tycho family. As Tycho, I am here to resume service under the contract with Mag Force 7."

Jamil lowered the gun. "You mean you're Tycho's little brother?"

Tycho nodded. "In human terms, that would be a correct assumption. According to my own culture, I *am* Tycho."

"How many male members of the family are there?" Quong asked.

"Thirteen," said Tycho with a pleased smile. His skin color had changed to a rosy hue, matching the floral pattern on the drapes.

"And all of them are trained soldiers?"

"The elder seven. The other six are too young. But they will take the training when they are of age, for we are a soldier, yes."

"*A* soldier?" Jamil was having a difficult time with the concept.

"The entire family is considered a single entity," Quong explained in didactic tones. "In sociological terms, this would be—"

"Don't you have a spaceplane to catch, Doc?" Jamil interrupted.

"Ah, yes! Thank you for reminding me." Quong shook hands with Tycho. "Welcome to the team. Remember, all of you, that we have only seventeen days left to complete our mission in Del Sol. I have rescheduled my flight to arrive at approximately the same time as yours. I will meet you at the Del Sol spaceport."

The doctor hurried off. Raoul retired for a long, soaking bubble bath, necessary to soothe his shattered nerves. The Little One went back to nursing his headache. Jamil marched the new Tycho off to the study, intending to assess his technical expertise.

Darlene was heading for her bedroom when she came across Harry, standing in the now-darkened living room, staring despondently out the window.

Darlene laid her hand on his arm. "We're eight again, Harry," she said, hoping to cheer him.

He only shook his head. "Not without Xris, we're not. I don't care how many Tychos come back from the dead."

Darlene wondered whether she should try to explain to Harry that Tycho was not a messiah, but decided that she was too tired.

She went to bed and, eventually, so did Harry.

*   *   *

Dr. Quong was the last person to board the transport. He arrived at the gate at a dead run, was hustled on board by an irritated gate attendant, who slammed shut the door after him and departed, muttering something about passengers who thought that regulations about arriving at the spaceport early applied to everyone else except them.

Petronella watched him board in some surprise, verified his destination, and said grudgingly to herself, "Well, at least one of their stories checks out."

CHAPTER 19

The bird a nest, the spider a web, man friendship.
William Blake, "Proverbs of Hell"

"You have a visitor," said the guard. "Name of Quong. Do you want to see him?"

"You didn't give me a choice last time," Xris said, reaching for his crutch.

"Yeah, well, the last visitor seems to have done you some good. I figure the trend might continue. How's that crutch working for you?"

"Fine, just fine," Xris replied.

His new accommodations might have been termed luxurious by comparison with his old ones. The new cell had its own shower, its own vid machine. He had access to the prison library and had kept himself occupied by reading some ancient Earth literature that had been recommended to him by Lady Maigrey during their brief time together.

Puzzling through the archaic language and studying the voluminous annotations and footnotes accompanying the text diverted his mind from jumping on its hamster wheel and running around and around, going rapidly nowhere.

Who had tried to kill him, and why?

Xris didn't trust Amadi. No surprise there. But Xris had ruled Amadi out as the assassin—at least he wouldn't be until Xris's usefulness to Amadi was ended. Xris had no doubt that Amadi was playing a deadly, dangerous game, that he was using Xris as a pawn in that game, and that Amadi fully intended to sacrifice his pawn in order to win.

Xris was perfectly willing to be moved around the board, especially if that meant gaining easy access to the enemy's stronghold. Vengeance is sweet. Rotten, but sweet.

The guard solicitously offered a helping hand, a hand which Xris found great satisfaction in ignoring. He hobbled out of his cell on his own, followed by the guard, who was no longer carrying the stun-stick, but a weapon known as the "sneezy," useful in quelling unrest among the inmates. When activated, the "sneezy" emitted an ultra-high-frequency sound that triggered sneezing fits of such violence that all those afflicted were immediately incapacitated.

"Tampambulos here." The guard reported to the guard at the infirmary. "To see his doctor."

Prisoners in the infirmary, under constant watch by security cams, could supposedly hold private consultations with prison doctors. And while the term *private* might actually have some meaning for the majority of prisoners, Xris was under no illusions. His first night in his new cell after the attempt on his life, he'd discovered the listening device that had been planted in his new crutch.

Bill Quong was there, waiting for him, along with the cybernetic limbs, packed in two specially designed carrying cases.

As Xris stumped in, he watched Quong's almond eyes widen in shock.

"By the Maker! Harry was right!" Quong exclaimed. "You look terrible! I will give you a complete physical. What do they feed you here anyway?"

"The food's okay, Doc." Xris glanced at the crutch, tilted his head slightly.

Quong nodded and punched in the code that would allow him to open the cases.

"I just haven't had much appetite," Xris continued. "I don't need a physical, Doc. I'll feel a damn sight better once I have a leg to stand on."

"I am glad you can still make jokes," Quong said stiffly. "The rest of us do not see much humor in this situation."

"It's important for me to keep up my spirits." Xris eyed the leg as Quong removed it from the case. "I take it that passed inspection?"

"The guards went over every centimeter. That is why I am late. I was forced to spend an hour reassembling it."

The leg and the arm certainly looked plain and ordinary,

so plain and so ordinary that Xris was worried. Quong hadn't had much time, after all.

"Are you sure these are going to work for me, Doc? They look pretty cheap. I won't pay for shoddy workmanship. I can't afford to have them break down on me."

Quong drew himself up, offended. "They are not as fine as the custom-made models to which you are accustomed, my friend, but I believe that you will find them quite satisfactory." His tone was cold. "Especially for a murderer."

"Don't go all righteous on me, Doc," Xris returned. "Or I'll bring up that malpractice suit they nailed you with on Vangelis II. Just shut your mouth and hook me up, will you?"

Removing his prison uniform and his underwear, Xris laid down on the examining table and prepared to undergo the painful and humiliating experience of having his limbs reattached. He was well aware that this operation was being viewed on the security cams, could imagine the guards watching with interest and ribald jocularity. He set his jaw, conjured up the ghost of Mashahiro Ito, and endured.

He and Quong spoke only when necessary, the doctor asking terse questions about fit or movement, Xris keeping his answers brief.

But it was all worth it when he sat up and, for the first time in a over a week, was able to stand without assistance, to flex the fingers on two hands.

"Thanks, Doc," Xris said.

"Do not thank me," Quong said curtly. "I am being well paid for my work. I will forward your records to the Jango medical facility. Herewith, I tender my resignation as your personal physician." He tapped on the door, shouted, "I am ready to leave!"

The guards entered the room with such alacrity that it was obvious they'd been watching the entire proceeding.

"I assume you have a chapel in this prison?" Dr. Quong said sententiously. "If you would tell me where it is, I would like to pray for the soul of this unfortunate man."

"Yeah, you do that, Doc!" Xris sneered. "Say a few prayers for yourself while you're at it."

Back inside his cell, Xris turned on the vid machine, set the volume on high, and sat back to listen to a commentary on the poetry of William Blake. He trusted whoever was eavesdropping on him would find his mind improved.

"Let us examine this line from *Marriage of Heaven and Hell*," said the professor. " 'Note: The reason Milton wrote in fetters when he wrote of Angles and God, and at liberty when of Devils & Hell, is because he was a true Poet and of the Devil's party without knowing it.'

"Blake refers, of course, to Milton's poem *Paradise Lost,* presumably the story of man's banishment from the Garden of Eden, but one in which many readers, Blake among them, have come to see Satan as the hero, not the villain, as can be seen in the above verse. According to Blake, the poetic imagination and the energy of human desire are near allied. . . ."

Xris scratched his head, bemused, and managed at the same time to tap the commlink behind his ear twice. He waited; no response. He tried again and after about half an hour, during which he wondered if Quong had gotten lost or been hijacked, he heard Doc's voice in his ear.

"Blessed Maker," Quong was praying, "do what you can to salvage the blood-stained soul of this wretched human—"

"I can hear you, Doc," Xris said, speaking from the back of his throat, not allowing his lips to move. This meant that some of his words were a bit slurred, since it was difficult to speak words with consonants such as *b* or *m* in them, but Quong would understand him well enough to get by. "Cut the crap. You alone?"

"Yes, finally. Sorry it took so long. The chaplain wanted to comfort me. He has at last left me to my prayers."

"Let's hope you can answer mine," Xris said. "Tell me about the leg."

"First, tell me what happened to your face."

"Oh, that." Xris was nonchalant. "Some lunkhead tried to kill me. Fortunately for the future of mankind, I doubt if he'll be making contributions to the gene pool anytime soon."

"A hired gun?"

"Yeah."

"Who hired him? This Amadi person?"

"I don't think so," Xris said. "I've just agreed to do a really dirty job for Amadi. Why would he pay to have me eradicated? It doesn't make any sense. Any suggestions will be gratefully received."

"I'll take it under consideration. In view of this, do you consider it wise to continue? Darlene has already told Agent Rizzoli the truth—"

"I'm staying," Xris said firmly. "This is too good to pass up. Finally I'll be able to look into the eyes of the bastards who ordered Ito's death. Not only am I staying with the job, Doc, I'm looking forward to it. We don't have a lot of time." Xris cut off any argument. "They'll come to get me for dinner in about an hour. Now tell me about the leg."

"I've placed a universal lock opener, a very precise magnetometer, and a micro-sized light source in behind the servo central control panel in your calf. The magnetometer is the only item with which you won't be familiar. You can use it to find metal sensors either buried in the ground or embedded in the walls. Is all that clear, my friend?"

"Yeah. Thanks, Doc." Xris started to say he appreciated it, but realized that any word with two *p*'s would never be understood. Quong knew how he felt anyway. "Any news from the front?"

"Agent Rizzoli paid us a visit after receiving an invitation from Darlene. Rizzoli brought company with her, only she didn't know it. We thought it was someone dropping by to see Darlene, but the Little One said no, he was interested in Rizzoli. We tried to hang on to him, but he got away."

"Amadi's having her followed," Xris observed. "With what Darlene told Rizzoli, that should have convinced her that she should be suspicious of her boss."

"I don't think we convinced her of anything except that we are bungling idiots," Quong returned ascerbically. "I am ashamed to say that we did not handle ourselves in a professional manner. There is more news. Tycho is with us."

"What?" Startled, Xris spoke the word aloud. However, it fit in with what the professor on the vid was saying, and so he hoped no one watching or listening would get suspicious. "You started believing in ghosts, Doc?"

"I have always believed in supernatural manifestations," Quong replied. "This does not happen to be one of them. Our current Tycho is actually our former Tycho's younger brother. It seems that the senior male of the family takes on the responsibilities of those who precede him. His hobbies are blowing things up and breaking into banks."

"I like him already. You might need him for this job."

"Then it is okay if we go ahead with the assignment?" Quong said. "We had planned to do so but I wanted to check. We have lost a great deal of time."

"Yes, we signed a contract. We have, what—sixteen days from today to overthrow Kirkov? Can you handle it?"

"We have, of necessity, revised our plan. But we believe that we can accomplish our goal."

"Fine. Oh, and you'll have to give up Harry. I'm going to need him. Stash him on a planet near Jango. Tell him to find a spaceplane with room for five passengers and that has EVA, stealth and jamming capabilities, and is fast and maneuverable both in planet atmosphere and in outer space."

"Certainly," Quong returned. "Perhaps we can pick one up at Rummage-O-Rama. Along with a new suit for Harry."

"Talk to Olefsky," Xris suggested. "The Wolf Brigade probably has a couple of spaceplanes they're not using. Tell Harry someone will be in touch with him. The code word is *Hogan*. Got that?"

"You should spell it."

Patiently, Xris spelled it.

"Harry is not taking this well," Quong observed as he prepared to depart.

"Yeah, I figured as much. I saw him at the sentencing. This job should make him a lot happier."

"What do we do about Agent Rizzoli?"

"Keep her nose pointing at Amadi. Eventually she's bound to get a whiff of something foul."

"How do we do that if we are busy overthrowing a small government?" Quong demanded.

"Beats me, Doc," Xris said cheerfully. "You'll figure out something. I have every confidence in you."

"I must go. The chaplain is approaching. Good-bye, my friend. Take care of yourself."

"You, too, Doc," Xris said, realizing at that moment how much he missed being with them, how much he hated being shut up in this cell, how much he hated being alone. "Give my best to everyone."

There was no reply.

CHAPTER 20

Man needs to suffer. When he does not have real griefs he creates them. Griefs purify and prepare him.

José Martí, *Adultera*

The prison trip to Jango wasn't any luxury cruise, but it wasn't bad, either. Their transport had been a passenger freighter and, once upon a time predating the Revolution, had probably been a pretty classy lady. She was old now, slow and shabby, but her crew took pride in the ravaged beauty—the transport was practically an antique—and had gone to great lengths to refit her and keep up with maintenance.

The prisoners were held on the lower decks, not permitted to come anywhere near the bridge. All access to the upper decks was sealed off, except for one lift that was guarded twenty-four hours by living, breathing guards as well as guard 'bots.

Due to the fact that this ship had once transported passengers, the prisoners' quarters were much better than the prison cells, the food was really quite good, and the guards were at least polite. Xris was locked up in a large room— it had once been a gym—along with the five other prisoners being taken to Jango. They showered in what had once been the men's locker room and slept in bunks bolted to the walls.

Vids and mags were provided for their entertainment, but the vids were old, the mags outdated; Xris found one that featured an interview with the late and unlamented President Robes. Three of the men played bridge, however, and when they found out that Xris knew something about the game, they badgered him into being a fourth. Of the other two prisoners, one spent most of his time napping in his bunk. He woke up only for meals. The other was hunched over a small computer. He said he was writing a book.

Xris appeared almost human in his new cybernetic leg, arm, and hand. Covered with fleshfoam and plastiskin, his limbs looked and felt like real flesh and blood, muscle and bone. They were even warm to the touch. His companions had no idea he was a cyborg.

He agreed to play bridge with them, not because he particularly enjoyed the game—he had learned it only to please Marjorie—but because he needed to know these men. One of them might be an assassin, sent to finish the job.

After their first morning together, however, Xris determined that his fellow incarcerees—as they preferred to be called—were petty crooks, not assassins. If there was a hired killer in the group, he was such a consummate actor that Xris would never penetrate the disguise and he might as well quit worrying about it.

The five had names, presumably, but Xris didn't pay any attention to them. He didn't intend to entangle himself in the lives of any of these men. He wasn't going to be around them that long.

Xris would have liked to have continued in solitary. Company grated on his nerves, interrupted his thought process. But he was well aware that loners tended to lead short and miserable lives in prison. Even in a so-called white-collar institution like Jango. it was generally advisable to have someone watching your back. Xris went out of his way to be accommodating, therefore, although given a choice, he would have preferred to pace the floor, stare out the window at the passing stars, and try to sort through this mess.

"Jango has one of the top-rated golf courses in the galaxy," said his partner, a young man of about twenty-eight, lean and tan with blond hair of which he was obviously very proud, for he kept drawing attention to it by affectedly shaking it out of his eyes.

"My attorney showed me a brochure," said the man to

Xris's left, who was forty and a bit on the pudgy side. "They have two swimming pools, an outdoor and an indoor, and a sauna. There's a weight room and a putting green, daily aerobics classes, and a jogging track." He patted his rotund stomach. "I promised the wife I'd lose a few kilos. It cost me some extra to get sent here, but I figure it's worth it."

"Not only the amenities," agreed Pudgy's partner, who sat to Xris's right, "but you want to make certain you get in with the right class of people. I've heard that the business contacts you make in places like this can be of immense benefit."

Xris listened, sorted his cards.

"What are you in for?" Pudgy asked his partner.

"Embezzlement." The man was in his mid-thirties, with skin the color of cappuccino and shapely hands with long, deft fingers. "I had a girlfriend with expensive taste. Yourself?"

"Tax evasion." Pudgy grunted. "My accountant assured me it was all perfectly legal, then he skips the planet."

The other two made sympathetic murmurings.

"Securities fraud," Blondie said, adding, aggrieved. "Everyone was doing it. I just happened to get caught."

The other two sighed and nodded in understanding.

"What about you?" Cappuccino turned to Xris with a pleasant smile.

"Murder," Xris said. "My open? Two hearts."

Silence. One might say dead silence.

Xris looked up. "Anyone else bidding?"

"Pass," said Pudgy, staring.

"Pass." Blondie gulped.

Xris frowned at him. "Two hearts is a demand bid, partner."

Blondie paled, looked distractedly at his cards. "I . . . I beg your pardon. Two diamonds."

"Three diamonds," Xris corrected. "They're a minor suit."

"Yes, you're right," Blondie said faintly. "I don't know what I was thinking. Three . . . three diamonds."

"Pass," said Cappuccino, exchanging glances with Pudgy.

Xris took the bid to game in diamonds and they played

the hand out in silence. Xris made the bid, despite the fact that his flustered partner had named a suit in which he was void.

The hand completed, Xris excused himself to go to the bathroom. Activating his augmented hearing, he was amused to listen in on the frantic, whispered conversation that took place in his absence.

"Maybe he's joking?"

"Are you kidding? Did you see his eyes?"

"They must be sending him to another prison. What's he doing on our transport?"

"Shouldn't he be in leg restrainers or something?"

"I'll speak to the captain."

"This is an outrage! My attorney will hear about this."

"Perhaps we could ask him. I don't think he'd be offended. . . ."

Xris returned. The conversation took a sudden lurch.

"You played that very well," Blondie said, desperately casual.

"Thanks." Xris looked politely at Pudgy. "I believe it's your deal."

Pudgy dealt the cards, sneaking sidelong glances at Xris's partner, urging him to ask.

Xris sorted his cards, pretended to be absorbed in his hand.

"Uh, Xris . . ." Blondie smiled in a ghastly, friendly manner. "I was wondering if you'd mind answering a question."

"Shoot," said Xris.

Blondie flinched.

"Just a figure of expression," Xris said, apologetic. "What do you want to know about? My conviction?"

"Manslaughter, was it?" Blondie asked hopefully.

Xris shook his head. "First degree. Premeditated. Whose bid is it?"

"Then this transport's taking you to a different prison?"

"Nope. Jango. Same as you. Maybe we'll be cell mates." Xris gave them a friendly wink.

"That's not possible!" Blondie cried, losing control. His voice was tight, constrained, and squeaked. "They don't send violent offenders to Jango! My attorney told me so!"

The other three regarded him in shock.

Realizing what he'd just said, Blondie took out a pillbox, threw several capsules into his mouth. He swallowed them with a grimace.

"I'm sorry, Xris," he said. "It's my nerves. Ever since the trial. If I said anything to offend you—"

"Sit down," Xris ordered. "And let daddy explain the facts of life. You two." He glanced over at Sleepy, who was now wide awake, and at young Hemingway, who was no longer writing. "Listen up.

"You've all been suckered. Get that into your heads right now. Jango's a nice place, sure. But it's not filled with nice people like yourselves. You paid extra to get sent there, right?"

They nodded.

"So did I," Xris said. "And so did half the other inmates in Jango. It may look like a country club in the brochure, but they average about twenty killings a year in Jango. Twenty unsolved killings."

"Oh, God!" Blondie whispered.

"In fact, you'd probably be safer in a maximum-security prison like Sandusky's Rock, where the guards keep close watch on all the inmates and everything they do."

"Then why did *you* arrange to come here?" Cappuccino asked, clearly not believing a word of it.

"Like you said—business connections." Xris smiled.

"Oh, God!" Blondie repeated, leaning his head on his hand.

Pudgy's jowls sagged; his skin had a gray tone. He didn't look well. Blondie was a nervous wreck; his pills weren't helping. Cappuccino's mouth twisted derisively. His thin fingers deftly sorted and resorted his cards.

"All right, Xris, you've managed to scare the crap out of these gentlemen with your stories. But I don't buy it. The government wouldn't allow it."

"The government has a hell of a lot to do trying to clean up the corruption left over from the old Democracy. His Majesty's making headway, but let's face it, cleaning up the prison system is on the bottom of his list."

"But we're not murderers! We didn't hurt anyone!" Blondie whined.

"No, of course you didn't," Xris said, his sympathetic

tones mocking theirs. "What about the company whose funds you embezzled? What happened to it? Did it fail? Were its owners ruined? Did people lose their jobs? And the securities fraud racket. How many poor saps fell for your slick line and lost everything they've worked for? They're destitute and you've got money enough to pay a high-priced lawyer to get you off with a couple of years in a cushy prison." He snorted in disgust. "No, you fellows aren't a bit like me."

"What do you want from us?" Cappuccino asked, frowning. "Money? Is this some type of extortion?"

"I don't want anything from you," Xris replied. "I don't need anything from you. I can take care of myself. I'm just giving you a friendly warning. You don't believe me?" He shrugged. "Fine. Let's play bridge."

He glanced over at Pudgy. "Your bid."

The game continued, but nobody's heart was in it anymore.

As a matter of fact, Xris was exaggerating about the horrors of Jango. He knew nothing at all about unsolved killings, would be surprised if they had even one. From all Xris had ever heard, Jango wasn't a bad place to spend your five to ten with no time off for good behavior. But these bastards were so damn smug, with their brochures and their handicaps, he figured a few sleepless nights would be good for them.

Unfortunately, Xris would prove to be one heck of a prophet.

CHAPTER 21

Shades of the prison-house began to close
Upon the growing boy . . .
William Wordsworth,
> "Ode, Intimations of Immortality"

The three days aboard the prison transport passed pleasantly enough. After the initial shock, the others came to the conclusion that Xris was lying. They discussed it often in private whispering sessions, whenever Xris was in the head and they assumed he couldn't hear. Cappuccino maintained that Xris was just attempting to intimidate them with a view to extortion. The other men agreed, although just exactly what Xris might extort and his motive for extorting it were rather vague in their minds.

They read over their brochures, talked about golf, and, after some whispered discussion, continued the bridge games. They didn't like Xris, but they did like playing bridge and were desperate for a fourth. They played for money to be paid on account, and by the end of the trip Xris and his partner were the big winners; when Blondie recovered from his scare, he was a good bridge player and more than made up for Xris, who was merely adequate. Sleepy slept and Hemingway worked on his novel with, he said, a new twist.

On the third day, the transport left hyperspace and entered into orbit around Jango. Even Sleepy woke up enough to take a look out the viewscreen, where the others were crowded, peering down at a grayish green ball of a planet that was rapidly growing in size as they descended.

The sight had a sobering effect on the little group. Jango had been a colorful brochure up until then. Now they were about to see the reality and more than one was thinking about what Xris had told them. Even Cappuccino looked unusually thoughtful and grave.

"Is it true that there aren't any cities on Jango?" Blondie asked. "That the only people who live on this planet are the socially maladjusted?"

"You mean convicts?" Xris grunted.

"I don't consider myself a convict," Cappuccino said sharply. He glanced at Xris, seemed about to add something, but politely refrained.

Xris shook his head. It would be funny if it wasn't so damn tragic. "Yeah, it's true. Unless you count the guards. No cities mean no people, and that means no support—willing or otherwise—for an escapee. The land surrounding the prison is nothing but swamp and forest. You might manage to live on your own for a day or two, especially if you've had survival training *and* you can avoid the surveillance satellites that home in on the microchip they'll shove up your butt on your arrival. But what's the point? You're just as much a prisoner out of prison as you are in. There's nowhere to go on the planet and no way to get off.

"You see those satellites? Not only do they help keep track of the prisoners, they also detect the approach of any unauthorized plane or ship. Those spaceplanes that came to take a look at us earlier were patrol planes. If we'd been anything else except this transport they'd have either escorted us politely out of the area or—if we caused trouble—shot us down."

As Xris spoke, he was taking a good, long look at the satellites; made a mental note that he'd need the access codes to bypass the early-warning system.

"You certainly know a lot about this facility," Cappuccino remarked caustically.

"*I* did my homework," Xris returned.

"Gentlemen," came the announcement over the comm, "we will be boarding the shuttle to the surface in half an hour. Have everything packed and ready to go."

They gathered up the few possessions they'd been allowed, and then returned to stare out the viewport. The men talked lightly about how soon they might be on the green, bemoaned the fact that they hadn't been permitted to bring along their own golf clubs, but would have to use the prison's—undoubtedly inferior.

The lighthearted talk ceased when the guards entered. The others watched in shocked silence as one of the guards placed restrainers on Xris's hands and ankles.

"We'll get Tampambulos settled, then we'll be back for the rest of you," said the guard. "Everyone have their gear packed?"

The others nodded. No one spoke.

"Move it along, Tampambulos," the guard ordered.

Xris headed for the door, moving slowly and awkwardly with the metal restrainers around his ankles.

One guard followed him, holding a beam rifle. The other guard kept the remote control for the restrainers in full view. With a touch of a button, Xris would be lying helpless on the floor, unable to walk, unable to use his hands.

Xris winked as he passed the little group.

"My God," said Blondie unhappily.

Cappuccino frowned, worried.

Pudgy looked away.

The shuttle was older than the transport and not nearly as clean. The passenger compartment was a cylindrical metal tube with benches on either side and no windows. It smelled of vomit, which gave some hint of what the trip down through the atmosphere was going to be like. Xris sat at the rear of the tube. In addition to the restrainers, his legs and arms were bolted to the shuttle's bulkheads. He watched the others being herded on board.

Cappuccino wrinkled his nose. Blondie gagged and clapped his hand over his mouth. They sat down on the benches.

"Put your right hand up," ordered the guard.

"What for?" Cappuccino asked, startled.

The guard jerked his thumb in the direction of a metal clamp attached about shoulder height to the shuttle's bulkhead.

"Is that necessary?" Cappuccino demanded.

"Regulations," said the guard.

Cappuccino looked for a moment as if he were going to argue. The guard brought the beam rifle up with a snap, aimed it at him. Cappuccino glowered defiantly, but he lifted his right hand. The guard thrust Cappuccino's wrist into the clamp and fastened the clamp over it. The rest submitted to the shackling in silence.

"I guess you boys must feel like prisoners about now," Xris called out cheerfully.

Outside of a few bitter glances cast his direction, no one had the heart to respond.

The shuttle was not equipped with any inertial dampening devices over what they used for launch, unlike those aboard the commercial shuttles, and the ride was as bumpy and uncomfortable as the smell had forewarned. Xris was reminded of the trip he'd reluctantly made aboard a military drop ship. The ride in the drop ship had been terrifying—rocketing through the atmosphere, the drop ship engulfed in flame. Compared with this ride—jouncing and bouncing off the metal walls of the shuttle, watching his fellow prisoners turn sickly green—Xris would have traded places with himself in a nanosecond.

The guards had handed out barf bags before they retreated to the front of the shuttle, ensconcing themselves behind a steelglass barrier. Soon nearly every prisoner on board had lost his lunch, with the exception of Xris, who would have given—and could have given—his left arm for a breath of fresh air.

The landing was bone-jarring, further shaking the already demoralized incarcerees. Blondie struck the back of his head against the bulkhead, a good solid hit that brought tears to his eyes. Xris expected him to complain of whiplash and threaten to call his attorney, but he was apparently too weak to do anything at the moment except groan.

The shuttle door opened. Rain-freshened, cool air filled the cabin and Xris sucked in a welcome breath. Two guards entered, accompanying a man in a business suit. Broadshouldered, neatly dressed, the man cast a disparaging glance at the disheveled, smelly, and half-dead inmates, then launched into his speech, which he rattled off by rote in a rapid-fire monotone that left the prisoners blinking.

"I am Deputy Warden Montieth. Welcome to the Jango Rehabilitation Facility. You men will be assigned to a blockhouse, where you will live and sleep. You men will be assigned to a cafeteria, where you will eat. You men will be assigned to a work detail, where you will work. Work is needed in the following areas: the plastic-injection molding factory, the garment factory, the hydroponics farm, the offices, the kitchen, and the laundry. You men do not have a choice of jobs. These jobs will be assigned to you. You men will be paid wages, what is known around here as Jango dollars. This currency has value only on Jango and can be used to purchase sundries, toiletries, candy, and snacks from the commissary. The currency is not to be used for gambling. Gambling is prohibited on Jango. Anyone caught gambling or wagering will have time added on to his sentence."

Montieth paused, fixed his gaze on each one of the men in turn. Xris admired the warden's style. He had accosted the prisoners at their lowest point psychologically. Now he was using his eyes to intimidate them. Only two people met and held the warden's gaze: Xris and Cappuccino.

It was to these two that Montieth, his voice hardening, spoke next.

"I can't imagine that any of you would be so foolish, but I am required to issue this warning: If any of you are thinking of trying to escape from Jango, please disabuse yourselves of the notion. The prison is surrounded by swamps and a jungle that is filled with various life-forms, most of whom happen to be carnivores. There is no way off the planet. These shuttles are the only vehicles permitted to land on Jango. We don't rely on supply ships. We are completely self-sufficient here on Jango, producing the food, the clothes, and other items we need on site.

"All shuttles are attached to their transports, like this shuttle that brought you here. The shuttle pilot is not permitted to either land or depart unless he receives an 'all clear' from Prison Control. Prisoners are not permitted to come anywhere near the landing platform. You will be fitted with a monitoring device that will allow us to pinpoint your location at all times. If we notice your blip in a restricted area, you will be brought before me and then you'll see my unpleasant side.

"Further, there will be no fighting, brawling, threatening, intimidating, pandering, stealing, swearing, fornicating. We have a complete list of regulations, which you will be expected to follow, or, again, you will be brought before me."

He smiled, a thin-lipped smile, ice-coated. "But I'm sure I don't need to worry about you gentlemen. Five of you are serving five-year sentences. You'll find that the time passes quickly. Before you know it, you'll be on this shuttle on your way back home. Don't make things hard on yourself. Don't screw up. It's not worth it."

He shifted his gaze to Xris and the smile disappeared. "You're going to be with us a bit longer, I understand. We'll be keeping an extra close watch on you. Just don't say I didn't warn you."

"Any questions?"

Cappuccino raised his left hand. "According to the brochure—"

"What brochure?" Montieth snapped.

"The . . . uh . . . brochure my attorney showed me, which had information about Jango. . . ." Cappuccino's voice petered out.

"*That* brochure," said Montieth with a slight sneer and a nasty emphasis. "It's outdated. We've made some changes."

"The golf course?" Blondie spoke faintly.

"Is currently closed," said Montieth. "We've been having a problem with snakes. Any more questions? Fine. The guards will show you to the blockhouse."

The shuttle guards removed the restraining devices from everyone, including Xris, then herded them out of the shuttle. They walked down a ramp onto a broad tarmac just as a rain squall ended. The clouds were beginning to break up. In the distance, a reddish sun gleamed, bathing the landscape with a pink tinge. The air was humid and hot, tropical.

Teams of inmates could be seen mowing, pruning, and weeding the manicured lawn, which was crisscrossed with sidewalks. The lawn and the sidewalks came to an abrupt end when both neared the jungle, which was partitioned off from the prison by an electric fence. According to what Xris had read, the fence was there more to keep the jungle predators out, as opposed to keeping the human predators in.

A quadrangle of tall buildings rose from the center of the

rolling hills. Resembling dormitories, they reminded Xris of
his university days. In fact, the entire complex might have
been an educational facility. The buildings were painted
white with black trim, looked clean and well-kept. A large
office complex, probably the administration buildings, stood
on a higher hill. A series of domed buildings with glass
walls that reflected the red sun with blinding intensity must
be the greenhouses. There were no walls, no guard towers.
Nothing but jungle and what looked like an air-traffic control tower in the very center.

"This doesn't seem so bad," Pudgy said, brightening.

"It matches the brochure, even if the brochure is outdated. And like he said, five years goes pretty quickly,"
Blondie agreed.

"All those regulations, it sounds as if they run a real
tight operation," Cappuccino said, with a glance at Xris.

"We'll see," was all Xris said.

The guards, dressed in gray, each with an I.D. card
attached to his uniform and a beam rifle in his hand,
marched them off toward the Quad. As they walked past
one of the work groups, the men looked up from digging
weeds, regarded the new arrivals with curiosity sprung from
boredom, glad for any break in the routine. Their uniforms
were soaked. They'd obviously been working in the rain.
A wet, bored-looking overseer ordered them to quit gawk-
ing and get back to business.

The guards led Xris and his companions to the third
blockhouse on the quadrangle.

"Each blockhouse has a central monitoring station," announced the guard, halting his prisoners so they could have
a good, long look.

A guard sat in what appeared to be a bunker surrounded
by monitors that provided a view of every cell in the blockhouse, shifting from one cell to another every few seconds.

"A security cam located in each cell keeps its eye on you
and the guard keeps his eye on the cam," stated the guard.
"Any questions? Move along."

They were marched halfway down a corridor on the first
floor and here the guards stopped. Using their badges as a
passkey, the guards opened two doors, one on either side
of the corridor.

Inside were two sets of bunk beds, two desks, four chairs, two closets, and two chests with four drawers each. Another door opened into a minuscule shower stall. There were no windows, and no door to enclose the sink and toilet.

"These are your quarters. Four to a cell, each cell with a separate wash facility. It's your home for the next few years, so keep it clean. Inspection and head count at 0600 hours. You will stand here, at the foot of the bunk, neatly dressed, with your bed made and the room spotless. Head count at 2200 hours, which is 'lights out,' and again at 0200 hours. If any man is found missing from his bunk during head count, the alarm will sound, lockdown will occur, and that man will be found."

Pudgy, Xris, Cappuccino, and Blondie were assigned to one room. Sleepy and Hemingway were assigned to a room across the corridor. Xris entered, looked around curiously, opening drawers. While he was checking out the shower, he could hear Blondie speaking in a low voice to one of the guards.

"That man is serving twenty years for murder. I'm certain he doesn't belong with us in our room. There must be some mistake."

The guard shrugged, answered in a loud voice. "You four are assigned to this room and that's all I know. You got a problem with a roommate, take it up with the warden."

Xris returned. Blondie glanced at him, saw that he had heard, and flushed deeply.

The guard indicated a keypad next to the door. "There are two keypads, located inside and outside. These lock and unlock your door. Punch in five numbers in sequence and the door opens. This is during the day only. After 'lights out,' you will be denied access.

"You men decide on the code you want to use. We suggest that you change the code at least once a month. Control Central can lock or unlock the doors at any time. Don't forget your code! If you do and we have to let you in or out, it's five Jango dollars the first time, twenty dollars after that, plus twenty demerits. All of us guards have our own code that can open the doors at any time.

"All rooms are subject to random inspection at any time, day or night. You will note the security cam in each room.

That is there for your protection. If the view of the security cam is obstructed or if the security cam is disabled, an alarm will sound and the guards will investigate."

He handed each of them an electronic scheduler. "Here's your job assignments, work times, mealtimes, table numbers. You will be on time for work and for meals. Five dollars and five demerits fine for every five minutes you're late. Twenty-five demerits and you start losing privileges, starting with free time. You each have two hours of free time per day, from 2000 to 2200 hours. You may use this time to attend classes, visit friends, go the gym, rent a vid, or participate in team sports. Twenty-five demerits, you lose one hour of free time.

"You may go anywhere in the facility with the exception of the shuttle pad, which is off limits; the administration buildings, unless you have a work permit; and the Control Tower.

"Turn in the clothes you are wearing. You will wear prison-issue clothing. It's there on the bed. Lose any article of clothing and it's twenty-five demerits. Here's the doctor to inject the monitors. Drop your drawers and bend over."

Once this humiliating procedure was done—with Pudgy, Cappuccino, and Blondie now looking very much as if they deeply regretted their life of crime—the guards left them. They had the rest of today to look around and become acquainted with their new environment. Tomorrow they would start to work.

The four stared at each other in uncomfortable silence, until Blondie felt compelled to offer a lame explanation for trying to ditch Xris, an explanation Xris didn't want to hear.

He turned his back, walked over to one of the unmade bunk beds, and selected the lower one. He didn't figure either of the other three were going to argue with him and he was right. Blondie stammered on for a few minutes, then dried up.

Stacked neatly on the ends of the beds were two piles of clothes and linen. One pile contained bedsheets, pillowcases, and towels. The other pile was made up of two sets of cotton knit track pants, a pair of denim work overalls, two T-shirts, four pairs of underwear and socks, and two pairs of vacuuform adjustable sneakers. A sweatshirt and a pullover nylon jacket completed the wardrobe.

Xris moved the clothes from the bed to one of the drawers, leaving out the track pants and shirt, which he intended to wear. He was going to undress in a moment and his roommates would discover that not only was he a murderer, he was also half machine. This should just about finish them off, he was thinking, when a voice came from the door.

"So, look at our new little jailbirds. Ain't they cute."

Xris turned to see four men standing in the corridor outside their room. Xris had seen some big men in his time, but the man who'd made the comment was certainly impressive. He stood taller than Xris, was broader than Xris through the shoulders—and Xris was no shrimp. The man had no neck to speak of, what neck he'd started out with at birth having been swallowed up by the muscles in his shoulders. Given the dull, mean look in his little squinty eyes, that muscle extended well up into the man's head. Bleached hair flowed in a mane down his back.

The three flanking him were obviously his flunkies. They stood grinning, prepared to enjoy the show. In their arms, they held four pairs of shoes and a couple of sweatshirts.

Xris's three roommates stood gazing at the apparition uncertainly, not knowing how to respond. Xris ignored the comment, began to roll his socks into neat balls.

Muscle Head sauntered into their room, pivoting sideways to fit his massive bulk through the door opening.

"Me and the boys here want to welcome you fellows to Jango. My name is Slovenski, but you can call me Master. I run a charitable organization here on Jango and I know that you boys will be happy to donate your shoes and sweatshirts to the needy."

"Needy? What needy?" Blondie made the mistake of asking.

The Master came toe to toe with Blondie, whose nose was level with the huge man's breastbone, barely visible beneath his swelling pecs.

"The poor fellas who ain't got any shoes," said Slovenski, looming over him.

"But that will be us, if we give you our shoes," protested

Blondie. He took a nervous step backward, ran up against his bunk.

"Yeah, ain't it a shame," Slovenski jeered. "But you can buy 'em back. Fifty dollars for the shoes and one hundred dollars for the sweatshirt. Real money. Not this Jango crap."

The others gawked. Blondie went whiter than the bed-sheets. Pudgy broke out into a sweat, while Cappuccino looked as if someone had mixed his coffee with green Jell-O. Xris put his socks in the drawer, along with his sweatshirt and the extra pair of shoes.

"Uh, Master, look there." One of the flunkies pointed to Xris and giggled. "I guess this one don't hear too well."

Slovenski rounded just in time to see the drawer close on the sweatshirt. Glaring at Xris, Slovenski leered down at him.

"Are you deaf, boy? Is that your problem? I guess you must be, since you're putting on those shoes."

"I heard you," Xris said pleasantly. Smoothing the Velcro strap around his ankle, he stood up. "I just didn't hear you say anything particularly intelligent."

"Yeah? Well, maybe your ears need cleaning." Slovenski lashed out with an enormous hand, aiming a blow at Xris's head.

Xris caught hold of the man's fist in his left hand, his cyberhand, and began to squeeze.

It was interesting to watch the varying expressions on the Master's face. First there was laughter, as he figured he'd easily break Xris's hold. The laughter darkened to anger when he found he couldn't. Anger increased to fury. He brought up his other fist.

"Don't even think about it," Xris warned, and markedly increased the pressure on the clenched fingers.

Slovenski crumpled. "Ow! Oooow! Hey! Aaaagh. Let the hell go of me, you son of a bitch! Let go!"

"I prefer giving to a charity of my choice," Xris said, maintaining the pressure. "I'm keeping my sweatshirt and my shoes. The same goes for my friends. Right?"

The Master cursed and spluttered. The flunkies stared, aghast. None of them seemed inclined to come to the rescue of his leader.

Xris increased the pressure. Something snapped. The Master gasped and gave a little gurgle.

"Right?" Xris repeated.

"Right! Right!"

Xris released his grip.

Slovenski groaned and fell back, nursing his bruised fingers, which were already starting to swell. His squinty little eyes regarded Xris with inveterate hatred.

"Fucker," Slovenski snarled. "You'll pay for this."

"But not today," Xris said, smiling.

"Hey, Master!" one of the flunkies hissed. "The guard!"

Slovenski backed out of the room, nursing his injured hand. He and the flunkies departed, the Master moving with as much dignity as he could muster, considering that four of his fingers were now turning an unbecoming shade of purple.

The guard looked in the door. "What's going on?" He cast a grim glance around. "This has always been a quiet floor. I hope you boys don't plan on being troublemakers. One more incident like this"—he glared at Xris—"and you'll find yourself in solitary."

"Us!" Blondie cried. "It wasn't us! That maniac—"

"Be quiet," Cappuccino said, seeing the guard's eyebrows pull together in a frown. "You're only making things worse."

"But . . ."

"We're sorry, sir," Xris said contritely. "It won't happen again."

"See that it doesn't." The guard departed.

Blondie collapsed onto his bunk. "What's going on?" he demanded plaintively. "I don't understand!" He pointed to the security camera. "They saw that monster try to steal our shoes! They saw him threaten us. He was going to hit you, for God's sake! And *we're* the ones who get into trouble."

"Welcome to Jango," Xris said, putting sheets on his bunk.

Across the corridor, Sleepy emerged from his room, wandered disconsolately down the hall in his stockinged feet.

CHAPTER 22

Lava Quod est sordidum . . .
Wash what is dirty . . .
Stephen Langton, Archbishop of Canterbury,
"The Golden Sequence"

The inmates ate together in one large room, sitting at assigned tables, twenty to a table. On entering the cafeteria, they walked down a line of steamer tables, made their selections from a variety of nutritional and unappetizing food, which was cooked by the prison staff, served by inmates. During dinner, the inmates were allowed to talk freely. The room was a hubbub of voices that all stopped when Xris entered. Word had spread fast, apparently.

Heads turned, men craned their necks to catch a glimpse of him. Xris wondered if he should tip his hat to the crowd, like the laser-ball players. Ignoring the stares, he took his place in the food line.

Xris watched closely and noted that his tray was shoved out just a bit too enthusiastically by the prisoner at the end of the line. Xris picked up his tray, bobbled it clumsily, and managed to spill most of the food on the floor. He earned a five-dollar fine, which was marked against his name by the guard on duty, and another tray of food.

He doubted if the meal had been poisoned, though that was a possibility. But it probably had some other nasty surprise, like ground glass in the hash or needles in the apples. Xris moved off, thinking that if he had to dump his food every night, he would soon have to file for the prison's version of bankruptcy.

All eyes were on him as he walked through the hall to his assigned table. Some regarded him with respect, though they shook their heads as he walked past, predicting in low voices that within a week he wouldn't be holding his head so high. Most seemed to find him amusing. He'd taken their minds off their own misery for a moment and they were grateful.

The Master entered, with his hand bound in an inflatable splint. All eyes turned his way and, at his scowl, the eyes quickly found something else to look at. One of the flunkies carried the Master's tray, since he was incapacitated. Xris felt almost friendly toward the poor Master, who had inadvertently made Xris's job in this prison a hell of a lot easier. Everyone was talking about him, which meant that the Hung leaders would be listening and they'd be impressed Xris just had to make sure that one) they stayed impressed, and two) he stayed alive. Not necessarily in that order.

His fellow prisoners weren't the only ones talking. When he sat down, his roommate, Blondie, blurted out, "You're a cyborg! I found out! The guard told me."

"Pass the catsup," said Xris.

"The doctors did a very nice job on you," Pudgy added politely. "I couldn't tell."

Xris shoveled in food, eating rapidly on the theory that the less time the bland and tasteless mass spent in his mouth, the better.

"You're in danger," Cappuccino leaned over to whisper, under the pretense of grabbing a hunk of bread from the basket in the middle of the table. "I've been doing some listening. It seems that this Master bastard has already sent three guys to the infirmary. One of them had to be airlifted to a special hospital on Firma Prime. His spine was broken in three places."

"I can take care of myself," Xris muttered through the overcooked corn and lima beans.

"Yes, I know you can. It's just . . ." Cappuccino paused. His lips tightened. He seemed to find the words he had to say tasted worse than the food. "I've been a fool. I should have known the truth about this place, but I guess I didn't really want to. I may be a crook"—he smiled thinly—"but I'm not a coward. If you need help . . . well, I know you don't think much of us and I guess I can't blame you. We must seem pretty soft and, well, naive, to you. Though why I should care what a murderer thinks . . ."

Sighing, he shook his head. "Sorry. No offense. It's just . . ." He glanced sidelong at Xris. "I get the feeling you're not exactly what you seem to be."

This was getting too close to the truth. Xris chewed the stringy meat, swallowed, then said, "What's your name?"

"Huh?" Cappuccino looked startled. "But you've been with us . . ." He stopped, smiled slightly, then said, "I'm Malcolm. This is Alan"—he indicated Blondie—"and Kenneth." That was Pudgy.

Xris nodded. "We'll talk later," he said and set himself resolutely to the task of finishing his meal.

During recreation time that evening, Xris sat down with his new "team" in their cell and laid out their strategy.

"The 'Master' as he calls himself won't take this lying down. He can't afford to. He'll be after me. The rest of you may come in for some harassment, especially if you're determined to stick with me."

Malcolm, formerly Cappuccino, looked determined; the other two, unhappy and resigned. Apparently it had occurred to them that they didn't have much choice.

"Okay, here's the plan. We change the code on the lock every day. You, Blon— I mean, Alan. You good with numbers?"

Alan nodded.

"Fine. Can you figure out a code sequence that we can change every day, but which is easy to remember?"

Alan thought a moment, then said, "Yes. We pick a five-number random sequence: 4, 96, 32, 75, 16. That's the code for the first day. The second day, the code changes to 96, 32, 75, 16, 4. The numbers move up one digit, the first number moves to the last. The third day the code is 32, 75, 16, 4, 96. And so on. After each number rotates through once, we change all the numbers and start again."

"Good." Xris approved. "I take it everyone can remember that. Now, you can bet your shoes that the Master either owns one of the guards' security passkeys or he has access to one, which means that he can waltz in here anytime he pleases. We also know the guards are pretty damn slow to respond. It won't matter so much during the day—even the Master has to take his work shift. But it will at night."

"Do we keep watch? One of us stay awake?"

"A good idea, Ken, but we've all got to go to work in the morning. What I propose is to set up an alarm system. Something simple that would alert us to intruders."

Metal wastebaskets would have been ideal, but the cells were all equipped with trash compactors, so that was out. Eventually they ended up removing, with much difficulty, a metal slat from underneath one of the bunk beds. They balanced the slat across the seat of a chair, which they placed next to the door. Any movement of the door would bump the chair, jostling the metal slat and sending it clanging to the floor.

Xris figured the noise alone would frighten off any intruder—the first time, at least. His cell mates agreed and went to bed feeling safe and secure. Xris didn't tell them what might happen the second or the third time. He didn't tell them about zip guns or cross-bows or knives made from the very same bed slats they'd used. Let them enjoy one night's peaceful sleep at least.

The metal slat hit the floor around 0200. Xris was up and out of his bed and across the floor before the vibrations had ceased, but there was no one in the room. The door, which was automatically shut and locked at 2200, had been pulled shut again. Xris couldn't open it to look outside.

"You see, it worked," he told the others. "Go back to sleep."

It would not work the next time. Lying in the darkness that smelled of three other bodies, listening to Malcolm snore, Xris faced the undeniable truth that he'd made a dangerous enemy. But then, he'd known that the moment he'd decided to keep his shoes. He'd also known at that moment that he was using the Master, that if the Master hadn't taken it upon himself to be a jerk, Xris would have been forced to invent one. If he was lucky, the Master would continue to play into Xris's hands.

And, before he broke out of here, Xris would probably have to kill him.

* * *

Wake-up call came at 0530. They had thirty minutes to shower—all four of them—and shave. By 0615 they were expected to be standing in line for breakfast. Xris grabbed his food, gulped hot coffee and downed a couple of hard-boiled eggs, bacon, and biscuits. Breakfast was the best meal of the day.

The inmates were expected to be on the job at 0700.

Xris had been assigned to laundry detail, a job which required heavy manual labor. The prison authorities knew he was a cyborg and had apparently decided to take of advantage of the fact. Two of his cell mates were working in the administration building—the job Xris had been hoping for, since it gave him access to the prisoners' records. Xris knew the names of the Hung leaders, but he had no idea what they looked like, what cell block they inhabited, or how to gain access to them. There were over ten thousand prisoners on Jango, which ruled out a door-to-door search. He didn't want to arouse suspicions by asking around.

Amadi was scheduled to visit the prison in the next day or two. Xris would ask to be reassigned. He had two weeks to the day to bust out the Hung leaders, according to Amadi's time schedule. Right now, Xris would have been happy to have moved that timetable up by about fourteen days. He had never loathed anywhere as much as he was starting to loathe Jango.

The laundry facility was located in the basement of the dining hall. No windows, no ventilation. The washing machines took up one entire wall, the dryers—which used the old-fashioned method of heat drying as opposed to evaporation—lined another wall. The laundry room was hot, humid, and noisy.

Xris was given the task of loading clothing into the enormous industrial washers. Each prisoner's laundry was placed in a net bag, which was tossed straight into the washer. In addition, there were bed sheets and towels and the guards' uniforms, plus the clothes of the prison administration and hospital staff.

"This morning's workload is light," said the foreman, after showing Xris how to load and operate the machines. "Only one blockhouse sends their laundry in on Mondays.

This afternoon will be busy, 'cause we get the stuff from the dining halls and the infirmary. Tomorrow is sheet day."

Xris faced a mountain of bags and more were being trundled in on carts. He couldn't wait to see a heavy day.

He grabbed the first bag and it was then that he realized he'd hit pay dirt, so to speak. Each bag was marked with the prisoner's name, cell number, and bunk number. Xris didn't need to ask to be reassigned. All he had to do was keep a lookout for the Hung leaders' dirty shorts, and he'd find out everything he needed to know.

The physical labor—hefting the bags, tossing them into the machine, reaching for another bag—was mind numbing—'bot work as it was known in the industry. Robots could have performed the task, but that would have deprived the prisoners of something to do. Xris wondered just exactly how loading washing machines was going to help a hardened criminal such as himself lead an honest life. Probably it had something to do with the symbolism of cleansing—washing the soil from his darkened soul.

In the meantime, he bent and lifted, swung and threw until the machine was filled. Closing the door, he hit the soap and water buttons and watched as the giant machine started its cycle. Moving to the next machine, pushing the cart filled with bags, Xris blessed the need to look for names on the bags. If he hadn't had that diversion, he would have soon been as empty-headed as any ordinary work-'bot.

Twenty other inmates were on laundry detail, some shifting the wet clothes into the dryers, others helping to load. Conversation was permitted, but it was futile. The huge metal washing machines knocked against each other when they were in operation, water splashed and frothed. The dryers made a high-pitched whining sound, similar to an artillery shell in flight. Those inmates who needed to talk did so by shouting. Xris finally turned off his augmented hearing, and occupied himself by reading name tags.

The routine continued all morning. Xris was accustomed to physical exertion, but not the constant, repetitive movement required by this job. By lunchtime, his back muscles were ready to stage a revolt, while his shoulder muscles were seriously considering dissolving parliament and calling for new elections. On the good side, he was too tired and too hungry to notice the taste of the food.

He was delighted to find, on his return, even more laundry than when he'd left.

According to the tags, the load in this cart contained laundry from Blockhouse Five. Gritting his teeth against a shooting pain which had developed in his right shoulder, he grabbed a bag and automatically glanced at the name tag.

"By god," Xris said, catching hold of the bag in the act of tossing it.

MACDONALD was the name on the tag.

Macdonald was one of the names of the Hung leaders.

Macdonald was also a fairly common name. There were probably kilos of Macdonalds in Jango. Xris glanced around to see if any of the guards was watching. Apparently it was time for their afternoon naps, for they were nowhere in sight. He set the bag aside, reached for the next.

MAIR. This was better. There couldn't be many Mairs and, according to the tag, this Mair was in the same cell as Macdonald. The third bag clinched it—BECKING.

Xris started up the washing machine. Under the cover of its splashing and banging, he ducked behind the half-filled laundry cart, knelt down, and dumped out the contents of each bag onto the cement floor. Macdonald's clothes showed him to be a man of nearly two meters in height, on the thin side, to judge by his waist size, but with a heavy upper body, to judge by his shirt size. Becking was about one point eight meters, and a little stockier. Mair was the shortest, at about one point six meters. Lifting Mair's T-shirt, Xris whistled in surprise.

Blood.

Blood stained the front of the T-shirt and the front of the sweatshirt which was also in the bag.

Either Mair was the clumsy type or he wasn't a regular contributor to the Master's shoe fund.

Xris committed the cell number to memory and was about to start shoving the clothes back into the bag when he felt a heavy hand grab hold of his sore shoulder.

Checking the reflex that had his cybernetic hand grappling for the man's throat, Xris pivoted to his feet.

The guard was glaring at him. "I'm talking to you, 97602!"

"Sorry, sir," Xris said and tapped his left ear. "Hard of hearing. What did you want with me?"

The guard pointed to the clothes on the floor. "What the hell are you doing? Looking for something in your size?"

"No, sir," Xris said politely. Reaching down, he picked up one of the bags, held it out for inspection. "This one's defective, sir. So are the other two." He indicated a large rip in the netting, a rip he'd made himself, just in case.

The guard peered at it, peered at the other bags. He had the brains the size of a piece of space dust, for he didn't bother to check the cell numbers on the bags, or he might have thought it odd that three defective bags came from one cell.

"You'll find replacements in that bin over there. Transfer the name, number, and cell block. Indelible ink pens are on that table."

He walked off.

Xris replaced the bags, carefully printed the names and numbers on each one.

MACDONALD, BECKING, MAIR.

Xris went back to work.

CHAPTER 23

Freedom has a thousand charms to show,
That slaves, howe'er contented, never know.

William Cowper, "Table Talk"

"Oh, ick!" cried Raoul, on entering the terminal building on Del Sol. Shuddering, he drew back. "What are those creatures?"

"Keep your voice down! *Those creatures*," Jamil said, "are the people we've come to save."

"Save from what?" Raoul wondered. "If it's ugliness, there's not a thing to be done."

"Tycho and I will see to the luggage," Quong offered. "Everyone, give me your baggage tags."

They had cleared customs and immigration on the cruise ship itself. Their luggage, including Raoul's twenty-six suitcases, two trunks, and seventeen hat boxes, had been searched and had passed inspection, though there was some question by the officials as to the quantity and type of "medications" brought along by the Adonian. Raoul couldn't understand the problem and it appeared for a few tense moments that he would be barred from entering the world.

Jamil had spent three days with Raoul aboard the cruise ship, endeavoring to keep him from insulting most of the other passengers by offering to give them advice on their makeup or making disparaging remarks about their attire. Last night Jamil had been forced to haul Raoul off the stage when he felt like he needed to "join the dancers!" Jamil had been quite willing to toss Raoul to the drug-sniffing 'bots.

Wondering how and why Xris put up with the Loti, Jamil

had spent four hours explaining matters to the Del Solian officials. He assured them that Raoul was a danger only to himself. Considering Raoul's true occupation, this was not precisely true, but the officials, after spending an hour talking with Raoul, were ready to believe anything. Eventually Raoul and his "medicine" were allowed to enter the planet. The weapons, which would be used by the dremeck revolutionaries, had been previously smuggled into the world disassembled, the cartons labeled TOYS.

"If our friend Jamil ever had any ambitions for taking over Xris's leadership role, I will wager that he has since abandoned them," Quong said in a low voice to Tycho, who nodded and smiled.

Tycho's older brother Tycho had given the younger Tycho one piece of advice: The only way to live among humans and retain your sanity was to keep your translator turned off as much as possible, nod and smile if anyone said anything to you, and don't drink the water anywhere, ever. Consequently Tycho had no idea what the doctor had said, but he nodded and smiled. He understood from Quong's gesture that he was supposed to accompany the doctor and so he went, a bundle of plastic chits in his thin-fingered hand.

Jamil, in the meantime, was arguing with Raoul. Or rather, arguing *at* Raoul, since Raoul never permitted himself to become involved in an argument. Arguing, he said, caused wrinkles.

"I briefed everyone on the situation on this world on board the cruise ship," Jamil was saying, his voice rising with increasing anger. "Weren't you listening?"

"No," Raoul replied complacently.

Removing the mirror from his handbag, he looked anxiously at himself to make certain the rigors of travel had not ruined him utterly. Tenderly patting down a few wisps of misplaced hair, he assured himself that he was still beautiful, then he closed the compact and returned it to his purse.

"But please do not take offense, Jamil," Raoul added, on seeing that Jamil resembled one of the more picturesque thunderclouds that were occasionally allowed in the skies above Adonia. "I rarely listen to Xris Cyborg, either. My

friend"—he tapped the Little One on top of the fedora—
"keeps me apprised of developments. Just now he tells me
that we are here to save these people from being massacred
and also to free them from tyranny and oppression."

At that moment, a group of the "creatures" was being
marched past. They were manacled hand and foot, chained
together with old-fashioned leg irons around their ankles.
There were about twenty of them and they were being
escorted by two humans carrying stun-sticks.

"Adonians have heard of slavery, I presume," Jamil said,
his voice cold and harsh.

"Oh, yes!" Raoul was enthusiastic. "At the age of eigh-
teen, all Adonians enter a period of enslavement. It lasts
about a year—"

"What?" Jamil demanded, incensed.

"Don't pursue this," Darlene cautioned.

Jamil ignored her. "What do you mean, you Adonians
practice slavery? That's not possible! Adonia is officially a
member of the Empire and slavery is illegal—"

"The enslavement lasts a year," Raoul continued gravely,
"unless both parties mutually consent to continuing the relationship. It's all part of our education system." A blissful,
nostalgic shimmer glistened in his unfocused eyes. "My own
master was a remarkable woman. Such a hand with the
paddle. I was her favorite. She had a golden collar made
for me, with rubies and a golden chain. The gold looked
quite stunning against my bare skin. When she took me for
walks, everyone we met was quite insanely jealous—"

"That's enough!" Jamil said hurriedly. "I understand.
And I'm sorry I do."

"I warned you," Darlene murmured with a wry smile.

"But not soon enough." Jamil tapped one of the Del
Solian spaceline employees on the shoulder. "Excuse me,
but those people who just passed us—are they prisoners?"

"What people?" The Del Solian glanced around.

"Those people." Jamil pointed to the chain gang, which
was clanking its way through the spaceport.

"Oh, those aren't people," the woman said with a laugh.
"Those are dremecks. Luggage handlers. It must be
lunchtime."

"They go to lunch chained like that!" Jamil glowered dangerously.

"Jamil . . ." Darlene said in a low tone, tugging on his sleeve.

She started to add that they weren't supposed to draw attention to themselves, but since everyone debarking was looking at Raoul and either glaring or waving—the entire troop of showgirls showered him with kisses—she abandoned that as useless.

"It's for their own good," the woman explained. "Dremecks are very easily distracted and they don't have much common sense. If we permit them to roam free, they become a nuisance to the passengers. And they'd never return to work. We had a terrible time with them wandering out onto the tarmac to watch the cruise ships take off. A great many of them were killed and that caused flight delays. It annoyed the pilots. We've found this solution is best all around."

"Chaining them up like animals!" Jamil said savagely.

"Jamil, please . . ." Darlene attempted to intervene.

"You off-worlders are always very quick to judge us," the woman said coldly. "Wait until you've been here awhile. You'll see what it's like."

"Patience, Jamil," Darlene said softly. "Put racial memory on hold, will you? You're not going to help these people by antagonizing their rulers. Remember this is a police state. Don't look now, but those two women in dark clothes with the wires running into their ears are taking a great deal of interest in us."

Jamil glanced at them. The women were indeed watching them; one was speaking into a headset. Jamil rearranged his face into a carefree smile and retrieved Raoul, who had been about to depart with the showgirls.

"We're supposed to meet Doc down in the baggage area."

The team followed a trail of icons symbolizing suitcases, and soon caught up with the dremeck chain gang, shuffling and clanging its way through the spaceport. Another chain gang being led in the opposite direction passed the first. The dremecks smiled and nodded to one another in passing. They looked remarkably cheerful as they marched along, each with one three-fingered hand on the back of the shoulder of the dremeck in front, their manacled feet swinging in time so that they did not trip each other with the chain.

Their human guards, herding them from behind, were grim-faced and serious, obviously taking no chances with their charges.

Jamil gave the dremecks a look of eloquent sympathy as he walked past them. He would have raised his clenched fist in a fierce expression of power and solidarity, but Darlene, guessing his intention, took hold of his arm.

"Now is *not* the time," she said firmly.

The men and women with the wires running into their heads were everywhere. Highly visible in their dark suits and white shirts, with the emblem of Del Sol emblazoned upon their left coat pocket, they kept watch on everything and everyone in the spaceport. Their faces were cold, impassive, forbidding. Anyone who laughed, sneezed, coughed, or spoke drew their attention; they seemed particularly offended by laughter.

Anyone who deviated from the marked routes was approached and questioned. New arrivals, who had debarked with cheerful faces and eager looks, were already starting to wilt in the dark shadows cast by these denizens of Kirkov's authority. It was easy to tell the Del Solian population from the tourists. They kept their heads down, glanced up only occasionally to see where they were going, and never, never spoke to or looked directly at any of the people with wires in their heads.

"Two of them are following us," Darlene said softly. "Probably because of Raoul. We should send him to the hotel while we meet with the dremecks."

"I don't suppose we could send him to the Void while we meet with the dremecks," Jamil said gloomily.

"He does come in useful sometimes," Darlene reminded him.

Jamil grunted.

Raoul was giving the luggage handlers a wide berth; they had a most peculiar smell. He held a hankie to his nose and clutched his floral print duster close to his body, fearful that the blue tones of their skin might rub off on the fabric.

The Little One made a sound that might have been a laugh and made a motion with his hand in Raoul's direction.

"What do you mean, they think *I'm* ugly?" Raoul cried, staring down at his friend, appalled.

The fedora nodded up and down emphatically.

"Ah, poor things," Raoul said softly, much affected. He favored the dremecks with a pitying glance. "Jamil is right. It is our duty to free them. From those dreadful clothes, if nothing else."

Perhaps due to the deplorable fact that the luggage handlers were forced to work chained to one another, the unloading of luggage from the cruise ship was taking an interminable amount of time.

Aware that allowing oneself to become stressed in a situation over which one has no control is a contributing factor to elevated blood pressure, with the possibility of stroke or seizure, Dr. Quong refused to allow the delay to annoy him. He sat down in a metal chair, which was chained, like the dremecks, to a line of metal chairs.

Two men with wires in their heads strolled past. Quong smiled at them politely, wished them a good day. Not only did they fail to return his pleasantry, they seemed to find it highly suspicious. After a searching perusal, they continued their walk.

Tycho had gone off in pursuit of chocolate, to which, he had admitted, he was particularly addicted. Quong had begun to issue his standard warning on the subject of sugar and caffeine when it occurred to him that he had no knowledge of how these substances might affect chameleons. The other Tycho, the first and original Tycho, had never shown the least proclivity for anything other than spaghetti. Quong allowed the new Tycho to eat his chocolate, though the doctor made a mental note to consult certain scientific journals on the subject.

Sitting in the chained chair, Quong watched the dremecks good-naturedly untangling themselves from their chains. He took this opportunity to study the race, which was a new one in his experience.

The doctor had, of course, done his research and, unlike

Raoul, Quong was prepared for the odd sight of the small, stocky humanoid beings with their blue-gray skin. What he had not been able to ascertain from the vids he had watched was the unique texture of the skin, which appeared to be the consistency of bread dough and which flowed in soft folds around their large eyes, their most prominent facial feature.

A dremeck's mouth was completely enveloped by the folds of skin and was visible only when he or she smiled. The smile completely rearranged the skin folds, making a startling difference in the expression. When a dremeck was not smiling, it appeared to be in the depths of gloom, because the folds of its face all flowed downward. A dremeck smile acted like a mud slide, causing the folds to expand outward in all directions.

The dremecks' teeth were small and very blunt; they were not meat-eaters, but subsisted entirely on a diet of plants and fruits native to their world. Young dremecks did not have teeth at all, but attained them when they reached maturity.

Dremecks burrow. They have always lived underground, not for any special reason—the air on their world is not poisonous, the sun is not too hot. The dremecks live underground because they like living underground. It makes them feel more secure. It was therefore theorized that the dremecks had once been the food source for large predators. The dremecks had escaped this enemy by going underground and had apparently out evolved this enemy, for there were no large predators left on Del Sol.

Unfortunately, the dremecks could not escape their current enemy—humans—so easily. The fact that they were excellent burrowers had proven their downfall.

Early space explorers had found no signs of life on the surface of Del Sol—no cities or towns or villages, no cultivated fields, no oceanfront resorts, and therefore the dremecks' planet went unnoticed by the rest of the civilized galaxy for any number of centuries. The dremeck world was finally discovered by human scientists searching for the Bulgarvian wormhole. They named it Del Sol, after the noted philanthropist Ferdinand Del Sol of Mengus Seventeen.

It should be noted here that the dremecks had their own name for their planet. The dremecks believed that their world was responsible for giving them life; therefore, the name they called their world had come across to human translators as "uterus." This name was deemed unacceptable by map makers and travel agents. GNN said they could not report on such a planet during the "children's hour" of vid viewing. The Navy pointed out that, should war prove inevitable, they could not possibly attack with dignity a planet called Uterus. The name was therefore changed officially to Del Sol.

Further investigation by the scientists revealed that Del Sol was a treasure trove of minerals, including precious and semiprecious gems, gold and silver. The amounts discovered appeared so vast, at first, that the discovery was kept secret for fear that gold prices would plummet. Later it was found that the gold was of inferior quality, its molecular structure being just a tiny bit off, making it brittle instead of malleable, and so the currency standard was saved.

Diamonds and emeralds, rubies and sapphires, silver and uranium were discovered in abundance, however, and more than made up for the brittle gold. Early entrepreneurs were especially pleased to find that the ignorant dremecks had no idea what these minerals were worth. The dremecks used the gems to make body adornments, worn by both the males and the females for no particular reason sociologists could determine except that the dremecks thought they were pretty. The dremecks willingly traded baskets of precious jewels for their most valued commodity—vegetables, which the humans were only too happy to provide.

The humans were baffled, however, to discover that the dremecks left all the vegetables they'd been given to rot. The report came back that the dremecks didn't like the vegetables because they were "dead," which led scientists to discover that the dremecks ate only living vegetation. They grazed.

It was undoubtedly this unfortunate resemblance to cattle that gave the first humans to visit the planet the idea that the dremecks were subhuman, ranking somewhere above rats and rock-and-roll singers in intelligence; equal, perhaps, to those other herd animals, politicians; but below the rest of humanity.

Comforted by the knowledge that they were saving the dremecks from themselves, the humans moved in during the time of the corrupt Democracy. Using the dremecks as miners, they looted the planet of its mineral wealth, becoming very rich themselves in the process. Almost overnight, Del Sol emerged as one of the galaxy's financial capitals. Not being particularly scrupulous people themselves, the bankers were not much interested in the scruples of others, particularly if such scruples could adversely affect profit. Advertising for Del Solian financial institutions read: "The bank where nobody knows your name."

As for the dremecks, they were easily subjugated. Enslavement was made all the easier by the fact that the elder dremecks were an extremely gentle people and didn't believe in resistance—ever. The younger dremecks were, according to reports, becoming restless.

Dr. Quong mused on all this as he watched the dremeck baggage handlers unload the metal bullet-shaped suitcases of the passengers, standing them on end so that the phosphorus lights flashing the baggage numbers were visible.

Quong had mentioned the dremecks' nonaggressive trait to Jamil, suggested that this might be a problem in training them as soldiers. Jamil merely brushed the information aside, thereby offending Dr. Quong. He said no more about it, but was looking forward with perverse pleasure to the first meeting of the gung-ho mercenary and the grazing revolutionaries.

Quong was startled from his reverie by a touch on his foot. Looking down, he saw a dremeck crouched on the floor, polishing the doctor's boot with a rag.

Embarrassed, Quong started to draw his foot away. "No, really, that's not necessary." He fumbled for a coin.

The dremeck lifted his head. His eyes, which were round and black and very liquid, protruded slightly, causing the folds around the eyes to flow backward like a receding tide. He had a flutelike voice and spoke Standard Military— taught to them by the humans—with a lilting accent that was really quite enchanting.

"Please permit me to continue my work, sir. This is the

only way we will have a chance to talk without arousing suspicion." The dremeck paused, then said carefully, "It is a very sunny day outside, with not a cloud in the sky."

That was the code which meant that all was going well, they were not being watched, were not in any danger. If the dremeck had said, "It is a very sunny day outside, but rain is predicted tonight," then Quong would have known that someone was on to them. At the words, "There is a terrible storm raging," the Doc would have made certain his weapon was fully charged and close at hand.

Since the weather was sunny, Quong relaxed.

The dremeck proceeded to shine his boots and talked at the same time. "I recognized you by the description given me. It was said you had shifty eyes."

"Shifty eyes!" Quong repeated heatedly, then suddenly realized what was intended. "Ah, perhaps you mean slanted eyes? Yes, my eyes are slanted—a natural and, to my mind, quite attractive feature of my race."

The dremeck lifted its own incredibly round eyes. "Have I offended?"

"No," Quong said, smiling. "Well, maybe. *Shifty* means . . . But that is not important." He glanced around. No one, including the wire-heads, was paying any attention to them. Leaning forward as if to study the dremeck's work, Quong lowered his voice to ask, "What is the plan?"

The folds of the dremeck's face melted like sand dunes at high tide. "Plan?" he repeated in a tremulous voice.

"Where are your headquarters?" Quong pursued. "And how do we arrive there without arousing suspicion?"

"We don't really have a 'headquarters,' if I am understanding the word correctly, but I assume that you will want to discuss matters with the One who guides us. He awaits you in the Xynx Burrow, which is located about three hour's foot journey from here. The One says that yourselves, the Army leaders, should travel to the burrow on the Uglies train. You will not be noticed. Many Uglies visit our burrow, which is also what we have been told is the galaxy's largest diamond mine."

"By Uglies, I assume you mean humans?" Quong said mildly.

The dremeck's round eyes widened, then vanished as the

folds of its face crumpled. His hands holding the rag began to tremble. "I forgot! I am sorry, Overseer. I did not mean it. Please forgive me—"

"There, there." Quong would have laid a soothing hand on the dremeck's shoulder, but the human guards overseeing the luggage handlers were starting to take an interest in him. He knew enough about this world to understand that any friendly overture to a dremeck would be viewed with suspicion and perhaps hostility. "I feel much the same about many members of the human race myself. Especially now. And please do not call me Overseer. I am Quong. Dr. Quong."

He rose to his feet. The luggage was at last sorted. People from their cruise ship were already gathering to retrieve their possessions. Quong made a show of taking the change from his pocket, picking through it.

"The guards are watching us. We will retrieve our luggage and take the Uglies train to the Xynx mine. Is that correct— I beg your pardon. I do not know your name."

"My what?" The dremeck was startled and uneasy.

"Your name. I told you mine. It is Quong. William Quong. And you are?"

"Remer," said the dremeck in immense confusion. "I— I am called Remer. Forgive me for seeming startled, but no human has ever before asked my name."

"Hopefully that will change," Quong said, and pressed a coin into the dremeck's hand. He noted, scientifically, that the body temperature of the dremeck was apparently quite low, judging by touch, and that the blue-gray skin had a certain moist quality to it. Clammy, the Uglies would term it. "I look forward to meeting you again, Remer. Ah, there is the rest of the team!"

Quong waved to draw their attention. Jamil waved back. The dremeck, clutching his rag in his hand, stared at the small group.

"Is that all of you?" Remer asked, dismayed.

"Another member of the team, Tycho, is standing over beside the juice machine." Quong peered that direction, squinted. "At least I think that is where he is. It is difficult to tell. He comes from a race known as chameleon and at the moment he is blending in with his surroundings. That may be him beside the water dispenser. And now I must go. Farewell for the moment."

Quong started to walk away, but the dremeck made a frantic gesture with the rag.

Quong glanced at the guard, who was saying something to his companion and pointing at them.

"What is it?" Quong said softly. "Be quick! They are watching!"

"Where are the rest of you?" Remer asked, his words tumbling over each other in his haste. "Where is the army?"

"Army?" Quong frowned. "What army?"

"The army you promised to bring! The army that will save our people."

Quong looked at the dremeck. He looked at the guards and he looked at Jamil, who was walking, unsuspecting, down the corridor.

The doctor understood. Chuckling, he rubbed his hands together.

He could hardly wait to break the news.

CHAPTER 24

Other Voices, Other Rooms
Truman Capote, title of novel

"Hello, Sam," Petronella greeted the secretary guarding Robison's office from behind a massive oak desk. "How're things going?"

Sam shrugged. "Same as always." He glanced at his calendar screen, which glowed a faint iridescent green. "You have an appointment?"

"No, but I was hoping I could see him," Petronella said in wheedling tones. She glanced significantly at the open door, peered inside. "There doesn't seem to be anybody with him. . . ."

Sam was shaking his head. "Sorry, but he has an appointment in—"

"Rizzoli? Is that you?" Robison yelled out from the office.

Sam lifted an eyebrow, gave a wry smile. "Go right in, Agent."

Petronella entered the office, which was habitually darkened. Robison disliked bright light, held that semidarkness was more conducive to thought. The windows in his office were tinted a dark charcoal gray and even then he generally kept the shades activated. Computer screens glowed eerily from dark corners. The only light was above Robison's desk and he had it situated so that it shone brightly on the face of the person in the chair opposite his desk. The odd shadows cast by the single bright light and the glowing computer screens gave the room a secretive air, or so Petronella had always imagined. The darkened room always gave her an adrenaline rush, always made her work—which was usually mundane, often uninteresting, and sometimes just plain grubby—seem more exciting than it really was.

She shut the door behind her and walked quickly to stand in front of Robison's desk.

"I know you have another appointment, sir. This won't take long. I didn't want to send it through the usual channels—"

"Sit down, Agent Rizzoli," Robison said affably. "My next appointment can wait a few moments." He grew more serious. "What is it? What have you found out?"

"A lot, sir," said Petronella, sitting in a chair across from Robison's desk. She kept her voice low, despite the fact that the room was sound proofed, and drew her chair closer. "For starters, you were right. Dalin Rowan is Darlene Mohini. I met her, talked to her."

"Excellent. Where is she?" Robison activated his electronic notepad.

"I met her on Adonia, along with the rest of the team, at the chateau of one of the team members, Raoul de Beausoleil."

"Expert poisoner," Robison said, bringing up the file with a touch of his hand on the nearby computer console. "Used to work for the late Snaga Ohme. We suspected him in the poisoning of the wife of the president on Modena, but we couldn't find enough evidence to make a case."

He paused, lips pursed, staring at a vid shot of Raoul, who would have been highly flattered by the attention.

"I assume you have Rowan stashed away somewhere safe. I'd like to talk to her. If you could—"

"Sorry, sir," said Petronella, "but Rowan refuses to co-operate with us."

"The devil she does!" Robison frowned.

"You can't really blame her, sir," Petronella said. "There've been two attempts on her life. Which reminds me, sir, did you have me followed?"

Robison snorted. "Why would I have you followed, Agent? No, of course not. What made you think that?"

"Someone came to de Beausoleil's house, pretending to be a pool cleaner. The Adonian spotted him and he ran—"

"Probably another Hung assassin."

"Yes, sir. That's what they thought at first, but that telepath of theirs claimed that the man was following me."

"Did you spot him when you drove to the house?"

"I . . . uh . . . forgot to check, sir," Petronella said, flushing. "It's just that . . . no excuse, sir. I'm sorry."

"What made you believe this telepath of theirs?" Robison asked acidly.

"Well, sir, Rowan suggested that it might have been Amadi, and I must say that I agree with her. After all, I did discover those files—"

"If you were followed, which I very much doubt, then that must be the answer. Which means that Amadi suspects you. You'll have to be more careful from now on."

Petronella swallowed the rebuke in silence.

"Now," Robison continued, "as to Rowan, we could offer her protection—"

"Begging your pardon, sir, but Rowan knows that someone high up in the Bureau is tied in to the Hung. She knows that we can't guarantee her protection and that she's a lot safer with her mercenary friends than she would be with us. She knows about Amadi, sir," Petronella finished.

Robison shook his head and swore softly. "Son of a bitch. They're all in this together."

Petronella was troubled. "That means that Rowan and Tampambulos set up their friend Ito to die. I find that hard to believe, sir."

"Don't be naive, Agent!" Robison snapped. "Ito found out about them and they had to get rid of him. Just like they got rid of Armstrong."

"But Tampambulos was in that factory, too, sir—"

"So their plan went awry." Robison was impatient. "Consider this. Tampambulos is carrying the bomb. He plans to stash the bomb in the factory, knock Ito unconscious, leave him there, and escape. Tampambulos explodes the bomb, blows up his partner, and claims that Ito was caught in a booby trap. Instead, the bomb goes off before Tampambulos can escape and he ends up critically injured. Rowan feels the heat and decides to turn on her former employer, the Hung. She doesn't do any real damage, however. Maybe she and Amadi and the Hung had it all arranged. When the heat's off, she and Tampambulos get back together again. Amadi's there to welcome them home and they take up where they left off."

Robison gave her a shrewd look. "We have information that a large sum of money has been deposited in the Mag Force 7 account."

"Tampambulos was transferred to Jango, where the Hung leaders are imprisoned," Petronella said reluctantly, still not wanting to believe the ugly picture that was taking shape on her mental screen. She had found herself liking Darlene Rowan. She could still hear the pain in Rowan's voice when she talked about Ito's death. Hard to believe it was all an act. But what other explanation could there be?

"I'd say that clinches it," said Robison coolly. "He's there to break them out. Amadi suspects that you're on to him and he had Rowan try to throw you off the track."

"I suppose you're right, sir," said Petronella. "What do we do to stop them?"

Sam's voice came over the comm. "Sorry to interrupt, sir, but the Home Secretary is here—"

"I'm in an important meeting," Robison told him. "I'll be with her when I can break free." He was silent a moment, marshaling his thoughts, then said, "Get a Crown warrant and return to Adonia. Pick up Rowan. I want her in my office—"

"We can't arrest Rowan, sir."

"Why not?" Robison glared at her.

"Rowan's not on Adonia now. The team left on an assignment."

"You know where they went?"

"Yes, sir. I planted a listening device."

"Then get a warrant for whatever planet they're on!" Robison rose to his feet. The interview was at an end. "Thanks for bringing this information to me, Agent. You have your orders—"

"It won't be that easy, sir," Petronella protested. The chair beside her hopped and skittered. She laid a hand on it. "Rowan's gone to a planet called Del Sol. It's outside our jurisdiction."

Robison frowned. "Del Sol?" he repeated. His eyelids with their sandy lashes flickered. "Never heard of it."

"Not surprising, sir," said Petronella. "It's this little

dinky planet in the Rotarian Sector, a part of a hegemony known as the Seven Sisters. The trouble is that it's not part of the Empire. It's independent. We have no jurisdiction on that planet—"

"What are they doing on Del Sol?" Robison demanded abruptly.

"Apparently it's a job they took on before their leader was arrested. I'm not certain what they've been hired to do. They didn't discuss it."

"You're sure that's where they went?"

"Yes, sir. I followed them to the spaceport, saw them board the liner. It's a nonstop flight. I plan to check again to make certain they disembarked—"

"Don't bother," Robison said curtly. "It's too much trouble. We could never justify the expense. We'll find some other way of dealing with Amadi." He smiled at her. "Thank you, Agent Rizzoli. You've done a fine job on this case. I have something else in mind for you. I'll be transmitting the facts in a day or two."

"Is . . . is that . . . it, sir?" Petronella stammered, shocked. "Am I being taken off this case?"

"It doesn't seem that we have much of a case left, does it, Agent Rizzoli?" Robison returned, his tone cool with an irritated edge. "On your way out, tell Sam to connect me with the Home Secretary, will you?"

"Yes, sir." Petronella stood up, walked to the door. Halfway there, she halted. "If I've done something wrong, sir—"

She stopped talking. He was looking at the computer screen, deliberately ignoring her.

Petronella turned and continued to walk across the floor, which suddenly seemed to be as long and wide and empty as a spaceport tarmac. She was dazed by the suddenness of it all, puzzled and confused. Her face felt flushed; she was unsteady on her feet. All she could see was her career swirling around and around in the toilet, then vanishing down the drain.

And as far as she could tell, she'd done nothing wrong!

The door slid silently open. Petronella stumbled through.

She needed to sit and calm down, but not with the sympathetic eyes of the secretary on her. She managed a smile that felt tight enough to snap like a rubber band and stalked, straight-legged and straight-backed out of the office. She made it out of the building, found a small coffee bar, and sat down to recover from the shock. Only then did she realize she'd forgotten to give Sam the message about the Home Secretary.

Screw it.

Petronella ordered coffee, but by the time she got around to drinking it, the liquid inside the cup was cold. She was listening to voices, a great many voices, yammering in her head. Robison's dismissal, over and over. Her own voice, repeating everything she'd said, trying to determine just what the hell she'd said wrong; and another voice, saying something in the background.

The voice was trying to tell her something and she had to make all the other voices inside her head shut up so she could listen. She wasn't certain whose voice it was.

Robison's?

She went through his explanation of the facts again.

Her own voice? She hadn't said anything all that intelligent.

Darlene Rowan? Jamil? Dr. Quong?

Petronella closed her eyes, relaxed, and concentrated, and suddenly all the other voices fell silent. One voice spoke. Raoul's voice, interpreting the Little One, and it came to her with the scent of gardenia.

"*. . . the pool cleaner was, in reality, an Adonian private detective hired by someone—he's not clear who it was—to keep watch on you and to record what you said and to whom you said it.*"

That was it! That was what had been nibbling at her, like mice in her brain.

"If someone went to the trouble of hiring an Adonian private detective to spy on me," Petronella said to her coffee cup, which now held extremely cold coffee, "then someone had to have known *in advance* that I was traveling to Adonia. Amadi didn't know that! I didn't tell him. I didn't tell McCarthy or anyone in the office where I was going on my 'vacation.' "

Only one person had known she was going to Adonia. Her superior. Andrew Robison.

CHAPTER 25

You know my methods, Watson.
   Sir Arthur Conan Doyle, *The Crooked Man*

Petronella knew the moment she walked into her apartment that someone had been there, someone had searched it.

The place was just too neat.

The dwelling of a Talisian appears chaotic to most non-Talisians. Why bother to pick up articles and put them away when a whirlwind could strike at any moment? Whoever had searched her apartment and riffled through her drawers had left most of her things in standard Talisian disorder. The mags were still strewn about the floor of the living room. The teakettle was upended in a corner of the kitchen. But the lamp shade had been straightened, her bed made. Her underwear was in a drawer, not shoved under her bed, where it usually resided. A few pieces had even been neatly folded.

Petronella hurried to check her computer. Piles of papers littered her desk, along with a three months' assortment of sticky notes, game manuals, books, wadded-up Kleenex, half-full coffee cups, and warranty cards she was always going to fill out and send in. Someone had been here, spent time examining everything on her desk. Her apparently disordered piles had actually been in a sort of order—to her, at least. The recent stuff was on the top while the stuff that she'd meant to do three months ago was on the bottom. Now the three months stuff was on top and the immediate stuff, like a recent bank statement, was on the bottom.

Of course. They had been searching through her personal things for some key to her password, to break into her files.

Did they really think she was that incompetent? Did they actually believe she'd be stupid enough to write it down, leave it lying around?

The insult angered her almost as much as the violation of her apartment.

At least her files were safe, she thought, until she saw the cable neatly coiled beside the lamp.

The searchers hadn't been able to break into her files, and so they had simply copied them onto another computer and carried them off, to break into them at their leisure. They had made a complete electromagnetic copy. Analyzing it would provide them with all the data in the computer. All they needed was the encryption code. That would take time, but they'd crack it. They always did. She knew; she'd done it herself.

"Why?" she asked the computer.

"Hello, Petronella," the computer said brightly, activating at the sound of her voice and reciting its customary message. "Welcome back!"

"The computer was a lame-brained model, but it was all she had been able to afford after graduating from college. Her salary was such that she could afford better now, but she'd grown rather attached to this one, which suited her needs and, unlike some models she'd seen, didn't try to be her friend.

Right now, however, she could have wished for a computer that took a more active interest in her life.

"Computer," she began, knowing this was hopeless but forcing herself to try, "I need to know if anyone other than myself had access to my files." She went on to provide the computer with specified parameters, giving it the dates she'd been gone. "Who logged on during my absence?"

The computer did a brief search, then replied, "You logged on via a remote unit five days ago."

"Yes, that is correct. Next."

"You activated us yesterday, this location."

"No, I did not."

"Yes, you did," said the computer, adding in hurt tones, "You never believe me."

Petronella didn't bother to argue. She wouldn't win, and besides, she'd found out something interesting. Whoever had broken in had done so yesterday. Not earlier. Yesterday.

"What time did I activate you yesterday?"

"At 0100 hours," the computer replied.

Petronella made the time-difference calculations. The break-in had occurred almost exactly one hour after she had made her report to Robison.

He didn't waste any time. But then he was noted for his efficiency.

What the hell was going on? If he had a question, why not ask her?

Fighting the urge to leave the apartment, which didn't feel like hers anymore, Petronella went into the kitchen and punched up a pot of coffee. Whoever had been here had searched the kitchen, too, perhaps thinking she customarily stashed important information in the vegetable crisper.

Sipping her coffee, she tried to convince herself that it must have been Amadi who was having her followed, having her apartment searched, stealing her files. She almost had herself believing it, could even hear herself telling Amadi that she was going to Adonia. She wanted desperately to believe that he was the one at fault, not her respected and admired superior.

She was forced to face the fact that Amadi wasn't the person who had ordered the break-in of her apartment. If Amadi had wanted to do so, he wouldn't have waited for four days to do it. He would have broken in the moment he was certain she was off-planet.

So what did it all mean?

A crash came from the bedroom. In the living room, the recliner scooted back a foot and bumped up against the wall. The doors to all the kitchen cabinets swung open. Petronella wasn't aware of the disturbances. She concentrated on the puzzle, going so far as to note down the known facts on a paper towel.

Fact: Amadi had caused Xris Tampambulos to be arrested for the murder of Dalin Rowan.

Fact: Dalin Rowan hadn't been murdered. Dalin Rowan was alive and well, but wouldn't stay that way long if the Hung found her.

Fact: Xris Tampambulos knew he hadn't murdered Rowan, yet he went meekly off to prison.

Fact: The prison Xris Tampambulos went off to so meekly was the prison holding the leaders of the Hung.

Conclusion: Through coercion or some other means, Amadi was using Xris to break the Hung leaders out of prison.

Fact: Internal Affairs suspected Amadi, Tampambulos, and Rowan of being linked to the Hung.

Conclusion: Amadi, Rowan, and Tampambulos are linked to the Hung.

Problem: If Rowan is working for the Hung, why have they tried twice to kill her?

Problem: You have only Rowan's word that the Hung tired to kill her.

Fact: Rowan and the Mag Force 7 team have gone to a small, nonaligned planet, Del Sol. Exception: Harry Luck, pilot.

Fact: Harry Luck had not gone with them.

Petronella had checked their arrival at the spaceport through the cruise line and discovered that only six members of the team had arrived on Del Sol.

Query: Where is Harry Luck and what is he doing?

She put a question mark next to that and moved on to the next item.

Supposition: Robison is having me followed.

Petronella gazed at that long and hard and eventually altered it.

Fact: Robison is having me followed.

Fact: I reported to Robison that the team has gone to Del Sol.

Del Sol. She stared at the words, slowly underlined them. Her conversation with Robison had gone into the toilet the moment she'd mentioned Del Sol. She thought back, tried to remember his reaction. He was a nondemonstrative man, not given to hand gestures or displays of emotion. She didn't know him well, but she guessed that he was adept at concealing emotion. Talisians are sensitive to the energy emanations of others, perhaps because their own can be so destructive.

There had been a flow of energy between them prior to that moment, a flow that fairly crackled with excitement. When she mentioned Del Sol, the flow had decreased, and by the end of their conversation it had diminished altogether.

Fact: After I reveal what I know to Robison, my apartment is searched.

Conclusion: Unable to trust Robison. Unable to trust Amadi. Unable to trust Rowan.

Frowning, Petronella looked back over her scribblings. She put circles around three large question marks at critical points, then tucked the paper towel in her purse and, although it was after midnight, she left for the office.

Query #1: Jango.

"Warden Montieth?"

The man in the vid nodded coldly.

"I am Agent Rizzoli, FISA. You'll find my credentials in the upper right-hand corner of your screen. We have information that a prisoner, one Xris Tampambulos, may be plotting an escape for himself and three other prisoners: Becking, Mair, and Macdonald, if you—"

"Thank you, Agent Rizzoli." Warden Montieth spoke coldly.

He was an all-around cold bastard, Petronella decided. Cold voice, cold eyes, cold and lifeless expression. She got the shivers just looking at him.

"We have the situation well in hand," he added.

"Yes, sir," she said. "I was wonder—"

The screen went blank.

She crossed out one question mark on the paper towel.

Query #2: Jafar el Amadi.

Petronella scrolled past the date of birth, planet of origin, personal background of Jafar el Amadi. Under religion, Muslim, he described himself as a believer, but not devout. She read about the private schools, read about the university degrees—several of them. Cum laude. Salutatorian. Master's. Doctorate. FISA Academy. High ranking. Married fifty years, six children, fourteen grandchildren. Owned a dog.

Medical record excellent. No health problems. Always met weight requirements, physically fit and active. Belonged to a fencing club.

Service record: exemplary. Several citations for meritorious actions. Promotions; praise from superiors and co-workers. The one blot on an otherwise perfect record was a note to the effect that he had ordered his agents into a suspected Hung ammunitions factory, which had then blown up, killing one agent and maiming another. There had been an inquiry, some question as to whether or not Amadi should have obtained more information about the factory before ordering his men to enter it. The FISA panel investigating the matter could not reach a conclusion.

Amadi had devised the idea of sending Dalin Rowan undercover. Amadi, along with Rowan, was credited with having sent the Hung's three top leaders to prison. Following that, Jafar el Amadi had retired, with a full pension and many accolades. He lived quietly with his wife and dog in a upper-middle-class suburban neighborhood.

When several years later it was discovered that news of the Hung's demise had been greatly exaggerated, Amadi had come out of retirement—reluctantly, to judge by the correspondence on file.

According to Robison, Jafar el Amadi, a man who lived modestly, was a traitor raking in millions. Jafar el Amadi, who had dedicated his life—and who had, on several occasions, nearly lost that life in the line of duty—was helping criminals escape justice. Jafar el Amadi was a foolish man, a desperate man.

Now that she had studied his record, Petronella couldn't bring herself to believe it. Yet she was faced with the fact on her paper towel that he had been the one to arrest the cyborg on a charge that Amadi himself must have known wouldn't stick.

Petronella let that question mark remain where it was.

Query #3: Del Sol.

According to the reports of those who had been monitoring the cyborg during the time just previous to his arrest, he had been discussing the team's next job. That job was on the nonaligned planet of Del Sol.

Petronella read through the transcripts of the team's conversation about Del Sol, a conversation that had been recorded by surveillance, a conversation that had been interrupted by the arrest.

The team was going to help the oppressed dremecks overthrow a purportedly insane dictator. All this with the blessing of the Royal Navy, if not something more substantial. Tampambulos did not know the name of the person hiring him, only communicated with that person through a third party, and that only by coded transmission. Tampambulos obviously had a pretty good idea who this person was, however, otherwise he would not have accepted the job.

On questioning following his arrest, Tampambulos had refused to speculate as to the name of his mysterious employer and the arresting agents. Figuring logically that this had nothing to do with a ten-year-old murder, they had not pressed the cyborg for the information.

Petronella scanned through the statements taken from the rest of the Mag Force 7 team, but also drew a blank. They appeared to know even less about Del Sol than their leader. They had been hired to do a job and they intended to do it, unless FISA could find a law to stop them.

FISA either couldn't or wouldn't— perhaps also had some idea of the important personage who had hired the Mag Force 7 team. Xris Tampambulos was known to be a close personal friend of His Majesty the King and several of the king's ministers and advisers, including the powerful monarch Bear Olefsky and the Lord Admiral, Sir John Dixter.

Xris had gone to prison. The Mag Force 7 team had gone

to Del Sol. Was there some sort of connection? Or was it coincidence?

Petronella was about to log off when, on a hunch, she asked for a record of the name of the person who had last accessed this particular file. The holding computer came back with a security query. She typed in her log-in and password, then her position number at FISA.

The answer came back: Internal Affairs, Level One.

Somebody else besides her believed there was a connection, and that somebody came from the office of the director of Internal Affairs.

Petronella called up her travel agent and asked for the transport ticket prices to Del Sol. At the answer, her stomach heaved, her hands grew sweaty. My God, that was a lot of money!

"It's not part of the Empire," said the travel agent apologetically. "There's nothing of interest to do or see on the planet. We cater mostly to business people. Shall I reserve a seat for you?"

"I should let it go," Petronella muttered. "So what if someone searched my apartment and is right now probably reading through my personal computer files? It's not my problem. I've been ordered off the case. If I'm wrong, I'll lose my job and be in debt up to my ears.

"But if I'm right . . ."

She paused, sucked in a deep breath, and made a reflexive catch of the suddenly airborne staple gun.

"One round-trip ticket to Del Sol, please," said Petronella to the smiling travel agent, who could probably retire on the agency fee he'd earn from this one.

Petronella flashed her FISA I.D. "Earliest departure possible. The matter is urgent."

CHAPTER 26

You and what army?
American slang, circa twentieth century

"What do you mean, you won't fight?" Jamil demanded. "They're planning to exterminate you!"

"Am I not using the word *fight* correctly? Do you not understand me?" the dremeck known as the One, whose name was Marmand, asked anxiously, his face-folds twitching. "What I intend to say is—"

"You're using the word correctly," Jamil said grimly. "I know what you mean. What you mean is that you won't fight your own battles."

"We had never heard of 'battles' until recently. I did some research on them," Marmand explained, referring to warfare as he might have referred to some type of interesting, albeit disgusting bug he was investigating. "I have asked our human overlords to explain to me how 'battles' work, and from what I gather, we would make extremely ineffective battlers. We do not kill."

According to Quong, who was the only one who had taken the time to study the dremecks, Marmand was an elder of his race. His age was not readily apparent—the only difference between very old dremecks and very young dremecks appeared to be height, as far as Jamil could see. He could find no difference at all between the males and the females, but he presumed that the dremecks knew, which was all that really counted. All dremecks wore the same coveralls over their wrinkled bodies and they all wore some sort of glitzy jewelry. Once the jewelry had been the beautiful gems the dremecks mined. Those had all been taken away by the humans, replaced with cheap plastic.

Unlike the jewelry, the coveralls were not native to the race. The dremecks generally wore no clothes at all. The temperature in their underground burrows was constant, they were protected from the elements, and they'd had no reason to wear clothing until the humans arrived. The dremecks could understand why the humans wore protective covering—their skin was soft and flabby, easily punctured, burned, and blistered.

The dremecks could not understand why they themselves should wear clothes, which were not nearly as tough as their own skin and which required a lot more effort to keep clean. One human overlord had endeavored to explain to the dremecks the concept of nudity and shame, but the dremecks remained baffled.

After speaking with Marmand at some length, Jamil came to realize that Marmand had more face-folds than the others and that all the folds seemed to be drooping, giving him the mournful air of a dyspeptic beagle.

"You'll shoot back quick enough when they are shooting at you," Jamil predicted. "You'll kill when they start killing your people."

"They have killed us," Marmand said with gentle dignity. "And we have not killed back."

"But . . . didn't that make you angry?" Jamil asked, amazed by this response. "Angry enough to lash out?"

"It made us feel very sad," Marmand conceded. "And there was some anger, particularly among the young."

He indicated several dremecks standing in a group nearby, a group who looked embarrassed. They shuffled their feet and seemed to wish that they had decided not to attend the meeting.

The conversation between Jamil and the One was being held in the open, in a large cleared area of the burrow, known as the Talk Room. All the dremecks not currently working in the mines were gathered here—several hundred, by Jamil's guess. He and Marmand and the rest of the team stood in the center of the domed rock room; the other dremecks formed neat concentric circles around them. The acoustics of the underground Talk Room were so good that the dremecks in the last circle could hear just as well as those in the front row.

"Do you mean that the young dremecks want to fight?" Jamil asked, his spirits improving. He could work with this.

"No, the young wanted to run off into the outback and hide," said Marmand. "We persuaded them that this was not a wise course of action. There are several thousand of us. I think our presence here in the mines would be missed, don't you?"

Jamil grunted glumly. "Yeah, maybe."

"And then the Uglies would come searching for us in anger and many more of us would be killed."

Jamil stared hard at the young dremecks, hoping that he might see some signs of murderous rage barely held in check.

The young dremecks, seeing him look their direction, grinned at him—sending their face-folds into amazing convolutions—and wiggled their fingers in what he had come to know was a dremeck form of greeting.

Jamil sighed deeply and turned back to Marmand, who was regarding him with sympathy.

"I am sorry. We appear to be a disappointment to you."

"I don't understand you people," Jamil said accusingly. "You let yourselves be treated like animals—worse than animals, for the humans let their pet dogs ride on their comfortable, luxurious trains, while they force you to travel in what were once termed 'cattle cars.' They have enslaved you. They make you perform menial tasks for no pay. They chain you together like criminals. They beat you. Now they're planning on slaughtering the lot of you and you won't fight to save your own lives?"

"Oh, we do not like the Uglies," Marmand said, "present company excluded." He gave a bob of his head, which sent the face-folds flopping. "Although we do like some of the things the Uglies have brought to us. The Burrows That Reach Into the Sky, for example, are quite remarkable. Not that we would want to live in them, but we like to see them. We wouldn't even mind if the Uglies continued to remain here, but we don't want to be their slaves anymore. Nor," he added as an afterthought, "do we want them to— how was it you put that—'space' us.

"But," Marmand continued, "I do not see how killing

them will stop them from killing us. If anything, it will make them angrier."

"No, it will make them respect you. If you dremecks band together and fight the Uglies, they'll listen to your terms," Jamil argued.

"You are saying that you humans have no respect for us because we do not want to slaughter you?" Marmand was asking for clarification.

"If you want to put it that way," Jamail answered harshly, "yes. I'm sorry, but that's the way it is."

"Do not be sorry. We understand. Humans are good killers. You kill your food before you eat it. You kill each other. And that is why we have brought you here," said Marmand cheerfully. "*You* humans will fight for us!"

"You want me to risk my ass for your cause?" Jamil asked, stunned. "While you hide here in your burrow, safe and sound?"

"You appear to be upset. Is that wrong?" Marmand seemed confused.

"Yes, it's wrong," Jamil stated.

"But how can that be? You humans do this all the time," Marmand protested. "The overlord explained it to me. You always hire others to fight your battles for you. You call them 'soldiers.' Is that not true?"

Quong chuckled. "He has you there, my friend."

"Whose side are you on, Doc?" Jamil demanded angrily. "If you can't help me, maybe you should just pack up your medical kit and go home! And take Miss Universe there with you!"

"My, we're in a mood today, aren't we?" Raoul said. He had his feet propped up on a packing case and was painting his toenails with red lacquer, much to the delight and admiration of about twenty dremecks, who were gathered around to watch.

"Jamil . . . Doc . . . This isn't helping," Darlene admonished. She put her arm soothingly around the Little One, who was withering in the hot winds of anger swirling through the group.

"I am sorry, Jamil," Quong apologized. "I will do what I can, although I must confess the situation does not appear promising. Somewhere something was miscommunicated.

The dremecks don't want to *be* soldiers. They want to hire soldiers."

"Excuse us a moment, will you?" Jamil said to Marmand. "Conference. Everyone." He glared at Raoul, who started to protest that he would mess up his toenails. Seeing Jamil's dour expression, Raoul stood up and walked gingerly on his heels—wads of cotton stuck between his toes.

Jamil led his team to the part of the burrow that had been designated their living quarters. The burrow was honeycombed with these small caverns, which is where the dremecks lived. They did not live in family groups, but were grouped together by age.

"Time is running out," Jamil said to them. "Kirkov's birthday is thirteen days from today and—"

He stopped, glared at Tycho, who was nodding and smiling. "Turn on your translator!"

Tycho nodded and smiled.

Jamil glowered. "I said, turn on your translator!" He pointed.

Tycho, looking guilty, hastily switched it on. "Sorry, Jamil. I keep forgetting."

"We were supposed to act as military advisers to an army," Jamil continued. "Now I find out we *are* the army! What are we supposed to do? Fight the whole damn war by ourselves? Is there any way we can get hold of Xris?" He looked hopefully at Darlene.

"It would be difficult," Darlene said. "And what good would it do? Xris can't help us. Not from prison."

"He might be able to contact the person who hired us."

"We all know who hired us. Someone *very* high in the court," Darlene emphasized "Very, *very* high. And if we approach this person about this job, my guess will be that this person will deny ever having heard of us *or* the dremecks."

Jamil sighed and shook his head in wordless exasperation. He massaged, ineffectually, his aching neck and shoulders. "The question is, what do we do now?"

"I have a question." Raoul raised the nail polish. "Why didn't the king—"

"We don't know that," Darlene interrupted.

"I beg your pardon. Why didn't this very, very high-level court person hire an army, if that's what is needed?"

The Little One twitched one shoulder and gave his nose a violent rub.

"Thank you," Raoul said to his friend. "Now that you explain it, I understand."

"I'd be interested to hear that answer," Jamil stated.

"Would you?" Raoul appeared pleased. "The Little One says that His Majesty the King must not seem to be in the business of overthrowing the governments of other worlds, particularly those worlds that are not in the Empire. No matter how badly they need overthrowing."

"That makes sense," said Quong.

"Of course it does," said Darlene. "If the Dremecks themselves overthrow the dictator, His Majesty is observed watching the game from the sidelines, applauding politely. He steps forward after it's all over to present the trophy and his congratulations, then the Royal Navy comes in to sweep out the stands and dismantle the goalposts."

"Which is all fine except that now we have the dremecks watching the game from the sidelines, applauding politely!" Jamil growled.

"Why don't *we* hire an army?" Raoul suggested. He sighed. "I've longed to be a soldier. Tight-fitting uniforms . . . large guns . . ."

"Do you have any idea how long hiring an army would take or the logistics involved or the money it would cost?" Quong asked, amused.

"Not to mention the fact that we're back to obfuscating the high-level people," Tycho pointed out.

"*Implicating* high-level people," Quong corrected. "Though the other might also apply."

"Thank you, Doctor." Tycho changed color with pleasure, his skin deepening to a rich brown. "It would be said, and rightly so, that those at the top are the only ones who have the money and the means necessary to bring in an army."

The Little One shrugged his shoulders and lifted his hands to the air.

"You are wrong, my friend," Raoul said in a stern tone which caused everyone to regard him with amazement.

"We cannot simply pack up and go home. We cannot leave these poor dremecks to suffer under this oppressive regime."

"Raoul, I'm proud of you," said Darlene, impressed. "I didn't think you'd care about them."

"Not care!" Raoul's eyes opened wide, carefully, so as not to disturb his mauve eyeliner. "Not care! My dear Darlene, any dictator who would force people to dress in those . . . those ill-fitting, shapeless, and dingy coveralls"— he shuddered—"should not only be overthrown but should be made to wear Harry's suit for a year as punishment."

"I agree with Raoul. Not about the coveralls," Quong amended hurriedly. "But that it is our duty to help these people. I find the fact that they refuse to kill even in their own defense quite commendable. Humanity would be better off if we had evolved believing in a similar credo."

"No, we'd all be living in burrows beneath the ground," Jamil countered. "But I agree. I'd like to overthrow this Kirkov. Not only for the stake of the dremecks, but because the humans on Del Sol—the ordinary humans, not the ones aligned with His Eminence—don't have life so great. The wire-heads watch and listen and spy on every thought."

"And we should not forget that we are being paid handsomely for this assignment and that we will lose a lot of money if we quit," Tycho observed.

"You remind me so much of your brother," Quong said in emotional tones.

"Thank you." Tycho nodded and smiled.

"Perhaps we could convince the humans to join the fight," Darlene suggested. "They're not happy about the current situation, at least the ones I saw at the spaceport."

"They won't. Why? Because they're scared," Jamil said flatly. "Good and scared. You saw them skulking around with their heads down, afraid to look directly at anything in case they might be looking at the wrong thing. Kirkov's smart. He doesn't shoot rebels or throw dissidents in prison. He ships them off-planet with bad job references and worse credit ratings. They're ruined financially; they lose their homes, their families break up. Shooting them would be the quick way out. And so, to keep living the good life, these people have to support him. And they don't dare cause trouble."

"But if we could persuade the dremecks to rebel," Quong suggested, "then the humans might join them."

"Maybe." Jamil was skeptical. "But that's one hell of a big *if*."

"War of the Worlds," said Darlene.

They all stared at her.

"War of the Worlds," she said excitedly. "I read once that on ancient Earth, actors performing a play that was being broadcast by radio actually convinced people that they were under attack by aliens from Mars. There was panic. People armed themselves. Some even committed suicide, rather than let the aliens capture them."

"Considering that at the time the only life to be found on Mars were one-celled organisms, this was quite a feat," Quong observed.

"Isn't that interesting," Jamil said sarcastically. "Now that we've played a round of Media Trivia, can we get back to the problem at hand—"

"But that's the answer," Darlene said insistently. "We stage a made-for-vid revolution."

Jamil scowled and Tycho's hand hovered uncertainly near his translator. Only Quong appeared interested, but that may have been from a medical standpoint. Raoul was waving his hands over his toenails to induce them to dry.

Darlene carried on, undeterred. "We convince the inhabitants of Del Sol that the dremecks are staging a *coup d'etat*. We don't have to hire an army. We train the dremecks to act like an army. The first thing we do is capture the vid station—"

"Now, wait a minute," Jamil cut in. "Kirkov knows the dremecks. He knows that they're pacifists. He's not afraid of them—"

"Yes, he is!" Darlene stated emphatically. "I'll bet my share of this paycheck on it. Most beings in the galaxy are naturally xenophobic. We're afraid of all foreigners, of anyone different from ourselves."

"I know that I find most of *you* extremely frightening," Tycho said helpfully.

"Think about it," Darlene continued. "That long-ago

actor caused people to fear aliens they had never even seen! Humanity hasn't changed that much over the centuries, unfortunately. The guards at the airport carry stunsticks when they guard the dremecks, keep them chained together. If they're not afraid, then they're nervous."

"Guilty conscience," Quong added succinctly. "The dictator of Del Sol and his followers know deep down that they themselves would rebel should they find themselves in a situation similar to the one in which they have placed the dremecks. Kirkov expects the dremecks to rebel, for it is what he would do himself. He will readily believe it when it happens."

"The first thing we do is capture the vid station," Darlene explained. "At the same time, we slip into the dictator's palace, take him and his entourage hostage. Hopefully, since we have the element of surprise, we can accomplish this without bloodshed. Once we have the vid station, we broadcast vid shots of the dremecks marching victoriously through shopping malls and down the main streets of town."

"I think you're on to something, Mohini," Jamil admitted. "The only problem is, how do we force Kirkov to relinquish control? We're going to have to act fast, while everyone's off balance. If this revolution drags on a long time, people are going to figure out the truth—that it was all a sham."

"We could threaten to kill him if he doesn't surrender power," Tycho suggested.

Quong shook his head. "I have researched this man Kirkov. He is a bully and a tyrant and, some believe, a megalomaniac. He will not surrender under a mere threat of force. A threat which we are not prepared to carry out."

"Oh, yes, we are," Jamil said emphatically. "I'd be glad to make him see the light, so to speak." He patted his lasgun.

"Xris already ruled that out, remember? Killing Kirkov is not the answer," said Darlene. "He has a successor and loyal followers. "We'd have to kill all of those people, as well."

"Then we would lose the dremecks," Quong stated. "They would never permit a bloodbath."

"Speaking of actors—" said Raoul.

"We weren't," Jamil snapped, in no mood for the dreamy ramblings of the Loti.

"Speaking of actors," Raoul continued, plucking wads of cotton from between his toes, "I have seen pictures of this Kirkov—you can't miss them. He has plastered them all over the city. There was even one in the little boy's room at the spaceport and I saw another as we entered the mine shaft. He is really quite handsome. His uniform fits him superbly. I should like very much to meet his tailor, if that could be arranged. However, that's not the point, which was . . ."

Raoul paused, thoughtful.

"Thanks, Raoul. Give me a call the next time you're in town," Jamil said. "Now, look, Doc, what if—"

The Little One waved his hands frantically and stomped his feet. He pointed emphatically to Raoul, who had just recaptured the butterflies in his head.

"I have it! We were speaking of actors. And I remember thinking, 'That dictator fellow. He looks rather like Rusty Love, not counting the hair and the teeth and their physique. Other than that, the two could be twins. Perhaps they are. A good twin and an evil twin.' So you see," Raoul said, regarding them limpidly from beneath gold-shimmered eyelids, "that's the solution."

"What is?" asked Darlene.

"We don't shoot the dictator fellow," said Raoul, patient with the slow learners. "We snatch him, bag him, and put Rusty Love the actor in his place. Rusty Love surrenders power to the dremecks. Then he steps into the gondola of the balloon and floats off—I saw that in an old vid once and it was quite effective. We film the balloon ascension with the cams and show it to all and sundry on the evening news with follow-up coverage on the morning talk shows. As for the dictator fellow"—Raoul's hand fluttered—"once he provides me with the name of his tailor, you may do what you like with him."

The Little One clapped his hands and then gestured proudly at Raoul, as if he were presenting him to cheering crowds. The rest of the team gazed at Raoul in stunned, even awed silence.

"You know," said Quong at last, "Kirkov *does* look a lot the actor Rusty Love. Now that you mention it, the resemblance is quite remarkable. And the parts that don't work could be overlaid with makeup. Raoul, that is a brilliant plan."

"Thank you," Raoul replied modestly. "I thought it up all by myself."

"The Loti may be on to something," Jamil admitted. "Of course, we can't get Rusty Love, but there must be some tall, handsome, blond hunk in the city who would—"

"If you want Rusty Love, you can have him," Raoul said. Having finished with his toes he was painting his nails the same shade of red.

"I suppose you know him," Jamil retorted bitingly. "And I'm sure he'd be glad to drop everything he's doing and travel to some remote part of the galaxy to do you this little favor."

"Oh, yes." Raoul was complacent.

"And what would it cost us?" Tycho demanded. "According to my calculations, we have only five thousand eagles left for extraneous expenses. If we go over that, we cut into our profit margin."

"So like his brother," Quong murmured.

"It won't cost us a thing," Raoul said, daintily dipping the brush into the bottle. "He will be only too happy to perform this small task for me. He is an Adonian, you know."

"And he'd go to all this trouble to free some dremecks from slavery?" Jamil asked skeptically.

Raoul smiled, smoothed polish on his index finger. "Let us say that he would go to all this trouble for *his* master. Rusty Love was once *my* slave."

CHAPTER 27

The quietly pacifist peaceful
always die
to make room for men
who shout. . . .

Alice Walker, "The QPP"

"That's the plan," said Jamil. He looked intently at Marmand. "Can your people handle it?"

Marmand didn't respond immediately. Jamil didn't want him to. Jamil wanted the dremeck leader to consider every angle, to make certain he understood what he was committing to before committing to it.

"We wouldn't be expected to really use the weapons," Marmand said. "Just march around with them."

"And sometimes point them at people. Don't worry," Jamil added, seeing Marmand look unhappy, "we'll make certain that the beam rifles can't possibly harm anyone, unless maybe you clobbered someone over the head with one. They'll be like toy guns, like the ones the human children play with. They'll just *look* real."

Marmand shook his head sadly. "Humans teach their young to kill. You must know that to even pretend to do harm to another living being would be extremely repugnant to us."

"Well, then, we'll just pack up and go home," said Jamil, losing patience. "And you and your children can see how long you can hold your breath in the vacuum of space, which won't be that long because the cold will be so intense it'll probably crystallize your blood unless your bodies explode due to the sudden change in pressure."

"You think we are being difficult," Marmand said, with

a deprecating smile that caused the sagging folds of his cheeks to lift momentarily. "I have not said that we would not do what you require of us. I simply wish to point out how hard it will be for some of our people to do what you ask. I don't suppose that you, for example, could strangle a human baby with your bare hands."

"Of course not," Jamil said shortly.

"Or even pretend to do so?" Marmand persisted.

"Well . . ." Jamil hesitated.

"You see? Even pretending to commit such a heinous act would make you uncomfortable, wouldn't it?"

"Change requires sacrifice," said Jamil. "The price of freedom and your lives comes high. Even pretending to use these weapons will put your people in danger. If you point a gun at someone, you've got to expect them to figure you mean it. I'm hoping that the sight of a few hundred armed dremecks will cause most humans to join up with us, but I can't promise that none of your people will get hurt or that they won't inadvertently hurt someone."

"Perhaps we could negotiate with His Eminence," Marmand suggested pleadingly. "Assure him that we are not a threat to him, that we will remain his slaves, if that is what he wants."

"Is that what *you* want, Marmand?" Jamil asked grimly. "Think it over. How do you think it makes your children feel when they see their parents chained together and led off by human guards with stun-sticks? You're saying to your children, 'We're not equal to the humans. We're a menial, subservient race. We don't deserve to hold our own beliefs or to pass on those beliefs to you. We are slaves, we were meant to be slaves, we will always be slaves. You children and your children's children will be slaves because we adults don't care enough about you to struggle for your freedom.'

"Is that how you think, Marmand?" Jamil concluded. "Is that how your people think? Have they completely lost all self-respect? Because if that's true, then there's nothing I can do to help you. There's nothing an army of hired guns could do to help you, because you're not willing to help yourselves. Even if an army did free you, you would still be slaves."

Marmand was thoughtful, sadly thoughtful. The face-folds seemed to sag down to his knees. At length he sighed. "I have watched our little children playing at being slaves. They chain themselves together with lengths of rope and are led off to 'work' by children playing the overseers." Marmand looked directly at Jamil, the liquid eyes round and intent and filled with pain. "The most coveted position in this 'game' was that of the human overseer. The winner got to be the human. The losers were the dremecks."

Jamil had to bite his tongue to keep from saying something sympathetic. This story was a powerful reinforcement of his own arguments. He kept his mouth shut.

Marmand sighed again. "You could not have known this, of course, but one thing I have noticed about you humans—even the worst of you—is that you have a most frightening way of digging up those thoughts we most want to keep buried. You do this to each other and torture each other quite effectively."

"Yeah, and sometimes we help each other, too," Jamil said gruffly. "And that's all we want to do. We want to help."

"And earn your fee, which is substantial," Marmand added with a slight smile.

"*You're* paying our fee?" Jamil asked, amazed.

"A portion of it," Marmand replied. "Along with another party."

"Do you know the other party?" Jamil was intensely curious.

"An anonymous benefactor," Marmand answered with a twitch of his face-folds. "We honestly do not know who it might be, though we have our suspicions."

Jamil grunted. "Yeah, us, too. Do you"—he paused, glanced around to make certain that none of the rest, Tycho especially, could hear him—"do you have the money? Because if you don't, we could make an arrangement—"

"No, no. Money is not a problem." Marmand waved his hand to brush away the unspoken offer. "We have resources. The humans would say that we have been stealing from them, but the diamonds were here before the humans were and so we do not consider the appropriations we have made to be theft. Also, we have been told that if we succeed in overthrowing this current government and replacing it with one of our own, we will have the ability to seize the money that is kept in the steel-lined burrows and use that to aid our people."

"Nationalize the banks." Jamil nodded and made a mental note to call his broker and make certain he didn't have any funds in Del Solian banks. "That's true, although you're going to make a lot of humans out there very upset. Still, I don't suppose you really care about that, do you?"

"Not much, no," Marmand said, and the face-folds rippled in a wide smile, which very quickly vanished. "Our people will do what you want. The young are especially eager to be free of the humans and"—he sighed deeply, so deeply that the sigh seemed to come from far beneath the ground, where the dremecks lived and worked—"we will pretend to fight."

He shook his head sadly, the face-folds flapping back and forth. "We may be saving ourselves, saving our race from extinction, but if this rebellion changes us, changes who and what we are, then I think those who come after us may look back and curse us."

"Your culture has survived for centuries," Jamil said, vastly relieved. "I don't think a few weeks of military training and a couple of mock battles will affect it."

"Military training." Marmand repeated the words with dread. He shuddered. "What happens if our young come to enjoy it?"

Jamil grinned. "With me in charge? I don't think that's likely!"

The training of the first and hopefully last dremeck army began the next day. Jamil studied various locations to hold his drills and finally chose a gigantic cavern in a played-out diamond mine located about two hundred meters below ground level. Kirkov's surveillance satellites would not detect them down there. Quong went over the cavern with his equipment to make certain that the humans had not left behind any listening devices.

Darlene began trying to find ways to invade the Del Solian government and military computers. She didn't have to delve deep into the systems, just deep enough to plant viruses that would, in two weeks' time, bring the military and government computer networks to their knees. This done, she was planning to tour the vid station and return with a detailed map and access into their computer files.

Raoul contacted Rusty Love's publicist, who put him in touch with Rusty Love's agent, who thought it all quite ludicrous and refused to admit to Raoul even that Rusty Love was alive, much less where to find him. After much persuading and a bribe of a case of Adonian champagne, the agent agreed to pass the message on to Rusty Love that an old friend was attempting to get in touch with him, and that was the best the agent would do.

The date for the video-revolution was set for twelve days hence, on a night known to the dremecks as Rock Slide Night, commemorating some dire event in dremeck history.

Jamil's immediate problem was how to pull two hundred able-bodied dremecks from the workforce without arousing their overseers' suspicions. The team members, with the exception of Raoul, were passing themselves off as sociologists and cultural anthropologists, engaged in studying the dremecks. Raoul had offered to appear in the guise of cultural anthropologist, but once it was explained to him that this had nothing to do with skin care products, he had decided it would be better if he were to say he was here to visit Del Sol's galaxy-famous diamond merchants. His story could always be altered to fit the Rusty Love scenario, and thus Raoul and the Little One had taken a room in the city's most expensive hotel. Their visits to the burrows were under the guise of wanting to see the diamonds in their natural setting.

These were the stories the team members had given the wire-heads during their routine interrogation at the spaceport. In addition, Dr. Quong had made an erudite and didactic speech to the overseers the first day of the team's arrival at the burrow, managing to bore the overseers thoroughly and making them late for work. After that, the overseers had been careful to keep out of Quong's way, had even taken to fingering their stun-sticks when they saw him approach.

But that did not solve the problem of how to effect the

disappearance of two hundred members of the dremeck workforce. Quong and his team of "ologists" had been permitted to stay in the burrows only on the condition that their studies didn't take the dremecks away from their jobs.

It was Marmand who provided the solution.

"Humans can never tell us apart—" he began.

"I am extremely sorry about that, Marmand," Dr. Quong interrupted, embarrassed. "I had assumed that I was talking to you, when I discovered that the one to whom I was speaking was your mate. I did not mean to offend her. It's just that you dress alike and—"

"Please do not feel the need to apologize, Doctor," said Marmand gently. "We would probably find it hard to tell you humans apart, as well, except for the fact that your females have ugly protrusions on their bodies, which allows us to distinguish them from the males, and that all of you have a wide variety of skin colorations, to say nothing of the unsightly growth you encourage on your heads."

"I can hardly wait to tell Raoul," Jamil whispered, grinning.

Quong nodded. "Especially the part about 'unsightly growth.' Business before pleasure, however."

"The humans do not consider the elder among our species suitable for hard labor," Marmand was saying. "The elder dremecks, therefore, remain in the burrow and take care of the children or tend to the farming of our food supplies or perform other tasks that do not require exertion or endurance. The elders have volunteered to take the places of the young dremecks at work, so that their presence will not be missed."

"But won't that be hard on them?" Jamil asked. "I appreciate their offer, but two hundred elderly dremecks collapsing on the job would look about as suspicious as two hundred young dremecks reporting in sick."

Marmand's face-folds rippled in sly amusement. "You humans equate our elders with your own. The truth is that our elders are stronger than our young. Our bodies do not degenerate with age. The reverse happens, in fact. The bodies of the young are not fully developed; neither are their brains. They are weak compared to their elders, who are strong in order to care for them."

"Doc?" Jamil was dubious.

"I have noted that Marmand appears to be in excellent physical condition," Quong said, "but I had assumed that this was the reason he had been chosen as the One. Now it appears that Marmand is the rule, not the exception."

"Maybe we should put together an army of grandparents," Jamil suggested.

Marmand shook his head, the face-folds swaying from side to side.

"The elder are very much opposed to the idea of an army. They will do their part by taking the places of the young, but that is all they will do, and they are not happy about doing that much."

"They don't have to be happy, Marmand," said Jamil. "All they have to do is—"

"Excuse me," Quong interrupted. "Tell me this, Marmand: If you dremecks grow stronger as you age, are you immortal?" He took out a recording device and activated it. "Speak distinctly, will you, please?"

"Not now, Doc," Jamil snapped. "As I was saying—"

"No, in time we all will die—as you humans term it," said Marmand, seemingly relieved to be speaking of something other than the army. "Once a year, we enter the Birth/Death Cycle. That is when all dremeck children are born and, during that time, a proportionate number of elder dremecks die."

"What is the manner of death?" Quong asked. "I must assume that they don't commit suicide."

"Of course not." Marmand was shocked. "We had never even heard of such a thing until you humans arrived. The bodies of certain elder dremecks simply cease to function. The breakdown happens very rapidly, beginning with a weakness in the limbs and always resulting in death. Those affected sink gradually into a deep sleep, from which they do not awaken. We are aware of the onset of death about two days in advance and thus we have time to bid farewell to our loved ones before proceeding on to the next stage of existence."

"And the number of those who die corresponds exactly to the number of births?" Quong asked. "Fascinating. Absolutely fascinating. No other humans have done any studies on this? No, of course not. Because they do not know! You have kept the truth about the elders hidden! I will be the first to study this phenomenon. Excuse me. I must go and retrieve my instruments. You will not mind if I run a few tests, will you, Marmand?"

"Not now, Doc!" Jamil repeated loudly, his voice grating. "First the revolution, then the *Journal of the Galactic Medical Association.* I need you to start turning those beam rifles we brought into toys!"

"But this could be of great importance in scientific research into the aging process!" Quong argued. "This is the first race we have ever encountered that grows stronger as it ages, not weaker. My studies here may make medical history. If Xris were here, he—"

"Xris isn't here!" Jamil shouted savagely. "I'm here. And what am I doing? I'm going along with a plan thought up by an Adonian Loti whose remaining brain cells couldn't outfit an amoeba! I'm training an army of pacifists! I'm hiring a movie star to overthrow a dictator! I wish Xris was here, Doc! I wish to God he was here!"

Quong took a moment to let the outpouring of anger and frustration flow past him, then said quietly, "I am sorry, my friend. I spoke without thinking. You are right, of course. I will begin to dismantle the beam rifles."

"You do that, Doc," Jamil said, suddenly ragged-edged and tired. "God forbid we should actually kill anything."

CHAPTER 28

I was in prison, and ye came unto me.
The Bible, Matthew 26:15

The inmates of Jango were permitted two hours of recreation time before lights out. Some of the prisoners attended classes, some watched vids. Those who had enough energy left after work sweated out their frustrations in the gym. There were swim teams and boxing teams, wrestling teams and chess teams, bridge clubs, guest lecturers, and a group of would-be actors rehearsing for a production of *Our Town*. The golf league had been disbanded after it was rumored that one of its members had died of snakebite on the fourteenth hole.

Although the time was supposedly "unstructured," each prisoner was required to participate in one of the activities, which were designed to improve health both mentally and physically, according to the brochure. Xris's butt-beeper, as the devices were affectionately known among the inmates, would report his location to Command Central. He was supposed to be attending a class in Zero-Gee Calculus. He was going to be late to class today, however. Probably earn himself another ten demerits.

Changing out of his sweat-soaked clothes, he took a shower, making certain that one of the cell mates was in the room keeping watch. Not that he counted on them in case of attack, but they could at least scream. Nobody came around to shoot holes in his mattress. Coming out of the shower, Xris thanked Alan for standing guard duty, put on his sweatpants and sweatshirt, and left for class, making a small detour on his way.

Cellblock Five was located across the quadrangle from

Xris's cellblock, the third building of a second quadrangle. The rain had started again. Xris had been on this planet a week to the day and it had yet to stop raining for longer than twenty minutes. People didn't die on Jango; they mildewed. Those attending class were running through the downpour across the wide expanse of lawn toward the education building. Its lights shone brightly in the gray gloom, something the brochure would probably cite as symbolic.

Xris entered Cellblock Five, walked up to the security post that stood in the center of bisecting corridors.

"I need to see inmate Mair," Xris said respectfully.

The guard glanced up from his portable vid; he was intently watching a soccer match being played on some distant planet. Looking annoyed, he waited until a commercial break, then grunted. "He won't be there. This is rec time. What do you want to see him for?"

"I was worried about him," Xris said. "He fell and hit his head a couple of days ago and I heard he wasn't doing too well. Besides, he's got some notes I need for class. Look, sir, I'm late as it is—"

The guard shrugged. He wasn't the one who would be getting the demerits. Besides, the game was about to resume. He jerked his thumb at an electronic pad on the desk. Xris pressed his thumb on the pad, leaving behind a faintly irradiated imprint that quickly faded. Then he was off down the hall.

According to their laundry tags, Macdonald, Becking, and Mair shared the same room, located on the first floor. Xris walked down one corridor, turned right, and entered an adjoining hallway. He halted when he saw a small knot of men standing around a doorway. Although he couldn't be certain which room the doorway led to, he could make a pretty good guess.

Xris waited in the angle formed by the convergence of the two corridors while he decided on a course of action. His original plan had been to reconnoiter the corridor, determine the exact location of Mair's room, maybe even have a chance to talk to Mair, who—to judge by the T-shirt in his laundry—had lost a lot of blood and might not be feeling up to either physical or mental stimulation. Xris was still trying to decide how to introduce himself, wondering how to worm his way quickly into their confidence. He had come up with a few ideas, but so far he hadn't liked any of them. Now, however, God was smiling on him, giving his enemies into his hands. Or maybe it was Mashahiro Ito. Xris remembered reading about a ghost known as a revenant, who could not rest until it had exacted revenge on its murderers. . . .

Three men stood outside the cell door, blocking the entrance. They were probably supposed to be keeping an eye out for the guards, but they were too busy watching, with leering grins, whatever was happening inside. Xris recognized the three—the Master's flunkies. Judging by the sounds his augmented hearing was picking up, the Master was having a conversation with a gentleman who occupied that cell. A rather strenuous conversation, one punctuated with thumps and groans.

The flunkies were enjoying the show, weren't aware of Xris's presence until he peered over their shoulders into the room. The Master was inside the cell, enjoying his rec time talking with a short, tubby man with graying hair going thin on top. Becking, Xris guessed, by his shirt size.

The Master had hold of what little hair Becking had left. The conversation they were holding was rather one-sided. The Master pounded Becking's head into the concrete wall while he recited a litany, which went: "Tell me what I want to know." Thump. "Tell me what I want to know." Thump. "Tell me—"

Becking's face was covered in blood. He couldn't have answered if he'd wanted to, because every time he opened his mouth, the Master would bounce him off the wall again. The eye of the security cam roamed around the room, saw what was going on, but was apparently not interested.

As entertaining as all this was—Xris could have cheerfully watched Becking's head being used for racquetball all night—this was the perfect opportunity to ingratiate himself.

Xris placed his hand, his cybernetic hand, on the shoulder of the nearest and skinniest flunkie.

The man gasped, jumped, goggled.

"Excuse me," Xris said politely. "Would you mind stepping to one side? I need to get in there."

"You can go to—"

"Thank you." Xris lifted the flunkie off the ground and tossed him down the corridor. The flunkie slammed up against the wall, then slid to the floor with a groan.

"I only ask nicely once," Xris informed the other two.

They glanced at their crumpled comrade and backed off down the hall.

"Hey, Master," one yelled. "It's the Tin Man."

"Inaccurate and not highly original," Xris said, stepping inside the cell. "Mostly I'm plastisteel, but then I guess it would be too much to hope for you to have brains as well as beauty."

The Master looked around, annoyed.

"Fuck off, asshole," he said, and bashed Becking's head into the wall. "You and me'll settle what we got to settle later. This is none of your fuckin' business."

"Well, in a way it is," Xris argued. "I work in the laundry. Do you have any idea how hard it is to get bloodstains out of those cotton T-shirts? You're putting me to a lot of extra trouble. So why don't you let the man go."

Xris noticed that the security cam was now suddenly an interested spectator. Somewhere in the distance, an alarm was buzzing. Xris didn't have much time.

The Master grunted, made an obscene gesture, and turned away. He was in the act of knocking Becking's head against the wall yet again when Xris drove his cybernetic fist into the Master's stomach.

The Master was in excellent physical condition; Xris's clenched hand encountered solid muscle. But muscle is malleable and Xris's fist wasn't. The Master gasped in speechless agony and doubled over. A chop to the back of the neck drove the Master to his knees. Clutching his gut, he sucked air and glared at Xris in impotent fury.

Becking sagged down the wall and sat there, leaning his bloodied head against the bed frame. His eyes were alert, though shadowed with pain, and those eyes regarded Xris intently.

Xris was about to introduce himself when a blast from a stun gun hit him from behind and the only thing he met was the floor.

*   *   *

Opening his eyes, Xris thought at first that he was still inside his dream. He hoped he was still dreaming. A kaleidoscope of dazzling colors burst before his eyes, whirling and shifting, splitting and merging. Realizing he was awake, Xris panicked. He grabbed wildly for the sides of the bed, clutched them tightly, for he had the terrible impression that he was going to fall into this vat of swirling electric color and never emerge.

The panic subsided when a portion of his brain that wasn't engaged in running around screaming and banging on the inside of his skull told him to calm down. There was a rational explanation. Some of his optic circuitry must have been damaged. Fighting the nausea, he tried turning his head ever so slightly.

The colors vanished. He was looking at nothing more exciting than a gray wall in a very small room, a room with a single bed, a sink, a toilet, and a vidscreen in a corner near the ceiling. A force field bathed him in an annoying red glow.

Xris turned his head back and the fireworks display burst into view.

"Great!" he muttered, closing his eyes. "A broken connection somewhere. Either that or a crossed wire. Or maybe something pressing on a nerve."

He didn't know, couldn't begin to fix it, and there was no way to reach Dr. Quong, who was presumably on Del Sol by now, preparing for the revolution. Xris considered briefly having the medical staff at the prison examine him, but he put that thought immediately out of his head. They might find the little presents Quong had tucked inside Xris's leg.

Xris sat up, blinked, and the colors disappeared. Making a few experimental moves, he discovered that the fireworks display didn't begin as long as he remained upright and held his head relatively still. A wrong move, a too-quick turn of the head, another bump, and he'd find himself stepping into something akin to one of Raoul's more interesting flashbacks.

Xris opened a small panel on the inside of the wrist of his cybernetic arm, punched in the command to run a systemwide diagnostic program. He hoped it would locate the problem, fix it, and do so quickly. At least there was no one around to ask stupid questions or make imbecile remarks.

Solitary, Xris realized. They've put me in solitary confinement.

He rose gingerly to his feet, instinctively careful not to move his head. He walked over to the toilet, relieved himself. Returning to his bed, he glanced at the vidscreen and saw a man watching him.

The face of Robert Montieth, the warden, filled the vidscreen.

"If you are experiencing any discomfort, the full effects of the stun will wear off in about half an hour," Montieth informed him.

No, it wouldn't, but Xris couldn't tell this bastard that. Xris sat down on the bed and carefully tilted his head to see the screen.

"As you have probably surmised, you have been placed in solitary confinement," the warden informed him. "You have only been here a few days, Tampambulos, and already you've been involved in two incidents. First you attack a fellow inmate without provocation, an action that resulted in broken bones. I let that go with a warning, since that was your first day and I make allowances. But this second assault will be punished. You are a troublemaker and this is what happens to troublemakers."

Xris started to shake his head, thought better of it.

"I wasn't the one who started the trouble, sir," he said, sounding contrite. "The first time, that muscle-bound lunkhead tried to shake us down for our shoes. Next I go to visit some friends and I find him playing hockey using my friend's head for a puck. None of the guards seemed to care, so I did something about it."

"I'm afraid that explanation won't do, Tampambulos," Montieth said coolly. "Inmates Becking and Slovenski have both testified that they were having a quiet conversation when you burst into the cell and made an unprovoked attack. Their testimony is further corroborated by several other inmates who were witness to the disturbance and by the guard who was watching the security monitor.

"Further, I want you to know, Tampambulos, that inmate Slovenski is a model prisoner. His work for several charitable organizations has won him acclaim here at Jango. We are very proud of inmate Slovenski. All of us benefit from his efforts."

Some of us more than others, Xris thought. So that's why the guards are blind half the time. Slovenski's paying them to keep their eyes shut. And how much do you make off the shoe fund, Warden Montieth? Except that Slovenski's got to be handing out more than petty cash. It would be interesting to find out how he's making the big money around here.

Not that it's any of my business, Xris remonstrated with himself. I've got my own problems.

"You will spend fifteen days in solitary confinement, Tampambulos. I hope you will use this time constructively to rethink your attitude. You will be provided with vid-books and other educational material, of which I trust you will take full advantage."

The vidscreen went blank.

Fifteen days! Way past the deadline.

Xris laid back on the bed. He wasn't overly concerned. Once Amadi found out, he'd see to it that Xris was back on the job. In the meantime, Xris would catch up on his calculus.

Solitary meant solitary. If there were other prisoners around, Xris couldn't hear them or see them. Same with guards. There were no windows in his cell. The only way he could tell day from night was by the digital clock on the vid machine.

Dinner arrived in his cell via a automated conveyer system. A metal hatch on the back wall slid open, a food tray appeared. When he was finished, Xris touched a gray button. The door opened. Xris placed the tray on the belt and the door closed. The food served in solitary made the food in the cafeteria look like gourmet night in the best restaurant on Adonia.

Xris slept soundly—at least no one snored in solitary. The next morning he opened his eyes with trepidation and was relieved to see nothing more colorful than gray wall. He was deeply involved in his mathematics lecture, was actually enjoying it, when a voice interrupted his studies.

"Hey, you."

Xris peered through the red glow of the force field. A prisoner stood outside his cell, guiding an automated mop around the floor.

"Hey, you," repeated the prisoner in a low voice, with a glance down the hallway. "Come over here where I don't have to shout."

Xris cast a glance in the direction of the vid machine.

"Don't worry," the voice assured him. "They don't keep watch on you. Why should they? You're not going anywhere."

Xris stood up, approached the force field.

The prisoner plied the mop. He was a tall man with muscular arms and chest, thick dark hair, and a tanned face. The eyes were blue and unblinking, reminded Xris unpleasantly of the eyes of a corpse.

"My name's Macdonald." The eyes held a tiny flicker of interest. "What's yours?"

"Tampambulos. But don't worry about pronouncing it. Everyone calls me Xris."

"Do I know you, Xris?" Macdonald asked, staring.

Yes, you know me, you bastard, Xris said silently. You see this leg? It's there because you blew off the real one. See this arm? That's there for the same reason. You know Mashahiro Ito, too. And all the others you've murdered over the years.

"No, you don't know me," Xris said with a smile.

"You're a friend of Becking's, then?"

"No. I haven't had that pleasure. Mair either."

Macdonald's staring eyes narrowed. He hadn't blinked once during this conversation and Xris's own eyes were beginning to water in sympathy. "Then why did you tell the guard you were coming to see us? And why risk your own neck to save Becking's?"

"Let's just say that we have a mutual friend."

"Who?" Macdonald demanded.

Xris cast a significant glance at the vidcam.

"They're not paying attention. They never do. You're in solitary, for God's sake!" Macdonald said, adding impatiently, "I switched jobs with a guy today specifically to have this talk. I can't afford to do it two days in a row. Answer my questions."

Xris shrugged. "Amadi."

"Never heard of him," Macdonald said. The eyes still didn't blink.

"Oh, uh, sorry," Xris said. "My mistake. Make that Trevor. Archibald Trevor." This was the code name Amadi had given him.

"Why didn't you say so in the first place?" Macdonald snapped. "I don't play games, Tambompol." Evidently he wasn't as sure about not being overheard as he let on, because he glanced up and down the hallway, then asked quietly, "Are you the man Trevor hired for the job?"

Xris nodded. "And, as I said, you can call me Xris. I'm the one who's going to bust you out of here."

"When?"

"You've got to be patient, Mr. Macdonald. I have my own arrangements to make." Xris shrugged. The less anyone knew about his plans, the better. "You've been here ten years. I wouldn't think a few more days is going to matter much."

Macdonald finally blinked. Lines on his forehead creased and wrinkled. "Trevor gave you a deadline. I know because we gave Trevor a deadline. A week from tonight. Can you meet that?"

"Not while I'm in here," Xris said.

Macdonald was silent for a moment, shoving the mop back and forth, then he said grudgingly, "Thank you for helping out Becking. That bastard Slovenski. That's the second beating he's given Becking. I think he might have died if you hadn't come along."

Ain't that a shame. Aloud, Xris asked, "Is he okay?"

"Yes, a slight concussion. Nothing more serious, thanks to you."

Xris did his best to look sympathetic. "What's going on here anyway? Ama—Archibald gave me to understand that you fellows had a good thing going here on Jango. He showed me the brochures. I know something about the corporation you own," Xris said mildly, "and I know you've been running it and doing a damn good job with it for years. Now you're letting a muscle-bound thug push you around? What's the deal?"

Macdonald's face flushed with anger, while the blue eyes paled—an odd and unnerving contrast. In those corpselike eyes, Xris saw the man who could casually order the death of two federal agents in a weapons factory. The man who could send assassins to kill Darlene.

But the anger flashed and burned out, leaving only a middle-aged man looking slightly ridiculous holding on to an automatic mop. Macdonald even managed a wry smile.

"We ran the universe from our prison cell. You think I'm exaggerating? I'm not. There's only one organization who wields more power than we do, and that's the Royal Navy. People ask us how we can stand it, cooped up on this planet." Macdonald shrugged. "Hell, if you were making ten million an hour, you wouldn't mind shoving a mop around for it, would you?"

"I'm not sure that even ten million an hour would compensate me for a bed that would be more comfortable if it was filled with rocks, and food that makes rat poison look appetizing by contrast." Xris shook his head. "Not to mention a few other amenities, such as female companionship—"

Macdonald looked disgusted. "What did you think I was doing with some of that ten million? Saving for my retirement? We had a good thing here. *Once.*" He laid emphasis on the word. "Private cells, furnished and decorated. Our own gourmet chef. Playing golf every day. Little vacation trips now and then. And what safer place to run our operation? Whenever any of our plans went a little bit awry, we were never suspected. We had the perfect alibi! We're in prison!"

Macdonald grew bitter. "But all that changed. About six months ago. First that bastard Montieth was made warden. He began to make life miserable. He started small at first. He got rid of our cook. Then he shut down the golf course with that ridiculous tale about a snake. He forced us out of our private cells. I don't know how that bastard did it, but he managed to discover every guard we had in our pay and he got rid of them. Same with the inmates. They were either transferred to other facilities or given early release."

"I'm surprised that Montieth hasn't met with a little accident before now," Xris said.

Macdonald snorted. "Don't think we didn't try! He has shut down many of our lines of communication, seriously crippled our operations! He never goes anywhere near the prison facilities. He has four armed bodyguards. He doesn't eat or drink anything that's not analyzed first. Then, to make matters worse, that psychopath Slovenski gets himself transferred off death row and sent here!"

"He must be a rich psychopath."

"He didn't pay for it!" Macdonald snapped. "Montieth brought Slovenski here to make certain everyone stays in line. Slovenski beats people to a pulp and if you fight back, you're the one who ends up in solitary."

"Tell me about it," Xris said feelingly.

"He's beaten up both Mair and myself. I was in the infirmary three days with a broken nose and four broken ribs. Like I told you, that's the second time he's attacked poor Becking."

"It seems to me that the public would benefit if Slovenski's death sentence were carried out," Xris observed.

"We tried. The fellow we sent after him was our best man and he's in the hospital with a broken spine. Everyone's scared. No one'll touch him." Macdonald's eyes took on a hungry gleam. "Except maybe you. You're not scared. You've managed to do more damage to Slovenski in a week than any of our men did in three months."

Macdonald moved closer, his hands closed over the mop handle. "I hear you're a cyborg. Those cybernetic hands of yours—they could crush that thick neck of his easily."

Xris shook his head again.

"What's the matter?" Macdonald demanded. "You the squeamish type?"

"Let's say I'm the doesn't-plan-to-end-up-in-the-disrupter type. I may have to kill this bastard, and if I do, I do. But that's between him and me. If he leaves me alone, I'm not going to go looking for trouble.

"Look, sir," Xris added, seeing Macdonald's pale corpse eyes take on a dangerous life, "you hired me to break you out of here this time next week and that's what I'm going to do. What happens if Slovenski is found dead with a broken neck? Who are they going to suspect? And what's going to happen to me? I'm either going to be dead or locked up for fifteen billion years and where does that leave you? Sitting in your nice crowded cell with Montieth watching on the vidcam while his newest bully-boy uses your head to mop the floor. You can't afford to indulge in personal revenge, sir," Xris said, adding in tones low and solemn, "Too many people are counting on you."

Macdonald stood scowling, his hands white-knuckled on the mop. The blue eyes were still alive with rage and Xris was afraid that the man was too furious to listen to reason. But he hadn't become the head of a multibillion-dollar organization by having oatmeal for brains.

"You're right," he conceded, though Xris could see that it took a struggle to let go of his fantasy of Slovenski writhing on the floor with blood gushing out of his mouth. "Of course, you're right. I wasn't thinking." He was silent a moment, still enjoying the fading picture, then he said, "What do you want us to do?"

"Sit tight. I'll be in touch."

"You can't do much from in here," Macdonald pointed out.

"Don't worry. You get the word to Trevor that I'm stuck. He won't let me rot here for long," Xris said.

"I wouldn't be so certain," Macdonald growled ominously.

"Trevor got me sent to Jango, didn't he? He'll find a way around Montieth."

"I hope so."

Macdonald didn't sound convinced, and after he left, Xris had to admit he wasn't, either. He turned off the mathematics lecture and sat down on his bed to try to solve the more complex equations he was encountering here on Jango.

This warden, Montieth, risks his life to shut down the Hung's prison operation and then what does he do? He brings in his own personal attack dog. Of course. A minus B equals A+. Montieth minus the Hung equals Montieth's own profitable enterprise. Xris was willing to bet that most of the money from Slovenski's charitable enterprises was finding its way into Montieth's pocket.

Xris was divided. Part of him applauded the fact that

Montieth was making life miserable for the Hung—even if the warden did have his own personal agenda. Unfortunately, Montieth could get to be a real pain in the ass. He wasn't likely to take kindly to the fact that Xris had let everyone in this prison know that Slovenski could be hurt, that he was vulnerable. Montieth and Slovenski both were bound to retaliate, if only to prove to the rest of Jango that they were still in control. Montieth was quite capable of leaving Xris in solitary confinement and forgetting about him.

Not a pleasant thought.

Presumably, "Mr. Trevor" would solve the problem. Amadi must have something on Montieth. Someone has something on everyone. That's what makes the universe go 'round.

There was nothing Xris could do but wait.

And at least he wasn't loading laundry.

He laid down on his bed, put his hands behind his head, and wondered how his team was getting on with the revolution.

CHAPTER 29

For now I see
Peace to corrupt no less than war to waste.

John Milton, *Paradise Lost*

Seven days. Jamil had seven days to turn grazing dremecks, who never so much as squashed a fly, into what must pass on the vidscreen for highly efficient soldiers. Not only that, but he was going to have to give them a certain amount of training in self-defense, an unknown concept to the dremecks. He laid out a time schedule and a plan in his head as he descended into the depths of the burrow to his underground training center, traveling in the rickety metal cage the dremecks termed proudly their elevator.

Fortunately, Jamil was not claustrophobic. The ride down in the jolting, bumping, creaking cage was not pleasant, but then neither was the fiery descent through the atmosphere in a drop ship, and he'd done that often enough. Jamil allowed himself to think just once about the horrific fall he would experience if one of those cables—which appeared to have been installed somewhere around the time of Napoleon—broke. He allowed his stomach to shrivel at the thought, then firmly put the fear out of his mind.

He had enough other, more important, worries than the possibility of ending up smashed to a pulp at the bottom of a dremeck mine. He had trained raw recruits in his days in the Army, but those had been recruits who were expecting to learn how to kill the enemy. Now he was teaching recruits how to pretend to kill the enemy.

First Jamil decided he would conduct a little experiment. If the plan for the peaceful revolution went wrong—and Jamil always assumed the plan was going to go wrong—the danger wouldn't be pretend danger and he had to know if the dremecks were all likely to turn and run shrieking for their lives at the first sign of trouble. He and Quong had spoken with several of the younger dremecks and Jamil had been pleasantly surprised. He had the impression that the young dremecks were more militant than Marmand wanted to admit.

Jamil was under no illusions, however. Not even the most radical of the young dremecks would kill an arachnid if it crawled down his neck. Jamil had proof of that, because he watched Trella, a female dremeck, gently remove a large hairy and vicious-looking variety of that genus from her shoulder and place the spider carefully upon a flat rock.

Jamil's conscience jabbed him occasionally, but he told it to shut up. He had one consolation. Marmand wanted him to make sure the training was an experience the dremecks wouldn't enjoy.

Jamil could personally guarantee that.

The mine shaft was pitch-dark. Jamil had not thought to wear night-vision goggles and he couldn't see a thing—not the cage around him, not the walls, not the dremecks. He had an eerie sense of descending into time itself, and since he was thinking of revolutions, he wouldn't have been overly surprised if the cage door had opened up onto a bunch of old women seated around a bloody guillotine, knitting.

He was picturing the doomed aristocrats walking up the stairs when the elevator lurched to a stop with a suddenness that sent Jamil staggering. The rusty hinges of the cage door opened, emitting an ear-splitting shriek. Lights flared in his face, blinding him. He blinked, waited tensely for his eyes to adjust to the light.

"Where are we?" he asked, moving cautiously out onto a small platform of rock. "The center of the planet?"

"Oh, no, sir." Trella made a sound that Jamil had come to know as a dremeck equivalent of a chuckle. "We have to transfer to the other lift for the second descent. The cables aren't long enough to reach this far down."

Jamil took a step forward and banged his head on the crossbar of the cage. He cursed, ducked, and walked into the cavern, massaging his aching forehead. He'd have a lovely bump there tomorrow.

"I am sorry, sir!" Trella gasped. "I should have warned you!"

"No harm done. These . . . um . . . elevators weren't built for humans. I should have watched where I was going." Jamil entered the second cage.

Trella slammed the safety door closed and pushed the control over to the down position.

"Yes, sir," she said, subdued.

Jamil could see her in the lights of the platform. She hung her head, causing her face-folds to bunch up on her neck. Female dremecks resembled males in every aspect that Jamil could see, although Quong had assured him that the anatomy beneath the concealing coveralls was quite different. Jamil had taken Quong's word for it. He knew Trella was a female only because she had volunteered the information.

The cage began its descent: the lights soared up and away and soon they were in darkness again.

"By God!" said Jamil, in sudden understanding. "You did that on purpose! You *wanted* me to hit my head!"

"Not you, sir! Never! I should have warned you. I am truly sorry, sir," said Trella miserably. "It's just that we don't . . . I mean, with the other Uglies . . . the ones who aren't nice to us, like you . . ."

"No, no!" Jamil rubbed his hands. "Don't apologize! This is great! What you're telling me is that when the human overseers escort you into the mines, you 'forget' to warn them to duck. You deliberately let them wang their heads! I take it the One doesn't know about this?"

"None of the elders do," Trella said, her voice small in the vast darkness. "They would be very ashamed of us."

"Do you do anything else to harass the Uglies?" Jamil asked. "Dig holes in the cavern floor for them to stumble into or loosen rocks in places so they'll tumble down and strike the Uglies on the head?"

"They wear helmets," Trella said defensively. "It doesn't hurt them . . . much. And it makes us feel good, which is something we don't like to talk about, because it is wrong to feel good when someone else is in pain. The elders would be most unhappy if they knew. Unhappy and disappointed. It is a terrible thing to admit. I hope *you* are not very disappointed in us, sir?" she asked anxiously, having heard Jamil sigh. "So disappointed that you might leave?"

"I'm not disappointed in you dremecks,' said Jamil. "I'm disappointed in us, Trella. The Uglies. We did this to you and I'm sorry. I'm really sorry."

He was heartily ashamed of himself and all humans in general at that moment. They had taken gentle, peace-loving beings and taught them the sweet pleasures of revenge. He was going to take that training another step further. Maybe in a hundred years or so the dremecks would be happily flinging nuclear bombs at each other.

It was a damnable situation. He could tell himself that it wasn't his fault, that he wasn't corrupting the dremecks; they'd already been corrupted. But he sure as hell wasn't going to help matters any.

Do I have a choice? Jamil asked himself. Yes, of course. I can stop this godforsaken elevator, send it back up the shaft. I can walk away from this planet, walk away from the dremecks.

He could see the future clearly, as if the cage were now hurtling forward in time instead of backward.

Thousands of these people are going to die. Of course, I won't be here to see it. I won't know about it unless there's a report on GNN. And then I can shake my head and say sadly, "What a shame!"

Their innocence has already been destroyed. I can't give that back. But maybe I can teach them to use their new-found knowledge wisely.

The cage lurched again; this time Jamil was hanging on tightly to the railing, prepared for the jolt because he'd seen it coming. The cavern area was well lit with large nuke lamps, which the dremecks had probably stolen from work areas.

Trella opened the cage door and this time she warned Jamil about striking his head on the crossbar.

Stepping out, he felt as if he had truly been in some sort of time-travel machine. He was a much different person at the bottom than he had been at the top.

The two hundred young dremecks clustered in small groups, chatting cheerfully, eager and excited at the prospect of a holiday, for that's what this amounted to for them. As

Jamil approached, they turned from their conversations to face him. A low murmur, almost a growl, went through the crowd.

"What's the matter with them?" Jamil asked Trella, who was standing beside him. "Did I do something wrong?"

"They are cheering you, sir. I guess it doesn't translate well." Trella walked over to join the rest of the dremecks, who were all looking expectantly at Jamil, their face-folds taut with anticipation and enthusiasm.

Jamil cleared his throat, shouted to be heard over the low growling. "Thank you! I am glad to be here."

He had forgotten he was in a cave. The echoes that thundered back were quite startling, even to the dremecks, and he paused to allow the rebounding sounds of his own words to dissipate.

"We don't have much time, and so we are going to start work immediately," he said, speaking in a normal tone. "Can you all hear me? Good. Now, if you'll all gather around, everyone sit down, I'll explain the plan of action. . . ."

Half an hour later, he asked the dremecks if they understood what they were supposed to do.

Two hundred heads and innumerable face-folds nodded and flapped in answer. He asked for questions. There were none, probably because this was all so completely new and foreign to them they had no idea what to ask.

"There will be no killing," he said, and he repeated it. "No killing. I know that you don't believe in taking life and I want you to understand that I respect your beliefs. I don't want to do anything to cause you to change those beliefs or to doubt them. More important, I don't want any of you to get killed. I intend to strike so swiftly that the humans will not even consider fighting back.

"But if something goes wrong, you dremecks have to have confidence in yourselves. You have to know that you can handle the situation, even though all hell's breaking loose around you. That's what I'm here to teach you—that and a few military-type maneuvers which will convince the Uglies that you mean business.

"If you don't remember anything else about what I'm going to teach you today, I want you to remember one fact and I want you to concentrate on that fact. It is this: The Uglies are afraid of you."

The young dremecks made sounds expressive of disbelief.

"No, I mean it," Jamil insisted. "Think about it. The humans chain you together. They post guards to watch over you. They carry weapons when they're around you. Isn't that true? Why would they do those things if they weren't afraid?"

The young dremecks discussed his logic, turning to each other and talking in loud, excited voices. The babble ceased almost immediately and Jamil realized, when the eyes all turned back to him, that they all agreed and were pleased with themselves.

"We are going to use their own fear against them. Their fear will be our greatest weapon," Jamil said.

A ripple of doubt sent the face-folds twitching.

"Yes, what's the matter?"

Trella responded. "But *we* are afraid of the Uglies, sir. Won't they use that fear back on us?"

"They will if you let them." Jamil lowered his voice, crouched on his haunches, and made himself one of the group. "Look, I know about the 'fun' you've been having with your overseers. Rocks hitting them on the heads, holes for them to fall in. Don't worry"—a murmur of alarm had swept through the group—"I won't tell the elders. You're afraid when you make these booby traps, aren't you? Afraid that the humans will catch you? Afraid of what they'll do to you? You're also afraid of what the elders will say if they catch you, aren't you?"

The dremecks hung their heads, face-folds sagged.

"But you do them anyway. You overcome your fear. Fear is good. Fear is healthy. Fear keeps us alive. Fear gives us all sorts of benefits—I'm not sure how your anatomy works, but for us humans fear makes our heart pump faster, we get more blood to our limbs. Fear even releases a chemical called adrenaline that makes us stronger. Fear can work for you, but it can also work against you. That's called panic.

"I want you to be afraid—that'll keep you alive. I don't want you to panic, which is as good a way of getting killed as I know of. Now, are you afraid of me?"

Jamil looked around. The dremecks, round-eyed, all nodded yes emphatically.

"Why?"

"Well, sir, you are bigger than we are and your weapons are not toys." Trella pointed to the lasgun in Jamil's holster. "Your human weapons will kill us. We have seen it."

"We've brought you some body-coverings called armor that will help to protect you against our weapons. As for physical advantages, some of us are taller than you are, but we're not necessarily stronger and we don't have your endurance. The humans have made you feel inferior because that's how they're controlling you. You're not, and I'll prove it to you."

At least, I hope I'll prove it, Jamil silently amended. This was the test. This was where he found out more about the dremecks than they knew about themselves. Unfortunately, if the test proved positive, he would be teaching them things about themselves that it might be best if they never learned.

"Trella. Come here." Jamil motioned.

Trella, looking worried, but also a little pleased by the attention, came to stand beside him.

Jamil put both hands on the young dremeck's shoulders. "Now, put your hands on my shoulders, too." He bent forward so that she could reach him.

"Good," Jamil said, resting lightly on the balls of his feet. "When I say the word 'go,' I want you to try and knock me to the ground. I will try to do the same to you."

Trella nodded to indicate that she understood.

Jamil opened his mouth, but he didn't say go. Instead he kicked Trella's legs out from under her and shoved hard with his hands. The young dremeck tumbled heavily to the floor, where she lay glaring at Jamil and catching her breath.

The dremecks murmured uneasily.

Trella jumped to her feet. "That wasn't fair!" she cried. "You didn't say 'go'!"

"Didn't I?" Jamil was contrite. "I'm sorry. This time I'll say 'go.' I promise."

Hands to shoulders, he and the dremeck squared off. Once again, Jamil's foot shot out and Trella went down.

"Go!" said Jamil, grinning. "There—I said it."

Trella picked herself back up, her face grim. The crowd's murmur had deepened in tone. The dremecks didn't like this.

Jamil crouched, reached out his hands. "Once more. This time I'll let you say— Oof!"

Trella lifted her hands, but she didn't put them on Jamil's shoulders. She shoved them into his chest, putting all the force of her stocky, well-conditioned body behind the blow.

Jamil lay on his back staring up into the darkness of the cavern ceiling. After a few tense moments wondering if he was ever going to breathe again, he gulped air, then regained his feet.

"I'm sorry!" Trella was trembling all over. "Oh, sir, I'm so very, very sorry! Are you dying? I didn't mean to hurt you, I swear it! I only wanted you to stop knocking me down!"

"I'm all right," he gasped, wheezing. "Don't worry, Trella. You did . . . what I wanted you to do."

"You wanted me to knock you down?" Trella was amazed.

"Yes," said Jamil, and wished like hell he was telling the truth.

The young dremecks had given their version of a cheer when he went down. But now they were silent, fearful. At the same time, he could sense they were excited about what Trella had done.

You didn't start this, he reminded himself. It's obvious these dremecks can be pushed only so far before they begin pushing back.

At this point, some questions occurred to him: Do the elders know what the young have been up to? Do they know about the booby traps? Do they know that the young are ready to rebel? If the answer is yes, then maybe Marmand brought in outside help in order to forestall the young from acting on their own.

"Were you afraid of me when you knocked me down?" Jamil asked.

"Yes," said Trella, thinking back. "But I was more angry than I was afraid. What you did wasn't fair. And I didn't want you to knock me down anymore. It didn't hurt so much, but it made me feel bad."

"Were you afraid of me when I was lying on the ground?" Jamil asked with a smile.

"No," Trella said, her face-folds spreading away from her mouth in a dremeck grin.

"Congratulations, Trella," Jamil said. "You're no longer a slave. To the humans or to your fear."

Jamil kept the young dremecks hard at work the rest of the week. They practiced drilling and marching, giving fierce-sounding yells (one of the more difficult assignments). They practiced twisting their face-folds into ferocious scowls (accomplished after much laughter) and to charge forward en masse screaming at the tops of their lungs, after which they solemnly "accepted the surrender" of those dremecks detailed to playing Uglies.

Jamil taught them how to use the useless beam rifles, how to pretend to fire them, pretend to recharge them. Quong and Tycho had even rigged the guns to emit light and a burst of sound when "fired." The light was an eerie green color, like no light ever before seen coming out of a beam rifle, and the sound was something between a burp and a gargle, but the dremecks loved it and, thought Jamil, it was at least guaranteed to confuse the enemy, if it did nothing else.

He didn't have time to train the dremecks to be soldiers. He had time to train them to look like soldiers—enough to fool human civilians into thinking the dremecks were a fighting force. If they came up against a real army, God help them!

According to the plan, they wouldn't come up against real soldiers. But the first lesson Jamil had learned in the Army was that the plan never survives contact with the enemy.

The dremecks in training were ordered to remain down in the caverns, isolated from the rest of the dremecks, especially the elders. Jamil slept with them, but he didn't eat with them. During their eating periods—dremecks eat twice daily—the young dremecks went off to one of their "pastures," food-growing areas located in the burrows, where they plucked the leaves and flowers from some sort of plant life that apparently thrived in darkness (Quong was collecting samples) and devoured them on the spot.

While the dremecks grazed, Jamil went topside to report to the rest of the team and discover the success of their various missions.

The news was good—sort of.

"Quong, you first," said Jamil, ignoring Raoul, who was

patting the air with his fingertips, a gesture indicative of strong excitement and violent emotion, which would have been more fully exhibited but for the fact that he might ruin the line of his hand-tailored suit. "You've been talking to some of the Uglies. How did that go?"

"*Trying* to talk is more like it," Quong grumbled. "I have never seen such pervasive fear in any population. The few who are willing to speak on the subject are those from the very dregs of society, who have nothing much to lose. But from them I gather that there is a certain amount of sympathy for the dremecks on Del Sol. Kirkov has his supporters, but those are mostly found among the upper classes, whom he courts, and the Army, which is extremely loyal to him.

"The general populace would be pleased to have Kirkov removed. However, while they do not like to see the dremecks used as slaves or 'relocated,' they would not be particularly pleased to have dremecks as rulers. At least not now. The humans, even those who like the dremecks, have no respect for them.

"It seems that there was a resistance movement started several years ago by some humans," Quong stated. "A group formed to try to gain more rights for the dremecks. The dremecks at first promised they would participate, but at the crucial moment they all disappeared, leaving the humans to face arrest and subsequent deportation and incarceration."

"Oh, goody," said Jamil in gloomy tones.

"They didn't have you for a leader," Darlene said, patting his shoulder comfortingly.

Jamil only grunted.

"At any rate," Quong continued, "I believe that most of the humans on Del Sol will go along with us, if for no other reason than the chance to rid themselves of Kirkov, whom they describe as a bully, a thug, and a criminal, surrounded by a highly trained and highly motivated Army, which doubles as a police force."

"This just gets better and better." Jamil shook his head.

"Me next!" Raoul was panting with eagerness.

"In a minute. Darlene. Your report."

"The military commlink system was a bitch to break into,

but I managed, after two days and a sleepless night. This is the way it will work: When I send the command, all calls coming into the military HQ—which, as Quong says, doubles as the police station—will be routed into a voice-mail system that will be very polite but won't let them speak to any live person in the known universe. Outgoing calls will be scrambled, so that when the general issues the order to his troops to hit the streets, he'll find himself speaking to the cook in the mess hall. The next time he tries, he'll get the commissary, and so on."

"Why not just cut communications altogether?" Quong asked.

"Because the military would immediately view that as sinister, the prelude to trouble. The way this is set up now, they'll think it is just a screw-up. The general's calls aren't going through. Something's wrong with the system. It's a job for the engineers. Eventually the army brass will figure it out and realize that they've been sabotaged, but by that time it will be too late. The next thing they know, Kirkov is seen surrendering to the dremecks."

"What about the Army brass?" Jamil asked worriedly. "Will they refuse to accept defeat? Hang around to fight? Quong says they're loyal—"

Darlene grinned. "To Kirkov and the life he's providing them. Once he's gone—or rather once they think he's gone—they'll be on the first transport out of here. According to what I've discovered snooping around in their personal files, every one of them is up to his or her eyeballs in graft and corruption. They figure it's just a matter of time before someone moves in and ends the good life. They've all got secret bank accounts, houses built on other planets, and one-way tickets for themselves and their families off of Del Sol."

Jamil nodded, grudgingly optimistic. "We'll let the Crown deal with them. Next."

"Me, me!" Raoul begged.

Jamil had been putting this off, because he was certain he would be in for a barrage of excuses and evasions, all adding up to the fact that Raoul had, and after much work, obtained an autographed vid of Rusty Love. Nothing more.

Which meant that Jamil would have to figure out some other way of dealing with Kirkov. He had a few ideas. . . .

"Me, me!" Raoul said, wriggling with excitement.

"All right. Raoul. Have you contacted your dear friend, Rusty Love, and will he agree to come to Del Sol and perform this little charade for us?" Jamil didn't bother to hide his sarcasm, knowing that Raoul wouldn't notice it anyway.

"Yes! And yes!" cried Raoul ecstatically.

"He will?" Jamil asked, astonished.

Raoul preened, smoothing his long, black hair and reading from a note written in his delicate handwriting on the back of a shopping list.

"My dear friend Rusty Love"—Raoul glanced at Jamil, eyes glittering from beneath blue-tipped eyelashes—"will arrive in Del Sol on the date specified. We will meet him at the spaceport—he will be in disguise, naturally; you've no idea how he suffers from the tabloids. We will take him to the hotel, where he will be available for briefing and rehearsal.

"The next day, he will make the switch, as arranged. He will be driven to the palace and will there surrender to the dremecks. After which, he will depart."

"Is this on the level?" Jamil asked Quong and Darlene. Both nodded.

"I spoke to Mr. Love on vidphone myself," Quong said. "He said he would do anything for Raoul."

"He even began to elaborate," Darlene added, "explaining what he would do and how. At which point we ended the conversation. Quickly."

The Little One sidled up to Jamil and punched him in the thigh with his fist. Jamil couldn't see much beneath the brim of the fedora, but he was positive the Little One was smirking.

"Okay," Jamil said magnanimously, "I admit it, Raoul. I doubted you and I'm sorry."

Raoul rose to his feet and made a graceful bow. The Little One punched Jamil again.

"Ouch. Okay. I apologize to you, too. Let's get on with this. My army will be back from gently nibbling tender plants any minute now. Tycho?"

The chameleon smiled and nodded.

"Turn on your translator." Jamil sighed and gestured.

Tycho switched it on. "Sorry, boss. Were you talking to me?"

"I want your report. The others have given theirs. Weren't you listening?"

"But I have already listened to them once. To hear them again would be abundant."

"Redundant," Darlene corrected.

"Thank you. My report. In my guise as tourist, I traveled to the Royal Palace and joined a group who were being given the standard guided tour. Vids were not allowed, of course, but I had the doctor's concealed vidcam and so that was not a problem. We were shown the office of state, where Kirkov performs all official functions, and I was able to obtain excellent vid footage of the desk, the throne, and the background. I also took vids of certain portraits of Kirkov in ceremonial uniform, which I have given to Raoul, who is in charge of the costumes.

"Next I took vids of major intersections and other prominent buildings in the city itself, for use as backdrops. Finally, I have vids of the vid station, both its interior—Darlene and I took a tour—and its exterior, and also its grounds and environs. You will find it all here." Tycho handed over a portable vidviewer.

"Well done," said Jamil. "And after this, keep your translator on, will you, Tycho? One of us might, by accident, say something important." He stood up, prepared to make his way back to the cavern.

"How are the troops shaping up?" Darlene asked.

"Fine," said Jamil. "Don't worry. We're coming along fine. I'll make killers of them yet."

"Jamil—" Darlene began.

"Good work," he said, interrupting her, and left before she could finish.

Back down in the cavern, he had the young dremecks pretend to club each other with the butt end of their useless beam rifles.

CHAPTER 30

God sends meat, and the Devil sends cooks.
John Taylor, *Works*

"Tampambulos."

The force field shut down, the red glow fading, along with the very faint buzzing, which Xris had not even been aware he was hearing until it ended.

"Yeah?" Xris said, not looking up from his vidbook.

"On your feet. Warden wants to see you."

"Tell him I appreciate the invitation but I'm otherwise engaged."

The guard grunted, didn't even bother to respond. He must have heard that one a million times. Xris tossed the book aside, pushed himself up off the bed. As he started to leave the cell, the guard gestured with the stun gun toward a neatly folded pile of clothes.

"You want me to bring those?" Xris asked.

The guard nodded.

Xris was surprised. "Am I being released from solitary?"

The guard shrugged, shook his head.

"I guess that depends on how my meeting with the warden goes, doesn't it?" Xris suggested.

The guard shrugged again and gestured with his stun gun.

Grabbing his small bundle of underwear, Xris limped down the corridor. After two days of enforced idleness, his joints—his real joints—had stiffened up on him.

"I hope they're not paying you by the word," Xris said politely.

The guard grunted again and this time he almost smiled.

After a long walk through a sterile corridor, branching off into a maze of cells, Xris was brought to a halt at a security post. While they passed him through, he glanced around. This cellblock was located below ground level; he hadn't even been aware that it existed. The guard at security gave Xris the okay. A massive steel door swung open, and he stepped outside.

Rain pounded down on his head, soaking him. For once, he didn't mind. He paused to enjoy the smell of the rain-wet grass, enjoy the sight of the gray clouds scudding overhead. More than once, alone in his cell, the thought had occurred to him that Amadi had double-crossed him, that this might be Amadi's way of getting rid of him, that he might never see the outdoors again. As it was, rain running down the back of his neck felt wonderful.

He and the guard slogged across the yard, heading for the administration building. A group of prisoners, clad in plastic ponchos, were outside shoveling mud off the sidewalks. Since it was still raining and more mud was washing down the hillside every second, their job seemed futile. They didn't look happy about it and neither did their guard.

By the time he reached the administration building, Xris was having second thoughts about the delights of a rainy day. His clothes were soaked. He was soaked. The water ran off him in rivulets, dripped onto the floor. And, of course, the building was air-conditioned.

He was shivering so hard by the time they had taken the elevator up the thirteen stories to the warden's office that even his plastiskin had goose bumps.

"Sit there," ordered the guard.

Xris glanced around, saw a chair, sat down. The guard tromped over to report to a man seated at a desk.

"Prisoner Tampambulos."

The man nodded. "I'll tell the warden."

The guard stepped back to stand beside Xris.

The man touched a button, reported to Montieth, who mumbled something that no one, including his secretary, could comprehend. The secretary didn't care, apparently. He went back to work, reciting a long a list of numbers into a computer.

Xris waited, clutching his soaked underwear and shivering.

The secretary looked up, fixed Xris with an accusing eye.

"You're dripping on the floor."

"Sorry," Xris returned pleasantly. "I fell off my yacht while I was deep-sea fishing. I didn't have time to change."

"Get him a towel," muttered the secretary.

The guard clamped ordinary metal restrainers on Xris's wrists, even the cybernetic wrist—not too bright, this guard—and tromped off down the hall. He returned from the men's room with a handful of paper towels, which he handed to Xris.

"I can't very well . . ." Xris exhibited the restrainers.

The guard glared and tossed the towels into Xris's lap. He unlatched the restrainers, but by that time the paper towels had sopped up the water from Xris's uniform and were now as wet or wetter than he was.

"Could I trouble you for few more towels?" Xris asked. "Oh, and make them heated this time, will you?"

The guard glowered. "Stuff 'em up your—"

"The warden's ready," the secretary interrupted coldly. "Take him in."

The guard relatched the restrainers. Xris dropped the soggy paper towels onto the floor. He grinned at the secretary's yelp of irritation, realized then how low he'd sunk. A man who had helped bring a king to power was now snickering at watching some poor dilbert in a cubicle wipe up a mess on the floor.

"Sorry," Xris said, and his apology was sincere.

Warden Montieth sat behind a desk that was absolutely empty; nothing on it, not a phone, not a computer terminal, not a drinking glass or a picture of the wife and kids. Montieth was leaning back in his chair, watching the rain fall. He glanced at Xris over his shoulder, stared at him without interest a long moment; then, with a sigh, he shifted his bulk around in his chair to make the stare personal and concentrated.

"It seems you have friends in high places, Tampambulos. I just want you to know that they may not be high enough. I'm letting you off this once because I don't have much choice in the matter. But if you go around beating up any of your fellow inmates again, the Lord Almighty Himself could come down off his throne and ask me to spare you and I'd spit in His face."

Montieth swiveled in his chair, clasped his hands over his belly, and went back to watching the rain.

Xris had been entertaining himself during his walk through the rain with the witty things he intended to say to warden Montieth. The man's cold nonchalance and supreme dispassion were so impressive that Xris could think of only one insult out of an entire repertoire, and somehow, "You're even uglier in person"—though delivered in admiring tones—would have seemed flat and uninspired.

The guard marched Xris into an adjoining room that contained a metal table and two metal chairs and Jafar el Amadi, who might have passed for metal. Xris went on high alert, forgot that such insignificant assholes as Montieth and his pet pit bull existed.

"Leave us," Amadi said to the guard.

"You want me to activate them restrainers, sir?"

"That won't be necessary." Amadi smiled ingratiatingly. "I'm his attorney. I don't think he will harm me."

"He'd like to," Xris assured the guard. "But he won't."

The guard, looking dubious, stepped through another door that led to a hallway. "I'll be right outside. Watching the monitor." He pointed to a vidcam on the wall.

Amadi was setting up a portable computer, which he carried inside a plastisteel briefcase.

"Sit down," Amadi said.

Xris sat. Resting his arms on the table, he let his wrists fall. The restrainers hit the metal tabletop with a bang.

Amadi glanced up. He got the message, apparently, for he smiled briefly and without humor, then looked back at his computer, which—Xris noticed—Amadi was careful to keep shielded from the cam.

"We're discussing your case," he said with a sideways glance at the guard.

"Can he hear?"

"No. The room is soundproofed. Attorney-client privilege. But he can see. So don't go for my throat."

"I won't. But consider it merely a pleasure deferred. What about Ghengis Kahn in there?"

"Montieth?" Amadi shook his head, his gaze still fixed on the computer. "He couldn't care less. He probably wouldn't mind if you did go for my throat. He and I don't exactly get along."

"But he takes your money quick enough. How much did you pay him to let me out of solitary?"

Amadi glanced up again. "I really don't think that's anything you need to know."

"Yeah, I guess not. Say, you wouldn't have a twist on you, would you?"

"Not allowed." Amadi continued to search his files. Apparently he found what he wanted, for he frowned at the screen.

"I have contacted Harry Luck, given him the date and time, told him what to do. He's going to ask Bear Olefsky to loan him a suitable spaceplane." Amadi's frown deepened. "I don't doubt your judgment, Xris, but Harry Luck is . . . well, he's . . ."

"My friend," Xris said quietly. "Don't worry, Amadi. Harry'll get the job done."

Amadi shrugged. "You know him best, I suppose. All right. He'll be here at 0200 hours Friday morning."

"What's today? I've lost track of time."

"Wednesday."

Xris stared. "That's damn quick! Why the rush?"

"Things are happening. Sooner than we'd anticipated," Amadi said. His gaze shifted back to his computer screen.

"Yeah? What things?"

"Nothing you need concern yourself about. Now, here's the plan. Harry will land his spaceplane on the golf course at 0200, somewhere around the fourteenth hole. You and the three Hung leaders will be there to meet it."

"Provided Slovenski doesn't kill them first."

Amadi glanced up, perplexed. "Who the hell is Slovenski?"

"The prison bad boy. He's been beating them up on a regular basis. Not that I really minded seeing them get the crap beat out of them, but since I'm being paid by the head, I'm bound to lose money if one of them ends up with his head pounded into his shoes. I put a stop to the beatings. That's how I ended up in solitary. Didn't Montieth tell you?"

"I didn't ask for details," Amadi said dryly. "You'd been here nearly one week. I figured it was about time you got into trouble. Look, Xris, see if you and your little friends can't play nice for the next few days, all right? I don't want anyone to get suspicious. Just make sure you get them on that goddamn plane!"

Xris grunted. "Speaking of the plane, it's going to be fairly difficult to take off in it after it's been attacked by the patrol planes, then vaporized by the lascannons and the surface-to-air missiles and God knows what else they've got in the way of security devices. Or do you plan to ask Montieth if he'll be an angel and shut them down for that night?"

"Shutting the ground weapons down is your job, Xris." Amadi smiled faintly. "As for the patrol planes, I've given Harry Luck the access codes to the early warning system. Once he disables it, you won't be bothered by patrol planes. What's the matter, Xris? I thought you might find disabling lascannons a welcome change from sorting the colors from the whites."

"It will be." Xris's hand reached automatically for a twist. He halted the hand's progress, annoyed at himself. "But I think the guards might get suspicious if I start tossing wet clothes into the lascannons to dry."

"I'm going to show you something, Xris," Amadi said, resting his hands on the briefcase. "This cost us a fortune. You'll have to memorize it. I don't dare make a hard copy."

He swiveled the briefcase for Xris to see. It took Xris a moment to figure out what he was looking at, then he realized it was a diagram of the power grid for the prison. He stared at it for a few seconds, blinked twice, then nodded.

"I got it."

"Are you sure?"

Xris tapped his enhanced left eye. "I take the term 'photographic memory' literally."

"I'm impressed," said Amadi.

"Yeah, I got myself blown to bits in that factory just so I could take digital shots of my kids on holiday."

Amadi said nothing. Xris and Marjorie had once planned on a having a large family—something that wasn't likely to happen now or ever. Amadi hit the delete button and the diagram of the power grid disappeared.

"I presume you have some means of shutting the grid down? I told Dr. Quong what might be required—"

Xris grinned. "That's something you don't need to concern yourself with, Mr. Trevor."

Amadi gazed at Xris in silence, probably wondering if it was worth his time to argue. Amadi knew Xris, however. He shut the briefcase.

"What about backup systems?" Xris asked.

"There's only an instant's delay in bringing the lights to the buildings and the compound back on. It takes longer to switch over power to the lascannons and pulse cannons. They suck up a hell of a lot of juice."

"How much longer?" Xris asked.

"Ten minutes," said Amadi.

"So I have ten minutes to get everyone loaded onto the plane, lift off, and escape out of range of lascannons?" Xris ground an imaginary twist between his teeth. "It can't be done."

"Sure it can." Amadi smiled expansively. "My experts say five minutes with a fast plane and a good pilot. That gives you a whole extra five minutes to relax."

"Thanks a lot." Xris grunted. "Maybe I'll use them to work on my putting."

"I'm going to be in that plane, too, Xris," Amadi informed him, more gravely. "I'm seeing to the . . . um . . . 'arrests.' "

"You and me and the leaders of the Hung in a spaceplane with six lascannons pointed right at us. Hell, it must be my birthday!"

Amadi didn't reply. Shutting the briefcase, he rose to his feet. "Friday night, then. At 0200."

Xris stood up. He was tired for no reason at all, since he'd done absolutely nothing the last few days. Nothing except daydream that he was back at that house by the beach, sitting in his chair, watching the waves chase each other to the shore. A stupid dream. He'd been angry at himself for thinking it up. But it was like one of those irritating songs—it was in his head and he couldn't get rid of it.

"What happens after we board the plane?" he asked.

"You'll receive your instructions."

"Oh, and about that assassin—"

"What assassin?" Amadi stared intently. If he was acting, it was damn good.

"Oh, hadn't you heard?" Xris feigned surprise. "The one who thought he was going to turn me into a colander there back in the holding prison."

"I didn't hear about it. Good God, Xris. You don't suspect me? Why would I want you killed?"

"You tell me, Amadi."

"I swear . . ." Amadi paused. "I know you hate me, Xris, and that you'd sooner trust the devil himself, but I give you my word that I didn't set you up for the kill. Think about it, Xris. If I'd wanted you dead, there are any number of ways—" He stopped.

"Yeah. Like maybe rig a factory to blow up when I'm inside."

"Xris—"

"Hey, look. Forget it. I have. You're saying you didn't pay to have me killed this time and, you know, for once I believe you. But then if you didn't, who did?"

Amadi's face was gray and troubled. "Have there been other attempts?"

Xris thought back, remembered the enthusiastic food tray, the setting off of the chair alarm in the night. He nodded. "Yes. Twice. Not very serious, though. Or very professional."

"I'll see what I can do," Amadi said. "In the meantime, take care of yourself."

"That's it?" Xris was angry. "Take care of yourself? Now, look, Amadi! If you know—"

"Guard!" Amadi tapped on the plastisteel window.

"Wait!" Xris said urgently. "One more thing we have to get straight."

The guard stepped over, began to punch in the code that would open the door.

"The Hung leaders. They're going to die, Amadi," Xris said. "They're not stepping off that plane alive. I just want to make that clear."

Amadi twitched down the sleeves of his expensive suit coat. He smoothed imaginary wrinkles from his silk tie.

"Death is only one way to die, Xris," he said softly. He picked up his briefcase. "You should know better than anyone."

CHAPTER 31

... he was ... of the Devil's Party without knowing it.
William Blake, *Marriage of Heaven and Hell*

Petronella's passage to Del Sol was quite luxurious. As it should be, she thought resentfully, considering what she was paying for it. For the price of this ticket, she could have purchased a small house. She tried her best to enjoy herself her first night on board, but the mystery in which she was involved kept intruding.

She wasn't in the glass-glittering, silver-gleaming wait-staff-groveling dining room. She was inside the office of Jafar el Amadi, trying to find a clue in something he'd done or said.

She wasn't listening to her dancing partner's whispered words of seduction. She was hearing Andrew Robison take her off the case.

Consequently, the people at her table thought her a crashing bore—*crashing* being the operative word. Due to the emotional turmoil she was in, the Talisian part of her seemed to be in overdrive.

Having figured she'd broken enough crystal for one night, Petronella retired to her stateroom early. She wasn't sleepy. Her mind was wound too tight to release and start slowing down. She roamed around the small cabin, watched a nebula float past, and deliberately did not sit down at her computer, because she knew if she did, that meant she'd made a decision—and she didn't think she had, yet.

In twelve hours, the ship would make the Jump to hyperspace. The decision would be taken out of her hands. Once in hyperspace, she wouldn't be able to make contact with anybody.

But she had twelve hours. . . .

Petronella's pacing carried her past the tiny desk that folded down from the wall. Her computer was on the desk. The business card with Darlene Mohini's personal computer uplink was on the computer.

Petronella walked past it six times. At the seventh, she reached for the card, activated it.

The business card was not glitzy and flamboyant as some: It sang her no songs, it sent her no animated creatures to cavort across the small screen. Darlene's name appeared in a soothing shade of deep blue. That was all. Just the name.

Petronella held fast to the card, almost as if she were a psychometrist, willing it to reveal something about its owner. The card gave her nothing more than the name, however. Sighing deeply, Petronella inserted the card into her computer.

Darlene had said to call her anytime; if her computer wasn't on, the incoming message would alert it, cause it to turn itself on. If she wasn't awake or wasn't there, her computer was linked to her commlink and would let her know that she had a message waiting. Petronella hoped Darlene would be asleep or gone somewhere, taking in dinner and a show. That would give her some time to reconsider.

But Darlene was neither asleep nor enjoying a pleasant evening's relaxation. She must have been working on her computer, might almost have been waiting for this call, for she appeared on the screen before Petronella was ready to see her.

Petronella gave a little start of astonishment. Her water carafe slid off the table and landed on the floor, splashing water over her bare ankles. Fortunately the carafe was made of plastic.

"Ms. Rizzoli," said Darlene, smiling. "What a pleasant surprise. You look very nice in that dress. It must have been a great party."

"What?" Petronella asked. Then she remembered; she was still wearing her evening gown. Looking down at the silk and sequins, she flushed in embarrassment. She supposed she *could* have appeared more unprofessional; she could have been in her pajamas. The flannel ones.

"I'm on board ship," she said in apology. "We had to dress for dinner."

"Taking a vacation?" Darlene asked coolly. Her eyes darkened and a tiny crease pulled her brows together.

"I need to know if I can trust you," Petronella said quietly, urgently. "I can't trust anybody else, it seems. So far you're the only people who haven't lied to me. At least not that I know of. But that's just it. I don't know! And I'm staking my job, my future, maybe even my life on this. You have to admit that you're a pretty weird bunch. . . ."

"I'm afraid you've started in the middle. What are you talking about, Ms. Rizzoli?"

"I know I've started in the middle. I can't tell you the beginning. Not yet. Please, I need to know. Can I trust you?"

"Yes," said Darlene gravely. "Though I'm not sure how I can prove it."

Someone—another member of the team, presumably—said something in the background.

"One moment, please," Darlene said, and, switching her computer to soothing music and a blank screen, she turned away.

"Would a reference help?" she asked, returning. She didn't give Petronella time to answer. "Tell me how you can be reached."

Petronella sent her access code. "But I'm not sure—"

"Thank you. Someone will contact you," Darlene said, and the screen went blank.

"References?" Petronella said to the empty screen. "I'm not hiring a nanny, for God's sake!" Irritably kicking the water carafe out of the way, she roamed back over to stare gloomily out the viewscreen. "I shouldn't have called. Or if I did call, I should have known what I wanted!"

And now, of course, since she had to stay awake to wait for this next call—a call she didn't want to receive, but which she couldn't very well avoid—she was suddenly sleepy.

She yawned. Yawned again.

"Damn!" Petronella muttered. Picking up the water carafe, she carried it to the replicator and filled it with coffee. She change out of her evening dress and into blue jeans and a floppy-sleeved shirt. Not quite appropriate, perhaps, for receiving references, but she was feeling put-upon and didn't much care. Propping herself up with pillows, she stretched out on the bed and began to read the latest trashy romance, confident that between the coffee and the titillation she'd remain awake.

A buzzing sound startled her.

She sat up. Apparently the love scenes hadn't been all that arousing. The champagne and her unexpected nap had left her with a nagging headache.

The incoming message light was flashing on her computer. Petronella jumped off the bed, indicated she was ready to receive. Glancing at the clock, she was startled and not particularly pleased to see that almost six hours had passed. Either the team had experienced difficulty getting in touch with their reference or they had experienced difficulty finding a reference! This was ludicrous. Petronella was now extremely sorry that she had called Darlene. She was sorry she had traveled to Del Sol, sorry to have wasted her money.

An official looking symbol flashed on the screen—a bright golden sun with a lion's face, the sun's rays forming the lion's mane. The symbol was very elegant, very impressive, and Petronella was trying to prod her sleep-befuddled brain into thinking where she'd seen it before and what it meant when the symbol disappeared.

A blond and slender man, dressed in an elegant white suit, white shirt and a crimson red tie appeared on the screen. Petronella had a confused impression of warm wood, fine furnishings, rich draperies in the background.

"Ms. Petronella Rizzoli?" asked the man in a clipped, well educated, and pleasingly modulated voice.

"Yes, I'm Petronella Rizzoli," she replied.

"My name is D'Argent. Please hold one moment for His Majesty."

The man vanished. The official symbol was back on the screen.

"What?" Petronella demanded, shocked. "What did you say?" She tapped on the screen. "Hello? Come back? What? I— Oh!"

The official symbol had disappeared.

D'Argent was back, but only for an instant.

"His Majesty, King Dion Starfire."

And there on her screen was a man she had seen many times, but only on GNN news reports. She recognized him immediately, despite the fact that he was not wearing his crown or his robes of office. The red-golden hair and the blue, blue eyes, the famous Starfire eyes that were part of his heritage, were unmistakable. He was dressed quite casually in a beige cardigan sweater and open-collared shirt. Judging from the shelves of ancient books in the background, he was in his famous library.

Panicked, Petronella wondered if she was supposed to curtsy, couldn't figure quite how to manage that while seated in a chair. Her face burned, little prickles tingled through her body, her hands were chilled.

"Ms. Rizzoli," said His Majesty. "We are pleased to make your acquaintance."

"Your Majesty! I'm . . ." *Flabbergasted* wasn't what one said, she supposed, although that was what came to mind. "Honored," she finished lamely.

The king came right to business. "We understand that you are seeking references for a group of mercenaries who call themselves Mag Force 7."

"Yes, Your Majesty," Petronella said in a small voice.

"Ms. Rizzoli, I don't know whether you are questioning their efficiency or their courage or their honor or their trustworthiness. It doesn't matter. I can answer for them on all counts. I am not at liberty to discuss the nature of the services they have performed for me, but I can assure you that in all respects they performed selflessly, professionally, courageously."

The king had been grave and serious up to this point, but now he smiled, a radiant smile, very much like the sun that was his symbol.

"I admit that they can seem a little strange, Ms Rizzoli," he said, and his voice was as warm as his smile. "Their methods are unorthodox and occasionally illegal. But I would trust them with my life. I have, in fact, trusted them with my life. Not only that, I would trust them with the lives I hold more dear than my own—the lives of my wife and my child. Does this help you, Ms. Rizzoli?"

"Yes, Your Majesty," said Petronella faintly. "Thank you for taking the time."

"It was our pleasure. Good evening, Ms. Rizzoli."

D'Argent was back on the screen.

"The audience with His Majesty, King Dion Starfire, is concluded."

The screen went blank.

Petronella sat staring at the blank screen until an announcement over the shipboard comm alerted her to the fact that within a few hours they would be making preparations for the Jump to hyperspace. This meant that she would have to be in her cot, with the safety webbing over her. There would be no chance for further communications.

She fumbled for Darlene's card, inserted it into the computer.

Darlene was there immediately. "Did you talk to our reference?"

"Ms. Mohini," said Petronella, anxious not to waste time, "I'm on my way to Del Sol."

"You are?" Darlene looked amazed.

"I know this sounds bizarre, but I think that there's a connection between Xris's arrest and your being hired to go to Del Sol. I don't know what it is yet. I think the answer is on Del Sol. I can't talk about it now. I want to arrange a meeting with you when I arrive, which will be about twenty-four hours from now."

"Certainly, Ms. Rizzoli. We should meet in public. There's a large shopping mall known as the Bayside Plaza. I'll meet you at the scarf counter in Bergdorff's for lunch. Twelve hundred hours."

Petronella made a note. "Fine. I'll be there. Your friend, Tampambulos. He's in prison on Jango?"

"Yes?" Darlene was concerned. "What about him?"

"I don't suppose there's any way you can contact him, but if you can, warn him that he's in danger. Very great danger. That's all I can say. I have to sign off now. We're going to be making the Jump to hyperspace. I'll see you on Del Sol."

"Ms. Rizzoli!" Darlene said urgently. "Tell us—"

Petronella switched off her computer.

She had abandoned the side of the angels.

CHAPTER 32

Give me a man that is capable of a devotion to anything, rather than a cold, calculating average of all
the virtues!
      Bret Harte, *Two Men of Sandy Bar*, Act IV

"What the hell is that?"
      Harry looked up and up and up at the monstrosity
that had just lowered itself from the skies and was, at present, parked on every single landing pad at the admittedly
small local spaceport and was lapping over onto several
nearby corn fields.

"It's what you requested," said the commander of the
Wolf Brigade. He glanced at the behemoth proudly. "It's
a prototype. The new Xena class. Not even in production
yet."

Harry scrunched his eyes against the blazing sun. He was
reminded of a fish he'd seen once at an aquarium. Quong
had called it a manta ray. This ship resembled a manta ray
in shape, or rather the shadow of a manta ray, because it
didn't look substantial. It sort of wavered and shimmered
darkly. Harry had the feeling it might dissolve into the
tarmac.

"I don't think I asked for anything this . . . well . . . big,"
he said.

"You said you wanted a ship designed for speed, with
stealth capabilities, to haul men and machinery. That's the
biggest armored transport there is in the universe. It's completely undetectable by most standard planetary radar. It
isn't the fastest ship in the universe," the captain admitted,
"but then its armor is so heavy and its shields are so strong
that it doesn't need to be able to outrun anything in the

universe. It can take a direct hit from a lascannon and maybe bounce you around in the cockpit some, but other than that, no effect."

Harry wasn't really paying much attention. He was thinking back to the request he'd left with Bear Olefsky. "I said I needed a ship with room enough to carry six men, one of *them* a machine."

The commander frowned. "That's not what we heard." His frown darkened, looked particularly formidable coming from the depths of his gleaming plastisteel helmet, which was fashioned to resemble the head of a wolf, complete with teeth. "Are you saying you don't want it? Do you know how much trouble and expense the Bear went to in order to deliver this to you on time?"

"I appreciate it. I really do," said Harry. "It's just . . . I don't suppose . . . you'd have anything smaller? Along the same lines, of course. This is really amazing. Just . . . smaller?"

"No," said the commander grimly. "We don't. Not that we could have it here on time. This came from halfway across the galaxy, you know."

"It seems pretty slow on landing," Harry ventured.

"It weighs more than some moons," the captain said in frigid tones. "What do you expect? It's faster on takeoff. And, in case of an emergency in space, the cockpit detaches. Men are worth more than machines, I always say."

"That's a good saying," Harry said. "Men are worth more than machines." He repeated it to himself a couple of times, glancing at the commander out of the corner of his eye, hoping the commander would be impressed.

The commander wasn't.

"Sign here to indicate that you received delivery and that *everything was satisfactory.*" He emphasized the last, glared at Harry, and held out a pad.

Meekly, Harry pressed his thumb on it. "Thanks." He looked back at the monster, blinked a couple of times, trying to take it all in. "It's really a . . . a beauty."

The commander snorted and stalked off.

"Hoo, boy," said Harry, and sighed.

He was preoccupied, still thinking about the gigantic transport, when he entered the small motel room he'd rented near the spaceport. He'd just come from arguing with the spaceport manager, who was trying to charge Harry for every single one of the parking spaces the transport ship was occupying.

The phone was buzzing when he entered.

"Yeah?"

"Is this Harry Luck?"

"Yes. Look, this better not be any more excuses about my interplanetary vid hookup—"

"This is Mr. Tampambulos's secretary, Archibald Trevor. We spoke before."

"Oh, hi." Harry forgot about his vid hookup and about the manta ray transport. He pressed the phone closer to his ear. "How is Xris?"

"He's fine, Mr. Luck. He's looking forward to that round of golf."

"Golf?" Harry repeated, not understanding at first. Then it struck him. "Oh, yeah. Golf."

The voice was a man's voice, deep, pleasant, but it had an edge to it that always made Harry's neck hairs itch. He scratched the back of his head.

The voice continued. "If you'll recall, Xris has asked that you meet him and a few of his friends at the golf course near his new home, Mr. Luck. You know where that is?"

"Yeah, sure." Harry was quiet a moment, then said, "They got a golf course there?"

"I will transmit the landing coordinates and the exact time and date of your expected arrival."

"Thanks. Say, listen. I've heard about that spaceport," Harry said, still scratching.

He noticed, as he was talking, a light flashing on his phone. Someone had left a message for him. He made a mental note to find out who. Unfortunately, Harry's mental notes didn't have much glue and kept falling off.

"Landing a spaceplane there can be a real pain in the ass," he continued, "or at least that's what people say. Lots of local interference, stupid questions. One guy I know says they even threatened to shoot him down."

"The people at the pro shop can be a little touchy, Mr. Luck. In the transmission, I've provided you with information that should help, and Mr. Tampambulos will make prior arrangements with the greens manager to deal with the situation. You won't have any problems."

"Okay, fine. Thanks. . . ."

But Harry was already talking to dead air. He wasn't worried, however. Xris was making the arrangements and that was all Harry needed to know. If he had been told that Xris was making arrangements to get him in and out of hell, Harry would have packed his suntan oil and been ready to go.

The phone buzzed again.

"Mr. Luck?"

"Yeah. Glad you called back. I had a question about that golf course. Are there any landing lights—Oh, it's you. Listen up! You bastards promised me you'd be here to hook me up a week ago! I've been stuck in this damn motel room with nothing to watch but six hundred and forty-eight channels and I— Oh, you will? Well, fine. I'll be here."

Harry jabbed the phone button to with extra pressure, just to show them he meant business. After that, he stood for a moment, knowing he had to do something but unable to remember what. He looked at the light flashing on the phone. Someone had left him a message. He should really find out who.

His computer buzzed.

"Incoming transmission," he said, and went to his computer.

He downloaded the files. The prison break was set for tomorrow night, which meant that he'd have to leave tonight in order to reach Jango in time. As Mr. Trevor had instructed on his previous phone call, Harry had rented a small apartment on a weekly basis, an apartment near a private spaceport on a planet in the Jango system. Harry copied the landing coordinates into a computer remote that he would transfer to his plane.

A map had been provided, showing the location of all the security satellites, as well as their electromagnetic search frequencies. Another map revealed the location of the air-to-ground batteries. Harry didn't need to worry about any of those. Xris would handle that part. But he transferred the map to the remote, just to be safe. Not that Xris ever made mistakes, but other people had the nasty habit of interfering with his plans.

Harry checked his watch. He had plenty of time to pack, recharge his weapons, eat a couple of replicator pizzas, and pack a snack in case he got hungry on the way to the spaceport, which was located across the street.

He was spreading mayonnaise and lettuce on a peanut butter sandwich—Harry was very particular about his sandwiches, never trusted the replicator, which always argued with him about the mayonnaise anyhow—when the phone buzzed.

Harry slapped the other slice of bread down and went to answer.

"Eye on the Galaxy," said the man. "I'm in my hover, on my way to repair your vid hookup."

"Shit," said Harry. He'd forgotten all about that. The bastards *would* show up just as he was leaving.

"Look, never mind. I've been called out of town."

"See here, Mr. Luck, I'm making a special trip just to do your hookup. It'll only take a few moments."

"I'm leaving town," Harry repeated. "I don't plan on coming back. I'm sorry, but—"

"Mr. Luck. I am here at your insistence. You'll have to pay for the service call anyway. And since it's after hours, that'll be triple overtime."

"Jeez," Harry muttered.

If the new Tycho was anything like the old one, Harry probably wouldn't get reimbursed for the extra charges.

"Well, at least the next poor sucker who rents this dump will have decent vids to watch."

He gave the man directions to the apartment and went back to making his sandwich.

The sandwiches were in his duffel bag, along with his clothes and his weapons, a Marcus quad-shot minigun and a snub-nosed .38-decawatt, his computer remote, shaving kit, and helmet. He was already wearing his flight suit.

"Vid man," came a voice calling through the door.

Harry glanced out, saw a man in uniform carrying a toolbox. He opened the door.

"Come on in. I hope you don't mind, but I gotta leave. The vid's over here."

Harry turned to lead the way out of the entry hall into the motel room. He was just about to point out the location of the vid set when he felt something hard press into his back.

"Hey!" Harry complained. "Watch it! You're sticking me with your toolbox!"

"It's not a toolbox, Mr. Luck," said the man. The hard pressure transferred from Harry's back to the bare skin on his neck. He had no difficulty recognizing the feel of cold metal against his skin. "It's a .50-decawatt hand cannon. There won't be much of your head left if I fire this. Follow my orders and no one will get hurt. Put your hands up in the air and turn around slowly. Very slowly."

"Who are you?" Harry asked, pivoting slowly, as ordered. He felt the gun on his skin as he turned, felt it swipe past his ear. The gun backed off only when he was facing the man. Harry looked at him closely, didn't recognize him.

"Is this a robbery? If so, it's a mistake, 'cause I don't have any cash on me. . . ."

"This isn't a robbery, Mr. Luck," the man said. "You're taking a trip in your new prototype transport ship tonight. By the way, it's a little big for the job, isn't it? And slow? But then, they said you weren't too bright. That's one of the reasons I want to go along."

"And I'd love to take you," said Harry earnestly, thinking to distract the man and knock the gun away. "Nothing I hate worse than traveling through space by myself." He tensed, ready to swing. "But I'm supposed to pick up some people and I don't have room—"

"Don't do anything stupid, Mr. Luck," said the man with the gun. "Either now or when we're in the spaceplane. Your mother wouldn't like it if you did anything stupid."

"My mother . . ." Harry went cold. His hands clenched to fists. "You fucking bastard! What—"

"Don't get excited, Mr. Luck. Your mother is fine. I'll even let you speak to her when we're on board the plane. Some people from my organization are paying her a little visit. They'll leave when I give them the word.

"Now, Mr. Luck," the man added, stripping off his uniform, still keeping the gun aimed at Harry, "we're running behind schedule. Here, let me carry that."

"Thanks, but I can manage," said Harry.

"I insist." The man picked up the duffel bag. He unzipped it, glanced inside. Seeing the guns, he smiled and zipped it back up. "I'll be glad to carry it. Keep moving, Mr. Luck. Your mother's waiting for your call."

"Fucking bastard," Harry said again. He started out the door, stopped when his phone buzzed.

"Answer it," ordered the man.

"Hell, it's probably just the vid people. The *real* vid people," Harry emphasized.

"I said answer it. Who knows? It might be Mr. Tampambulos's secretary, Mr. Trevor. You wouldn't want to miss that call, would you?"

"Fucking bastard," Harry muttered, and went to answer the phone.

"Yeah?"

"Harry, this is Darlene. Where have you been? Don't you check your messages? I've been trying since yesterday—"

"I can't talk now, sweetie," Harry said loudly. "I gotta go. Good-bye—"

"Harry, damn it, wait! We've heard that Xris might be in danger and—"

"Yeah," said Harry. "I know." He ended the connection. "All right," he said glumly to the man with the gun. "Let's go."

CHAPTER 33

El pez muere por la boca.
The fish dies because he opens his mouth.

Proverb

Xris's cell mates were happy to see him. So happy, their pleasure in his return was touching. He might have been coming back from the dead.

"C'mon, guys," Xris said, embarrassed. He mopped his bald head with a towel. "It was only a few days in solitary. I don't recommend it, but at least I caught up on my sleep."

"You're a hero," said Malcolm, grinning. "Everyone's talking about how you took down that fat bastard."

"Great," Xris said bitterly. "Now Slovenski will go out of his way to prove to everyone that he can take me."

The three sobered.

"I guess we never thought of that," Malcolm admitted.

"Has he been around?" Xris asked.

"It's hard to beat up on people from your hospital bed," Alan said.

"Yeah, but he'll get better, unfortunately." Xris never would have believed it, but he was starting to feel something for these men. Affection? Too strong. Pity? Yeah, maybe. They were a lot different from the three cocky bastards he'd met on the transport.

Xris tried to think of how to say what he had to say. "Look," he said finally, awkwardly, "if something happens and I'm gone for a long time—a real long time . . ."

The three gazed at him somberly, troubled.

"Will you three be okay?"

"What are you going to do?" Malcolm demanded.

Xris shook his head. "Nothing I don't have to. Answer

my question. Rec time's almost up and I have business to attend to."

"We'll be okay," said Malcolm, and the other two nodded. "Reality was a tough pill for us to swallow, but we choked it down. You do what you have to do and don't worry about us. We can take care of ourselves."

"I believe you can," Xris said.

He restrained the urge to pat them on their heads. Putting on his jacket, he prepared to go back out in the rain.

Malcolm stopped him at the cell door. "Xris, it's not worth it," he said in a low voice. "Killing Slovenski, I mean. Montieth will crucify you. Slovenski's working for him. Everyone says so. Sure, it may be self-defense, but you'll never even have a chance to stand trial. Montieth will put you away for good. Don't risk it."

"I know what I'm doing," Xris said.

Maybe if he repeated that often enough, he'd come to believe it.

Becking, Mair, and Macdonald were also glad to see him, although they weren't quite as disinterested as his cell mates.

"Anyone want to go jogging?" Xris asked.

"I would," said Macdonald, and grabbed a towel.

He and Xris slogged through the rain to the gym, joined the group of prisoners who were running around and around the track, going nowhere in a tremendous hurry. The track circled the upper part of the gym. On the floor below were basketball hoops and weight machines. Guards kept an eye on everyone from a room at the top, which overlooked the entire gymnasium. Macdonald and Xris fell in at the back of the pack.

"I spoke to Mr. Trevor," said Xris beneath the cover of thudding feet and the echoing shouts from the ball game. "The pro shop on the golf course. 0200 hours."

Macdonald nodded. He was running easily, maintaining a good pace, his stride long and even. Xris ran clumsily. He had never run all that well; the flesh-and-blood part of his body was always engaged in a hopeless contest with the artificial. The damp was having an effect on his joints, probably a touch of arthritis. Just what he needed to make his day, a reminder that he was growing old.

"What's the plan?" Macdonald asked.

"All arranged."

"How?"

"Leave it to me."

Macdonald wasn't pleased. His corpse eyes flicked over to Xris. "Trevor says we can trust you."

"Does he? Gosh, that's sweet of him," Xris said, gulping air. "I'll have to remember to send him a thank-you card."

Macdonald apparently had no sense of humor. The two continued jogging. Macdonald wasn't even breathing heavy, hadn't broken into a sweat. Xris was already winded and wondered if he could survive another fourth of a kilometer.

"I want to know the plan," Macdonald said, his voice grating.

"Yeah, and so would every prisoner in Jango," Xris returned, loping along. "I'm not saying"—he had to suck in a breath—"that you would let word of this out"—he sucked in another breath—"but maybe you talk in your sleep."

Xris called it quits. Wiping his face with a towel, he stood panting at the side of the track, out of the way of the other runners. Macdonald jogged on a few paces, realized Xris wasn't with him, left the track and jogged back.

"You bastard!" Macdonald was angry. "How dare—"

"Look, sir," Xris said in mollifying tones, trying to catch his breath. "you're not thinking straight. Do you want it to look like the finals of a GGA tourney on the first hole Friday night? What do you think will happen if even one person found out we were making a break for it? He tells his buddy, then *he* tells his buddy, and pretty soon we have five thousand guys out there all trying to get on our plane."

Xris shrugged. "I know I can keep it secret. I know you can keep it secret. But what about Becking? What about Mair? Do you trust them implicitly?"

By the look on Macdonald's face, he did not.

"So what happens when they ask you what the plan is?" Xris persisted. "You say you know, but you're not going to tell them. And then—"

"Hey, you two on the track!" The guard's voice boomed over the comm. "Break it up!"

"All right." Macdonald was still angry, but he was forced to admit that Xris had a point.

The Hung leader wasn't the type to forget the insult, however. Xris would be made to pay, though not until after he had served his purpose. All a matter of timing.

"I take it you fellows can escape from your cell, sneak out of the cellblock and onto the golf course without my help?" Xris asked.

"We can," Macdonald said. His look and tone made rigor mortis seem a warm and friendly state. "Just don't ask how."

"I wouldn't dream of it." Xris smiled. "We all have our little secrets. The guard's getting suspicious. I'll be in contact. The pro shop, Friday night, 0200. We have a ten-minute window. I'm not waiting for stragglers."

"We'll be there," said Macdonald. He continued his jog.

Xris watched the Hung leader make another circuit of the track. Then, putting the longing for a hot shower firmly from his mind, Xris went back out into the rain.

He had one more hour before he had to return to his cell. Once outdoors, he brought up Amadi's diagram of the power grid, which was now a photographic image stored in his brain, available on command. Xris crouched down to tie his shoe. He glanced around. No one but himself was stupid enough to be out in the rain during rec hour. Even the guards had sought shelter inside.

Reaching under his sweatpants, he popped open a small compartment on his cybernetic leg, fumbled until he found the switch, and activated the magnetometer. This done, he finished tying his shoe, stood up, started off at a gentle lope.

One of the devices Dr. Quong had installed in Xris's leg—presumably on Amadi's advice, although Xris was certain Quong himself had foreseen that Xris might have a need for it—was this magnetometer. As Xris took his walk around the compound, the magnetometer in his leg triggered a pulse whenever it passed over a buried power cable.

The pulses corresponded precisely with the diagram Amadi had provided. Not surprising. Amadi must have known Xris would check things out. Xris gazed at the golf course, now off-limits to the prisoners. According to the diagram, he would find a power grid junction box just north of what was termed the "pro shop" by the prisoners. Here golf clubs and shoes were stored; for obvious reasons, it would never do for prisoners to keep nine-irons in their cells. The pro shop was locked up. No one was supposed to go near it.

Xris considered making the attempt, abandoned that idea quickly. His butt-beeper was being monitored. The warden would very reasonably want to know what the hell Xris was doing wandering around a golf course in the rain—particularly a golf course that was off-limits.

Xris could only hope that Amadi's diagram was accurate, that the junction box was where he said it would be. He was fairly certain now that on this, at least, Amadi was playing straight. Amadi knew and respected Xris's abilities. Hell, as Xris's boss, Amadi was responsible for Xris possessing those abilities. If Amadi planned to double-cross Xris, planned to wipe out Xris in a "botched" escape attempt, he would wait until Xris had served his purpose. It was all a matter of timing.

He headed back for his cellblock.

He arrived there in time for lights out, too late for a hot shower.

He was cold all night.

CHAPTER 34

Depend upon it, sir. When a man knows he is to be hanged in a fortnight, it concentrates his mind wonderfully.

Samuel Johnson, from James Boswell, *Life of Johnson*

"Something bad's happened," said Darlene. "Something's wrong. I finally got through to Harry and—"

"What did he say?" Jamil interrupted.

"I'm telling you," Darlene said shortly.

Not only was she worried, her nerves frayed, but she hadn't taken a proper shower or washed her hair since their arrival. The dremecks bathed in underground streams that were icy cold. Quong maintained that they were invigorating; Darlene pointed out caustically that she hadn't seen him jump in yet.

"Harry couldn't talk. When I said we'd heard that Xris might be in danger, Harry said, yes, he knew, and he hung up on me. That's not like Harry. Something's gone wrong."

"You know how screwed up Harry gets things. Maybe he was just confused."

"He didn't sound confused," said Darlene. "He sounded scared. I've never heard Harry sound scared before."

"All right, so maybe something has gone wrong," Jamil conceded impatiently.

Shoving his hands in the pockets of his fatigues, he paced irritably about the small subterranean room provided for their use by the dremecks. The room served as communications room and sleeping quarters for everyone except Jamil, who was still bivouacking with the dremeck army, and Raoul, who was establishing his guise as an advance member of Rusty Love's entourage by occupying the best hotel in the city and drinking champagne with the showgirls.

"There's something else," Darlene said.

"What? The sun going to go nova?" Jamil glowered. "We have ten minutes to evacuate the planet?"

"Close. The deadline's been moved up."

Jamil stared, his jaw going slack. "What? How? Who—"

"There was a message. Our anonymous employer. Intelligence has discovered that Kirkov has moved up the operation. The transports will be coming for the dremecks *this* Friday night."

Jamil said every swear word he knew and added a few exotic ones he'd learned from Tycho.

"Is it just me," Darlene added, when Jamil's supply of expletives was exhausted, "or has it occurred to the rest of you that someone is using this revolution for his own personal benefit, that to him it has nothing to do with saving the dremecks. And somehow Xris is involved and in danger."

"It's occurred to the rest of us," Jamil said gloomily.

"We could fly to Jango," Tycho suggested. He was learning to keep his translator turned on. "Rescue Xris."

"And do what once we get there? Go in with guns blazing? Maybe blow Xris's entire operation? Remember, we don't know exactly what he's doing there! We could mess things up good." Jamil halted his pacing. "This puts us in one hell of a spot. Are we working for the good guys or the bad guys? Will saving the dremecks help save Xris? Or harm him? And who is this other person and what is his private agenda?"

"I think Agent Rizzoli has the answer to most of these questions," said Darlene. "We shouldn't make any decisions until we meet with her."

"Which is when?"

"Noon today. At the shopping mall. The scarf counter at Bergdorff's. Lots of people and lots of noise to distract the wire-heads."

"The scarf counter!" Raoul cried, ecstatic. "They carry the most exquisite silk scarves. You must see them, Darlene. A scarf would add a softening touch to your jawline. . . ."

* * *

The Bayside Plaza on Del Sol was located at one end of an artificial lake named Lake Kirkov. The lake had once been blue and lovely, when it was first built. Since then, however, the underground systems that were supposed to feed fresh water into the lake kept clogging up with some sort of local fauna. The lake had gone stagnant, with green gunk and dead fish floating on its surface. Kirkov was furious over this. He guessed that comparisons were being made between himself and this unfortunate body of water and he had declared all-out war on the fauna, which was, however, withstanding the assault with remarkable tenacity.

The shopping center itself was a gathering place for the people of Del Sol, mainly, as Darlene had said, because the wire-heads couldn't listen in on the conversations of a thousand people, though they did their best to try.

After reconnoitering, the team decided the best place to hold a conversation with Agent Rizzoli was a table in the outdoor café, which had been built directly overlooking the stagnant lake. As one can imagine, the café was not particularly popular and there were plenty of empty tables where they could hold at least a semiprivate conversation.

"See if the waiter can give us a table as far from the water as possible, Doctor," Darlene suggested. "I'm just going to show dear Aubrey the scarf I picked out."

"I do not think finding a table will be a problem," said Dr. Quong wryly. "Don't be long."

Tycho and Quong headed for the restaurant. Jamil and Darlene sauntered off in the direction of the stores. Raoul and the Little One were already inside, the Little One listening in on the thoughts of those nearby while Raoul reveled in the feel of silk against his skin.

"This is a test," Jamil said, using their implanted commlinks. "Everyone reading me?"

"I am here," said Quong.

"And myself," said Tycho.

"I keep hearing voices," said Raoul. "Oh, ouch! I remember!" he said huffily, presumably speaking to his small companion. "There's no need to strike me!"

"I'm on," said Darlene.

"Anyone following us, Doc?"

"Not that I can see."

"Okay, everyone. We're on our way. Stay in touch."

"The vibrations make my scalp itch," Tycho could be heard complaining.

"Your brother had the same reaction. You'll get used to it. Come along, my friend, and keep your translator turned on."

"Aubrey?" Jamil demanded in a scandalized tone. "Where'd you come up with a silly-ass name like that?"

"Aubrey has always been one of my favorite names," Darlene returned. "I think it sounds very distinguished."

Jamil grunted. "Sure thing, Dagmar. It's one of *my* favorite names," he added with a grin.

The two entered the megadepartment store, where they were immediately set upon by sales 'bots. Having barely escaped with their lives, they made their way through a veritable maze of women's clothing. A wrong turn brought them to shoes, not scarves, but they doubled back on their trail and eventually discovered the right department. Here they found Raoul, standing at the corner of a display case, lapping up praise from a fawning mannequin.

"Such lovely eyes and hair," the mannequin was saying in its mechanized voice. "Try on the orange silk. There!" The mannequin's robotic hands fussily draped the scarf around Raoul's shoulders. "It looks adorable on you. Simply adorable."

"I don't wear orange near my face as a rule," said Raoul, peering intently into a mirror as he arranged the scarf picturesquely on top of his green chiffon blouse. "It fades my complexion. What do you think?"

"With those golden tones in your complexion you should wear orange all the time," the mannequin gushed. "Observe the effect when we add this cunning little green pillbox hat."

Darlene glanced around for the Little One, found him seated on the floor at Raoul's feet. The Little One had his head buried in his arms. Even the fedora looked bored.

"The place is empty," said Jamil in low tones, speaking over the commlink.

"No wonder," Darlene replied. "Did you see the prices?"

"Too empty." Jamil glanced around. "Not even any wire-heads. What have you spotted?"

"A salesman in the men's department to our right, a saleswoman in lingerie to our left, and two men riding down the elevator. One hundred gold eagles for a scarf!" Darlene exclaimed. "A *scarf,* for God's sake! Look at this red one, darling."

"I don't like it," said Jamil. By his grim tone, he was not referring to the scarf. "Any sign of Rizzoli?"

"Let me show you the cutest new way to tie a knot," the mannequin offered. She leaned over the counter, put her hands on the scarf, which was around Raoul's neck.

The Little One leaped suddenly to his feet, waving his hands in alarm. Whirling, the raincoat whipping around him, he pointed frantically to the two men on the elevator.

"Down!" cried Jamil, grabbing hold of Darlene's shoulder and pushing her bodily to the floor.

"That's scarf's a little too tight, my dear!" gasped Raoul.

A blast from a lasgun shattered the plastiglass case where Darlene had been standing. Jamil crouched over her, his lasgun in his hand, returning the fire, which had come not from the men on the elevator but from the lingerie department. The saleswoman was no longer in sight. Another blast came from that direction. A second shot, from the opposite direction—men's wear—took out a display of silk ties.

"Behind the counter!" Darlene shouted, crawling on her hands and knees.

Jamil dove headfirst over the counter, just seconds before it exploded in a flash of iridescent light, showering them both with hot plasma, bits of plastic, and melted silk. Darlene drew her lasgun, kept low. Another shot smashed into the display directly overhead.

"Where did that come from?" she cried.

"The two on the elevator. You hit?"

"No, I'm okay. You're on fire, though!" Darlene used her hand to extinguish a small flicker of flame on Jamil's shirt.

"Help! Help!" The croaking sound came from above and slightly behind them. "It's choking me!"

Darlene looked behind then to see Raoul struggling frantically with the mannequin, which had tied the orange scarf around his neck and was slowly and most assuredly strangling him with it. Raoul grappled with the 'bot, trying desperately to break its grip. The Little One, swarming up onto the counter, began pummeling the murderous mannequin with his hands and kicking at it with his feet.

The robot clenched the scarf tighter and tighter. Raoul was turning a most unbecoming shade of blue.

"That thing's strangling Raoul!" Darlene raised up, hoping to go to his aid. A lasgun blast nearly took off her head. She ducked back down. "I can't get to him!"

"Where are you? What's going on?" Quong's alarmed voice came over the comm.

"We've been ambushed," said Jamil. "Four of them! They've got us pinned down."

"Tycho and I will be there!" Quong promised. "We're on our way."

But they would never make it. Not in time.

"I'll draw their fire," Jamil said. "You help Raoul."

Darlene nodded.

Jamil jumped to his feet. Firing as he ran, he dashed across the aisle and dove for cover behind a counter featuring leather goods. Purses and handbags tumbled down on his head as the case blew apart. Lasgun fire poured in on him from four directions.

Crawling on her hands and knees, Darlene circled around the counter, hoping to get a clear shot at the mannequin and not kill Raoul in the process. He was losing consciousness; his hands were going limp. The Little One had taken off the fedora, was beating the mannequin with it, to no avail.

"Get back!" Darlene shouted, raising her gun.

The Little One scrambled backward, fell off the counter. Darlene fired.

The mannequin's head exploded. Wires popped and lashed. The hands no longer moved, but they didn't let loose, remained locked in position, holding the scarf tightly around Raoul's throat. Its power supply gone, the mannequin slumped sideways, its lifeless hands dragging Raoul's head down onto the counter. He no longer struggled, but lay quite still, his long black hair falling in disarray over his shoulders.

There was gunfire all around her and then suddenly everything went quiet. A bad sign, but Darlene couldn't take the time to see what was going on. She lunged for the mannequin. Grasping its hands, she tried to break the grip, but failed. She plunged her fingers between the scarf and Raoul's neck, wrenched the scarf as hard as she could. The material gave way. She waited an anxious second and was relieved to see his eyelids flutter. Raoul moaned, his rib cage expanded with a gasping, indrawn breath.

Satisfied that he was alive, Darlene was about to go back to help Jamil when a flash of color caught her eye. Reaching down, she plucked an object from the breast of the mannequin.

"Son of a bitch," she said, staring at it. She tucked it into a pocket.

Leaving Raoul to the care of the Little One, Darlene crawled back to the front of the wrecked leather-goods counter. Jamil lay in a pile of smoldering handbags. A woman bent over him, her hand on his neck.

"Hold it right there, Rizzoli," Darlene shouted, aiming her gun.

"I'm on your side!" Petronella cried. "Come here and help me! Keep your head down. I took out two of them, but the other two got away and I don't know where they went!"

Darlene hesitated. Keeping her gun aimed at the agent, she crept out warily from behind the counter, crossed over to Jamil.

Alarms were going off. The air was filled with smoke. The sprinkler system activated and now water rained down gently on them. Jamil was already starting to come around, shaking his head groggily. A large patch of black hair had been burned away and the side of his face was covered with blood.

Quong and Tycho arrive at that moment, guns drawn.

"Solidify!" Tycho shouted, aiming his weapon.

"What?" Petronella looked up.

"He means freeze," Quong explained. "Don't move, Agent Rizzoli."

"She claims she's on our side," Darlene said.

"Is she?"

"Who knows? We don't have time for an interrogation. There're two assassins down but still two to go and we have no idea where they are!"

"I quite understand." Quong crouched, swiveled with his gun in hands, searching. "What is the matter with Raoul?"

"A mannequin tried to kill him. Honest, Doc. I swear it. You help him. Tycho, cover us. Rizzoli, keep your hands where I can see them. Jamil, can you walk?"

"Right! About face. March." Jamil staggered to his feet, clutched at the broken counter to keep his balance. He blinked confusedly as water trickled down his nose. "Carry on, men. A little rain never hurt anybody."

"Oh, dear," said Darlene. "We can't carry him!"

"I'll take one of his arms. You take the other," Rizzoli offered.

"This way," said Quong, hurrying past with Raoul—a limp mass of green chiffon—in his arms.

The Little One, his hat battered and askew, trotted after them, tripping over his raincoat in his haste, one small hand clutching at Quong's trousers leg.

Darlene and Rizzoli followed, with Jamil between them. He was able to walk, but he had no idea what was going on, kept asking Petronella where the reviewing stand was located and if the general was there yet.

Tycho brought up the rear, guarding their backs.

The team had reached the housewares department when they met up with the police, wearing body armor and helmets and carrying beam rifles.

"They will want to question us. And we don't have time!" Quong muttered. "Stand aside!" he said loudly. "I am a doctor."

"What happened in there?" the policeman asked.

"Someone tried to kill us!" Quong stated. "There may be two assassins still inside. I am sorry, I cannot stay to elaborate. I will make a full report for you later. These people need medical treatment."

The policeman gazed at them intently, then motioned them past. "Sure, Doctor. The paramedics are waiting for you. Berserk dremecks," he reported into his comm. "They've tried to kill some of our people."

"Dremecks! That's not true!" Quong protested.

"Doc!" Darlene said urgently, coming up behind him, half dragging a groggy Jamil. "Keep moving!"

"Central, we have a situation on our hands," the policeman was saying. "Dremecks, armed and dangerous. They've killed two people and taken hostages."

"I do not understand what is happening," Quong said angrily, personally affronted. "*Were* you being shot at by dremecks?"

"No, Doc, of course not," Darlene returned. "The police were in on it! They had to be!"

"I see." Quong grunted. "Then we must still be on our guard."

Outside the store, police were attempting to herd the curious away from the site. Jet-powered ambulances were circling overhead, searching for clear landing zones. One dropped down almost directly in front of Quong. The paramedics jumped out, ran to the back, and flung open the doors.

"Don't get in there!" Rizzoli warned. "It's a trap!"

"I know what I am doing," Quong said curtly over the blast of the engines. He continued walking straight toward the ambulance.

Two paramedics were unloading an air-cushioned stretcher.

"I am a doctor!" Quong told them. Shouldering them to one side, he placed Raoul gently on the stretcher. "I will tend to these people. There are other members of our group still in the building! You are needed in there!"

The paramedic looked at his partner. "You stay here. I'll check it out." He headed off toward the store, which the police now had cordoned off.

"What's the matter with him?" The remaining paramedic looked at Jamil.

"Concussion," said Quong. "Similar to this." He punched the paramedic squarely and solidly in the jaw, caught the man on the downward slide, and dragged him underneath a bench.

"Good work, Doc," said Darlene.

"Hurry up!" he replied. "We don't have much time. His partner will soon discover he has been duped and will return."

Darlene and Petronella helped Jamil climb into the back of the ambulance, wedged him in among the heart monitors and resuscitators.

"It's a goddam mess in here," Jamil said, glaring around angrily. "Where's my driver?"

Quong activated the stretcher containing Raoul. The stretcher glided inside the ambulance, settled into place. Darlene and Petronella secured it. Quong hoisted the Little One in after.

"Tycho, you are with me. Hold on, everyone. This is going to be a rough ride."

The doors slammed shut. Darlene and Petronella made certain that Raoul was strapped securely to the table. He opened his eyes once during the process, looked at the leather bands across his chest, murmured, "How sweet of you," and lapsed into unconsciousness again.

"Activate!" Quong snapped at the computer. He climbed into the driver's seat of the ambulance. Tycho jumped into the passenger seat and slammed the doors.

"You are not the authorized driver of this vehicle," said the computer. An alarm began to blare. "Exit immediately. You are not the authorized—"

"Emergency code 0/79921," Quong returned, punching buttons. "Override. I'm taking manual control."

The alarm shut off. The computer fell silent. The ambulance lifted off the ground and soared into the air at a high rate of speed, sirens wailing.

"Tycho, my friend," said Quong, guiding the ambulance into the lane reserved for emergency vehicles, "you may put away your weapon. For the time being, we are safe."

Darlene slid aside the steelglass panel that separated the driver from the back of the ambulance. "That was pretty impressive, Doc. How did you know the override code?"

"This was how I earned my way through medical school," Quong replied, entering the coordinates of the burrow into the ambulance's computer.

"You were an ambulance driver?" Darlene asked.

"No," Quong replied. "A car thief."

Darlene sat back down.

"He's kidding, right?" Petronella asked.

Darlene shrugged, shook her head, and rearranged the blankets more comfortably around Raoul.

"How are you feeling?" she asked gently, seeing his eyelids flutter.

"Orange," he murmured brokenly. "Terrible color . . . makes me . . . turn blue. . . ." His gaze wandered to Petronella. His eyes opened wide, then he closed them. "Oh, God," he whispered. "My poor vase."

Police cars sped past them, heading toward the Bayside Plaza, where, it was now being reported, berserk dremecks were holding off police in an armed confrontation.

"Power to the people," said Jamil, weakly raising a clenched fist.

Darlene looked at him closely. "You back with us?"

He nodded, grimaced in pain, gingerly touched his head where a bump the size of a small planet was rising. "Have I been out long?"

"Not very. That's a nasty crack. Doc, Jamil's making sense again."

"Excellent. Keep him still, keep his head stabilized, and tell him to stop talking," Quong ordered.

"You heard the Doc?"

"Yeah," Jamil said, wincing. "Just answer one question. Who the hell was trying to kill us?"

Darlene retrieved the object she'd found on the mannequin, held it up.

"It's a playing card," Jamil said, squinting at it. "You're saying some deranged poker player wanted to gun us down?"

"It's not a playing card," said Petronella, staring at it. "It's a tarot card. The Hanged Man. Where did you find this?"

"On the mannequin," said Darlene.

"A Hung hit squad," said Petronella.

"I don't get it," said Jamil.

"This is the Hung's calling card," Darlene explained, holding up the image of a man hanging upside down from a tree. "They leave them on the bodies of their victims for the police to find. A warning to back off." She sighed.

"They must have tracked me down, although I can't imagine—"

The Little One jabbed a finger at Petronella.

"Her?" said Darlene, frowning.

"She broke my vase," said Raoul weakly. "She's capable of anything."

"He's right. It was my fault," said Petronella. "I inadvertently told someone where to find you. I thought I could warn you before the Hung struck, but I underestimated them, it seems. At least," she added softly, "now I have the proof I need to hang *him*."

Darlene eyed Petronella. "You're not some rookie bumbling around on this case, are you, Agent Rizzoli?"

In answer, Petronella reached into her purse, drew out an identicard, and handed it to Darlene.

"Whew." She gave a low whistle.

"What is it?" Jamil demanded, half sitting up.

"Stop moving!" Quong shouted, watching from the rearview mirror.

"FISA Internal Affairs. By God!" Darlene exclaimed in sudden understanding. "You're investigating Amadi, too!"

"I *was*," Petronella said pointedly. "Answer two questions for me. What are you people doing here on Del Sol and what is your man Tampambulos doing on Jango?"

"Answer me one question," Jamil returned. "What's keeping me from shooting you?"

"Nothing, I hope," Raoul murmured.

"I now have proof that the person I suspected in the Bureau is involved with the Hung," Petronella replied. "He's the only one who knew you people were on Del Sol, the only one who could have ordered you followed, the only one who could have ordered that hit. What I can't figure out is the connection between Xris on Jango with the Hung leaders and you people on Del Sol."

"I trust her," said Darlene to an obviously dubious Jamil. "We were thinking the same thing."

"All right." Jamil winced, put his hand to his head.

"We've been hired to foment a revolution on this planet," Darlene explained. "We are planning to overthrow this dictator Kirkov, save the dremecks before they're exterminated, and give them back their planet. But I don't know what that has to do with Xris."

"Let's say Kirkov is in league with the Hung," Petronella suggested thoughtfully. "You stage a revolution. He is deposed. The dremecks seize control—"

"Good God!" Darlene stared. "I think I know."

"What?" Jamil demanded, sitting upright.

"If you do not stop moving around," Quong said severely, "I will truss you up like a chicken. Darlene, be quiet. No more excitement."

"What is it?" Jamil whispered.

Darlene glanced at Doc's back and shook her head.

"Poor Xris," was all she said.

CHAPTER 35

Struggling in my father's hands.
Striving against my swadling bands.
Bound and weary I thought best
To sulk upon my mother's breast.

William Blake, "Infant Sorrow"

"You have a concussion," said Dr. Quong. "You should rest and take it easy."

"Sorry, Doc, but I have a revolution to stage tonight. Besides, that instrument you stuck on the back of my head did the trick. No headache. No dizziness. I slept fine. How's—"

"I relieved the symptoms. I did not cure the condition," Quong said ominously. "The tissue in the affected area is still—"

"Thanks, Doc," Jamil interrupted, patting Quong on the shoulder. "Send me your bill. How's—"

"If you fall into a coma, do not blame me," Quong continued.

"I won't, Doc. I promise. How's Raoul? He's suppose to meet Rusty Love's private barge in less than four hours. What's wrong? What is it?"

Quong was shaking his head. "I believe that Raoul may be dying."

"Dying?" Jamil was shocked. "But he was doing okay when we hauled him out of the ambulance. Well, when he saw the bruises on his neck last night he fainted, but bruises aren't fatal! What's wrong?"

"He has developed a dread of shopping," said Quong solemnly. "A phobia. He says that he can never go into a shopping mall again and therefore he sees no reason to live."

Jamil breathed a sigh of relief. "Is that all?"

"He is an Adonian, my friend," Quong reminded him. "First Harry's obnoxious suit, now an attack by a mannequin, a being in whom all Adonians place their trust. Raoul has suffered severe torment—by his standards, at least."

"He hasn't seen anything yet," Jamil predicted, looking grim. "Are the vids finished?"

"They are finished," said Quong. "Tycho and I completed them last night. We have some very nice footage of the dremecks marching through the main streets of the capital, dremecks surrounding the Royal Palace, dremecks rejoicing when word of Kirkov's surrender is broadcast. The dremecks are terrible actors. But they will be adequate for the purpose. Speaking of dremecks, the One has been here asking for you. He is very upset, my friend."

"Tell him I fell off the planet." Jamil hurried away to deal with his next crisis.

He passed Darlene and Petronella, huddled together over Darlene's computer. The two had been working on the computer since the team's return from yesterday's disastrous shopping expedition. They had been there when Jamil had gone to bed last night and they were back at it again early this morning.

Jamil knew better than to ask them what they were doing and how they were coming along with it. He had tried twice already. The first time they hadn't heard him—or if they had, they were ignoring him—and the second time, when he'd insisted, they had said something to the effect that he wouldn't understand and it would take too long to explain and how was his headache and shouldn't he let Dr. Quong take a look at that nasty cut?

"I'd say that's conclusive," Petronella was saying as Jamil slowed his walk to overhear. "That's the account."

"Yes, no question," Darlene agreed. She looked tired but triumphant. "Of course, there's no name on it. We can't prove a thing."

"But if all this"—Petronella waved her hand at a few passing dremecks—"goes as planned, it won't matter."

"True," said Darlene. "Very true. Oh, Jamil. The One's been looking for you."

"I know. I'm avoiding him. How's it going?" Jamil asked, hovering.

The two women exchanged glances.

"Fine," they both said simultaneously.

"I'd be glad to tell you, Jamil," Darlene added, "but it's . . ."

"Restricted information," Petronella finished.

"Yeah. Right. Whatever. Just tell me one thing," Jamil said testily. The ache in his head was starting to return. "Does this restricted information have any bearing on what we've got coming down today?"

"No," Darlene replied. "It doesn't. Except . . ."

"Except what?"

"Except that it is now more important than ever that we proceed with our plans."

"Uh-huh. And you're not going to tell me why."

"Official business," said Petronella, and damned if she didn't reach for her FISA identicard.

Jamil ignored her. "Is Xris involved?" he asked Darlene. "You can tell me that much, I suppose."

"Yes, but we're not sure how. We think Harry's in on this, as well. That's why he sounded strange on the comm-link. We do know that there's nothing we can do for either of them, nothing except go ahead with what we're already doing."

She gave him a wary smile. "If it's any consolation, we *are* working on the side of the angels."

Jamil grunted, not impressed. "Are you going to be ready to leave on time?"

"After I take a nap," Darlene replied. "Then I'll be ready. How's your head?"

"The information's restricted," Jamil snapped, and continued on.

That was a cheap shot. Jamil had been in the military. He knew all about restricted information. This was government business and the government had a right to its secrets. What stung and rankled was the fact that he knew damn well Darlene would have told Xris. Jamil felt the first pang of jealousy he'd ever experienced in all his years working with the team.

He continued on to the team's quarters, in search of Raoul.

The Adonian, resplendent in a red embroidered silk bed jacket, lay in bed, propped up with at least six pillows—Jamil recognized his own special orthopedic pillow among them.

The Little One was seated at Raoul's side, holding his hand and gazing at him sadly.

"I will wear the black silk moiré at the funeral," Raoul was saying. "Not the one with the pearl bead cuffs. The one with the mauve crystals at the throat. You must send for Dallie Pah to do my hair and my nails. She'll cry and carry on, but you will be firm, my friend." He gave a delicate shudder. "I don't trust those so-called cosmetologists who work for the embalmers."

The fedora nodded.

"Now," Raoul continued, "you must keep a watch out for Raj Vu. If he attends the funeral wearing *his* black silk moiré tuxedo, you must run and let me know so that I can change—"

The Little One said something at this juncture.

Raoul listened, pondered, then sighed. "Quite right. I had forgotten." He almost frowned. Remembering in time that frowning caused wrinkles, he smoothed his hand over his forehead and said plaintively, "There *are* disadvantages, aren't there?"

He shifted on his elbow, appealed to his friend. "Raj Vu *wouldn't* wear his black silk, do you think? He *wouldn't* upstage me at my own funeral?"

The Little One shook the fedora, not at all sanguine as to Raj Vu's intents.

"You're right," said Raoul bitterly. "He would. Very well. I shall wear the purple taffeta."

The Little One made wild gesticulations.

"I know," said Raoul in martyred tones. "I was going to save that for the entombment in the Hall of Fashion mausoleum, but it can't be helped."

Jamil had been standing and listening in a certain horrible fascination, until he remembered that the minutes were counting down. Coming to his senses, he barged into the room, interrupting Raoul in his instructions on the various precious objects that were to be placed with him in his tomb.

"My makeup kit. That's a must. The beaded purse with the blue spangles. Yes, I know it's a bit formal, but we have always been told that heaven requires black tie. There is the chance that heaven might prove to be a masquerade, in which case you should include my feathered mask—"

"What the hell are you doing?" Jamil demanded.

"I have lost the will to live," Raoul replied with dignity, adding, "Hand me my blush, will you? No, not the coral. The pink—"

Jamil picked up the compact, prepared to throw it at Raoul's head as he unleashed the torrent of choice Army vernacular that would wash Raoul right out of his deathbed and slam him up against the far cavern wall. The Little One was already crawling under the bed. . . .

But Jamil halted, almost choking himself on the words surging up into his throat. He had always marveled at the way Xris handled Raoul, coaxing, pleading, and even tricking the Adonian into doing things he never would have considered doing. Such as wearing bright yellow overalls emblazoned with a large red beetle.

Jamil let the bad words escape in a hiss. He regained control of his temper, struggled to rearrange a furious scowl into fond compassion, and gazed down at Raoul.

"I heard," Jamil said in dirgelike tones. He rested a hand on Raoul's shoulder. "I'm sorry. I'll miss you. We all will. I guess . . ." Jamil choked, paused a moment to recover himself. After wiping his eyes, he carried on bravely. "I guess it's up to me to meet Rusty Love at the spaceport."

"Give him my regards," said Raoul, much affected by Jamil's emotion. He brushed Jamil's hand with his fingertips. "Tell him that when he speaks of me . . . and he *will* speak of me . . . to be kind. . . ."

"Yes, yes." Jamil blew his nose loudly. The Little One had emerged from beneath the bed, resumed his seat. He had pulled the fedora down his face. His shoulders were shaking. "I'm sure Rusty will be devastated. But there's this bar I know of in the city. We'll go there and drink a couple of beers in your memory—"

"Beer!" Raoul coughed up the word as if it were a hairball. "Rusty Love is an Adonian! He drinks only champagne! The *best* champagne. It is, after all, in memory of me." He modestly lowered his blue-glazed eyelids.

"Yes, you're right. We'll spare no expense," Jamil said, adding enthusiastically, "Wine coolers. This place has the best wine coolers. The coconut banana"—Raoul turned his face to the pillow—"really glues the old tongue to the pallet," Jamil continued enthusiastically. "After that, I'll drop Rusty Love off at his motel. The We're Not Inn. Get it? Pretty clever, huh? They have hot water . . . most of the time, at least . . . and he'll get a clean towel every other day."

"My poor Rusty," Raoul moaned.

The Little One patted his friend's hand.

"Do you think I should?" Raoul asked, shifting his head to look at his friend. "Consider . . . consider that I . . . I can never again go shopping!" This brought on a torrent of sobbing.

The Little One continued to press home his arguments.

"You're right," Raoul gulped, dabbing at his eyes with a tissue. "I suppose I *could* go in for therapy. It would take years, of course, but perhaps someday . . ."

The Little One spoke again.

"Coconut banana. I remember." Raoul gagged. Sitting up in bed, he reached out his hand, clasped Jamil's arm, and said dramatically, "I live."

"You'll meet Rusty at the spaceport, make certain he knows what to do and when to do it?" Jamil demanded.

Raoul sniffed and delicately blew his nose. "No one knows the sacrifices I make for my friends."

The Little One nodded emphatically.

If Xris had been there, Jamil could have expressed his doubts about trusting one Adonian Loti, much less two Adonian Lotis.

Xris would have reminded Jamil, reassuringly, that Raoul had never before let the team down.

Xris not being there, Jamil had to repeat this to himself. Somehow it lacked the proper ring of conviction.

"Oh, by the way," Raoul said tearfully as Jamil was leaving, "the One has been asking for you."

"Mr. Jamil!"
"Damn!"
Having spotted Marmand rounding a boulder, Jamil had tried to keep to the shadows. He was just about to duck into the elevator, hopefully without being seen. Dremecks have sharp eyesight, apparently.

"Mr. Jamil!"
Jamil backed into the elevator. "Listen, Marmand, I'd love to talk, but I'm extremely busy—"

The dremeck's face-folds were all pinched together and he was no longer blue. He was a mottled gray and his large eyes were wide open and glistening. He placed his three-fingered hand on the elevator controls, preventing Jamil from activating them.

"I am worried, Mr. Jamil. Very worried. I heard about that terrible battle at the Uglies burrow on the lake yesterday. Uglies firing guns and shouting about 'death to dremecks.' It is fortunate that no dremecks are allowed into that burrow or a great many people might have been killed."

"Look, it's not what you think—" Jamil began.
Marmand wasn't listening. "I have decided that this entire plan is far too dangerous. Nothing is worth risking so many innocent lives. Nothing. I thank you for all you have tried to do for us, but now you must go. Immediately. I fear you have done too much harm already."

The One stepped into the elevator. "I'm going to go down there with you today. I'm going to end this."

Jamil considered. Marmand was the leader of his people and he had the right—the absolute right—to send the team packing. Jamil might try arguing, but Marmand appeared about as easy to shift as that boulder.

To make matters worse, Jamil's conscience was bothering him. The team had been hired by an unknown someone, someone with the gods knew what motive, to come to Del Sol and conduct a revolution. Jamil couldn't be certain, but he was guessing—based on what Darlene and Petronella hadn't told him—that the purpose of this revolution was *not* saving the dremecks from extermination. Jamil was in a false position, he was lying to the dremecks.

Yet, while admitting that all this was true, he could still say with an absolutely clear conscience that the plight of the dremecks had touched him deeply and that he was committed to helping them now, if he hadn't been before.

"I am going to tell the young dremecks they must prepare to go back to work tomorrow," Marmand said stubbornly. "I will speak to Kirkov. I will promise him that we will be his slaves in perpetuity if he will only let us live."

"Live!" Jamil snorted, but Marmand had given him an idea. He left the elevator, walked over to a pile of leg-irons kept there by the human overseers to replace those whose locks didn't work. He picked up as many as he could carry, which was about seven. The damn things were heavy.

"What are those for?" Marmand demanded

"They'll need them for tomorrow, won't they?" Jamil said.

Marmand's face-folds twitched.

Jamil stepped into the elevator. It gave a lurch and began its slow, creaking descent. Marmand stood on the side of the cage as far from Jamil as he could get. He refused to talk. Jamil was just as glad to be silent. He stood in his own dark corner, brooding, wondering what the devil he was going to do if his plan failed.

The young dremecks were clustered together in small groups, some of them merrily tripping each other up, others practicing leaping on each other from behind, still others pointing the disabled beam rifles at their friends, who immediately flung their hands in the air in what Jamil had told them was a classic sign of surrender.

Marmand watched, appalled. He cast Jamil one reproachful glance, then stalked stiff-legged into the cavern. One of the dremecks caught sight of Jamil and yelled, "Attention!"

The dremecks halted what they were doing. Grabbing their toy guns, they scrambled and pushed and shoved. Soon they were standing in four lines, each in his or her proper place.

"What are they doing?" Marmand demanded.

"Bayonet drill," Jamil replied. "It dates back to the time

of Napoleon. I know that doesn't mean anything to you, but I think you should watch. They've been practicing really hard to show you," he added, seeing Marmand about to protest. "You don't want to disappoint them."

The One looked out into the eager faces, their face-folds bunched together into happy grins, which were not quite regulation.

"Very well," he said sourly.

Jamil took his place in front of the assembly. He drew himself up, barked out an order. "Close-order fighting, by the position. Carry arms!"

In near unison, the dremecks hoisted their rifles to the carry position and waited.

"Position one!" Jamil ordered.

The dremecks thrust their rifles out in front of them, held them in place.

"Position two!"

Dremeck rifles sliced through the air.

"Position three!"

Using an underhand motion, the dremecks used their rifle butts to strike an imaginary enemy in the jaw. The troops gave a loud yell, a yell which, for the soft-spoken dremecks, had taken more practice than all the rifle maneuvers combined.

"Position four!"

The dremecks returned their rifles to the carry position. Contrary to all military discipline, the young dremecks then turned around to nod, whisper, and grin at each other. They were obviously extremely pleased with themselves.

Marmand was horrified.

"What you have taught them is . . . to kill!" He could barely squeeze the word out through the anger.

"Yeah." Jamil acknowledged his guilt. "If they run into Napoleon, they can chop him up into little bits. Or rather they could if they actually had bayonets, which they don't. I haven't taught them to kill. What I've taught them is discipline, how to act as a unified whole. I've given them something else, too. Look at them, Marmand. Take a good look at them."

The dremecks, aware of their leader's scrutiny, had regained their order, were standing at what, for dremecks, passed as parade attention, which meant that half of them were standing stiff and upright, eyes forward, their face-folds quivering with the strain, while the rest shuffled their feet and giggled.

Marmand glowered. "They look like killers," he said in disgust. "Make them stop doing that."

"Right." Jamil stood in front of his command. In his hand, he held the leg-irons, chains dangling.

"That was rotten," he said, his voice harsh. "Rotten, lousy, clumsy, and stupid."

The dremecks were staring at him in bewilderment, their large eyes glistening, face-folds starting to droop.

"I don't know why I'm wasting my time," he went on. "I made a mistake. You were born slaves. You'll never be anything but slaves. Here"—he motioned—"put these chains on. You'll report to work tomorrow as usual."

The dremecks curled up, wilted, withered. It was like pulling out plants by the roots. Heads lowered, shoulders bowed, face-folds sagged. Here and there a rifle clattered to floor.

"We might as well start now." Jamil slid one of the leg-iron rings off his arm. "Trella, come here."

Trella stared at him, frightened.

"Trella!" Jamil barked savagely. He held the leg-iron ring open and ready. "You filthy dremeck! I said come here!" He reached out to grab hold of her by the arm.

Trella lowered her head. But instead of waiting meekly for him to fix the chains around her leg, she ran straight at him, head down, and butted him. Ramming her head into his solar plexus, she knocked the breath from his body, sent him sprawling backward on the rock floor with a melodic clang.

"I am not a slave!" she cried, stamping her foot on the chains. "I will never go back to being a slave! I would rather die!"

The rest of the dremecks surged forward, shouting and stamping and banging the butt ends of their rifles on the rock. Jamil was in peril of being trampled, and for a moment he feared he had gone too far. Hurriedly, he regained his feet, grimacing as he straightened, and looked at Marmand.

The One was cold and rigid, as if the rock had flowed down from the ceiling and formed itself into a dremeck.

"You say you would rather die," Marmand said gratingly, speaking to Trella, though his gaze included all the young dremecks. "Say instead that you would rather kill! Death is the price of freedom. Not only your deaths, but the deaths of other living beings! Is it worth it? Is your freedom worth ending the life of another? Think of it! We are given life once. We can never have it back, once it is gone. When you take a life, you take away a part of the future. You take away all that person would have dreamed or thought. Worse, you take away all the other people who might have been born of that person. When you end a life, you do not end one life. You end many. And what do you gain?"

"Dignity," said Jamil. "Self-respect. Some people would say that to live without that is not living."

"What do you say, Trella?" Marmand asked gently.

Trella did not look at the One. Her whole body quivering, she stared at the chains that lay on the floor.

"I will not put that back on," she said softly, so softly that she could barely be heard. "I will not."

Marmand looked at Jamil with utter loathing.

"No one's going to die," said Jamil lamely. "No one's going to kill or be killed. It's all going to be for show. . . ."

His voice trailed off. That wasn't the point. He had shown the dremecks a nice shiny red apple. He'd told them how sweet and juicy it tasted. He'd chopped it up and passed it out for their enjoyment. He could almost hear the garden gate slam behind him.

Trella had begun to pound the chains with her rifle butt. The other dremecks were joining her, pounding and smashing and battering the leg-irons that had marked their servitude.

Jamil should have stopped them in the mad fit of destruction—Trella had already broken the stock on her gun and the other dremecks were adding to the damage. But Jamil's head ached. His whole body ached.

Sitting down on a rock, he watched the dremecks and thought about nuclear proliferation.

CHAPTER 36

Would you realize what Revolution is, call it Progress; and would you realize what Progress is, call it Tomorrow.

Victor Hugo, *Les Misérables*

"Check weapons," Jamil ordered.

Tycho drew a minigun from an interior pocket. The minigun was small, easily concealed, and highly effective in close-quarters fighting. The minigun fired short, lethal bursts in rapid succession and could clear a hallway in milliseconds with minimum noise and maximum destruction. Tycho shifted the sleek little weapon to examine the power light at the bottom of the barrel.

"Off," he reported.

"Darlene." Jamil glanced at her. She was carrying the same weapon, concealed in her purse.

"Off," she said with a wry smile and a shrug.

Jamil checked his own. "Off." He slid it into the pocket of his suit coat.

"Can't we at least set them on stun?" Tycho pleaded.

Jamil shook his head. "There's no such thing as 'stun' to civilians. If you stun someone, what happens? There's a flash, a boom, and your man goes down. If you kill him, what happens? A flash, a boom, and your man goes down. Okay, the boom sounds different, but only to a pro. Seeing the target hit, watching him fly backward into a wall, most civilians will instantly assume the worst and then they'll go stupid on you."

"What if people shoot at us?" Tycho argued. "Their weapons won't be set on stun."

"We're thinking good thoughts today," Jamil admonished. "No one's going to shoot at us."

Tycho was not convinced. He had altered color to match the wall behind him and his skin was now pale blue, which was supposed to promote relaxed feelings according to the real estate agent who had been showing them the building. The room in which they were standing was part of a suite of offices available for rent in the building across from the vid station. It was empty except for the team members, who had left the agent standing at the front door, saying that they needed to confer in private. The relaxing blue was doing nothing for them.

"Your weapon will power up in thirty seconds," Jamil reminded him comfortingly. "In case we run into trouble."

"That's going to be a long thirty seconds," Darlene observed, not arguing, merely commenting.

Jamil knew very well how long those thirty seconds would be—eternity, maybe, if someone got the drop on them. He briefly reconsidered his orders, went over the same arguments he'd gone over a hundred times before now. Tycho was an unknown quantity, untested. His brother had been one of the best, but who knew if a cool head and nerves of steel were hereditary? If anyone died, it was going to make arguing the dremecks' cause a lot more difficult—maybe even impossible.

Besides, Jamil wanted to be able to show these people in a dramatic manner that he and his team were sincere.

And, after all, it was only thirty seconds.

"Doc, you ready?" He spoke into the commlink.

"Ready," Quong replied.

Dressed in a stolen overseer's uniform, Quong and thirty dremecks were waiting in a truck parked on the street across from the vid station.

"Make sure that they act like slaves, Doc. They looked like kids going to the fun park when we loaded up."

"I will do my best," Quong said. "But they are very excited."

"Fine, Doc. Remember, hit Maintenance first."

A moment's silence, then Quong said coldly, "Do you want to go over all my orders? Apparently we should, if I'm not to be trusted—"

"No, no, Doc," Jamil said hastily. "That's okay. I have every confidence in you."

He sighed, rubbed his hand over his sweaty face—it was damnably hot; they didn't turn on the air-conditioning just to show the place to prospective renters.

Jamil considered contacting Raoul to find out if Rusty Love's barge had come in and if it had brought Rusty Love with it. But though Raoul was fitted with an internal commlink like the rest of them, he generally forgot to turn it on, and if he did remember and anyone spoke to him, it might take him an hour or so to figure out which of the voices he normally heard in his head was speaking. Jamil abandoned the idea. He didn't have time to convince Raoul that he was who he claimed to be. Not God.

Jamil looked at his watch, noticed that Darlene was looking at her watch.

1500.

"There they go," Darlene said, pointing. "Right on time."

A long line of dremecks, led by two overseers, was shuffling out of the building, leaving by the side door. They were herded into a large truck parked in the alleyway.

When all the dremecks were on board and the truck doors were bolted behind them, the overseers climbed into the truck cab. The truck powered up its engines, rumbled off down the street, so heavily loaded that its jets couldn't keep it floating level. The truck bobbed and dipped, its frame occasionally striking the concrete.

Jamil pictured the dremecks jammed into the back of the airless, dark compartment. The truck had been parked in the sun. It must be hot as Raoul's red leather pants. Jamil had already seen the trucks arrive at the mines, had watched them haul the dremecks out unconscious, bruised, and battered.

"And there go the wire-heads," Darlene said. "Right on time."

Two of Kirkov's secret police were leaving the building. Their shift for the day was over. Their replacements would be along in a few minutes.

Jamil looked at his watch. 1505.

Quong pulled his truck into the alley. Jumping out of the

cab, he walked back, unlatched the doors. There was a moment's pause. Jamil could hear Quong over the commlink, reminding the dremecks of how they were supposed to act, what they were supposed to do. Quong backed up a step, his stun-stick held at the ready.

The dremecks jumped out of the truck in single file. Their leg-irons gleamed in the sunshine. There were a few more wide grins than Jamil thought appropriate, and some enthusiastic and good-natured jostling. Fortunately, no one was paying attention to the routine shift change.

Quong barked out a sharp command and the young dremecks fell into lockstep, hands resting on the shoulders in front of them, heads bowed submissively. Jamil heard the occasional smothered giggle over the comm, but, all in all, it was going better than he'd expected.

The dremecks, accompanied by their overseer, marched into the vid station by the side door.

"There goes the rest of the day shift," Darlene said, indicating a dozen people leaving the building.

"Right. Our turn," Jamil said.

"Thank you for showing us the office space, but the rooms don't quite suit our needs," Darlene said to the real estate agent, who was staring in considerable astonishment at Tycho.

"That's really an ugly shade of blue on the walls," Jamil added as they walked past. "You should consider changing it."

"Yeah," said the agent, agreeing wholeheartedly. "We'll do that."

They exited the building, crossed the street, and entered through the glass doors. Equipped with sensors, the door opened automatically whenever anyone approached.

The receptionist had looked up from her work, was smiling at them expectantly.

"Welcome to Vid Del Sol—" she began as the doors shut behind them. Catching sight of Tycho, her eyes widened.

"Damn! Rock in my shoe!" Darlene exclaimed.

The three halted just short of the weapons scanners through which they would have to pass to reach the reception desk. Darlene bent down, removed her shoe, and fished out the rock. While the receptionist's attention was divided between watching Darlene and staring at a blue Tycho, Jamil touched a control on the magnetic random scrambler that was attached to his belt. Darlene straightened, shoved her foot back into the shoe, and shook her head. Her face was flushed.

"Nothing like making a suave entrance," she said as she passed through the weapons scanner, which didn't emit a peep.

Jamil and Tycho followed. A security 'bot, its electronic eyes gleaming red, left its post and came over to inspect them. Again, Jamil touched the control. The 'bot stopped in confusion and began to pivot slowly in place, emitting a pathetic whine.

"Oh, dear," said the receptionist. "It's malfunctioning again. If you'll excuse me one moment, I'll call Maintenance. This happens all the time," she said with an apologetic smile. "It's an older model. We're supposed to be getting an upgrade— Hello, Maintenance? This is Reception. The security 'bot's on the fritz again. Thank you."

The receptionist looked up. "Welcome to Vid Del Sol— Oh, my goodness!"

A loud thud sounded behind them. The receptionist jumped to her feet. Jamil, Darlene, and Tycho turned to see a wire-head standing in front of the automatically opening doors, which unfortunately had not opened automatically. The policeman was holding his hand over his bleeding nose, while his companion beat on the glass.

"I guess your door's not working either," Jamil said helpfully.

The receptionist ran to the doors, tried in vain to shove the heavy plastiglass panels apart with her hands.

"I'm terribly sorry!" she shouted through the doors to the injured policeman outside. Holding a reddening handkerchief to his nose, he was being helped into a taxi by his companion.

Two more wire-heads, having seen the situation, approached the door.

"Out of service!" the receptionist yelled, motioning with her hands. "Go around to the side entrance!"

Human nature being what it is, the two attempted to

enter the doors anyway. After banging on them ineffectually, the two left.

"You should post a sign," Darlene suggested.

"That's a good idea." The receptionist headed back to her desk.

Before she could reach it, thirty dremecks swarmed into the lobby, moving at double quick time, with Quong trotting along behind them.

"Where do you want them?" Quong demanded.

"Not here!" The receptionist gasped. "Are you crazy? They're never permitted in the front lobby! Take them around to the back!" She gestured down a corridor.

"Sorry, lady. I'm new," Quong mumbled. "C'mon, you buggers."

The dremecks halted, wheeled, and milled about in confusion, tangling themselves in their chains. Quong—with threats and shouts—attempted to sort them out and get them moving again. Three people were now banging on the door, one of them red in the face and irate. The receptionist was feverishly writing the sign, all the while trying to raise Maintenance, who wasn't responding. Having met Quong on the way in, Maintenance was now in a closet, slumbering peacefully under the influence of hypnospray.

The three people who had been hammering on the door departed.

"Coast clear," Jamil announced.

"Where's the ladies' room?" Darlene demanded, leaning over the receptionist's desk.

The harassed receptionist lifted her face. Darlene sprayed her with hypnospray. Jamil caught the woman as she slumped backward, sound asleep. He lifted her in his arms, placed her in a comfortable position on a couch in the reception area. Tycho shifted the couch so that it couldn't be seen from the doors. Darlene taped the OUT OF SERVICE sign to the doors.

"Right. Move out."

Jamil gestured to Tycho. The three departed down the corridor on their right; Quong was marshaling the dremecks down the corridor to their left.

The Del Solian Public Records computer had provided Darlene with everything the team needed to know about the building, including a detailed blueprint, whose information was enhanced by the vids taken on the tour. Vid Del Sol was a small operation, funded and operated by Dictator Kirkov. All content was controlled. The nightly news always included a tirade against the Starfire monarchy, which tirade ended by praising Kirkov for saving Del Sol from being swallowed up by an unfeeling galactic empire.

It was difficult to control minds in an age when any kindergarten child could operate the family's satellite uplink. The people of Del Sol didn't need their minds controlled. They knew very well what was going on in the galaxy. Kirkov was quite clever in his rule. He trampled on no liberties and freedoms except those of the dremecks.

The economy was healthy, people were well fed. They lived in good houses, had good jobs. Their streets were safe, their kids were receiving an adequate education. The humans living on Del Sol were safe and they were prosperous, two words that many would have included in their descriptions of heaven.

Vid Del Sol was something of a joke. All broadcasts were censored. Kirkov himself wrote the script for the news reports, which no one watched, since they didn't tell the truth anyway. Vid Del Sol's highest-rated program was the local evening weather forecast. The next-highest ratings went to an early morning kiddie show featuring an oversized, hairy, and lovable tarantula whom preschoolers adored, for no reason any adult could fathom, providing the local psycho-analytical community with fodder for publications for years to come.

Station personnel records indicated only a skeleton crew of humans and dremeck slaves was on duty at night. The human crew included two wire-heads, who kept an eye on proceedings. The broadcasts were all prerecorded. The dremecks had been trained to run most of the electronic equipment, under human supervision. The news anchors were computer-generated—thereby saving a lot of money on highly paid and temperamental personalities.

Rumor had it that Vid Del Sol was sick and tired of being known as the home of Hairy the Airy Arachnid.

"Tycho, you cover the side entrance." Jamil pointed toward some stairs leading down to the lower level. They could hear pounding on the doors, which Quong had thoughtfully locked on his way inside the building. "That will be the wire-heads. Open the door, gas 'em, drag them inside, and clamp the restrainers on them. Don't give them a chance to report in! Got that? Then lock the door. When all's secure, join us in the studio."

Tycho nodded and departed, clattering down the stairs.

Darlene and Jamil proceeded along the hall. The studio itself was located at the end of the corridor.

"Twelve hours from now, the dremecks will be a free people," Darlene said. "You've done a good job, Jamil."

"We're not there yet," Jamil replied, pausing to peer in the offices they passed. "A lot could go wrong."

The station was closed for the day. Presumably the office staff—secretaries, advertising, scheduling, and administration—had gone home. Jamil kept an eye out for stragglers or extremely dedicated employees who might be staying on after hours.

Apparently no one at Vid Del Sol was that dedicated. The offices were empty. Voices could be heard, but they were coming from the studio.

"Nothing's going to go wrong. It's a good plan," Darlene said, smiling at him reassuringly. "Especially the abduction of the president."

"It's Raoul's plan," Jamil amended. "In my worst nightmare, I never thought I'd be carrying out an operation dreamed up by an Adonian Loti. And I do mean dreamed." He paused, activated his external commlink. "Time to check in with Rizzoli. Alpha One, this is Beta Two. Are you in position?"

"Beta Two, this is Alpha One." Rizzoli's voice. "I'm in position."

"Anything happening there?"

"People coming and going. Business as usual."

"Yeah, well, the shit won't hit the fan until Vid Free Dremeck starts broadcasting. With luck, I'll be there by then. Keep in touch."

"Right. Good luck, Alpha One."

Jamil ended the link. "I hope you and Rizzoli are right about this," he said to Darlene.

"So do I," said Darlene somberly. "For Xris's sake."

Jamil and Darlene rounded the corner, met Quong and his troop of dremecks marching down the hallway. At a signal from Jamil, Quong entered the control room. The dremecks filed in behind him.

Jamil and Darlene entered the studio.

"Good evening, ladies and gentlemen," Jamil said to the startled faces turned toward him. "We're here to institute a few programming changes—changes that I guarantee will increase your ratings one hundred percent.

"Tonight, Vid Del Sol is going to make history."

CHAPTER 37

We may live without friends; we may live without books;
But civilized man cannot live without cooks.

Owen Meredith, *Lucile*

"Welcome to Hernandez Valentino's. Ah! It is you, sir. So pleased. Madam looks charming tonight, as usual. Your table is ready. Alfonse will seat you. You are in for a treat this evening. Monsieur has heard?" the maître d' murmured.

Monsieur had indeed heard. The elite of Del Sol were talking of nothing else. Madam was overjoyed that they had been invited. Monsieur was highly sensible of the honor. When was Mr. Love expected? And was it true that His Eminence was to dine here tonight, as well?

Mr. Love was expected at 1800, but when he would arrive, the gods alone knew, Mr. Love being an Adonian. It was to be hoped devoutly that he would actually arrive this evening, and not two evenings from now.

This gloomy outlook rather dampened Madam's spirits, but Monsieur mentioned that no doubt Mr. Love had a social secretary who took care of these things, and if His Eminence Kirkov had been invited, surely Mr. Love would not wish to offend the leader of—slight cough from Monsieur, who was himself in the banking business—this influential planet.

The maître d' nodded and the two looked knowingly at each other. Rusty Love could tell the vid reporters that he was coming to Del Sol to investigate a possible location for a vid shoot, but the populace of Del Sol knew better. Del Sol was absolutely useless as far as local scenery, unless you happened to enjoy looking into vistas of gray buildings filled with even grayer suits that all smelled of money.

"His Eminence is indeed dining with us." The maître d' went on to favor Monsieur with his attention. "Mr. Love sent him a most elegant invitation, so I am told. His Eminence is not a fan of the vids." The maître d' emphasized this. "Not a fan. The dictates of his high office preclude such frivolous pursuits. He devotes every hour of his life to his people. Mrs. Eminence, however, is said to have persuaded him."

Monsieur and Madam understood completely. They themselves were not fans of the vids. Merely curious, could not turn down the invitation without offending, it would be something to tell their grandchildren.

Besides, to eat a meal prepared by Mr. Love's personal chef—the renowned Caligula Fox!

"That is not to say," Monsieur added hastily, seeing the maître d' frown, "that Chef Valentino is to be found lacking. Far from it. His *Haricots Verts avec Almondine* and his *Veau Flambé* are not to be equaled. Still, there is a lot to be said for trying something new."

At this juncture, the maître d' withdrew his favors, rather coldly, and said that Madam and Monsieur's table was ready. The maître d' summoned an attendant lord with a slight lift of his left eyebrow. The attendant lord, who was watching for the signal, launched into action. He apprehended the couple and, keeping them in strict custody, marshaled them through the candlelit landscape. Legions of other attendant lords bowed from their black cummurbunded waists, murmuring welcomes.

The instant the couple was seated in the crimson leather booth, they were set upon by hordes of underlings, who filled water glasses and placed Madam's napkin upon her lap, evidently under the impression that Madam was too weak to lift the bit of cloth to perform this duty for herself.

When the couple had been napkined and watered, the underlings melted into the shadows, hovering, waiting in tense anticipation to pounce upon the least crumb that might fall from Monsieur's roll or to refill Madam's water glass the moment she had taken a sip. The attendant lord summoned the wine steward, who conferred with Monsieur, and the brief eddy of excitement, which had sent ripples through the kingdom, smoothed out and vanished. All was again hushed, expectant, and exceedingly nervous. Chef Caligula Fox had not yet arrived.

The maître d' beckoned to one of the gentlemen-in-waiting.

"Is the table prepared for His Eminence?" the maître d' murmured.

He always murmured. He had never been known to speak aloud except on one dread occasion when His Eminence had refused a bottle of wine with the pronouncement that it was "corked." The maître d', on hearing of this, had said, "Ahem," in an extremely loud and violent tone, adding in a murmur that the wine steward was to be relieved of his duties on the spot.

Hernandez Valentino's was known to be the favorite restaurant of His Eminence, Dictator Kirkov. He dined there whenever his busy schedule permitted, preferring its dark, warm ambience to the vast, echoing gold-leaf-adorned and crystal-plated dining room of the palace.

His table overlooking the garden was always kept for him, even on those nights when he wasn't expected, even on those nights when it was known that he was off-world. If another party sat there, the maître d' was convinced that His Eminence would sense their emanations and be displeased, as the true princess in the children's tale had sensed the pea tucked beneath the very bottom of the twenty-five plastifoam mattresses.

Tonight the usual preparations had been made for both His Eminence's comfort and his security. Reservations for Hernandez Valentino's had to be made—by the ordinary people, at least—six months in advance. This permitted background checks to be run on all prospective diners. Food for the restaurant could be purchased only from local companies, who were first cleared by the secret police, and who then underwent periodic surprise inspections. All food served at the restaurant was sent through scanners that checked for everything from the occasional confused fly to arsenic and salmonella.

A portion of each dish prepared for His Eminence was passed around before his arrival to all the other diners. Not only were they much honored by this attention, but they were watched carefully by the wire-heads to make certain that they partook of the food. Anyone who refused a portion was whisked away to a back room and interrogated. The interrogation was not pleasant, and worse was yet to come. The offensive diner was not permitted to eat at Valentino's ever again. Consequently, everyone ate something of everything, with the result that all of His Eminence's food was tasted in advance by his loyal subjects.

No food left the kitchen but that a portion was first eaten by the cooks, under the watchful eye of the secret police.

As patrons entered, the maître d' greeted them with his customary aplomb, but he was seen to glance nervously at the doors to the kitchen. Chef Fox had yet to make an appearance. Dictator Kirkov and Rusty Love were expected within the hour and there was nothing to eat! Chef Valentino, who had stated loudly and emphatically that he had never heard of this Caligula Fox fellow and that he wasn't at all surprised the Adonian was late, was preparing to rush to the culinary rescue.

An elegant figure, draped in furs and saturated in expensive perfume, his fingers sparkling with jewels, glided into the restaurant. The figure was accompanied by a smaller figure clad in a battered fedora and a raincoat that was rather the worse for wear.

The fur-draped figure cast a bored glance around the restaurant, obviously not impressed, and said, "Caligula Fox."

The maître d' was startled, but accustomed to dealing with crisis situations. He replied in murmur, "So sorry. Chef Fox has not yet put in an appearance—"

"Yes, he has," said the figure, fixing the maître d' with violet-drenched eyes. "I am Caligula Fox."

The maître d' was shocked, appalled. He devoted a moment to recovering from this blow, then he murmured calmly and with immense dignity, "Chef Fox. You are needed in the kitchen. The service entrance is—"

"Kitchen?" Chef Fox's eyebrows arched. He was beyond amazement. "Whatever am I to do with a kitchen?"

"Cook in it, I presume," murmured the maître d', slowly

simmering. He beckoned and an attendant lord leaped to do his master's bidding. "Alfonse. Take Chef—"

The maître d' paused. This appeared highly suspicious. He left Alfonse hovering and looked about for one of the ever-present wire-heads. A slight nod and a flick of an eyelid and the wire-head hastened over.

"This person claims to be Caligula Fox," murmured the maître d'.

The wire-head looked Fox up and down, said calmly, "It's him."

The maître d' fixed the wire-head with an imploring gaze, begging him to change his mind. The wire-head shrugged and repeated, "That's him. We ran a computer check. Famous chef. Adonian. The other one in the raincoat. Alien. Pet."

Caligula Fox stood silently, untouched by this commotion, gazing vacantly at a bowl of yellow flowers.

"I beg your pardon, Chef Fox," the maître d' murmured distractedly. "It's just that I assumed that you, being a chef, would like to participate in the preparation of the food. Chef Fox?"

The small raincoated pet reached out a hand and tugged on Chef Fox's furry sleeve. Chef Fox gave a peremptory start and looked vaguely in the direction of the maître d'.

"Food? Thank you. I could do with a bite."

At this point the pet appeared to be imparting information to Chef Fox, who looked extremely astonished. "Truly? The kitchen." Eyelashes flickered. "Well, I suppose. . . . How amazingly *outré*. Where is it, my good man?"

"The service entrance is—"

"No," Chef Fox said, quite calmly. And that was all he said.

"Alfonse," murmured the maître d' faintly, "take Chef Fox . . . to the kitchen."

Alfonse, quivering in horror, hastened forward, bowed, and indicated the way. Chef Fox and his companion prepared to follow.

"I am sorry," said the maître d', "but your dog may not accompany you. Animals are not permitted in the restaurant. Board of Health regulations."

Chef Fox turned. His eyes, moist and unfocused a moment before, now glazed over and froze solid. "He is not an animal," Chef Fox said, and his voice was soft and yet hard and sharp, like a knife blade swathed in silk. "He is Rusty Love's dear friend and companion. You will show him to Mr. Love's table."

"I am sorry," said the maître d' firmly. He might not have been so brave, but he was confident in the backing of the wire-head standing at his side. "He will not be permitted to enter."

The pet held an unspoken discussion with Chef Fox—a proceeding which the maître d', the waiters, and the secret police all found quite alien and therefore highly disgusting.

"If he is not permitted to enter this establishment," said Chief Fox, "I can say with the utmost assurance that neither I nor Mr. Love will enter it."

Hernandez Valentino's could have borne up under the loss of Chef Fox, but Rusty Love was another matter. The terms were agreed upon. Chef Fox was led in fur-draped splendor to the kitchen, where he looked around in silent and profound amazement, as if it were the first time he'd ever seen such a place. The secret police searched Chef Fox, searched his clothes, searched the fur. The companion, also searched, was whisked off to the men's restroom, where he was sprayed with disinfectant and then escorted to Rusty Love's table, where the pet was admonished not to touch anything or breathe on anyone.

The maître d' ordered one of the attendant lords to bring him a restorative glass of sherry, which he drank to calm his nerves. He resumed his post just in time to welcome Rusty Love, who—being only an hour late—was considered by Adonian standards to be early. He apologized for such.

Word of the famous vid star's arrival spread through the restaurant, helped along considerably by the waiters, who increased their tips by passing the news to all their customers. Even those who claimed to have no interest in a vid star turned their heads or craned their necks to see.

"You are mistaken, my dear," said Monsieur to Madam. "He looks nothing like His Eminence."

Madam could only agree.

Raoul had taken considerable pains with Rusty Love's

makeup to ensure that this would be the case. Rusty Love's current hair was thick and batwing black; he wore it pulled back from his classically chiseled face in order to emphasize the classic chisels. His eyes were brown, tinted with flecks of gold, compliments of a few drops of pupil color enhancer. He was broad-shouldered, muscular, and his smile was warm and endearing.

That smile was his best point of acting. Rusty Love was an Adonian at heart, one might almost say the epitome of Adonia—self-involved, self-absorbed, cold-blooded, and calculating. He cared nothing at all for Raoul, and would not have come to his aid had not the dictates of Adonian social society required it. Even then, Rusty Love might have finagled his way around Adonian etiquette, but he thought his current vid shoot boring in the extreme and was glad for an excuse to take a break; never mind that his absence was costing the vid company billions.

Rusty Love was also intrigued by the element of danger, something he found quite diverting. Adonians do not react to danger as do other, more sensible races. They experience a small amount of fear, just enough to give them a mild adrenaline rush, which induces a pleasant feeling of excitement. There is no unpleasant clenching of the stomach, no unsightly perspiration on the forehead. The main reason for this apparent immunity to fear, so psychologists believe, is the Adonian ego. Adonians simply cannot believe that anyone or anything would want to harm them.

Robot cams surrounded Rusty Love, their lights providing a fitting halo for his exalted person. His bodyguards permitted the attention until the star himself reached the door to the restaurant, when the cams, which would have followed him inside, were driven away. Undaunted, the cams deactivated themselves and settled down on the lawn to await Mr. Love's departure.

The maître d' prided himself on the fact that he treated Mr. Love with the same cool and intimidating reserve that he used for all the other guests. Mr. Love was welcomed. He was given the best table (in reality the second best table). The only condescension the maître d' made to Rusty Love's star status was to personally escort him to his seat.

"Has Fox arrived?" Love asked negligently.

He was assured that Caligula Fox had put in an appearance and he had been taken to the kitchen.

"The kitchen?" Rusty Love found this highly amusing. "Fox in the kitchen. Imagine that," he said, and, giving his pet a pat on the fedora, Rusty Love deigned to be seated.

His bodyguards—enormous men, nearly four meters tall, built along the lines of an armored personnel carrier—took their places, standing behind him. The other patrons attempted to look as if they dined with vid stars every night of the week and either gave Mr. Love the faint smile of one who recognized him but couldn't quite place him or the beaming smile of one who had known him from infancy up.

"His Eminence will be honoring us with his presence this evening," murmured the maître d' confidentially.

"Eminently, I trust," said Rusty Love, who was known throughout the vid world for his sparkling wit. He glanced around to make certain that his comment had been appreciated.

His bodyguards laughed, as did the other guests, who had no idea what had been said, but found it funny.

The maître d' was not amused, nor were the secret police.

"Which Eminence would this be?" Mr. Love continued, casting an expert eye over the wine list. "I meet so many."

The maître d' paled. "His Eminence, the ruler of Del Sol," he said, and in his indignation he spoke aloud. "He dines here frequently."

"Does he?" Rusty Love continued reading the wine list. "Does His Eminence know anything at all about wine?"

"His Eminence is expert in his knowledge," said the maître d'.

"Then he must have his own private reserve," said Rusty Love, tossing the wine list contemptuously to one of his bodyguards. "There's not a decent bottle here. Bring me a bottle from His Eminence's stock. Have Fox choose it. He knows what I like."

The maître d' could do nothing but bow and summon the wine steward.

Rusty Love, smiling in his most charming manner, began to peruse the menu.

CHAPTER 38

He may live without books—what is knowledge but
grieving?
He may live without hope—what is hope but
deceiving?
He may live without love—what is passion but
pining?
But where is the man that can live without dining?

Owen Meredith, *Lucile*

"You must take off your rings, Mr. Fox," said one of the
wire-heads posted to guard the kitchen. "And give them
to me."

"What rings?" Raoul asked innocently, wondering what
in the universe the woman was talking about.

"*Those* rings, Mr. Fox," the wire-head said, pointing to
the three emerald, two ruby, and six diamond rings that
glittered on Raoul's fingers.

"My dear girl," Raoul protested most sincerely, "those
are not mere 'rings.' These jewels are a part of me, my
flesh, my bone, my blood. I could no more remove these
that you so crudely term 'rings' than I could snap off my
hand at the wrist. Still, thank you for thinking of me,"
Raoul added, pressing the woman's hand. "I assure you
that they won't come to any harm."

"The rings, Mr. Fox," said the wire-head, and she held
out a plastic bag. "Just put them in here, will you, sir? I'll
write out a receipt, then shut them up in the safe in the
manager's office."

"But . . ." Raoul's fingers fluttered in distress. "Why?
Why must you take my jewels?"

"Because, sir," said the wire-head with infinite patience,

"there have been certain unscrupulous persons in the past who have been known to stash poison in rings and then drop that poison into the food. We can't be too careful where the life of His Eminence is concerned."

"Poison! You horrify me!" cried Raoul.

You're overacting, came the Little One's warning voice in his head.

I know what I am doing, my friend, Raoul returned silently. *Trust me.*

The mental equivalent of a snort sounded in Raoul's brain.

Shuddering, he pulled and tugged and, with tears glimmering in his eyes, he sadly and reluctantly removed his rings and dropped them in the wire-head's plastic bag. Assuming an air of haughty injury, he accepted the receipt and tucked it into his handbag, which was the next item to be confiscated and removed.

"Do you want my shoes as well?" Raoul demanded coldly. "After all, I might knock His Eminence over the head with the heel?"

"That won't be necessary, Mr. Fox," said the wire-head, struggling to keep from smiling.

"Is that all?" he asked in martyred tones.

"Just a couple of more procedures, Mr. Fox," the woman said apologetically. "First, are you going to be tasting any of the dishes?"

"Of course," Raoul replied with disdain. "How does one cook if one does not taste the food to ascertain if one has perfected the balance of herbs and spices?"

"Exactly, sir." The wire-head handed Raoul a clean cloth. "Then I must ask you to remove your lipstick."

Raoul paused, sent a question flashing to the Little One. *Do they know the truth, my friend? Do they suspect me?*

No, came the Little One's reply. *This is a standard precaution.*

What do I do? Raoul was panicked.

Take off the lipstick, was the reply.

I will look hideous! You know how I absolutely fade away without it!

We have a higher purpose. We must sacrifice to attain our goal. Think of the poor dremecks.

Those dreadful coveralls. Yes. Raoul sighed. Accepting the handkerchief, he carefully removed the offending lipstick, although it was his favorite pearlized pink. Catching a glimpse of his reflection in a pot, he closed his eyes. *I suppose I have no choice but to throw myself on the altar of haute couture.*

"Now, if you'll just step through the scanner, Chef Fox, we'll let you get on with fixing dinner."

"Scanner?" Raoul eyed it with distaste. "What is that for?"

"Search for weapons, plastic explosives, small vials of poison concealed upon or inside the body."

"Inside! You are going to look inside me!" Raoul was horrified.

"It's routine procedure, Mr. Fox."

"It may be routine for you, but I have never been so insulted!" Raoul exclaimed, drawing back.

"It's routine procedure, Mr. Fox," the wire-head repeated in somewhat grimmer accents. She was finally losing patience.

"It's no reflection on you. We all do it, Mr. Fox," whispered the *sous* chef. "Whenever His Eminence dines here."

"You poor dear." Raoul patted the *sous* chef's hand in the utmost sympathy, but he did not enter the scanner.

"I do it myself," proclaimed Chef Valentino.

Raoul bowed to indicate his admiration, but he remained standing in the middle of the kitchen, surrounded by the staff.

The wire-head frowned. "Either enter the scanner, Chef Fox, or you will have to come with us to headquarters."

What's the matter? the Little One demanded. *Go through the blasted scanner! What you're carrying won't show up.*

I am aware of that, Raoul replied. *If you must know, it's . . it's my undies. Dr. Quong lost them when he was doing the laundry and I was forced to wear a pair that does not match—*

The Little One said something in return. Raoul didn't understand the meaning—the Little One was apparently speaking in his own language—but the picture it conjured up in Raoul's mind was quite graphic.

I didn't know you knew things like that! Raoul said,

shocked. *That is the last time I let you go to the vids with Harry Luck.* Raoul hesitated a moment longer. *You're certain they won't notice?*

Two more wire-heads stepped forward, obviously prepared to lay hands on him and remove him by force. Raoul submitted to the inevitable. "It seems I have no choice," he said bitterly, and, looking extremely dignified and uncaring, he walked through the scanner.

"Nothing. He's clean," said the policeman to his fellows, adding irritably, "What the devil was all the fuss about?"

"It's the principle of the thing," said Raoul. "I am not accustomed to being mistrusted. I find it deeply wounding."

"Now, if we could proceed with dinner," said Chef Valentino, barely able to contain his impatience. "What are you preparing, Chef Fox?"

"Me?" Raoul was astonished. "Nothing. I never prepare anything."

"But you call yourself a chef! What do you do?" Chef Valentino demanded angrily.

"I sit on this stool," Raoul said gravely, perching gracefully on a high wooden stool in the center of the vast kitchen. He was dressed all in white silk, with white silk flowing pants and a white silk shirt, tied around his slim waist with a white silk sash. "And I taste the food."

"And then?"

"Then I will make recommendations for improving it."

"Improving! My cooking! You reprobate! You charlatan! You mountebank!" Chef Valentino picked up a wooden spoon and waved it in a threatening manner, shouting to his underlings. "Remove this serpent from my kitchen!"

The doors swung open. One of the waiters hastened inside. "Mr. Love requests that Chef Fox select the wine from His Eminence's private reserve." Looking nervously at Chef Valentino, the waiter added, "Mr. Love says that Chef Fox knows exactly how he likes his food prepared and that he leaves everything in Chef Fox's hands. And"— the waiter gulped—"Mr. Love has been introduced to His Eminence and has been raving about Chef Fox to His Eminence. His Eminence requests that Chief Fox be permitted to do whatever he wishes."

"He may do so, then!" Chef Valentino flung his spoon to the floor. "I quit!"

"You cannot quit," said the *sous* chef. "You are the owner."

"Well, then. I take the night off!" Chef Valentino retreated to the back part of the kitchen, where he sat down at a table and ordered one of the staff to bring him bread and wine.

Chef Valentino turned his back on the lot of them, maintaining his disinterest, although the astute observer might have noticed that the chef could see everything that was going on, reflected in a large silver samovar.

"Send in the wine steward," Raoul ordered. "And tell me what you have planned for the various courses."

Raoul and the wine steward conferred while the rest of the staff, exchanging glances, proceeded with the night's dinner menu. The wine steward retired to the cellar with a list.

"Remember," called Raoul, "I will taste each one before it is served."

He sat back on his stool, crossed his legs, and dreamily watched the rest of the staff at work.

With some trepidation and a fearful glance at Chief Valentino's rigid back, one of the underchefs produced a bowl of salad dressing for Raoul's approval.

"Don't spill on me!" Raoul cautioned. "Hold the bowl beneath the spoon to keep it from dripping. They have developed hyperspace flight, or so they tell me, but they cannot yet find anything to remove olive oil from silk. And they call this progress!"

The chef did as she was told, positioning the bowl beneath the spoon to catch the drips. Raoul guided the spoon to his lips, tasted a tiny mouthful. He rolled it thoughtfully on his tongue. Everyone in the kitchen watched tensely, expectantly, including the wire-heads.

Holding the spoon over the dish of dressing, Raoul deftly moved his thumb under the handle of the spoon, slid the red-lacquered fingernail of his thumb under the red-lacquered nail of his little finger, and dislodged a small dollop of a clear, colorless gel-like mass. It fell into the salad dressing, where it instantly dissolved.

"Add a soupçon of ginger," he said.

"Ginger!" The underchef gasped.

"Ginger!" Chef Valentino leaped to his feet.

"You, sir, are not here," Raoul told him sternly.

Chef Valentino, mustache quivering, sat back down.

The underchef returned to her station, proceeded to add some grated ginger to the dressing, and tasted it with trepidation.

Raoul watched her closely.

"It's quite good," she said in astonishment. "His Eminence will be most impressed!"

"Of course," Raoul replied, clasping his bare and ringless fingers over a white silk-covered knee. "Now, the soup." *It is done,* he added, for the Little One's benefit.

The soup? The Little One was confused by the pronoun.

No, my friend, said Raoul, *the deed. The gel with the microtransmitters is in the salad dressing. Wait until the main course has been served and partially consumed, then you and Rusty Love may proceed.*

The dinner progressed from appetizer to salad to the fish course, with a wine selected to complement each. Raoul watched complacently as the wire-heads put each dish served to His Eminence through their analyzers. The waiters rushed in and out, bearing dishes and returning with His Eminence's compliments for Chef Fox and for Chef Valentino, who was now taking credit for having discovered Chef Fox.

Chef Valentino tasted the salad dressing and the soup—to which Raoul recommended adding a spoonful of vermouth. Clasping Raoul in his arms, Chef Valentino hugged him to his breast, being careful not to muss Raoul's hair, and declared that they were friends for life.

Raoul moved to the chef's table, where they shared a bottle of His Eminence's finest wine and were deep in discussion of how best to prepare *Filets de Soles Aux Moules* when their conversation was interrupted by a hovering waiter.

"Well, what is it?" Chef Valentino demanded irritably.

"Pardon, but Rusty Love is asking to extend his personal compliments to the chef," said the waiter.

Chef Valentino rose majestically to his feet. "Come, my dear friend," he said expansively to Raoul.

"No, no, my dear, dear friend," said Raoul in deprecating tones. "It is you who prepared this wonderful feast. You should receive the credit. What I did was nothing, minuscule, insignificant."

"Are you certain, my generous friend?"

"Please, accept the glory, my only friend. It is well deserved. Besides," Raoul added in an undertone, "I have to run to the little boy's room. Powder my nose. If I could have my handbag?"

Chef Valentino did not press the issue. He entered the dining room and was escorted to Rusty Love's table. The vid star was profuse in his praise and even offered to autograph this evening's menu. He drew a silver pen from the inside pocket of his jacket and, lifting the menu, he wrote his name upon it and handed it to Chef Valentino.

The chef was profuse in his thanks, when he noted a strange look pass across Rusty Love's face—the look of one who is suddenly intensely preoccupied with the functions of his internal organs.

"Excuse me," said Rusty Love. "But where is your men's room?"

One of the waiters indicated that the restrooms were located in the back of the restaurant, down a hall. Rising hurriedly to his feet, Love walked swiftly in the direction of the men's room. One of his bodyguards accompanied him, as did the Little One, trotting along after and tripping over his raincoat. The other bodyguard remained behind to make certain no rabid fan attempted to make off with the chateaubriand as a souvenir.

Rusty's Love's sudden illness must have affected his mental processes, for he took a wrong turn and ended up blundering into the table where His Eminence was dining. The bodyguard pointed out this error. His Eminence rose to meet the famous actor. Rusty Love was gracious, but obviously suffering. Fumbling with the pen he was still holding, he hurriedly signed an autograph for Mrs. Eminence.

Replacing the pen in his pocket, Rusty Love removed a handkerchief from his pocket and began wiping his perspiring face. He left as soon as he could, rushing off in the direction of the men's room. The bodyguard ran after him, leaving the Little One to keep up as best he could.

His Eminence was resuming his seat when suddenly he, too, looked deeply concerned about what was happening inside him. Manfully, he tried to ignore the rumblings in his bowels and sat down, took a sip of wine. His Eminence was up again instantly and now he also was heading at top speed for the men's room, his own bodyguards hastening along behind.

Chef Valentino, astonished and concerned that two of his most illustrious patrons had suddenly fallen ill, returned in haste to his kitchen.

Outside the restroom, Kirkov's wire-heads were twitching like dogs who scent a wolf in the fold.

"Your Eminence, do you think you've been poisoned?"

"How the hell should I know?" Kirkov responded, groaning. "Seal off the kitchen and stand guard outside here."

He pushed open the men's room door, nearly knocking down the Little One, who retreated to a corner. Two guards, looking worried, took up places outside the restroom door. Another ran to the kitchen.

Raoul, dabbing at his nose with a powder puff, looked up in astonishment as the dictator dashed past him and lunged into one of the stalls.

"Your Eminence! Are you unwell?" Raoul called out in concern.

His answer was another groan and the sound of retching, followed by other sounds that indicated His Eminence must be having a difficult time deciding whether he should be standing up or sitting down.

"Oh, gad!" Raoul snatched a handkerchief from his purse and clapped it over his face and nose. "The smell!" He repeated that quite loudly.

The Little One removed a handkerchief from his pocket, put it over his face, and pulled the fedora down almost to his nose.

Raoul opened his handbag, removed a can of air freshener, and began to spray the bathroom, filling it with the scent of roses. He concentrated the spray quite heavily over the stall where His Eminence was—as Raoul could tell by the view of the royal feet beneath the door—now seated on the toilet.

The sounds of groaning ceased quite suddenly.

Raoul opened the window a crack. The smell of roses dissipated, as did the hypnospray.

Raoul was waving his handkerchief to help it along when the door to the bathroom burst open.

"Your Eminence," cried the wire-head, about to enter, "are you all right?"

"Can't a man take a crap in private?" came a peevish voice from the stalls. "Get out of here, you imbecile! Tell everyone to quit worrying. I suppose they've put the entire kitchen staff under arrest by now."

"Yes, sir." The wire-head hesitated. "Then you don't believe that it was poison, Your Eminence?"

"I haven't been poisoned. Just a touch of indigestion. Probably those damn snails. Never could eat snails. Now leave me alone! And make certain that no one else comes in here!"

"Yes, Your Eminence." The wire-head withdrew, shutting the men's room door behind him.

"He's gone," said Raoul softly.

Rusty Love emerged from the stall. "Was he suspicious?"

Raoul glanced at the Little One, who shook his head emphatically.

"That was remarkable, Rusty, dear," Raoul said. "You sounded exactly like our poor Kirkov."

"I should sound like him," Rusty Love growled. "After all those damn newsvids you forced me to watch." He glanced with distaste at the closed stall door. "Do we really have to go in there and haul him out?"

"I'm afraid so. Let's get on with it. We don't have much time. The vidcast is due to begin in half an hour. You"—Raoul looked at the Little One—"block the door and keep your eye on the guard's thoughts."

After a brief pause, during which both Adonians studied their reflections in the mirror and took time to check their makeup, the two set to work.

Jamil would not have recognized this Raoul. Xris would have, however. This was the Raoul he had hired. As for

Rusty Love, his fans would have recognized him for the action hero they adored. His long-suffering directors would not have known him at all.

Working swiftly, efficiently, and silently, the two Adonians dragged the unconscious Dictator Kirkov out of the stall and spread him out on the couch. Rusty Love removed his black human-hair wig and stripped off his clothes. Raoul took a plastiskin mask from his purse and spread the mask over Kirkov's face, smoothing out the wrinkles and transforming the older man's features to those of the younger Rusty Love. Raoul covered Kirkov's buzz-cut blond hair with the black wig.

Rusty Love spent a moment again admiring himself in the mirror. "I like the new haircut," he said, running his hand over his now buzz-cut blond hair. "I think I'll keep it. They'll have to reshoot three-fourths of the vid, but"— he shrugged—"that's show biz."

"And the uniform looks wonderful on you, my dear," said Raoul, helping Rusty Love on with the jacket. "A bit tight through the shoulders. Don't move your arms a great deal or you'll split out the back. I always *did* love a uniform." He sighed blissfully as he stepped back to admire the effect.

The Little One gestured with one hand, thumb down.

"Oh, dear," Raoul whispered. "The guard is thinking that he should check on His Eminence. The guard is concerned that he hasn't heard any sounds from in here."

Raoul and Rusty Love looked over at the couch. His Eminence, now clad only in his underwear, was slumbering quietly. Rusty Love's clothes lay in a heap on the floor.

"The guard must not come in!" Raoul said. "Not yet! We're not ready! Say something!"

"I am feeling much better, Chef Fox," said Rusty Love using Kirkov's voice. He was just putting the finishing touches on a plastiskin mask that he had spread over his own face, a mask which added wrinkles and a certain sallowness to the actor's complexion. "Thank you for your concern. I am afraid I can't say the same for poor Rusty Love, though. He is quite ill."

"Don't worry about Mr. Love, Your Eminence," Raoul said loudly. "I will see to him. He is a fellow Adonian, after all. You don't suppose," he added in worried tones, "he has anything catching?"

The Little One motioned with his hand, thumb up.

"The guard is reassured, but only momentarily," Raoul whispered. "And my small friend has reminded me that it is nearly time for the news broadcast. Help me get him dressed!"

"How do I look?" Rusty Love asked, turning from the mirror.

Not only was Love's face transformed into Kirkov's, but it seemed that Rusty Love had poured his body into Kirkov's body, perfectly re-creating the set of the shoulders, the position of the arms, even capturing the slight sideways tilt of the head.

"You are truly gifted," said Raoul. "His own wife wouldn't be able to tell the difference. The only problem is that you seem to have gained a few centimeters across the chest. Perhaps you could stop breathing?"

"I have to breathe." Rusty Love sounded peeved.

"Well," Raoul said after a moment's thought, "don't breathe quite so . . . expansively."

The Little One made a growling sound deep in his throat. Rusty Love agreed that he would attempt to cut down on breathing and the two Adonians returned to business, dressing the limp and flaccid Kirkov in Rusty Love's clothing.

"How come he's not sick anymore?" Rusty Love asked, smoothing the black silk shirt over Kirkov's breast and adjusting the red cravat. "Can he get over the poison that fast?"

"It wasn't poison. It was machines. No, really, my dear! I'm not lying. Microtransmitters dropped into the salad dressing. Let me see if I can remember this. Dr. Quong explained it to me, but it all seemed so frightfully complicated. The transmitter tells the microtransmitters to go to the bowel system and there wreak havoc. When the microtransmitters are active, Kirkov needs to go to the little boy's room in a hurry. When they're off, he's just fine."

"I ate some of that salad dressing!" Rusty Love looked alarmed.

"Please do not concern yourself, my dear," Raoul said,

reassuring. "Everyone in the restaurant ate some of that salad dressing. I did myself. Recall what I told you earlier. The silver pen is the transmitter and it was set to transmit only on a narrow band, which is why we told you to hold the pen so that the clip was facing the dictator. After twenty-four hours, the microtransmitters will be flushed from the system."

Sounds of running feet could be heard. The Little One flung both arms over his head and scooted away from the door.

"The news has been broadcast. Here they come," said Raoul. "You know what to do from here. Good luck, my dear."

"It's been fun," Rusty Love said. "We must do this again sometime. We'll do lunch."

The two kissed the air somewhere in between them. Rusty Love straightened and assumed a dictatorial air. The Little One sat down on the couch beside Kirkov and stroked his hand.

"Excuse me, Your Eminence." The wire-head opened the door. "I know you said not to disturb you, but we have an emergency."

"Well," said Rusty Love-Kirkov, turning from the mirror, "what the devil is it?"

"The dremecks, sir," cried the defense minister, thrusting his way past the guard into the bathroom. "They're revolting."

"I know that," Love-Kirkov said testily.

"I mean, sir, they're in rebellion. Armies of them are marching through the streets. They're carrying guns, sir. There've been reports of humans being shot—"

"Freedom, eh?" Love-Kirkov looked grim. "I'll give them freedom. I'll free them from this life, if they don't like it. Put me through to General Karnack."

"We've been trying to raise the general, sir. Something must be wrong with the commlinks because we keep getting base Payroll Section—" The defense minister broke off, glanced at the slumbering Kirkov-Love. "What's wrong with Mr. Love, sir?"

"How the hell should I know?" Love-Kirkov glanced at

the vid star in disgust. "Drunk or drugged or both. He's a vid star. Send for my limo. We must return to the palace!"

"Yes, sir. We've done that. Excuse me, sir, but we can't just leave Mr. Love in the restroom. Think of the negative publicity if he should happen to die—"

"Call for his bodyguards, then! Have them take him back to his hotel."

"Revolution!" Chef Fox went pale. "God help us! The streets are not safe! Mr. Love must be transported to his private barge! Immediately!"

"Do what you want with the bastard!" Love-Kirkov thundered. "I have a goddam revolution on my hands!"

He charged out the bathroom. The guards and the defense minister trotted after. None of them gave a backward look at the true dictator of Del Sol, snoring and drooling on the couch.

The Little One opened the door to the restroom a crack. Sounds of voices and screams came from the restaurant, where people had brought out portable vid sets and were watching the first broadcast of Vid Free Dremeck.

"We are live from the corner of Main and Broad streets," came the voice of the excited newscaster. "You can see behind me thousands—literally thousands of dremecks—charging down the street. . . ."

"Mr. Love?" His two bodyguards nearly took the door off its hinges.

"There. On the couch," said Raoul, waving a languid hand. "It was the red pills. I told him, 'Don't swallow the red along with the blue and certainly not within an hour of downing the orange.' But does he listen? My friend and I will accompany him. He'll need me by his side when he awakens. Use the back door. We don't want the press seeing him in this condition."

He winked. Love's bodyguards winked back.

The two men picked up the unconscious dictator-turned-vid-star and carried him out of the restroom. The Little One led the way, showing the prearranged route to the back door.

"Is this the captain of Mr. Love's barge?" Raoul asked, speaking into the comm, as the unconscious Kirkov-Love and his entourage departed the restaurant. "There's a riot going on. Mr. Love is fine. We are on our way to the space-port. Please be prepared to blast off immediately upon our arrival. It would never do for these bloodthirsty dremecks to take Rusty Love—beloved of billions—hostage."

CHAPTER 39

Dust as we are, the immortal spirit grows
Like harmony in music; there is a dark
Inscrutable workmanship that reconciles
Discordant elements, makes them cling together
In one society.

William Wordsworth, *The Prelude*, Book 1

It was 0400, the night of the Revolution.

Contrary to the triumphant reports being broadcast on Vid Free Dremeck, the streets of Del Sol were relatively quiet. Driving the truck, Jamil floated over the occasional curious and confused onlooker, who had come out to witness the revolution but couldn't find it.

Just follow me, Jamil would tell them silently. I'm heading right for it.

This "assault" had not been part of the original plan. But Darlene and Agent Rizzoli were adamant that one building in Del Sol must be sealed off, no one permitted inside. That building was not the Royal Palace, where, according to one of his bodyguards, Rusty Love-Kirkov was now meeting with a delegation of dremecks and reporters. The building was not military headquarters, which was—Jamil fervently hoped—in a state of confusion due to Darlene's sabotage of their communications system. The building they were going to guard with their lives was a bank.

Guard with their lives. With their lives and toy guns.

"God help us," Jamil muttered. "Rizzoli, how does everything look?"

"Fine. There's an apartment building next door and some of the occupants are out on the sidewalk looking around, but they're not paying any attention to the bank. No one's paying attention to the bank. I suppose that's not surprising. Kirkov would have realized the danger, but Raoul reports that the Dictator is currently sleeping soundly aboard Rusty Love's private barge."

"Good. Let's hope everything stays quiet. Our ETA is fifteen minutes."

In fifteen minutes, Jamil drove the truck up to the front of a large, imposing-looking burrow—make that building; he was even starting to think like a dremeck—located in the heart of Del Sol's financial district. He found the apartment building; hard to miss. Every light in every window was turned on. The street was brightly lit as well, the street lamps illuminated a crowd of people milling about in front of the building. Every resident in that building must have been out on the front lawn, talking to his or her neighbor. Occasionally, the people would cast nervous glances in the direction of two wire-heads, who stood apart from the crowd, listening intently to all that was being said and taking notes on who said it.

Jamil shut down the air-jets. The truck settled to the curb. Rizzoli emerged from the shadows and waved. Jamil nodded to her as he stepped down from the truck cab. The apartment house residents had fallen silent, were watching in curiosity and some alarm.

Jamil opened the doors at the back of the truck. At his command, the dremecks—who were now quiet and subdued—jumped out. He'd brought as many as he could; they were practically stacked on top of each other, and looked extremely relieved to be out in the open air.

"You know what to do," he said to Trella, who was the first one off the truck. "But leave the guns in the truck."

"Sir?" She stared at him in astonishment.

"I was wrong to try to change you. I'm sorry."

"I don't understand, Mr. Jamil." Trella's face-folds gathered in a troubled bunch above her eyes.

"Leave the guns."

"If you say so, sir," she said. She tossed her useless weapon in the truck, ordered the other dremecks to do the same.

Jamil's heart ached. "Good luck," he said.

"You, too, sir," she replied.

Marshaling her forces, she bullied them into columns, marched them to the bank building.

Jamil watched them take up their position on the steps of the building, blocking the front door. Trella sent her troops around to guard the side and back entrances as well. Guarding the sides and back with nothing but their blue-skinned bodies. Sighing, Jamil walked over to the apartment building, where Rizzoli was attempting to quell the fears of the residents.

"They don't mean anyone any harm," Petronella was saying.

"Then why are they here?" cried one of the women.

Jamil faced the group of citizens—humans, Uglies. The two wire-heads were talking rapidly and excitedly over their comms. Nothing he could do about that short of shooting them, and his own gun was in the off position.

"I'm going to tell you people what's going on," Jamil said loudly, ignoring the wire-heads. "The dremecks have broken their chains. They've struck a blow for freedom. Why don't you people join us?"

"Chains?" said an older man in a bathrobe. "We're not wearing any chains."

"Aren't you?" Jamil cast a significant glance at the wire-heads. "Your chains may not be made of steel, like those of the dremecks. Your chains may not cut into your flesh when you walk. You may not have ever been prodded by stun-sticks if you stumbled and fell. But you are slaves. Slaves just like the dremecks. You're slaves to fear."

The wire-heads, their report made, drew the weapons which they kept concealed behind their backs—bolt guns, Jamil noticed. A bolt gun can fire in an instant. His gun would take thirty seconds to charge.

"The rest of you go back into your homes," the wire-head ordered. "The military will be here soon to deal with the situation. In the meantime, sir, you and the woman are under arrest."

As the wire-heads came to take them into custody, Jamil glanced around for help, spotted a large and heavy stone flower urn that decorated the front steps of the apartment complex. He was reminded of the urn in front of Xris's house.

"Rizzoli," Jamil said casually, "have you been keeping up with your medication?"

She followed the direction of his gaze, smiled. "No, as a matter of fact, I haven't."

The huge stone urn leaped into the air, sailed over the heads of the astonished spectators, and smashed into the backs of the two unsuspecting wire-heads, knocking them flat. One of them dropped his bolt gun. Jamil put his foot on the hand of the other, retrieved his weapon. Rizzoli wiped dirt from the smashed urn off their heads as she disconnected the wires linking them to their comms.

"He was right about one thing," said Jamil, speaking to the apartment residents. "Go back into your homes. There's probably going to be trouble."

The people stared at the unconscious bodies of the wire-heads, stared at Jamil and Petronella, and stared at the dremecks, who had taken up position in front of the bank.

"What are they doing?" the man in the bathrobe demanded. "Are they going to kill us?"

"You know the dremecks," Petronella said. "You've lived with them all your lives. Do you think it's possible that they could hurt anyone?"

"But the wire-heads said that the dremecks were marching though the streets, murdering people," said a woman, holding a child in her arms.

"Listen," said Jamil. "Do you hear explosions? Laser blasts? Do you hear sirens and alarms? No, you don't. This is a peaceful revolution. We've come this far without a single shot being fired."

"I've worked with dremecks," offered another woman. "God help me, I used to be an overseer once. I couldn't stomach it and I quit. This man is right. They're gentle people, gentle and kind. The way we've treated them is shameful."

"I hope the revolution succeeds," said another man boldly.

"You better watch what you say," warned one of his neighbors, frowning.

The man looked at Jamil and smiled faintly. "Chains. I see what you mean."

"Jamil," said Petronella, touching him on the arm. "You were right. Here comes trouble."

An armored personnel carrier soared around the corner, dropped down rapidly and heavily onto the street. Armor-plated doors flew open. Men and women in uniform jumped out and began deploying on the sidewalk in front of the bank.

"Call it a hunch," said Jamil, "but I have a feeling their beam rifles work. Go stand over there with the onlookers." He was on the comm, back to the vid station. "Delta Three, how close are we to Kirkov's surrender?"

"According to our reporter on the scene, the dictator and the dremecks are still in negotiation," said Quong, adding testily, "Rusty Love says that he must make his surrender appear convincing and I suppose that is true, but if you ask me, he is enjoying his role and is loath to relinquish the part."

"He may be upstaged. The Army's apparently solved their communication problems. They just made an entrance here and are undoubtedly on their way to the Royal Palace now, if they're not there already. See if you can hurry him along."

"You dremecks!" shouted a lieutenant, the platoon leader. "You have three minutes to surrender or we'll fire."

"That's him, sir," said another soldier, pointing at Jamil. "That's the leader. I recognize him from the vids."

Two soldiers approached, their rifles aimed at Jamil.

"Raise your hands."

Jamil did as he was told. "I'm not armed," he said, which wasn't exactly true, but these amateurs would never find it. "This is a peaceful demonstration."

"Search him," said the lieutenant. "Keep him covered."

One soldier searched him, patting him down. The other held his beam rifle on him.

"He's clean," said the soldier. "Keep your hands in the air, just in case."

Jamil did as he was told.

"It's not worth it, Jamil," said Petronella over her comm. The soldiers were taking cover, aiming their beam rifles at the dremecks. "Nothing's worth this! It will be a slaughter! Tell them to surrender."

Jamil looked at the dremecks. They stood together, facing the Uglies, facing the guns. Their eyes were large and gleamed in the white light of the street lamps. They weren't afraid and they weren't backing down.

I'd rather die than be a slave! Trella had said.

Because of him. She had learned that from him. What would she learn from him now, if *he* backed down? That he was a phony, a hypocrite, a liar, a coward. That he could talk glibly enough about his beliefs but he didn't have the guts to die for them.

"Two minutes!" the lieutenant shouted. "Two minutes and I will order my men to—"

"Hold your fire!" Jamil called. He walked forward, hands in the air. "Let me talk to them," he said. "I'm not armed. And neither are they. Let me talk to them."

"Go ahead," the lieutenant said. "I don't want to gun down unarmed people. But I will if I have to."

Jamil looked at the man intently. "They *are* people," he said. "Like us, only different. Remember that."

He could feel the beam rifles aimed at his back as he moved down a broad sidewalk toward the dremecks, who were now watching him doubtfully, uncertainly.

"We won't surrender, Mr. Jamil," Trella announced, before he'd even opened his mouth. "We've talked it over. They can shoot us if they want to. Maybe . . ." her chin quivered; she was trying very hard to be brave, "maybe our people will learn from our deaths. . . ."

"No one's going to die," said Jamil, and added mentally, From my mouth to God's ear.

Jamil reached the stairs, climbed them until he stood on the building's portico with the dremecks. He turned to face the soldiers. Holding out his hands, Jamil took Trella's hand in his right hand. He took hold of the hand of the dremeck Remer on his left.

"Link hands, all of you," he ordered, "and form a line."

The dremecks did as they were told. Holding hands, they stood tall and straight, facing the soldiers.

"We won't be slaves anymore," Jamil announced. "I guess you're going to have to shoot us."

"One minute," said the lieutenant grimly.

"Will any of you join us?" Jamil cried.

"I will!" Petronella shouted. "I know what it means to be persecuted because of who you are and where you're born." Walking in front of the soldiers, she took her place beside Jamil. "I guess you'll just have to shoot me, too."

"You can shoot me, as well," called the man in the bathrobe. He was short and balding, his feet in thongs that flapped on the sidewalk, but his courage gave him dignity and it was with dignity that he joined the end of the line. He smiled tentatively at one of the young dremecks and took hold of the blue-skinned hand.

"Me, too," said the woman who had once been an overseer.

One by one, then two or three at a time, the residents of the apartment building walked over to stand side by side with the dremecks. The only one who didn't was the man who had warned the others to watch what they said—along with the wire-heads, who were still flat on their faces in the middle of stone shards.

The soldiers gripped their beam rifles and looked uncertainly at their commander. Sweat gleamed on their faces; their hands clutching the rifles were white-knuckled. Jamil guessed that every one of them was wondering what he or she would do if the order to shoot were given.

They were, after all, trained killers.

The lieutenant was bright. He wasn't about to gun down humans on his own initiative. He was talking to headquarters. The conversation didn't last long. Jamil could tell by the man's grim expression what the order was going to be.

"Platoon, fire!"

The soldiers shifted uneasily.

"Begging your pardon, sir," said one, "but we could set our weapons on stun. . . ."

The lieutenant hesitated. He'd been offered a way out.

"I'll check with headquarters," he said, and began speaking into his comm.

A moment's silence. An expression of surprise contorted the lieutenant's face.

"He did? Is that for certain? Well, I'll be damned. Where the hell does that leave us? Yeah, with our asses hanging out." The lieutenant was not pleased. "Platoon, stand down."

The soldiers, looking vastly relieved, lowered the beam rifles.

Trella was clutching Jamil's hand so tightly he doubted if he'd ever be able to straighten his fingers.

"Did we win?" she asked in dazed tones.

"Yes," he said quietly, and he did not bother to add that they'd won for the moment but that any second things could still fall apart.

They had won. And even if they eventually lost, their victory could never be taken from them.

CHAPTER 40

Nos amis, les enemis.
Our friends, the enemy.

Pierre-Jean de Béranger,
Chansons de Dr. Béranger

Xris laid low during the next two days. He reported to the laundry at the usual hour, did his work, gave no one any trouble. When work was finished, he went back to his cell and stayed there. He avoided the gym, dropped out of his class. He ate in the dining hall with the others, but he ate in silence, keeping his gaze on his plate, ignoring the talk around him.

Slovenski had been released from the hospital. The big man's table was four behind Xris's. Slovenski never passed him but that he slowed down and either made some crude remark about "cybos," dumped hot coffee in Xris's lap, or spit in his food. The inmates and the guards watched with interest, knowing that a fight was inevitable and that it was probably going to be to the death. Bets were being placed, the odds changing daily. The smart money was on Slovenski as being a known commodity, but the cyborg had a loyal following.

Xris was going to disappoint them. He didn't think Montieth would toss him into solitary again; Mr. Trevor would see to that. But Xris was leaving nothing to chance.

By the time Friday came around, Xris was in line for Model Prisoner of the Year. The odds on him had dropped to almost nothing, as word went through the cellblocks that beneath the steel beat a heart of plastic. Even Xris's cell mates were starting to feel a little ashamed of him.

Xris wasn't interested. He felt almost sorry for Slovenski,

who was going to a lot of trouble all for nothing. This time tonight, Xris would be out of here—either that or he'd be dead, which amounted to the same thing. Slovenski would have to find someone else to intimidate.

Xris saw Becking, Mair, and Macdonald at dinner that evening. They exchanged glances. Macdonald nodded his head once. They were ready.

Xris returned to his cell after dinner, hoping for some distraction, some interesting conversation, or maybe a game of bridge. Anything to take his mind off the clock. But his cell mates were subdued and unhappy, in no mood to play games. They'd just received vids from their families that day and apparently the brochures hadn't mentioned anything about homesickness. Malcolm talked about his little girl, but only briefly, then he went to take a walk in the rain. The other two lay on their bunks and stared at the ceiling.

And then it was lights out. And that was the worst. Three hours to go, three hours of nothing to do but lie in the darkness and think about everything that could go wrong.

Xris stared up at the ceiling and played a game with himself to keep his mind occupied. He tried to hold out for exactly thirty minutes before he checked his watch. If he made it, he gave himself a point. If not, he deducted a point. By the time midnight crawled around, he was ahead of himself, three for two.

His cell mates were sleeping soundly, very soundly; not surprising, since Quong had thoughtfully included a vial of Raoul's bedtime "relaxant" as part of Xris's equipment. Xris had slipped the powder into their drinks at dinner. Nothing short of a bomb blast would have wakened them, and perhaps not even that.

Xris looked at his watch. 0100. A clear win.

He slid quietly out of bed, pulled on his black sweatpants. He put on his jacket, drew the hood up over his head. Wadding up his extra clothes, he arranged them on the bed, covered them with the blanket. The guards made a bed check every night at 0200, probably one reason Amadi had selected that particular time. The guards never looked too closely, didn't bother with heat-sensors as did their counterparts on Sandusky's Rock. Xris hoped the clothes dummy would keep them happy. If not, if they discovered he was gone, by that time he planned to be long gone.

He moved noiselessly across the floor, keeping watch on the ceiling-mounted vidcam. It would be sheer bad luck if the guard on duty tonight happened to spot him moving around his cell, but if that happened, the cam would suddenly start to swivel.

The vidcam didn't move. It stared fixedly at the center of the room, completely bored.

Avoiding its glassy-eyed gaze, Xris sidled around the wall until he reached the cell door. He had already removed from his leg another of Quong's blessed devices—a small metal tube about thirty centimeters in length with a button at one end and three metal filaments protruding from the other. Although somewhat cruder, the device was essentially the same type the guards used to override the controls. It would open the door for him and, according to his research, it would do so by bypassing the locking system. The cell door would think it was still shut and therefore, if it worked as he hoped it would, the device would not set off the alarm.

Activating his night vision, Xris inserted the three metal filaments into the minuscule space between the keypad button and the lock's cover. He touched the button on the end of the tube and waited for the red light on the keypad to turn green.

The light remained red. Xris noticed his hand was shaking. He forced himself to calm down, made a concentrated effort to hold the device steady.

Still red.

"Damn it, Quong!" he muttered. "I don't have time to screw around! Why the hell won't this work?"

Dr. Quong was not there to answer, leaving Xris to his own devices. He removed the filaments, carefully slid them in again, touched the button.

The light was red.

"Fuck!"

Xris glanced over his shoulder at the vidcam. It had not moved. He turned back just in time to see the light switch to green. He tensed, waited for the alarm.

Nothing but snores broke the silence.

"Sorry, Doc."

Removing the device, Xris replaced it in his leg compartment, closed the cover, rolled down his pants leg. He touched zero on the number pad and the cell door slid open. Xris slipped out, padded soft-footed down the corridor. He had only one obstacle to pass, and that was the night guard in the cellblock's central command post.

The guards were generally far more interested in their vidscreens than in monitoring the various consoles that provided them with views of nothing more exciting than a bunch of slumbering prisoners. But the sight of one of those prisoners trotting gleefully out the cellblock's front door would be enough to wrench the guard from even the most exciting soccer game.

Crouched in the shadows, Xris popped open his leg compartment, withdrew a small wooden tube and one of four wooden darts. He was extremely careful to touch the darts only with his cybernetic hand, because the tips had been soaked in another one of Raoul's slumber-time concoctions and Xris had no desire to take an unexpected snooze.

The guard—a nice, fat guard—sat at the desk, intent on his vid, which was showing the galactic heavyweight boxing match. His broad back was turned toward Xris. A vast expanse of bare neck protruding from the uniform collar provided an excellent target.

Much to the amusement of his cell mates, Xris had spent the last few days practicing shooting dried peas (salvaged from dinner) out of a straw at a bull's-eye drawn on the wall. Xris was not as proficient as the Little One in the use of a blowgun, but Xris eventually perfected his skills so that he could hit the target four times out of five. And the target he had been using was smaller than the guard's pudgy neck.

He placed the dart in the tube, brought the tube to his lips, and drew in a deep breath.

The clenched fist came out of nowhere, smashed into his jaw, slammed his head back against the concrete wall. He slid to the floor and lay there, stunned and dazed, as much from the shock of the unexpected blow as from the pain of the blow itself.

Strong hands grabbed the front of his sweatshirt, hauled him to his feet. Slovenski's little squinty eyes glinted in the lights of the security cams. Before Xris could regain his senses long enough to react, Slovenski's huge fist rammed into Xris's midriff.

Xris doubled over in agony. He knew that Slovenski was probably going to kill him, knew that he should make some attempt to defend himself, but right now breathing was his prime objective.

The noise of thumping and groaning had attracted the guard's attention. A real live fight was infinitely more interesting than a televised one. The guard stood up, peered out into the shadows.

"What the hell is—"

"Go back to your vid," Slovenski growled. "This ain't none of your concern."

Xris tried to stand up. Slovenski slammed his head back against the wall. Grabbing hold of a handful of Xris's jacket, Slovenski picked him up and heaved him over his shoulder, as if Xris were nothing more than a sack of laundry. Xris's head and arms dangled down Slovenski's muscle-bound back. Slovenski had one enormous arm clamped tightly around Xris's legs in front.

Slovenski eyed the guard menacingly. "I'm going to finish this outside. You plan on interfering?"

The guard shrugged, sat down. "Hell, it's none of my business."

"You never saw me," Slovenski said.

"Never saw a thing," the guard agreed, and went back to his vid.

Slovenski carried Xris out into the night. The rain had stopped, finally. The air was cool, reviving. Xris let himself go limp and flaccid, feigning unconsciousness. In order to start up where he'd left off, Slovenski would have to set his victim down on the ground. Xris's only chance against this monster was the element of surprise.

Slovenski strolled the grounds with as much confidence as if he had taken over ownership from the previous management. Reaching a clump of ornamental shrubbery that provided a haven of shadow from the bright security lights, he stopped. To Xris's astonishment, Slovenski lowered him to the ground as gently as any gorilla mother.

"You okay, Cyboy?" Slovenski sounded worried. "I didn't mean to hit you so hard."

"Huh?"

Xris sat up and stared at his attacker, tried desperately to bring Slovenski—a black shape against the flood of security lights—into focus. Another problem with his optic systems! Not surprising, considering the force of the blows he'd sustained. Not only was his infrared sight gone, but he was seeing two of everything. Which, in Slovenski's case, was not pleasant.

"Hey, Cyboy," said Slovenski softly, "just lay there and groan, would you? A guard's coming."

Baffled and confused, wondering if maybe some really important wires in his brain had shorted out and were causing him to hallucinate, Xris was only too happy to lie on the ground, press his aching cheek into the cool, wet grass, and groan obligingly.

The guard's footsteps crunched past on the gravel. Either the guard didn't see Slovenski, who was standing over Xris with his fists doubled, or the guard had developed convenient night blindness.

When the guard was gone, Slovenski knelt down beside Xris and placed a hand tenderly on his good shoulder. "Here. Let me help you up. Are you gonna be able to make it all right, Cyboy? I'm real sorry I hit you so hard. Sometimes I don't know my own strength."

"Yeah, I'm okay," said Xris, putting his hand to his swelling jaw. He didn't particularly appreciate Slovenski's commiseration.

"You sure? 'Cause I gotta go. At least now"—Slovenski grinned—"if you come up missing during bed check, no one'll bother to look for you until morning. Good luck, Cyboy."

Slovenski sauntered off.

Xris stood up, tried again to focus his eyes, but couldn't manage. He took a few steps, felt completely disoriented. He couldn't walk a straight line. He opened his arm, again initiated the emergency system-wide diagnostic and repair program. He waited with as much patience as he could manage. Picking out one tree that looked to him like two trees, he stared at it and slowly, slowly, a fraction of a centimeter at a time, the two trees merged into one tree again. He waited a few moments, but the infrared vision and augmented vision and other enhancements didn't return.

Xris shrugged. He had been downgraded to a normal human being. he'd live with it. As for Slovenski, Xris gave up on that. He thought maybe he was starting to see the whole picture, but it was fuzzy and was going to take a lot longer to come into focus than the trees. He didn't have time to waste worrying about it.

Nursing his aching jaw and his bruised ribs—real parts of him that only time would heal—Xris hugged the shadows and began the long trek across the compound to the golf course.

CHAPTER 41

I am escaped with the skin of my teeth.
                    The Bible, Job 19:20

Snakes on the golf course.

"Snakes!" said Mashahiro Ito, alarmed.

Xris started, turned to stare.

His partner, his deceased partner, was walking along at his side. Short, slender, straight black hair, dark, slanted eyes, and infectious smile—it was Ito, all right.

"You know how I hate snakes, Xris." Ito was grumbling and peering closely into every shadow. "Did you see something wriggle? Over there?"

Xris shook his head.

"I guess not. Must have been a stick. Say, Xris, you don't mind if I tag along on this one, do you?"

"No," said Xris after a moment's thought. "You've got a right to be here."

"Thanks, Xris," Ito said softly. "I appreciate it."

Xris nodded.

Ito said nothing more, and neither did Xris, who was searching for the power grid junction box. But from that moment on, he was conscious of his former partner at his side.

The low, squat square shape of the pro shop came into view, silhouetted against the stars. A fence separated the golf course from the jungle. Spotlights mounted on the fence illuminated the golf course. From the air, it would be seen as a black, vast expanse surrounded by lights—the ideal landing pad.

The lights gleamed off the sleek sides of multibarreled lascannons, snug in their turrets. If Xris couldn't shut down the electrical system that fed those cannons, Harry and his spaceplane would rain down on the golf course in little bits of charred flesh and metal. Xris looked at the bright LED lights of his watch for at least the forty-seventh time in as many minutes. 0130. Half an hour to go. Too soon for the Hung leaders to be here, but Xris risked a whispered call anyhow.

"Macdonald!"

No answer.

Xris removed the fleshfoam from the index finger of his cybernetic hand. He touched a tiny switch, switched on a beam of light. Flashing the light around, he repeated his call, just to make certain. When there was still no answer, he continued his search for the junction box.

And there it was, exactly where Amadi's diagram had said it would be.

The box was metal, three meters by two meters, built into the ground. A blast of hot air hit him in the face as he approached. He shone the light on the junction box, illuminated the fan assembly. The fan blades rotated at such a high speed that all he could see was a blur. Sucking the hot air out of the box, the fan kept the electronic circuitry cool, and at the same time prevented rain, insects, and golf balls from falling inside and damaging the equipment.

Xris reached into his leg compartment, selected various components. On a scanner, they appeared to be part of his own internal machinery. When assembled, they turned into a multihead screwdriver. He unbolted the fan shroud, stared down at the whirring blades.

"Good thing you spotted that snake, buddy," Xris said to his partner.

Xris ran back to where Ito had seen the stick. Picking it up, he returned to the junction box, looked again at his watch. Harry's spaceplane would be entering orbit. Which meant that at any moment the prison's radar would pick it up; the lascannons would start to zero in on their target.

Xris thrust the stick into the fan blades. The force of the blades hitting the stick nearly wrenched it from his hand. He held on desperately, hoped like hell the stick didn't break. The fan blades stopped turning. He could smell their motor already starting to overheat.

He peered down into the electronic switching circuitry below.

Xris stood up, opened the flap his sweatpants. For a panicked moment he thought he was going to fail and he swore grimly. It figured. Every single time before this, when he'd carried out a dangerous mission, he always had to pee. Now, when he needed to, when his full bladder finally might prove useful, he couldn't.

Harry was going to die, they were all going to die, all because Xris couldn't take a piss.

The absurdity of the situation struck him. He couldn't help but grin, and with that he relaxed, his bladder emptied. Urine streaked in a graceful arc down into the delicate electronics of the power grid.

Circuits shorted out with a hissing sound. Then came a crackling and ominous, angry buzz. Xris scrambled backward. He flattened himself on the green and covered his head just as the box exploded in a shower of sparks.

Xris was on his feet before the debris had quit falling. The fan assembly landed only about one meter away from him, its blades twisted. By some freak of the explosion, the stick was still firmly wedged inside.

Xris looked at his watch. It was 0156 and all hell was breaking loose. The lights had gone out in the compound, alarms sounded. Emergency strobe lights flooded the compound; Xris could have read tea leaves out there. Within seconds, the backup power generators kicked in. The lights in the cellblocks came back on. Guards were shouting, running from building to building.

The guards had heard the explosion—everyone must have heard the explosion—but unless someone had been staring directly at the golf course in the dead of night, no one had seen it. They had to figure it was an attempt at a breakout, but where? There would be an immediate lockdown. The guards would do a bed check, going to each cell and waking the prisoners. The search would take a long time.

But Xris had only ten minutes until the lascannons came back on line.

0158. Where the devil was Macdonald? And, for that matter, where was Harry? Xris listened for the spaceplane's engines, which he should have been able to detect even over the raucous screaming of the Klaxons. Perhaps his augmented hearing was malfunctioning, as well as his eye.

0159. It wasn't like Harry to be late.

0200. Something big, dark, and silent as the hand of God blotted out the stars above Xris's head. He stared at it, awed. The thing made no sound, had no lights, had no distinct shape. It took him a moment to figure out the thing was landing. Landing slowly, ponderously.

"*What* the *hell* is that?"

Xris, who had been readjusting his shorts, turned to find Macdonald standing at his shoulder, with Becking and Mair behind him. Either these guys were awfully good or his hearing *was* failing him. Xris glanced at their soft-soled shoes, their black sweats. They'd even blackened their faces. Pros, all right.

"What were you in the beginning—a goddam cat burglar?" Xris demanded, irritated at being caught—literally—with his pants down. He gave his sweats a twitch.

"We were hiding in back of the shop, watching. We saw no need to make ourselves known to you," Macdonald said in his chill voice.

"Checking me out, huh?" Xris tried to appear nonchalant, but he was worried. The ship was taking its own sweet time about landing, and by the sound of the shouts from the compound, the guards had spotted it.

"We only made one mistake in our lives," Macdonald said, by way of answering him, "and that was to trust someone who turned out to be a FISA agent. We let him get at our secrets. We won't make that mistake again."

At any other time, Xris would have found this conversation very interesting, but now he was engaged in mentally hurrying Harry Luck.

Xris calculated they had two minutes to go. The ship didn't appear to have moved at all in the last few seconds. He couldn't believe how enormous it was. It covered at least half the golf course. He could hear the ship's engines now, but just barely; it must have some sort of sound-dampening shielding. Xris was familiar with every spaceplane, shuttle, spaceship, and transport in the Royal Navy and he'd never seen anything like this.

"Harry, Harry," he murmured, shaking his head.

The shouts of the guards were closing in. Macdonald was breathing cold tomb breath on Xris's neck and swearing.

And then, suddenly, the ship gave a lurch, covered the last few kilometers in a split second. It settled gently on the ground, flattening out the rolling hills of the golf course which, snakes or no snakes, would not be playable for a some time. A rectangle of light appeared in the side.

Harry's bulky figure could be seen in the hatchway. "Xris?" he yelled, sounding worried.

"Come on!" Xris said, but he was talking to himself.

The Hung leaders hadn't bothered to wait around for his orders. They were already racing for the ship. Macdonald had the lead—no surprise, considering his expertise on the jogging track. Mair wasn't far behind and Becking, grunting and groaning from the aftereffects of his beating, brought up the rear. Xris exerted himself, but by the time he reached the hatchway, the other three were already inside.

"Go! Go back to the cockpit!" Xris shouted at Harry, who had his hand stretched out, wanting to help his friend up the stairs. "What are you standing around here for? Get this mother off the ground!"

Xris dove inside. The hatch swung shut behind him. He felt a gentle movement and realized that the ship was lifting off.

Harry Luck stood beside him. Harry's normally cheerful face was all twisted up with worry and anxiety, but Xris was too preoccupied, had too many worries of his own to notice.

"Who's flying this thing? The computer? You know I don't like computers doing the flying! That's why I hire you!"

"Yeah, Xris. I know. But, uh, Xris—"

"Where's Amadi?"

"Up front. Xris, there's something—"

"It can wait." Xris brushed him off. "In about five minutes, those lascannons are going to open up on us. Are the shields up? I want you at the controls of this contraption, not some computer."

Xris had Harry by the arm, was propelling him bodily through the empty, cavernous belly of the ship, steering him in the direction of the cockpit. The three Hung leaders clumped along behind; Xris could hear their footsteps ringing hollowly on the metal deck. Xris glanced around.

"What kind of ship is this, anyway?"

"This is a brand-new prototype cargo transport, Xris," Harry said defensively. "The new Xena class. Bear Olefsky loaned it to us. It's got all sorts of special features—"

"I hope strong shields are one of them!" Xris said grimly. Now that he looked at it closely, of course it was a cargo transport.

They were inside the belly of the transport now, moving away from the hatch at the back, heading toward what he presumed was the cockpit at the front. The overhead was far, far over his head. Heavy steel ribs gleamed in the semi-darkness. Giant hooks hung from the ceiling. Metal tracks ran along the deck. He could have fit the first four stories of his cellblock in this thing and have room left over.

"It'll hold forty T-26 Dominators—a whole regiment's worth," said Harry with a nervous glance at Xris.

"Fine!" Xris snapped. "When I want to haul around forty T-26 Dominators, I'll know what to buy. Where the hell *is* the cockpit?"

He had just stumbled into a metal bulkhead.

"Through here," Harry said, indicating another hatch. "Same as any transport. The cockpit is separate from the cargo hold so that the hold can be jettisoned in case of emergency. Look, Xris," Harry said, speaking in low, urgent tones, "we've got to talk."

The deck rocked beneath Xris's feet, throwing him against the bulkhead. The three Hung leaders staggered, reached out to grab on to each other for support.

"What was that?" Becking gasped.

"We're under attack," Xris said. "Lascannon fire."

"My God!" Mair was pale, his eyes rolling. "Do something! Get us out of here!"

"The computer can handle it," Harry said. "She's a really nice computer, Xris. Very polite and professional. I like her. And the shields—"

Another blast struck them. Macdonald was knocked to

his knees. Becking, clinging to a streel beam, was white and pasty.

Xris hit the hatch release, opened the hatch leading to the cockpit. A man holding a beam rifle stood framed in the hatchway.

Assuming the man was Amadi, Xris started to shove past him.

Not Amadi.

Xris came up with a jolt.

"Hello, Xris," said Andrew Robison.

CHAPTER 42

Show me a hero and I will write you a tragedy.
                    F. Scott Fitzgerald, *Notebooks*

"That's what I've been trying to tell you," said Harry Luck. "I'm sorry, Xris, but there wasn't anything I could do. They got my mom!"

"Shields holding, Pilot Luck," came the computer's voice, a female voice, calm and reassuring. "We will be out of range of lascannon fire in one minute. Do you want to return fire?"

"Do we?" Harry asked. He wasn't looking to Xris for the answer. Harry looked to Robison.

"No, don't bother. Take us out of here. Greetings, gentlemen," Robinson said to the Hung leaders. "I'm Mr. Trevor. The real Mr. Trevor. It's good to meet you face-to-face at last. Please take your seats and make yourselves comfortable. The trip will last about two hours. Sorry for the crude mode of transportation, but I didn't have much choice."

"As long as we're out of that hellhole, I don't care if I'm traveling by trash hauler," said Mair, sinking into his seat and heaving a sigh.

Macdonald strapped himself in, gazed into the cold empty vacuum of space, a vacuum that seemed cozy and cheerful in comparison to his eyes. Becking had located the head. From the sounds of it, he was busy losing his dinner.

There was one other passenger. Jafar el Amadi.

Amadi lay huddled between one of the passenger seats and a control panel. He had restrainers on his hands and feet. Blood covered his face, was matted in his silver-gray hair. His eyes were closed, his body limp.

"Is he dead?" Xris asked.

"No," Robison answered offhandedly. "At least I don't think so. He was waiting for Mr. Luck at the spaceport. My people arrived first. They had orders not to hurt him. I wanted information from him, but he put up a fight and they didn't have any choice."

"Where are the rest of your people?" Xris asked, glancing around.

"They stayed behind," Robison replied. "For security reasons, this needs to be kept quiet."

In other words, the lower echelons didn't need to know the names and faces of those who paid their salaries.

"We are out of range of lascannon fire, Pilot Luck," the computer reported. "Shall I lower the shields?"

"Yeah," said Harry dispiritedly.

Harry's greatest joy was flying, especially in tense situations. Now he sat slumped in the pilot's chair, unhappy and upset.

"Would you like the damage report, Pilot Luck?" asked computer.

"Whatever." Harry sighed.

"There is no damage to report," said the computer, who appeared to be genuinely fond of Harry and seemed to be trying to coax him into a good mood. "Would you like me to set the course and make the preparations for the Jump to hyperspace?"

"What is our course, Harry?" Xris asked, hoping to jolt Harry out of his lethargy.

"Beats the hell out of me." Harry looked up listlessly. "What is our course?"

"Del Sol," said Robison.

The shock was like a kick in the stomach and Robinson had done it deliberately. He was watching, waiting to see Xris's reaction. Xris gazed back blankly. Out of the corner of his eye he saw Harry jerk to attention, sit bolt upright, and open his mouth.

"Del—" Harry began.

Xris shifted his jaw a certain way and Harry's subdermal transmitter burst into a roar of static.

"Ow!" Harry clutched at his head and yelped.

"What's wrong with him?" Robison glanced around.

"Migraine headache. He gets them when he's under stress. He needs to learn to calm down," said Xris. "Not overreact."

Harry ducked his head, avoiding Xris's gaze, and hurriedly turned back to the computer.

"Enter a course for . . . what was the name of that place?" Harry asked.

"You know it. Your friends are there. Or should I say *were* there. Are you really that stupid or is it just an act?" Robison asked.

"It's not an act," Harry protested indignantly, and went back to plotting the course with the computer.

"As for Del Sol—that was the name, wasn't it?" Xris shrugged. "I've never heard of it."

"Uh-huh." Robison poked Xris in the small of the back with the beam rifle, indicated one of the passenger seats. "Sit down."

"What do you intend to do with that gun?" Xris asked, amused. "You certainly don't plan to fire it. If you do, you'll kill us all. You'll blow a hole in the hull. We'll decompress."

"Uh, no, we won't, Xris," Harry said, looking around. "That's one of the new safety features they've added. According to the head of the Wolf Brigade—"

He finally caught Xris's angry glare.

"Oops," Harry said meekly. "Sorry."

Robison shook his head. He attached a restrainer on Xris's good wrist. "Why the hell did you hire such a moron for a pilot?"

"I'm cutting back on expenses. Harry works cheap."

"I see. Take off your arm."

"Huh?" Xris played dumb.

"Take off the arm. I've read reports on you, remember?"

"If you have," Xris returned, "you know damn good and well I can't. What do you think it is? An overcoat? A surgeon has to remove the implants. Make a mistake and my entire system will go into shock. I could die."

"So what?" Robison sneered.

"So how much do I know about your operations?" Xris asked. "And who have I told?"

Robison cast a glance at Macdonald, who nodded.

"All right. leave it on. But I know damn well you can detach the hand!"

Xris couldn't argue with him on that one. He removed the cybernetic hand at the wrist. The fleshfoam hand looked particularly realistic and particularly gruesome, with wires dangling from the wrist like severed tendons, lubricating fluid dripping from it. Xris held out the hand to Robison, who looked disgusted.

"Put that thing on the floor."

Xris shrugged, did as he was told. Robison activated the restrainer on Xris's good hand. His fingers lost all feeling; the hand went limp.

"Let's discuss my fee," Xris said. "Without me, your friends there would still be squatting on the eighteenth hole. You can bet this fancy transport didn't come cheap. I expect to be paid for this job. Well paid."

"You'll get what you've earned," said Robison with an unpleasant smile. "Just like Amadi here. *And* your team."

"Team?" Xris repeated, shaking his head. "Why worry about them? They're not involved. Say, you haven't got a twist on you, by chance?"

"The hell they aren't. Or perhaps I should put that in the past tense. Amadi was the one who hired your team to go to Del Sol—"

"Del Sol!" Macdonald was on his feet. "Amadi sent a team to Del Sol?"

"Relax, Mr. Macdonald. Mag Force 7 has been eliminated as a threat. Permanently. Our hit squads don't miss."

Oh, yes they do. They'd missed Rowan twice. Still, third time was a charm. . . .

Harry shifted his big bulk in his chair, stared bleakly back at Xris, begging him to deny it, to say it wasn't true.

Xris avoided the pleading gaze. He couldn't offer Harry any comfort.

Amadi had hired them. Hired them to overthrow the government of Del Sol. What could a revolution on Del Sol possibly have to do with the Hung? Xris couldn't figure it out, but he told himself bitterly that he should have seen the two were connected. If for no other reason than that his arrest had come at precisely the time they'd been hired for the job.

Coincidence? He had always been the one to maintain that there were no such things. But he'd missed this one completely.

He'd given in to his emotion. He'd let his hate fog up his brain.

What a fucking, blind, stupid fool I've been! Xris berated himself. And my friends are the ones who've paid the price.

"I don't understand," Macdonald said. "What's going on? What does Amadi have to do with this? The last we were informed, he had retired."

"You don't know this, Mr. Macdonald," said Robison, "but this piece of scrap metal you see sitting here"—he gestured at Xris with the barrel of the beam rifle—"was once a FISA agent. He met with an accident. He and his partner were snooping around in a munitions factory when it blew up."

Macdonald stared, eyes narrowed. "What are you saying, Trevor? You hired him!"

"No," said Robison, and he looked nervous. "*He* did." He jerked his head at Amadi, who was groaning and starting to move.

"You have some explaining to do," Mair said.

"I don't have all the pieces yet myself, sir," Robison admitted. "That's one reason Amadi's still alive. At some time—I don't know how long ago—Amadi caught on to me. He intercepted the messages you sent to me. *He* became Trevor."

Macdonald stared at Amadi with a malevolency sharp as a knife's blade. "You say you don't know when this happened?"

"No, sir, I don't."

"A great deal of damage may have been done."

"It can be undone, sir." Robison shifted one hand off the barrel of the beam rifle, rubbed his palm on his pants. He left a streak of wetness. "Once we find out what he knows and what the cyborg knows. And we'll find out."

They began to discuss various methods of torture, arguing about which was the most efficient. The discussion sent Becking back to the head, but Mair and Macdonald were obviously enjoying themselves. Xris found the conversation boring. He'd spent a year in a hospital having most of his insides, not to mention a few assorted body parts, taken out, chopped off, disconnected, redesigned, rebuilt, reinserted, reattached. He could have given them a few ideas.

"Twenty minutes to hyperspace," said the computer. "All cargo should be properly stowed so that the load does not shift during the Jump. Pilot Luck, shall I run the cargo hold check?"

"We don't have any cargo," Harry felt compelled to point out.

"I know," said the computer gently. "I was only trying to help you take your mind off whatever it is that is bothering you."

"Thanks," said Harry, and he patted the console. "I appreciate it."

"Hey," Xris said, breaking into a conversation between Mair and Macdonald on the efficacy of electrodes attached to breast nipples. "I have to go to the head."

"So go," said Robison.

"I could use a hand." Xris grinned at him.

"Funny." Robison grunted. "Be creative. Oh, and leave the door open so we can see you."

"It's your funeral." Xris went to the head—a small compartment containing a toilet, a sink, and a tiny shower, located in the rear of the cockpit area. Xris stood by the door, waited for Becking to emerge.

"I hate space travel," said Becking as he left the head, wiping his lips with a trembling hand.

"Man was never meant to fly," said Xris solemnly.

Entering the head, he wrestled with his sweatpants and sat down on the toilet. Activating the internal commlink, he spoke between grunts.

"Harry, can you seize control of this monster from the computer? Fly it manually?"

"Yeah, I think so," said Harry, after some consideration. "You want me to try it now?"

"No. Let's get to Del Sol first."

"You got a plan, don't you, Xris?" Harry was excited. Xris hated to let him down.

"Not yet. But I'm working on it."

"They're not all dead, are they, Xris?" Harry asked plaintively. "Not Rowan and Jamil and Doc?"

"I wish I could say no, Harry," Xris answered. "But the Hung have killed good people before this."

Harry choked. "I'm worried about my mom, Xris."

"She'll be okay," Xris lied. "They won't hurt her."

"You sure? 'Cause—"

"Stop mumbling to yourself, you big ape." Robinson struck Harry hard in the back with the barrel of the beam rifle.

"Fifteen minutes to Jump," reported the computer. "*All* passengers must be in their seats with their safety webbing in place before the Jump sequence can commence."

Xris left the can, went back to his seat.

Robison and Mair lifted Amadi from the deck, settled him in a chair, and strapped his webbing over him.

Amadi's eyes opened. He blinked a few times, winced in pain from the bright light, and took in his surroundings.

"Hello, Xris," he said, glancing over at the seat near him. "Glad to see you made it."

"Hello, sir," Xris said.

Amadi gave a wan smile. "I even had you fooled, didn't I, Xris?"

"Yes, sir. You had me fooled."

Amadi sat back, sighed, and closed his eyes.

"Ten minutes to Jump," said the computer. "Starting Jump sequence now."

CHAPTER 43

Life . . . is a hand-to-hand mortal combat . . . between the law of love and the law of hate.
José Martí, Letter

"Del Sol tower, this is Wolf Two Two One Heavy, requesting clearance to Rimindar Field, Over."

There was a longer than normal pause. A controller came on the vidscreen. "Wolf Two Two One Heavy, you are not cleared. I repeat, you are *not* cleared. Del Sol is a sovereign world and will resist any attempts at illegal infiltration. We are under a state of emergency and cannot accept incoming traffic at this time. I repeat. You are *not* cleared. Do not attempt to land. Del Sol out."

"I don't understand! What's going on?" Robison demanded, frustrated. "Tell them it is imperative that we land! We have our own emergency."

"I'm sorry, sir," said the computer. "But they have ended communication. I suggest that we monitor local broadcast channels. Perhaps we could discover the nature of the emergency."

"I don't like the sound of this." Macdonald was out of his chair, pacing around the cabin. "Find out what's going on."

"Look at Amadi," said Mashahiro Ito, his voice strong and clear in Xris's head. "He's smiling. You know what *that* means!"

Xris knew what it meant. The boss smiled only when a case was closed, the verdict in, and he had won.

Amadi's blood-caked head rested against the back of the chair. His skin was ashen; he'd been sick during the Jump, vomiting on the deck. His eyes were closed. But he was smiling.

"I have the signal from the local vid channel," said the computer. "On screen."

"For those of you who have just joined us, I am Ron Sharp, general manager of Station Vid Free Dremeck, standing in for our regular anchors, who are on assignment. We are waiting for word from the palace, where it is reported that His Eminence, Supreme Ruler Kirkov, will be making a prerecorded broadcast to the nation. We have no idea what His Eminence will be saying or why he is not saying it live and in person. We assume that he will endeavor to calm the nation after this turbulent night of uncertainty and terror."

"What terror?" demanded Mair.

"Shut up," said Macdonald.

The face of a handsome man, somewhat florid and fleshy, with blond, buzz-cut hair, wearing a uniform decorated with ribbon and braid and innumerable gleaming metals, appeared. He was seated at a desk, against a backdrop of a gigantic flag. The man's face was rigid, stoic, expressionless.

"At 0600 hours, I, Gustav Kirkov, have surrendered power. Rulership of this world now lies in the hands of its oldest inhabitants—those known to use as dremecks."

Becking gasped.

"Shut up!" Macdonald snarled.

"I have resigned my position as supreme ruler of the world of Del Sol," Kirkov was saying. "Prior to my resignation, all military units under my command were ordered to stand down. The secret police have been disbanded.

"I ask the citizens of Del Sol to remain calm. I have received assurances from the leaders of the new government that you are in no danger. By the time this message is broadcast, I will have left Del Sol. I do not intend to ever return."

A momentary break, during which voices could be heard saying, "Can you confirm this?"

The obviously shocked and amazed news anchor was back on the screen, listening to reports over his comm, his hand pressed to an ear comm.

Shaking his head in wonder, he looked into the cam.

"Our sources confirm that Supreme Ruler Kirkov"—the man's mouth twisted slightly—"perhaps we should qualify

that and say *former* Supreme Ruler Kirkov—left Del Sol
in his private shuttle shortly after 0700 this morning. News
of his departure stunned his aides, who did not know he
was leaving. Apparently not even Madam Kirkov knew her
husband was intending to flee the world. She is said to be
making arrangements to join him."

He put his hand to his ear again.

"What does Kirkov think he's doing?" Becking squeaked.
"Surrendering to the dremecks! He's lost his mind!"

"The man's an idiot," said Macdonald. "I always said so.
But he's easily replaced. It will mean a lot of trouble and
expense." The cadaver-cold eyes went to Robison. "I
thought you said our people were on top of this situation."

"They were," Robison gabbled. "Something's gone
wrong. My reports—"

"Oh, hang your reports!" Macdonald snapped impatiently.

"No pun intended," Xris murmured, and turned his attention back to the vid broadcast.

"We have just been informed that one of the leaders of
the victorious dremeck Revolutionary Army has arrived at
our studios and is asking to speak to the nation."

A dremeck—at least Xris assumed it was a dremeck; he'd
never met one in person—appeared on the screen. Her
face-folds were all scrunched together in happiness and rippled excitedly as she spoke.

"My fellow citizens, I greet you in peace," said the dremeck. "My name is Trella and I am here as a representative
of the dremeck people. The free dremeck people," she
added proudly. "I want to first thank those humans who
helped us gain our freedom this night; the humans who
threw down their arms and refused to obey their leaders
when they were ordered to fire on us; those humans who
used their own bodies to shield us from the secret police;
those humans who marched with us on the palace and demanded the dictator's surrender. Thank you. We owe our
freedom to you and to one human in particular. He is very
modest and didn't want me to give his name, but he de-
serves to be known."

Trella turned her head and the vidcam followed her. The
cam focused on a black-skinned human dressed in combat

fatigues. He stood in a corner, looking extremely embarrassed and ill-at-ease.

"That's—" Harry gasped.

"Shut up!" Xris hissed into the internal comm.

"Jamil Khizr," said Trella. "Thank you, Jamil. We owe you our freedom. You will be a hero to the dremeck people forever."

Trella turned back to face the cam. "We want to reassure the human portion of our population that we intend to work together with you to form a coalition government of both humans and dremecks. As for planetary security, acting on the advice of Jamil Khizr, we have sent a request to His Majesty, King Dion, for Royal Navy protection. That request has been granted. It is our hope that Del Sol will apply for a position within the Empire, but that is something the people of Del Sol will determine in free elections."

"The Royal Navy!" Mair looked concerned.

Macdonald brushed it aside. "Don't worry. It will take them weeks to get organized. By that time, our people will be in place and their 'coalition' government will have voted to send the Royal Navy to hell."

"I don't think you'll find it's that easy," said Jafar el Amadi.

Macdonald lashed out with his hand, struck the injured man across the face.

"You've accomplished nothing except give us a little trouble."

Amadi didn't reply. He continued to smile, though blood trickled from his mouth.

"You know, Xris," said Mashahiro Ito suddenly, "I think I just figured out what the old man's up to. That secret bank account—"

"Harry!" Xris spoke urgently into the comm. "Do whatever you have to do, but end the transmission! Now! Shut it down. I don't care how! Break something if you have to!"

"But," Harry protested, "that was Jamil! On the vid! Maybe he'll be—"

"Damn it, Harry!" Xris said desperately. "Shut it down!"

"Too late," said Ito. "Looks like you may be joining me

sooner than you expected, my friend. Death isn't so bad. It's the waiting around that gets tiresome."

Trella was continuing her speech. "It has been brought to our attention that for the past several decades, private individuals, corporations, and crime organizations have been depositing money in the banks of Del Sol, thereby avoiding taxation and criminal prosecution."

Mair, Becking, and Macdonald were now staring silently and intently at the vidscreen.

"It's been proven that watching vids rots your brain," Xris said loudly, jumping to his feet.

Robison snatched up the beam rifle, aimed it at Xris. "Sit down," he yelled savagely.

Apparently Ito's ghost wasn't the only one to have figured out Amadi's scheme.

"Since much of the money has been illegally obtained, the new government has decreed that all financial institutions on Del Sol will be nationalized. The money belongs to the free people of Del Sol.

"The same holds true for off-world-owned corporations. We realize that in some cases innocent individuals will suffer . . ."

"We're ruined," Macdonald said coldly and dispassionately.

"Wiped out!" Mair gasped.

"We have payments due." Becking's lower lip trembled. His hands shook. "People we owe. When news of this gets out . . ."

Macdonald turned the corpse eyes on Robison.

"We can fix this, sir!" Robison cried desperately, lowering the beam rifle.

"How?" Macdonald demanded.

"I need time, sir! Time to think! I have contacts at the highest levels! I'm sure—"

A soft whoosh sounded in Xris's left ear, followed by a soggy plop. Robison gave a pain-filled grunt. He looked down at his chest. Blood bloomed like a terrible rose on his shirt front. He dropped the beam rifle. His hands went to his chest, but there wasn't anything for the hands to do once they got there. Robison grabbed hold of the back of a chair as he fell, but that was just a reflex action. He was dead when his body struck the deck. The bolt must have hit very close to the heart.

Xris glanced around, saw Becking holding a needle gun. Not a bad shot from a man whose hands were shaking. Becking turned the gun on Amadi.

Xris lowered his head and lunged. With one hand missing and the other incapacitated, his only weapon was his body, and he sent his full mass of flesh and bone and plastisteel plowing into Becking, aiming for the man's sore and tender rib cage.

Xris struck Becking, who shrieked in pain and went down. Unable to stop his fall, Xris landed heavily on top of the pudgy man. The needle gun flew from Becking's hand, landed on the deck, and skittered away, Xris had no idea where.

Not that it would do him much good anyway. He couldn't very well fire it with his teeth.

Xris rolled off Becking. By the sounds he was making—moaning, groaning, and puking—Becking was going to be involved with his own problems for some time to come, wasn't likely to interfere. Xris staggered to his feet.

Harry Luck and Macdonald lurched about in front of the console, wrestling for control of the beam rifle. Harry was the stronger of the two, but the rifle was covered with Robison's blood and Harry couldn't get a good grip on the slippery barrel.

Mair was watching, a needle gun in his hand, but he didn't dare fire for fear of hitting Macdonald.

"Pilot Luck," said the computer, "missiles on the planet below are locking on to us."

"Missiles?" said Harry, distracted. He turned his head.

Macdonald smashed Harry in the jaw with the rifle barrel.

Harry reeled backward, crashed into the console.

Macdonald aimed the beam rifle at Xris. "Don't move."

"Missiles locked on," reported the computer. "Commencing firing sequence."

Groaning, Harry sagged into the pilot's chair.

"What missiles?" Mair demanded, unnerved. "Why are they firing at us, for God's sake?"

"Standard defense procedure," said Xris. "We haven't

received permission to enter their atmosphere and we're entering it."

"But Kirkov ordered the military to stand down!" Mair protested.

"The missiles are programmed to react automatically. A fail-safe measure." Xris shrugged. "In all the turmoil, probably no one remembered—"

"Wolf Two Two One Heavy!" A panicked voice came over the comm. "Wolf Two Two One Heavy! We have just discovered that the missile launch sequence was accidentally activated. Four Proton V4 missiles have been launched at you. Suggest you take evasive action now!"

"Missiles launched," confirmed the computer. "Estimated time until impact: five minutes and twenty seconds. Raising shields and preparing to perform evasive maneuvers—"

"No," said Harry Luck.

The computer's lights burned blue for an instant, then brightened to green again. "Please confirm, Pilot Luck, that I am not to raise shields."

"No shields," Harry mumbled, holding his hand over his swelling jaw. "No evasive maneuvers."

Macdonald shifted the beam rifle, aimed it at Harry.

"Go ahead, shoot me." Harry wiped blood from his split lip. "I'll get to hell five minutes ahead of you. I'll let them know you're coming."

Macdonald shifted the rifle to Xris. "You're his commander. Tell him to raise the shields and get us the hell out of here. Or so help me I'll blow your head off."

"You can't kill a ghost, Macdonald," Xris said quietly. "I died in that booby-trapped factory of yours on TISor. I just haven't fallen down yet."

"Estimated time to impact: four minutes and thirty seconds," said the computer.

"Do something!" Becking whimpered. He was on his feet, shaking all over.

"Computer," Macdonald said, his voice tight, "raise shields and commence evasive maneuvers."

"I do not take orders from passengers," said the computer in lofty tones. "Estimated time to impact: four minutes and twenty-five seconds."

"I was in an explosion once," Xris said in conversational tones, thinking it might help to pass the time. "Let me describe it. First there's the blast, then white-hot pain as the metal and flame rip through your flesh—"

"Shut up," said Mair, mopping his sweating forehead with his sleeve. "Make him shut up. For God's sake, Macdonald, do something!"

"Estimated time of impact: four minutes," said the computer.

From his chair, Amadi chuckled. "Yes, Macdonald. You're the man in charge. The one in control. You have power over life and death. Do something."

"Pilot Luck," said the computer, "I have run an analysis on the four missiles. Two of them have faulty guidance systems and will miss us completely. One of them has a defective warhead and will impact but will cause no damage. The other missile will hit but its warhead will home in on the venting engine exhaust. The engine bay will be destroyed, resulting in loss of power to all systems except emergency—"

"Thanks, sweetheart," said Harry, patting the computer on the datalink manifold, "but I pretty well know what it'll do."

"Estimated time to impact: three minutes and thirty seconds," said the computer. "It is now too late to raise the shields or commence evasive maneuvers. All hands prepare to abandon ship."

"At least I'll have the satisfaction of killing you myself!" Macdonald said. "Starting with you, cyborg—"

"Abandon ship!" Becking shrieked. He grabbed hold of Macdonald's arm, jostling his aim. The beam rifle fired, blasted a burning hole in the copilot's chair.

"You fool!" Macdonald turned on him.

"You're the fool!" Becking cried, spittle flecking his lips. "She said *abandon ship*! That means lifeboats! There are lifeboats on board! We can escape!"

Harry Luck looked nervous. His hand, resting on the arm of the pilot's chair, opened and closed spasmodically. He couldn't meet Xris's eye.

"So that was your plan!" Macdonald snarled, putting the beam rifle to the back of Harry's skull. "You were going to escape in the lifeboats and leave us here to die. Where are they?" Using the barrel of the beam rifle, he slammed Harry's head down hard on the console. "Where are they?"

"Three minutes to impact," said the computer.

"Take me with you!" Harry whimpered, twisting around. His face was the color of wet clay.

"You bastard," said Xris.

"I'm sorry, Xris, but I don't wanna die! Take me with you," he said, pleading with Macdonald, "and I'll tell you."

"Sure, we'll take you," Macdonald said.

Harry jumped to his feet. "In the cargo bay. The lifeboats are in the very back. I'll show you—"

"We'll find them," Macdonald said, and drove the butt of the beam rifle hard into Harry's stomach.

Harry groaned, clutched his gut, and crumpled into his chair.

Becking and Mair did not wait for their leader. They bolted through the hatch, jostling each other in their panic. Macdonald, holding the beam rifle on Xris, edged after them. Reaching the hatch, he hit the closing mechanism. The hatch started to slowly shut.

Xris was missing one hand and the other was useless, but he started to dash out after Macdonald. They could shoot him full of holes. It didn't matter. He'd live enough long to see that they didn't reach the lifeboats.

"Two minutes and thirty seconds to impact," said the computer.

"Xris!" Harry moaned. "Xris, I'm hurt. Hurt real bad. Don't leave me! I don't wanna die alone! Xris, please!"

Xris hesitated, looked back at Harry.

The big man's face was smeared with blood and tears; his eyes were pleading.

"Two minutes to impact," said the computer.

"Xris, please!" Harry begged. He lowered his face to his hands, sobbed like a child.

Xris stopped. He could see, just as the hatch door was closing, the three Hung leaders racing for the back of the cargo hold.

Turning away, Xris walked over to the pilot's chair, laid his hand on Harry's shoulder.

"I'm sorry, Xris," Harry blubbered. "I'm sorry!"

"It's okay, Harry," Xris said softly. "It's okay."

"One minute and thirty seconds to impact," said the computer.

The hatch slammed shut.

Harry Luck sat up straight. Swiveling around in the pilot's chair, he wiped the tears from his eyes, gazed intently at the control panel.

"Excuse me, Xris," he said, elbowing Xris to one side, "but I have to get at the controls and you're in the way. You better find a chair and sit down. Mr. Amadi, sir, you strapped in tight? This is gonna be a bumpy ride."

"What the—" Xris stared, baffled.

"One minute to impact," said the computer.

"This is a *cargo* transport, Xris," said Harry. "No one cares about the cargo if you have to abandon ship. The cockpit separates from the body. Everyone knows that. And they called *me* stupid," he added, sniffing.

"That was all an act?" Xris still couldn't believe it.

"Well, of course it was," said Harry, glancing up from his work. He seemed hurt. "You didn't really think I'd fall apart like that, did you, Xris? You better sit down."

"Bless you, Harry Luck!" Xris said. lowering himself into the copilot's chair. "If you weren't so ugly, I'd kiss you."

"Aw!" Harry blushed. "It was nothing. Computer, I'm taking over manual control."

"Yes, Pilot Luck." The computer sounded extremely relieved. "Thirty seconds to impact."

"Here we go!" shouted Harry.

Xris hooked both elbows through the webbing.

Harry pulled the yellow and black emergency lever. Explosive bolts fired below the deck. Xris could feel what real internal organs he had left being pulled down through his rear end as the booster rockets kicked the cockpit clear of the massive body of the transport.

The cockpit pitched and vibrated violently. Even as well-built as this ship was, Xris didn't see how it could take the shaking; he expected to see cracks in the hull. Just when it seemed that the cockpit was going to shake itself to pieces, the vibrations stopped. The main engines had ceased fire. The cockpit, now a small, self-contained spaceplane, rocketed away under the power of the boosters. The g's pressed

Xris back into the seat, squashed him until he could hardly breathe.

He wasn't going to miss the last act. Exerting all his strength, he shoved himself up out of his seat until he could see through the viewscreen.

The cargo bay portion of the transport hung suspended in the black void of space, visible only because the dark and hulking mass of the ship blotted out the stars.

Inside that doomed transport. Macdonald, Becking, and Mair had probably discovered that they had been duped.

They had discovered that there weren't any lifeboats. Anywhere. Ever.

"Missile impact—now," said the computer.

An eye-searing flash of pure white. A roiling cloud of vapor and gases, whitish blue, tinged with red fire, expanded outward, and then, in a heartbeat, dissipated.

The stars shone, clear, bright, unchanging.

A warmth, as of a comforting hand, touched his soul.

"Thank you, my friend," said Mashahiro Ito. "I can leave now."

"Rest well," said Xris.

CHAPTER 44

Even his griefs are a joy long after to one that remembers all that he wrought and endured.

Homer, *The Odyssey*

"Help yourself to some of my salad, Mr. Amadi, dear,"
Raoul said. "It's walnut, soybean curds, baby squid, and
cranberry sorbet. The recipe was a present from Chef
Hernandez."

"I thought you said he liked you," Harry said innocently.

"He does." Raoul favored Harry with what was intended
to be an icy stare of disapprobation, but whose effect was
rather lost due to the fact that Raoul's eyes would not
focus.

"Maybe later," Amadi said politely. He speared a piece
of barbecued chicken with his fork, placed it on his plate.

"Tycho, you'll try some of my salad," Raoul said, and
held out a small squid on his spoon.

Tycho looked at the squid, blanched. "No, no! Thank
you, but . . . a friend of mine . . . an admiral . . . looks
very much like . . ." Averting his eyes, he left hastily, went
to sit beside a hibiscus bush, and was gradually lost to
their sight.

The team was once again back at the beach house. The
team members had arrived that day, coming in from their
various locations. Jamil, Tycho, Quong, Darlene, and Rizzoli came from Del Sol; Raoul and the Little One from an
unnamed location, about which Raoul was very mysterious;
Xris, Harry, and Amadi from the Royal Naval vessel that
had come to their rescue.

Xris had deemed it fitting that since their assignment had
started at the beach house, it should end there. He didn't

mention the fact that he'd spent those hellish hours in solitary dreaming of this house and looking forward to the day he could return.

"Thank you for coming, sir," Xris said as Amadi settled himself in a patio chair. "I've been wanting to have a chance to talk to you. How are you feeling?"

"Fine, Xris." Amadi smiled. "The skull fracture is a little slow to mend, but that's normal for a man my age. What did you want to talk to me about? This is really good chicken, by the way. Great sauce."

"I want to say I'm sorry, sir," Xris said. "I want to apologize."

"For what?" Amadi looked astonished.

"For not trusting you. For thinking you might have been the traitor. I had no reason, no reason to doubt you. You'd never let us down before. I should have known—"

"Nonsense," Amadi said crisply. "You had reason enough, God knows, not to trust anyone! And if it comes down to it, I'm the one who should apologize. For not trusting you. I considered telling you the whole plan. But I couldn't. I couldn't be sure."

Xris's expression darkened. "You didn't think I was working for the Hung, did you?"

"No, I knew better than that. But I wasn't sure who you were working for. Or should I say, who Rowan was working for. I knew that *you* trusted her, but how could I?"

Amadi glanced up at Darlene, who was standing behind Xris, her hand on his shoulder.

She smiled ruefully. "The feeling was mutual, sir, I'm sorry to say."

"I could certainly understand you bailing out after your testimony at the Hung trial," Amadi said, "but you left the Bureau in a hell of a spot. If you had come to me—"

"But I couldn't, sir!" Darlene replied earnestly. "Armstrong was dead and I knew the Hung hadn't killed him! I realized then it had to be someone in the Bureau. And . . . well, sir . . ." Her voice trailed off.

"All the evidence pointed to me," said Amadi. He sighed, then shrugged. "At any rate, all's well that ends better."

"What I don't understand, sir, is this: If you knew the

money was in the bank on Del Sol, why set the Hung leaders free to go get it? Weren't you taking a big risk?"

"Yes," Amadi admitted. "I had evidence that indicated their secret account was on Del Sol, but the evidence wasn't conclusive, and I had to know for certain. While the three Hung leaders were in Jango, they were in constant contact with 'Mr. Trevor'—"

"Who was really Andrew Robison."

"I intercepted Robison's transmissions to the Hung, substituted my own transmissions for his, sent my transmissions to the Hung, and picked up their replies. I sent Robison phony transmissions from the Hung to keep him happy. And so 'Mr. Trevor' began feeding the Hung leaders information about the political turmoil in Del Sol."

"Information you received from Sir John Dixter," said Darlene, in sudden understanding. "*That's* why he wouldn't do anything to help Xris! He knew what you were planning!"

Amadi nodded. "And Sir John assured me that I could trust all of you. So I *am* the one who should apologize."

"You told the Hung leaders that Kirkov was planning to exterminate the dremecks. Why should the Hung leaders care what happened to the dremecks?"

"They didn't. Kirkov was on the Hung payroll. The Hung told him to keep a low profile, not to do anything that would give the Royal Navy the slightest chance to intervene in Del Sol affairs. But Kirkov was psychotic. He refused to obey orders. When the Hung leaders found out, through Mr. Trevor, that Kirkov was planning to space the dremecks, they were furious, and I was sure I was on the right track. They knew the publicity that this incident would cause, the uproar throughout the galaxy. The spotlight would be shining on Del Sol and they'd be caught in the glare.

"You might be interested to know, by the way, that the secret account was in the names of all three. One couldn't access it without the other."

"I didn't get the feeling they were that attached to each other," Xris said wryly.

"They weren't," Amadi returned. "They arranged it that way so that one wouldn't kill the other two and make off with the loot. Charming bunch, weren't they? By now, though, they were worried about their money, but I still couldn't get them to leave their cushy prison. They kept trying to think of ways for Mr. Trevor to handle their problem."

"Cushy prison!" Xris snorted.

"You should have seen Jango before Montieth arrived," Amadi told him. "It was just like the brochures. The Hung leaders had life easy. Conjugal visits with their wives and girlfriends on a regular basis. Play golf all day, poker all night. You should have seen their cell. A penthouse. Montieth put an end to all of it."

"I'll be damned!" Xris stared. "Montieth was your man!"

"*And* Slovenski. Two of my best agents." Amadi grinned. "Between them, they made life hell for the Hung leaders. Macdonald tried to bribe Montieth. That didn't work. He threatened him. You met Montieth. You can imagine how he reacted."

"He said he'd spit in the face of God Himself."

"He would, too." Amadi chuckled. "Macdonald hired an assassin to kill Slovenski. The assassin is in the hospital. He now has regained the use of his arms. By that time, Macdonald was begging 'Mr. Trevor' to get them out of Jango."

"So will things improve back at Jango?" Xris asked. "I made a few friends there. They're not bad men. They just used bad judgment and I wouldn't want—"

"Slovenski is being 'paroled,'" Amadi assured him. "And Montieth will 'retire.' The old warden won't be back. He was so corrupt you could smell him in the next galaxy. A new one will take his place and Jango will be neither a dungeon of horrors nor a country club. It will be what it was meant to be—a correctional facility for first-time offenders."

"All was proceeding according to your plan, then," Xris said. "And it went straight to hell."

"Robison found out. I don't know what tipped him off. Something in one of those phony messages, perhaps. But he discovered that I was on to him. He was very clever, our Mr. Robison. Instead of using the Hung to deal with me, he made the case one for Internal Affairs to handle.

If the Hung had assassinated me, they would have confirmed all the evidence I had collected. I'd left it in a file that would be opened if I died."

"But by making it a case for Internal Affairs," Darlene said, "Robison not only got rid of you, he poisoned all of your information by making it look like you were the rotten apple."

"Precisely. Robison found out about the escape plan involving Xris. First he tried to kill Xris in prison. After that failed, he thought it over and decided to make the escape work to his own advantage. He used the Hung to kidnap Harry Luck's mother— How is Mrs. Luck, by the way? I hope she suffered no ill effects?"

"She's fine," said Xris, smiling. "Once the kidnappers discovered that they weren't going to be paid for their work, they weren't willing to risk their lives for nothing. According to Mrs. Luck, they were in a foul mood when they left."

"Yes, a lot of Hung employees are in a foul mood about now. We know of one gentleman who tried to set himself up as heir to Macdonald, Becking, and Mair. He was tossed out of a hovertaxi three hundred kilometers above a canyon without benefit of a parachute. No, the Hung are finished, at last."

"One more thing, sir," said Darlene somberly. "*Did* you kill Armstrong?"

"In my heart, many times," said Amadi. "I was at the hospital when they brought Xris into emergency. I was at the morgue when they tried to identify what was left of Ito. But no, Rowan. I didn't kill Armstrong. Robison took care of that for me."

"Champagne?" asked Raoul, coming by with a chilled bottle. "Hold out your glasses!"

"A toast," said Xris, raising his glass. "To you, sir. Congratulations."

"No, no," Amadi protested. "I can't allow that. The credit goes to you, Xris. You and Rowan."

Darlene raised her glass. "To Mashahiro Ito."

"And to all the others the Hung murdered," Xris added. "May their spirits find peace at last."

CHAPTER 45

Of freedom and life he only is deserving
Who everyday must conquer them anew.
　　　　Johann Wolfgang von Goethe, *Faust*

After everyone had eaten their fill of chicken and had secretly deposited the salad in the garden, so as not to hurt Raoul's feelings, the team assembled in the living room for the debriefing.

"First order of business," said Xris, settling himself into the leather easy chair which might have been selected with him in mind, "is to welcome Tycho to Mag Force 7."

"I am glad to be a part of such a lusterless team," said Tycho, rising and bowing.

"Illustrious," whispered Quong. "Illustrious team."

"Yes, that is what I said." Tycho reached out his hand, which had taken on the dusky rose shade of the couch's upholstery. "And I am proud to meet you at last, Xris Cyborg."

"That color is quite becoming on you," Raoul observed. "You should wear the couch more often."

Tycho smiled and nodded.

"Second," said Xris, "His Majesty King Dion sends his congratulations on a job well done. He appreciates our heroic efforts to help save the dremecks. He finds it especially meritorious that we did this all on our own initiative. He has sent a token of his esteem, which has been deposited in the account.

"Now, reports. Jamil. I understand that you have been involved in assisting the dremecks through their transition phase from slaves to masters."

Jamil had been sitting in a corner of the couch, brooding

over a bottle of bourbon ever since his arrival. He had refused dinner.

"The dremecks will do fine," said Jamil, not looking up. He swirled the amber-colored liquid in his glass so hard that he sloshed it over the sides, spilled bourbon on the couch. "Sorry, Xris. I'll pay for the cleaning."

"Don't worry." Xris smiled. "It's not my couch. So if the dremecks are doing fine, why the need to soak yourself in bourbon?"

Jamil made a frustrated gesture with the hand that wasn't holding the glass. "It's just . . . I'm a military man. My dad and mom were both military. I meet a people who are truly gentle, truly peaceful, truly believe that killing anything— even a carrot—is wrong. And what do I do? I train them to be killers."

"Nobody was killed," Darlene observed mildly. "No one was even injured, with the exception of that dremeck who got so excited he jumped off the troop transport before it stopped moving, and even he only had a broken ankle—"

"He is healing well," Dr. Quong added.

"See there," Xris said.

Jamil drank off his bourbon, set down the glass, poured himself another. "The dremecks are working with humans now. Soon they'll be living with humans. They won't be segregated anymore and they'll pick up our bad habits. The dremecks will learn to kill. Sooner or later. You just wait. And I'll be the one responsible."

"Look at it this way, Jamil," Quong argued. "Perhaps the dremecks will change the humans. Maybe Del Sol will become a peaceful planet of vegetarians."

"Poor Chef Hernandez," said Raoul sympathetically. "A lifetime of thinking up different ways to cook eggplant."

"Maybe," said Jamil, glowering darkly. "But I doubt it."

"Rowan and Rizzoli," Xris said, deciding it was time to move on. "You two have been working on the nationalization of the banks—"

"You are not smoking, Xris," said Dr. Quong suddenly.

"That's right, Xris!" Darlene was astonished. "You're not!"

"The truth is," Xris said, embarrassed, "Doc here has been after me for years to quit and, well, I went so long without smoking in Jango that I figured I might as well keep on going. I still get that funny metallic taste in my mouth—"

"Try peppermints," said Quong.

"I will, Doc. Thanks. Rizzoli, your medication seems to be working. I still have glassware."

Petronella laughed. Reaching out, she rested a hand on Quong's arm. "Your doctor discovered that the dosage I was taking wasn't adequate for my increased metabolic rate, or something like that. He adjusted it and now I can even enter china shops without making certain that my insurance is paid up."

"You have permission to visit me on Adonia," said Raoul graciously, "in about five years, during which time we will monitor your progress. Poor Hoskins. He was in such a state that he threatened to give notice and I was forced to send him on a cruise, all expenses paid, in order for him to recover from the experience, which I think I am not unreasonable in saying was a 'shattering' one."

The Little One, curled up on the floor, punched Raoul in the shins.

"It was too funny," said Raoul.

"Mr. Amadi." Xris turned to his former boss. "Would you mind if we listened in on what Rizzoli and Darlene have discovered?"

"Certainly not," said Amadi. "You have more than earned that right.

"Once we opened the records, we found the Hung account. Billions," Petronella said. "Billions and billions. The Del Sol banks had arranged financial transactions for the Hung all over the galaxy. They laundered money, converted gold to hard currency—charging exorbitant fees for the privilege, I might add. Kirkov came in for his cut, as did his staff and cabinet ministers.

"We're working with a committee set up by Parliament to place the money in a fund that has been established for victims of the Hung. There were some people who had legitimate accounts in the bank. The coalition government has promised to see to it that their funds are returned to them."

"There is more than enough money to improve the living

conditions of the dremecks," Darlene added. "Many of the older dremecks want to continue working at the same jobs, and now they'll be paid for their labor. Some of the young people, however, want to learn to work with the humans in the banks and the vid station, and"—she cast an uneasy glance at Jamil—"some of them want to form the first dremeck army."

Jamil just shook his head and drank off another bourbon.

"Now Raoul, your report," Xris said.

There was no response. Raoul was staring at himself in his compact, touching up a beauty spot at the corner of his eye.

Xris tried again. "Raoul!"

The Little One punched his friend on the toe.

"Now look what you've done!" Raoul said tragically. "I've smudged it!"

"Raoul," Xris said for the third time, "put away the mirror. You're lovely, as always."

Reluctantly, Raoul closed the compact, returned it to his purse. Then he was all attention, regarding Xris with a dreamy and flawlessly lip-glossed smile.

"First," Xris continued, "express to Rusty Love our appreciation. He did a fantastic job."

"Rusty Love was quite pleased to be of service," Raoul assured them, "especially after he received your most generous payment, which was quite unnecessary, since he did what he did out of gratitude for a valued mentor and teacher, that being myself. He found out that he prefers being involved in real-life action, rather than standing around watching his stunt double do all the exciting parts, and he asked me to tell you that if ever a job comes along where you might find him useful and you can assure him that it won't muss his hair or get dirt beneath his fingernails, he's your man."

"I'll keep that in mind," Xris said. "And how is our friend Kirkov enjoying his unexpected holiday?"

The Little One snickered and, bringing up one fist, he smashed it into the palm of his hand.

"Yes, quite," said Raoul in agreement. "His Eminence was not particularly startled to wake up and find himself in a strange bed, since I understand that this is a normal occurrence for him. It did strike him as strange that he was in bed alone. Further, that the stars outside his window were moving along at a considerable rate of speed. Surprised, he inquired as to the circumstances. I explained to him that he was on a private yacht about forty light-years away from his native planet, at which juncture His Eminence went from surprise to outraged in the shortest length of time it has ever been my privilege to observe.

"His reaction was quite entertaining for a few minutes, then it rapidly became boring. He seized a steak knife and came at me with the avowed intention of slitting my throat from ear to ear. My friend"—Raoul stroked the fedora—"biffed His Eminence on the head with a bottle of champagne. I was quite shocked at this act of violence on the part of my friend until I learned that, fortunately, it was domestic.

"His Eminence spent the night face-first on the floor, during which time I introduced a nerve-soothing potion into his water carafe. After that, we all got along quite marvelously. He didn't even put up a fuss when the agents came on board to arrest him for accepting bribes and racketeering. His Eminence gave a merry laugh and offered to pour them all a glass of water, which, acting upon my advice, they chose not to accept.

"His Eminence was quite sorry to leave us and actually kissed me on both cheeks when we parted," said Raoul, smoothing his hair. "It was really quite touching. When I saw him again during his trial, however, he wasn't looking nearly so cheerful. It seems that the drug I had used was addictive—a fact that had completely slipped my mind—and that his period of withdrawal had not been pleasant."

"Kirkov was sentenced to thirty years in prison," said Dr. Quong. "He has, of course, appealed. And he is attempting to have our friends"—he nodded at Raoul and the Little One—"brought up on kidnapping charges."

"How quaint," said Raoul, charmed.

"Maybe they'll send him to Jango," said Xris. "Hopefully before Slovenski is paroled. Harry, how did Bear Olefsky take the news that we blew up his brand-new transport?"

Harry, who had been lolling in the other easy chair

jerked to attention. He sat bolt upright, as he always did when Xris called upon him to make a report.

"I was sort of scared he'd be mad; it was a prototype, after all, and must have cost a bundle. But he wasn't. He wouldn't even take the money you offered him. Said it was worth it to find out that his innovations worked the way he thought they would and that now he could go ahead and put the Xena-class transport into production. He did say to tell you that the next time you wanted to borrow something, it had better be a cup of sugar." Harry looked puzzled. "Do you need sugar, Xris? 'Cause if you do, I could run out to the store—"

"No, Harry, what Bear meant was . . . never mind. I have plenty of sugar. Well, people," Xris said, "that wraps up another one. Thank you for everything. You've received your paychecks. I hope they were satisfactory?"

Everyone nodded, with the exception of Tycho.

"Excuse me, Mr. Tampambulos—"

"Xris," said Xris, smiling. "Just Xris."

"Yes, sir, Xris." Tycho paused to adjust his translator, then continued. "I was going over the accounts, and if you continue to pay people this generously, we are going to be running into a cash flow situation—"

"Just like his brother," said Quong fondly.

"You can talk about it later," said Darlene, yawning. "I don't know about the rest of you, but I say we call it a night."

She had noticed—and commented on the fact, when Xris was out of hearing—that he looked unusually tired. His good spirits seemed forced.

"What do you think's the matter with him, Doc?" Darlene asked in a low voice, after Xris had been called upon to kill what Raoul reported, in semihysterical tones, to be a spider of gigantic proportions haunting the bathroom.

"I am not certain," said Quong. "I will have to do a complete physical. It may be a shortage of potassium." He paused to finish his drink, then added offhandedly, "Unless you mean the depression."

"What depression?" Darlene asked sharply. "Why would Xris be depressed? The men responsible for what happened to him are now little globules of flesh adrift in space."

"Precisely," said Quong quietly.

"The spider was the size of the tip of my little finger," Xris said disgustedly on his return.

"You didn't kill it, did you?" Jamil asked anxiously.

"What do you mean, Doc?" Darlene drew Quong off into a corner.

"The party's over," said Quong, shrugging. "Xris has opened all his presents. He finally was given the one he wanted. Unfortunately, it isn't nearly as bright and shiny and wonderful as he had imagined it would be."

"I see," said Darlene. She and Amadi, who had been quietly eavesdropping, exchanged glances.

"Still, it may be the potassium," Quong said. "I will check the levels tomorrow."

"Doc, I need to talk to you." Xris broke in on their conversation. "See that Jamil gets back to the hotel okay, will you?"

"Come, my friend," said Quong, lifting Jamil by the shoulder and propelling him toward the front door. "I will fix you one of my patented hangover remedies. Not only will it cure your hangover, but I guarantee you will never touch alcohol again. Xris," the doctor added, "I will be back tomorrow to perform the blood tests."

"You better make it early, Doc," Xris said. "I'm leaving tomorrow afternoon."

"So soon?" Quong looked startled.

"This isn't my house, remember," Xris said.

"Yes, that is true. Come along, my poor besotted friend," Quong said, helping Jamil down the stairs.

"Good-bye, Rizzoli." Xris shook hands with the agent. "Good luck on your future career."

"She'll be Bureau director before she's finished," Amadi predicted. "Good night, Xris. Take care of yourself."

He paused in the doorway, regarded his friend intently. "I wish life was happier for you, Xris."

"Don't worry about me, sir. If a genie had come along and granted me one wish, seeing the bastards who blew up Ito blow up themselves would have been it."

"Would it, Xris?" Amadi asked.

"Well, maybe it would have been my second wish," Xris admitted, his hand automatically going to his pocket for a twist. The hand came back empty. "But I don't think even a genie would be able to grant my first wish. There's not enough magic in the universe would make that happen. Good night, sir. Say hello to your wife for me."

Amadi departed, waving good-bye to the others.

Darlene slipped her arm around him. He drew her into his embrace. She clung to him, resting her head on his shoulder, and broke into tears.

"It's over, Rowan," he said gently. "It's over. You're safe now."

"I can't believe it, Xris," she said, huddled against him. "I still answer the door with a lasgun in my hand. I can't sleep at night without wondering if I'll wake up to find someone standing over me—"

"It's over, Rowan," Xris repeated, holding on to her tightly. "Believe it."

"I'm starting to. But it's going to take a while." Darlene raised her head, smiled at him through her tears. "Do you think that somehow Ito knows?"

"He knows," said Xris, smiling back. "I'm sure of it."

"C'mon, Darlene," said Harry awkwardly, shyly. "The late showing starts at 2100."

"Harry's taking me to a movie," said Darlene. "Rusty Love's latest vid."

"Thanks for bringing me that autographed picture," Harry said as he proudly escorted Darlene out the door. "My mom was really excited. She's gonna put it in my baby book. . . ."

Xris walked back into the house. The smell of gardenia was still incredibly strong, but Raoul was nowhere to be seen.

"Raoul," he called. "Time to go."

Raoul, escorted by the Little One, came floating out of the kitchen. "I was just rescuing the salad," he said indignantly. "Someone had accidentally stuffed it into the trash compactor—bowl and all! However, I wrapped it up and placed it in the fridge. It will make a lovely luncheon for you. One can never tell about spaceplane food, you know."

Xris made certain they reached the door, Raoul having been known to veer off and end up in the garage, wondering where he was and how he got there. The Little One suddenly wrapped his arms around Xris's leg.

Xris reached down, gave the small shoulders an affectionate pat. "I'll be all right," he said. "Don't worry. I just need some time to myself."

Raoul touched Xris's hand, his good hand. Raoul's skin was soft and warm, his nails cool and sharp. He gazed at Xris and the drug-dilated, dream-laden eyes were suddenly sharp and cool as the exquisitely and carefully painted fingernails.

"Hatred is like the twist, my friend. It gave you a sense of well-being, yet all the while it was slowly poisoning you, body and soul." The nails and the eyes dug deep. "You will miss it for a time, Xris Cyborg, but you will be better without it."

"You're very wise, Raoul," Xris said. "Do you know that?"

"I try not to be," Raoul said with a delicate sigh. "You can't think how bad wisdom is for the complexion. Sweet dreams."

He kissed the air somewhere around Xris's left earlobe. Prying loose the Little One, who was in a most pitiable state of unhappiness, Raoul located the front door. He and his small friend drifted out into the night on a wave of gardenia.

CHAPTER 46

"Somehow I'll Find My Way Home"
                    Vangelis, Song Title

After everyone was gone, Xris shut and locked the front door. Quong and Darlene had cleaned up the dishes, so that was done. He moved chairs back to their original places, swept the sand off the patio, took down the umbrella from the patio table and stored it in the garage. He watered the plants in the garden.

He would leave the house exactly as he had found it and never come back. He needed one night here, one night sitting on the deck in the beach chair, watching the white foam on the waves, watching their quest to reach the shore, only to break and fall back, break and fall back.

His hand rested on the sliding plastiglass door as he was just about to step outside, when the doorbell buzzed.

"I found your eye shadow, Raoul!" Xris called. "I'll ship it to you!"

No response. He heard a thump, however, and the sounds of someone moving around on the porch.

"I'll take the medication you left, Doc," Xris said irritably. "No need to remind me."

The doorbell rang again, this time sounding tentative.

"All right, Harry, I'm coming," Xris said, exasperated.

He flung the door open.

"Now, look—" Xris stopped, stared.

The porch light shone on a face he knew as well as he knew his own. Knew it better, for he rarely looked at himself in a mirror. The face was older; sorrow and time had filled in the lines with shadows. She was too thin; she'd never gained back the weight she'd lost in the Corasian prison. But Xris had thought her the most beautiful woman he'd ever seen when he'd first met her and he had no reason now to change his opinion.

"Xris!" Marjorie exclaimed, trying very hard to look surprised to find him here.

She had always been a terrible liar. He was reminded of the time he'd come home after months in the hospital, the time she had said she was glad to see him.

"Hello, Marjorie," he said.

"I . . . uh . . . couldn't find my keys," she said with a strained little laugh. "I . . . I saw the light and thought . . . that maybe . . ."

"I guess I don't need to invite you inside." Xris reached down to pick up her luggage. "It's your house."

"Our house, Xris," Marjorie said softly. "Didn't you recognize it?"

He didn't answer, turned away. "Look, I was just shutting things up, getting ready to go back to the hotel. Thanks for the loan of the house. I hope we didn't mess it up too much. I'll put your luggage in the bedroom—"

"Xris," Marjorie said, reaching out and touching his arm—his cybernetic arm. "What's wrong? I know something's wrong! Amadi told me—"

He looked back at her. "Amadi?"

"Oh dear," she said, putting her hand over her mouth. "I wasn't supposed to say anything."

"He told you to come back," Xris said grimly. "Come back to your pathetic wreck of a husband."

"No, he didn't. He told me you were in some kind of trouble. And I had another note from Rowan saying the same thing—"

Xris reached again for a twist, saw that his hand was shaking, and shoved his hand in the pocket of his fatigues. "What about your studies?" he asked, his voice sounding harsh and gruff.

She shook her head. "My grades weren't all that good anyway."

"Liar," he said. "You had a scholarship. It was what you'd always wanted. It was important to you. You shouldn't have left."

"*You're* important to me, Xris," Marjorie said softly. Her

hand found his hand—his cybernetic hand. Her fingers locked over his, twined around them. "I'm sorry for what happened all those years ago, Xris. I'm sorry for hurting you. I tried to tell you that time you saved my life in the Corasian prison, but you wouldn't listen."

Hatred . . . slow poison . . .

"I've hated myself ever since then," she continued. "I've tried to understand why I acted that way and I have no excuse to offer. I hurt you, hurt you terribly, and I'm sorry. So very sorry."

"It was my fault," he said, and he realized for the first time in all these years that it really was. "You were only reacting to me. You did what I wanted you to do. I repulsed you, because I repulsed myself." He broke free of her grip. "I'll go get my things—"

"You don't have to leave, Xris," she said. "I wish you wouldn't. Whatever kind of trouble you're in, we'll work it out."

He started to tell her that he wasn't in any trouble—that a meddling old man and a meddling best friend had taken pity on him and . . .

His hand reached again for the twist.

"Here," said Marjorie, opening her handbag. "Try a peppermint."

"Quong, too, huh?" Xris asked.

Marjorie flushed. "*And* Harry Luck," she admitted. "And I had such a nice note from his mother. Mrs. Luck said that—"

Xris began to laugh. He laughed until the tears crept from beneath the eyelid of his one good eye—the other eye teared only on thirty-second cycles.

He put his arm—his good arm—around his wife.

"There's some salad left in the fridge," he said. "I'll split it with you."

MARGARET WEIS

New York Times Bestselling Author

& DON PERRIN

"Adventures and misadventures . . . plot twists and humor . . . sure to please Weis's many fans."
—*Publishers Weekly*

ROBOT BLUES

When a museum curator hires the Mag Force 7 to steal a robotic artifact from an excavation site, Xris feels this could be easy money. And when the mercenaries realize they've lost a deceptively dangerous antique, all havoc breaks loose. It's up to the Mag Force 7 to find it before the bloodthirsty Corasians—aliens bent on human annihilation–can use it for ultimate destruction. (455819—$6.99)

"Swashbuckling . . . makes one think of *Star Wars*."
—*Booklist*

THE KNIGHTS OF THE BLACK EARTH

They are Mag Force 7, the finest mercenary squad in the known universe. Their leader Xris is on a mission of vengeance against the comrade who betrayed him years before. Yet before Xris can claim his revenge, he and his men are recruited for a job they cannot turn down. And Xris's only hope of stopping them lies in joining forces with an old enemy.

(455142—$5.99)

from

*Prices slightly higher in Canada.
